# One Rode In

A NOVEL BY

Albert Zayat

This is a work of fiction. All of the characters, organizations, and events portrayed in this novel are products of the author's imagination or used fictionally.

ONE RODE IN



ISBN: 0983687323
ISBN 13: 9780983687320

Albert Zayat
one.rodein@yahoo.com
United States of America

# PREFACE

Great books are often great puzzles. ONE RODE IN is such a novel. If you enjoy figuring things out, like to search for symbolism, want to be taken on an intellectual journey you'll never forget, then ONE RODE IN is the book for you. All of this you'll get, plus an "AHA" ending. The time to begin this memorable journey is now. Joseph Conrad once said that his goal as a novelist was to make the reader "feel"; the goal of ONE RODE IN is to make the audience think and feel.

Professor W. J. Reeves

# ACKNOWLEDGMENTS

Anyone, who writes anything worth writing, understands how difficult it can be at times shouldering that boulder up such a steep hill, alone. To all mentioned below, and not, thanks.

Above all else to Professor W. J. Reeves of Brooklyn College: the bravest of confidants and friend. For without his invaluable knowledge of Literature, teaching technique of gentle suggestive nudges of "think about this," "One Rode In" takes longer and travels more difficult road than it was. And it was.

Harry Brey LCSW: a superior advocate, believer, and friend.

Marie Lynn, student: friend and for her stunning appreciation of "One Rode In" that put a large gust of wind in its sails.

Connie Baptist, a wonderful classy lady: for her friendship, and tolerant reading of my occasional late night text messages of experimental prose, and poetic verse.

Rebecca Crawley of RTC Publicity: for her advocacy, friendship, connections to good people, professional public relations competence, and understanding the changing landscape of the publishing industry.

Donna Zayat- ex-wife: friend, for her support, and her contribution to one heck of a milestone birthday party.

Suzann Ellingsworth-editor/book doc: friend and for surviving our multiple, ferocious, phone and e-mail conversations debating her exacting exemplary work.

Stephanie Ryan-graphic artist- plus: for taking "One Rode In" from a manuscript to a class "A" publication, her advocacy, friendship and professional dedication getting it correct.

Carolyn Haines-author: for her quiet- behind the scenes- advocacy and friendship.

# One

Raw bare skin poked through his size eleven. Cal's wing-tip stuck to the smothered gas pedal. He drove in a daze, through a black night, chasing a story, his last-second chance. Along for the night rode his other soul. Frail, thin, peppered with many well earned holes, from a life poorly lived. And, as many others souls have, it, began - to slip.

"I've stumbled on stories before, leads too. Chance counts of course. But this, come on, think man, why did this freakin story miss the headlines? Why am I so lucky to unearth it? Sure, vicious gun fights in bars happen, city or suburb. But innocents, assassinated, in a sleepy upstate New York country bar, that's big news man, or should have been."

Cal, a nervous self-talker, hung on tight to the steering wheel. Well hidden within the shadowy shell of his near dead car he sliced through a bleak night, somewhere, between here and there. Heavy pre-storm air hung over-head on a night reserved for only the desperate, and lonely. Two nicotine stained finger tips trembled as they frantically fumbled trying to spin the radio knob. Cal looked for the companionship of his first love, a whining blues guitar.

"Come on, come on damn it. Where's some god damn music?"

It was late, or early. Frayed speakers spoke only the whines of scratchy, static. Local stations went to bed early. No city stations dared to interfere.

"Give me a break damn it."

The only music he heard, memory. Trembling dedicated fingertips pinched the whining dial. Faint, floating, signals punched in, and out. Like a clever fisherman he finally hooked one. The husky female voice strengthened. Cal sighed. He tipped his head, pointed his weakening ear.

"You know Rachel we humans, well, we're much like crock-pots aren't we?"

"Doctor, really."

"Yes, yes, you see we simmer all that's put in us, and later? Well, that's why we all taste so differently–ha-ha-ha. In any case it's what gave me the final push, the encouragement. I knew I was on to something."

"Doctor, you mean what you told me off air, about that encounter, in the hospital, with the other doctor's patient?"

"Yes, my fine radio host, yes. That day my world turned upside down. Or right side up, hard to say. It's like that you know. Life, things just happen sometimes, no way to plan. It happened to me. That sickly patients thirty minute story, a story about three mother's sons. I'm convinced it wasn't a coincidence. I was meant to meet him. I was—told."

"Ladies and gentlemen, good evening. If you're just tuning in I'm sitting with Doctor Ja–"

"—Is it? And Doc Jack is enough, my throaty host. Heaven's, you tell them my last name and they'll be calling."

"Well, aren't you writing a book, Doc Jack? A theory, about how we come back, back from the dead?"

"I am, yes Rachel I am. However, it's far from complete. I don't need the goblins calling to raise Auntie Frieda."

"Please, Doctor Jack—tell our radio audience why you believe in reincarnation? What happened that day?"

"I didn't say I did, and please— humor me, use Doc Jack only. Now to answer your question, yes, I do. I not only think we come back, but, I know it. Not as you think though."

"Doc Jack, that sounds like double talk."

"Perhaps my buxom beauty, but you don't know what I do."

"Doc Jack– my word."

"Listen, I don't want to be rude, but it's what, one thirty in the morning? No one's listening, they never do. So don't worry about me disclosing your ample breast size. My guess is you have a full audience of say, three. One is likely an over-the-road truck driver. He kissed his wife good-bye twelve hours ago, rolled late night out-of-town to California. After he gets there and drops his trailer he's off to visit his girlfriend. Thirty minutes after he left, his wife, invited his best friend over. In thirty days that guy will be headed to six months, of a judge's time-out. Then we have a woman with more money than time. She just bought her fiftieth porcelain unicorn, television shopping. Last, a guy, driving alone all night on an adventure. He's listening to his beat up cars radio. The kind of guy with a lavender smile, detached, you know the kind. So lost he'd unknowingly walk in a gay bar and wonder, after twenty minutes, where the girls were."

Even Cal, with his weakening hearing knew this was not music to his ears.

"Jeasus save me, what a dopey Doctor, Dock Jack dick bag. Heeeyyyy, wait a sec; I'm up late listening, driving to wherever? You're the same SOB who woke me this morning, aren't you? Now take that back, I'd never do that?"

Cal dimly looked at the dim radio clock.

"And it's more like 2 a.m., buddy."

He tilted his ear to the radio.

"Maybe, hmmm, you know Rachel—I take that back. I'm sorry I said our driver would do that, he wouldn't. However, he'd run a garage sale full of used toasters, tagged for hundreds, and can openers at thousands, just to see the expression on the treasure hunters faces. You know the type. He's the kind who hasn't missed much of life's black ice."

"I would, yeah, and haven't." Cal smiled

"Doc—Doc Jack, very funny I'm certain our audience is much larger than that. No matter, please, go on. Please tell those who just tuned it what you told me. It's very entertaining, and how you happened to develop this, uh, theory of yours?"

"Madam, as a host, and a mother, I know you've learned some things. I have as well through my years in practice, stumbled on nuggets of information never known, or understood. You have to think, watch, and listen."

"Well of course you have to listen you're a shrink, ha hah ha."

"No, I mean we all, have to listen. More, than you know. We're told, we're more connected than we may think."

"Things, connected?"

"No more about that now. Soo, you want your audience entertained do you?"

Cal unknowingly ground his teeth, and had enough. Blinking Cal practiced his well used self talk, and self answer keeping himself company. Crap, used one too many times earned mother's soap. Carp it was.

"Music on my damn radio keeps fading, innnn, and oooouuuttttt, here in God's country. Well, go on blowhard. Let's hear. Some carp no doubt."

"Well my tolerant understanding radio host, here's how it happened. I was in the process of surrendering my regular practice to an associate. Time, I needed time to pursue my theory. On that routine day making my rounds, one of my last at the hospital, I passed an open door of a patient's room. An anguished man's voice called out. He wasn't my patient. I kept going. Three yards past a scent struck. Odd smelling cleaning or disinfectant I thought. A sliver of the acidic scent twirled, snaked and drilled through my chronically clogged nostrils, into my mouth and burned my teeth. I tell you, it stopped me cold. My legs deadened, felt like they had hundred pound bags of sand strapped to them. I couldn't lift my feet, couldn't advance as if paralyzed from the waist down. Feared what I inhaled was poison, or had a stroke, thought my death certain and would learn for myself if my research were true. Panicky perspiration ran from my forehead. Trying to break free I twisted around. Finally I broke from its grip going backwards. When I tried moving forward, again, the weight built on my legs as a warning. I took the hint, negotiated a few, escaping, back-paces. When I stopped I stood in front of the room where the cry for help came from, the one I ignored only moments earlier. My heart met my throat. A chill electrified my spine. The cry came again. Ecstatic I wasn't paralyzed charity filled my usually numb heart. I went in the room to see what I could do.

In the dim light of a night time hospital room I made out two fingers, on a left hand. They beckoned me closer. Dubiously, I shuffled to his mostly naked, languishing body. Soft light, from behind his bed, hazily spilled over him, shadowing what needed to be. A blind man could tell he was ill, very ill. He looked at me with a victim's protruding eyes, eyes that looked like he just got off the crazy train. Certain death wandered in his life.

I moved tight to the rails, asked what was wrong. In hindsight I could have asked a better question. My black shirt and pants were all I had clean that day. Likely he figured me for priest, minister, or rabbi. Displeased, his fingers beckoned me closer. I obeyed, bent, and suffered the odor of foul tobacco breath whispers as they passed through parched dehydrated lips. I listened. He told me, during the next half hour, he needed to confide a story to me about the three mother's sons, asked if I would listen. I could not have left, had I wished to. When he was done I looked at my watch. Exactly thirty minutes elapsed. I pulled back. We locked eyes. He held his fingers up again. I bent again. He whispered in my frightened ear, "It wasn't my youth I mis-spent." His tyrannized expression softened, as if he yielded to his punishment, his disease, for living an imperfect life."

"Did you answer back?"

"I did."

"What did you say?"

"I wanted, needed, to mercifully lighten his load. Wrestle his dying life's final companion, despair, from him."

"How?"

"I tipped, in his crusty elephant ear I whispered—the anguish you suffer is not as a result of this life. Then added– and, in many ways we never leave childhood, or it us, nor should we. He smiled."

"Doc Jack, what did he tell you during that thirty minute conversation?

Cal blinked.

"Forget that guy. Bunch of bunk, no damn music, and I'm stuck here listening to Doc crock.

"No, never mind, don't fade out. Okay, what did he say for heaven's sake? Finish it before I'm finished. Jeasus I wish there was some freakin music up here in chipmunk land." Exhaled cigarette smoke pounded against an already, yellow tinted windshield.

"In a minute Rachel, you goddess, now before I go on I need to know more about you. I'm not sure you're ready for this. As far as for your, eh hem, audience— they're on their own. All, whatever they count to.

Cal took the challenge.

"Go on buddy, I can take it. Hope a freakin deer doesn't jump in front of me. This car's taken all the hits it can."

"Now, my lady, your answers to three questions will help me decide."

"Questions, ah, go ahead, sounds like fun Doc Jack. First I do need to take a commercial break. What? Oh, okay, never-mind. I was told, go ahead."

"Fun madam, maybe, maybe not? Here's the first- What are you two favorite Beatles songs?"

"Yesterday, and Imagine."

"Two-Have you ever, purposefully, opened a window to hear the roar of a train's engine, the squeal of its wheels, and the shrill of its horn. If so, did it make you wonder where it was going? Wish you were on it?

"Often– Doc Jack, now, what in the world are we talking about?"

"Three-Do you think it wrong, if you loved someone, and they you, but you both are married to another?"

"I—-"

"—Hold your answer on that one till later. You need time to think."

"What about the first two questions then. Why?"

"Madam host– the first tells me if you have a pulse, and the second—its strength."

"We'll be right back everyone, but do stay tuned. Doc Jack thinks we come back, from the dead."

Cal winced.

"Man, he has some line of you- know- what. This morning I hated him, he woke me up with that tyranny of guilt bull. Man, he has everyone stumped. Ah, some music—no, more static, oh no not again, drat."

"And we're back, with Doc Jack as he wants to be called. A psychiatrist who thinks we come back from the dead, and is writing a book about his experiences. Doc Jack, you told us of your encounter with that sick man in the hospital. What did he say to you?"

"Rachel, I'll try to remember the best I can. First, in the interest of your sponsors, I will tell you, and, allll of your listener's, one of the–last things– he said. It sounded like complete gibberish at the time. After he said it I shook my confused head. He grabbed a pencil. Wrote, and then spoke it again as he handed the paper to me written with penmanship that looked like a frightened child's script. Then he made a proclamation of a sort, with words not of this world, this time. I saved the paper, gave to a colleague who studied ancient languages."

"What did it say?"

"I'm not completely sure, yet."

"What happened next?"

"I leaned over, whispered in his elephant ear."

"What, what did you say?"

"I said it was ok. He was not to blame, rest."

Cal wiped an itching nose with his sleeve.

"Jeeze, this is better than a game show."

He twisted the dial seeking music, banning Doc Jack, but found only static. When he switched back to the talk show, static interfered there also. Then, a high-pitched signal came back. Their conversation continued.

"Doc Jack, what did he tell you? What about- the three mother's sons?"

"Nooooo, come on, no static, pleaassse." Cal snorted.

"My apologies to all my listeners, we had a technical snafu. Again, please Doc Jack. What did he say?"

"Madam, my notes are fragmented, as was he. I can say he spoke of odd things. His first words to me I'll remember, forever. He said 'we all live somewhere between Che' and Scrooge."

"Che,' as in Guevara, that on top of three mother's sons, I mean really Doc Jack, what in the world are you speaking about, sir?"

"Odd, I know. Those were his first words, but his last were poetic. He finished saying 'a banquet of one's own words can be difficult to chew, hard to swallow, but often are digestible and nutritious.' Then he wrinkled my nose with his dirty dying breath saying, there was so much more to know. His last intelligible breaths renounced all he had previously renounced, wished he had a second chance. Then he gasped, and closed his eyes."

"Doctor Jack.

"Doc,"

"Doc, I confess. Your beside manner is, a bit unusual. As is all this. Did he die?"

"Yeah, what happened Doc gone job?"

Cal whipped his hands up. An old rock band drummers pose whipped the air.

"I don't know for sure. I think he died, again. Soon after, a round physician came in waving his hands, protectively shooing me away.

"He was portly?"

"No, fat, crowned with a lumpy bald head suitable for a mountain goat. A lime green tie covered half his globe belly. It was speckled with years of condiment mishaps, perhaps from food crushed by his fleshy jowls. His shirt's buttons fought to hold his pasty white blubber from escaping between them. Yes, fat, would be the appropriate term."

"What did he say?"

"He looked over a bulbous nose, and then broke into a discourse with the urgency of a house fire. He asked me what his patient said as he stroked his belly."

"And?"

"And, I said he said nothing. Then, fearlessly, I backed away. He smelled like three days."

"You lied, he did say something."

"I didn't. As I backed away I added, in a whisper, nothing you'd understand."

"His baloney lips flapped 'Whaaaa?' Then, in a counter-punch vent he said, 'I know you. I know your theories, and I think it rubbish.' "

"What did you say?"

"I told him– funny, I don't remember asking— your opinion."

"Really?"

"Yes—really. Yet he continued on ranting that he had a right to his opinion. I answered yes you do, as the owners of the White Star Line did about the buoyancy of Titanic."

"Eventually I grew tired toying with him, so I finished him with an assassin's wit. He asked, what do I seek—I said truth, and you—dinner. Then I added— by the way sir, you look like he night manager at the forty-dollar whore hotel. You know the one, it's down the block. Now, go home, wash. He left red faced, shoved chubby hands in his pockets."

"Doctor, you do believe in reincarnation?

"In some fashion, yes, and forty-dollar whore houses as well I might add."

"Doctor–"

Cal yawned.

"Carp, more static. I knew this was BS, where the heck is that map?" Cal fumbled with the papers on the passenger seat. "Second chance sounds good. Oh, good I'm getting the signal again."

"Doc Jack, indulge me, and my audience, please. We have less than thirty-minutes before the author of a new book, one about Martians, arrives in the studio. What can we learn from you today?"

"Rachel, we're going to find out, yes, yes we are, we're going into the next frontier of DNA investigation. I hope your new guest has a bigger audience."

Cal sighed a thank god.

"Damn, static. Now what am I going to do for entertainment." Cal grabbed a home-made Billy-club by its tapped handle, glared at the radio, then thought better. Affectionately he returned it.

"Doc Jack, before you said the man, well you said he died, again, though he had before?"

"I did madam, yes, I did. Some believe we spiritually pass this way again, and again. I'm not certain, but, I'm trying to find out. We do know, in a manner of speaking, we are reborn. That is our DNA is handed off to our issue, mentally and physically. You look in the mirror don't you? You see your eyes, skin, and nose. Maybe a little like Mom's, Dad's, or a little of each, maybe grandmothers or fathers?

You may, or may not, like them, but they're there and only with a surgeon's scalpel can you change them.

"This guy is nuts," Cal tapped the steering wheel "likely broke, has to pitch this deal. I wish there was some music."

"Listen, madam, and all, now we can trace our ancestral DNA."

"What?"

"Whaaa—" Cal agreed with the throaty host.

"Most really don't know where they came from. Oh yes, we know of our recent ancestry, ethnicity, nationally, culture, but that's just skims the surface. We travel back so much further. Markers, DNA markers help us plot our migration, as individuals out of Africa. Say fifty, sixty-thousand years ago. I told you before, I stumbled on something that went terribly wrong, or terribly right."

"You mean something that proves we come back, from the dead? How, how do you know this or think it."

"After that chance meeting, with that man, I wondered if it was so much chance."

Cal wrinkled his nose.

"This guy's full of it. I want to meet that chick buying the unicorns."

"Doc, are you sure—"

"By now madam, that guy, the one on his night-time adventure, is probably looking for the unicorn lady seeing as he's been married three times and now, dead broke."

"Hey, only twice damn it, and hey. You're a good guesser."

"Now, for your audience Rachel, get a pencil, and some paper everyone. Take some notes; I have permission. You too out there in audience land. Time you learn something. You may think me a crackpot, or a guardian angel. It's your choice, and frankly—I don't care. I'm here, on the air, with my audience of—well you decide."

"You're lame buddy. This is a hoax to sell a book. Back from the dead, really."

"But I warn you. This will shake what you hold holy. Oh, yes, one last thing, before you learn about the three mothers sons. The man, the sickly fellow said something you ought to know. He said you think your body old, but know your soul-its eldest brother."

Cal's eyes crossed. He flung enraged maestro hands from the steering wheel.

"Enough, I've heard enough."

"Hardly," Fluttered through the static.

A storm brewed. Lightning flashed her girlish temper. Keeping worn wobbling wheels on the road- straight- was difficult, but encouraged a mind to wander. An old memory, a long ponytail hooked behind a pair of soft brown eyes, curved an unfamiliar smile on Cal. He air rapped an unheard beat, to an unknown song. Thunder spoke. Cal winced, oncoming lights. The story he chased, and Doc's story about three mother's sons, started their duel for his attention, on the one road in- to Fate. He needed to dig up the story, about the shooting, quickly. Then, seek what many do, the one road out.

Lightening snuck a flash. Cal's thoughts retreated to morning, the previous day.

# Two

A simple early morning summer blue sky turned black. Outside Cal's Manhattan apartment window the electrical storm ignited. Cal was late to wake and late for work, as usual. Ominous rumbling storm noise snapped his eyes open. He pushed his feet against the belly in his mattress, sat-up, fell over. Slithering in a fetal position he sought safety under his ripped sheet that wrapped his head as if a mummy. His abused clock radio tortured him with a blaring talk show.

"We're back from our radio commercial break. If you just joined us we're talking with my guest, Doc Jack."

"Doc Jack has written one new controversial book, and working on another. Both make rather dramatic, unorthodox, conclusions about where some of our human demons come from. Doc, I confess. When we first contacted you to come on, well frankly, we had no idea how big a nerve this subject would hit. I'm so glad our originally scheduled guest, the author of, 'Why Nazis Were Just a Little Misunderstood,' cancelled. Just look at those switchboard lights, would you?"

"Hmmm, I see that, yes. Ah, well thank you. This is a better time slot than your late night show which I believe I'm scheduled for also. You must be desperate."

"We are not. Our research shows we have a very select, exclusive audience."

"Sure. Well, I thank your listeners for their interest! This is a difficult subject for many."

"Caaaarp...what time is it? Who the hell changed the station? Music – damn it, music is what I always wake up to. Who are these idiots! Ugh, I have to change these sheets, sometime." Cal flexed his right hand.

"Yes Doc, please go on. I'm sure all of our listeners will find this fascinating. Even those still in bed, late. It's a subject we've all wrestled with from time to time. In fact, I still struggle with some-hi-g I re—be- wh– I was a lit—e—"

"Yes, yes, very interesting but wh-n I talk about –ilt I refer to it as the absolute ru—

Tick, tick, Tick... Excuse me, my ce—phone"

"That's an interesting telephone ring you have there, Doctor. Sounds like a clock ticki–"

"Yes, yes it does, quite u–ful I find."

"Oh Jeasus, will you two shut the fuck up? Come on, shut u-u-p-p. I'm trying to sle-e-e-e-p."

"Doc, we're running late. I hear the storm is interfering with some people listening. We won't get to all the calls I'm sorry to say. Let me recap. Is it your contention that some of what troubles us in this life is carried forward from previous lives? Is that correct? How do you answer your critique's who argue you have no proof? What proof of it do you have? Let's –nish this -p for today!"

"Good! Good God damn it to hell. Isn't there any freakin, music on this thing? Dam blowhards! Thank god for the storm. At least that's blocking this hot air merchant from being heard." Cal kicked his legs like a foal trying to stand.

"Proof, what proof do I have? Listen, I've amassed a body of work over fifteen years. It's not just ones pa-t live- bu- p-rhaps oth—. One case took me to-"

"We're out of time, I'm sorry. Truly gives me the creeps. Doc Jack, for me and all our listeners I want to thank you for being with us for the last half hour. Come back, take us off the hook. Till then, I suggest to all my listeners who want to learn more, be on the lookout for our guest's new book titled—?" Rachel nodded, waited for a palpable pause to pass, then—

"The Tyranny of Guilt- thanks for having me on."

"Thank yo- Doc Jack."

"Dicks, tyranny of guilt, right. He's just trying to hustle a buck, that's all." Cal muffled into his tobacco reeking pillow.

Stirring, he slipped a hand from under his crispy, top, tented sheet. Blindly, he flung it in snaking wave, seeking the radio dial. Cal was late for work, again. His editor Big Pete waited for him, grinding his teeth, again. Cal glanced at the stack of bills on his desk. They stacked higher than the bills in his checking account. He groaned, rustled, tried but failed to sit-up again, and heard.

"Annnnd we are back from commercial break!"

"Damn, I thought you assholes were gone, The Tyranny of Guilt, the absolute ruler? Absolute bullshit you mean." Cal's hand waved in pursuit of the snooze button.

"Owwww, damn that hurts." the station changed, to static...

"Phew, thank friking Gawd. At least that's the end of them. I'm hungry. Morning I know, but could use a slice pizza. Hey look at that, must need a pee. Now where's my damn music?" Cal's hand stroked the radio searching for the station button.

Yielding, he struggled but wobbly sat on the edge of his sway-back, well-stained twin bed.

"Anyway what kinda carp is that? Tick tock yourself DICK DOC, or whoever you are, and get a real phone ring."

"Shit, its dark in here. What freakin time is it?"

"Later than you think, for most of us Rachel."

"Jeasus, I thought I got rid of you?"

"We're back with Do- J–k. So you were saying."

The radio show blared on. Cal's alarm clock ticked to 9:30 a.m.

"This guy is so full of it. Probably can't get a regular job, so he makes up this bull shit. Well, I have a few more buttons to push, buddy." Cal slapped the radio.

"There, you're history." Ocean waves crashing to shore and seagulls filtered through the scratchy speaker.

"Damn it, I knew I should have used my CDs. Give me my radio back-I want my music. I need some music juice to rally. Renegade would be good about now. Carp, Big Pete's gunna kill me." Cal knuckle swept his closed eyes.

"Oh, Mama, I'm in fear—"started singing Renegade.

Thunder spoke up. Cal came back, focused on a blurring road, listening to the late night talk show.

# THREE

"Rachel, I twitched. He told me about three Mothers sons, where they were supposed to be August 28th, 1970. Two were hunkered on a wicked dark night a long way from home, may not see the next day's dawn. The other lay safe in bed, woke to his future on a too bright day. He said those boys went about their business that day, and night, unaware providence spoke to destiny, and they agreed, two of the three were to meet thirty years later, in a storm. A highly charged electrical storm so damn powerful, and so god damn violent, it gutted their souls. Eternity bled from them. I didn't know what he meant for sure, but shivered."

"Gibberish- gutted their souls indeed. You need an honest job. This is carp. More book bullshit. What's that I smell? OH CARP, my coconut incense, forgot, in the glove."

Tick, tick, tick tock…

The weak car fan stirred soft pulsations of warm winged wind. It hung on Cal's sweating body.

"So Rachel, three mother's sons, different from one another as their black box of helixes said they could be.

"Huh, helixes, what the heck are you talking about?"

"Though different they were as common to one another as the chaotic 1970 world they lived in.

"I'll tell you how he told me. The first son came from a small town. Born lucky and bright, maybe too bright, it complicated his world some.

"Music I said. Jeasus H. Fucking Christ, where the fuck is the music?" Cal's hand double- slapped a drum beat on top of the dash above the radio.

"Back then there was big goings- on over in Southeast Asia in a place called the Viet Nam, called it a police action at first. The Army needed soldiers, so if you were eligible, and didn't have any kind of deferment–I'll explain in a bit– the government could draft you into the army to serve as a soldier pretty quick, and maybe be in a shooting war pretty quick. It's a long story, but they could do it."

"Hey, I remember that. Damn it-you know, buddy, if I ever see you, I'm gunna kill you. Now give me back my radio. Anyway, who are you talking about? Maybe I won't have to kill you after all. You're freakin nuts."

"Anyway, he called him Mr. Lucky. Six-feet-plus, blue- gray eyes mated to pale skin, a lucky wiry-lean body. The government identified him as 1A, he could be called, drafted, taken, by the military, at any time for active duty. His mom worried. You gettin all this....?"

"Who, the ffffuuu...ck are you talking to?"

"All set to get plucked and Mr. Lucky won the lottery. No not that kind but one just as good, maybe better. You see Rachel the system for drafting young men into the military changed from an old system to a new one thought fairer. The first lottery was held December 1, 1969.

This lottery assigned numbers to birthdates. If your birth date caught a low number you could be drafted. If you got a high number you wouldn't. Mr. Lucky was born May 27, 1948. That date netted 296, a high one. He won that lottery."

"Get on with this, so I can hear Renegade."

"So, the first mother's son, Mr. Lucky, wouldn't get called. He could enlist, but who would do that? What he couldn't get away from, the sweat of the wearing heat of New York City that Friday, August 28, 1970. Caused people to city shuffle, he said. He wasn't too bad with words it seemed.

"On a hot afternoon Mr. Lucky opened a letter and screamed. Good news. It flew out the door; almost beat him back to the choking smoke- stained air of his shared apartment.

This big city paper offered him a little job. Just a start, but a start it was toward a career as a writer. He leapt holding the job offer in hand. Waiting for him at the apartment sat an upset, overheated girlfriend. Listen in–"

'Come on, baaby.' Lucky pressed his luck.

'Get off me,' she shrugged his hug. 'Open these sticky painted windows, quickly, before I suffocate.' Mr. Lucky fist-pounded then open, then told her the news.

'I'm on my way,' he boasted, strutted.

'I?' wrinkled her freckled nose.

"Come-on Doc- you asshole, go ahead. Keep hiding in that radio. Don't ever let me catch you in an alley you son-of-a bitch! GIVE ME MY RADIO BACK!"

"Mr. Lucky was rarely aware. Today, no different, by nightfall he uncorked a grand bottle of cheap wine in honor of his great accomplishment, and anticipated forthcoming paycheck. Two glasses later, two joints later, and a bowl of strawberries with whipped cream came a lot of kissing, licking and another sort of ban-i-g, their l–t."

"Damn, that storm is back. Maybe for the best so I don't have to listen to this carp anymore."

"Air condit–ning w-sn't common back then so wi-dows we-e usually open. Sounds of the city, honking, trucks rumbling, kids screaming running through open fire hydrants as sprinkler systems, and oh yes, Mr. Lucky and girlfriend's passionate serenading screams. Sex sighs penetrated apartment walls, flew out the unstuck window, down the block and across the street.

The eavesdropping neighbors applauded from above in Italian, below in Irish and from different sides of the apartment in Polish and Yiddish. The street echoed approval from two buildings down, in German, Dutch, Ukrainian and Spanish, and anywhere and everywhere the grunting ooohhhhing and owwing reached. The two rested lying in summer sweat listening to the reviews, giggling at the approval rating that Saturday afternoon. Judges' score cards should have been held up."

"So who cares about all this carp?"

"Later that afternoon she told Mr. Lucky it was over. This never happens to him. In a fit of foolish rage he raised his right arm gesturing a slap the olive complexion he spent so much time kissing. The angelic, passionate creature he loved so much had her back to him packing her things. A powder keg of Irish, German, Italian and Syrian and when she turned she held knife in hand. Mr. Lucky's luck, changed."

"Some enchanted evening" Cal mocked.

"Around the same time Mr. Lucky was getting laid, and dumped, his roommates Remm the Gem, a tall, good looking blonde Norwegian, and Guitar Man Mike, a short, lazy, right-eyed bearded mix, quickly walked ten long blocks to their apartment. The deal went badly. Remm and Mike were good at smoking it. Not buying it. Seems the counter- parties in the drug deal were less than honest. At gun point robbed them of the purchase money. Besides the money and their dignity, the thief's stole a few other things."

"Clever crooks they were. They knew how difficult it would be to chase after them down the streets of Manhattan, on a hot day clothed, but naked?"

"When Mike and Remm walked out of the hotel, where the deal should have gone down properly, they wore only their tie dyed t-shirts strategically wrapped around their naked body's midsection, and two embarrassed smiles."

"Shortly after that day those boys mysteriously disappeared from the city. Talk was, they weren't as lucky in the draft lottery as Mr. Lucky. Said they liked the cooler weather anyway- wanted to visit Canada."

The sixties were technically over, but the Viet Nam war wasn't even close. One mother's son, Mr. Lucky, rested in his apartment alone on a hot afternoon in Manhattan's lower East Side, safe from an enemy's bullet on August 28.

"I can't shut this radio off, and he goes on and on and on. Look, I'm not religious, but I'm begging you Jeasus, kill this fucking guy." Cal ground his teeth.

"Rachel, on the other side of the world, in a place called Viet Nam, at 1:50 a.m. Saturday, August 29th 1970 best friends Malcolm McKeon and Johnny Shake, the two other mother's sons sat helplessly in hell suffering through one of Viet Nam's tropical storms, unsafe. Take a commercial break please, I need one."

# Four

"And we're back with Doc Jack and one heck of a story."

"Thanks brown eyes. He went on about those two. Fierce, stinging rain bore down. Punishing pellets rhythmically struck their helmets denying them sleep. Soggy wet, hunkered in a muddy bank, covered by GI ponchos. A tormenting mess, but happy they were it wasn't raining lead!

"The usual deal was Johnny talked and Malcolm, listened. Neither did either that night. The rain finally surrendered that Viet Nam Saturday. Good news to be sure. The boys pulled from the mud, left fossil imprints. The red tropical sun woke and percolated the wet ground, and the air steamy. Too far north of what was then called Saigon they bitched back and forth. What was worse, the heat or the rain?"

"This particular morning, the heat, nature's clothes dryer, was the favored choice. They'd curse it by noon. Either way- hungry- despised, bugs- were glad they were there."

"Excuse me Doc Jack, he told you all of this in thirty minutes?"

"Yes Rachel, but there is thirty minutes, and then again—there is thirty minutes. So shut-up and listen."

"Owwww, okay I'm sorry, but this is a strain, my friend."

"Die buddy, would ya. Put some music on." Cal blinked,

Doc continued

"Malcolm hailed from a small dairy farm community in upstate New York. At six- three, he was the taller wiry one. At odds with fair hair and boyish looks was an inexplicable seriousness. Who knows what happens to young people sometimes? Whatever his secret, he kept it, secret. Quiet tough Malcolm, usually knew there would be a fight ten minutes before, a lethal sharpshooter but a sucker for an injured dog, or a particular cow. Malcolm's instincts equaled Mr. Lucky's smarts. They were the same age."

"Johnny Shake stood a shorter five-nine. Dark curly hair sculpted army-style. His driver's license put him a few years older than Malcolm. What Lucky showcased with smarts, Malcolm with instinct, Johnny equaled with personality. The true NYC smartass's wit overcame a ninth-grade dropout education. He kept Malcolm laughing. In return, Malcolm kept him alive. The Viet Nam War was a raging rampaging rumble. The best of friends got their fair share of it. Their job: take lives-stay alive. Save souls- one in particular."

"Good name Johnny Shake. I like it. Bet he's cool. Malcolm sounds scary. Ok, go on Doc." Cal blinked.

"Both good soldiers, living soldiers, could be found taking breaks on a side of grassy hills when available. They only rested their bodies never their minds. Their eyes concentrated on big, broadleaved plants. Both knew they were predators, and prey.

"They stargazed when they could. Orion's Belt a favorite on star speckled evenings. During the day, Johnny blabbered on about his exploits as a NYC, in- tune guy. Malcolm never told him he knew something about it. The winds of a coming storm swept the boys' words to the listeners. Do you hear them?"

"Who's, Jeasus you're a gone-job?"

"Malcolm and Johnny's——"

"Damn static, damn country damn, damn, damn." Cal smacked the steering wheel.

"Ohhhh- carp. Okay, yeah. Wait, yes I think I can hear them getting louder. Clearer, yes I hear them. Shhhh, don't talk. I want to listen, yes- there they are—"

'It's what keeps us in the hunt, Johnny— what keeps us in the hunt. You know, God, Mother and Country. We're warriors –what we were always meant to be, always been. That's what Uncle told me."

'We gunna die today?'

'Dunno Johnny. Someday I guess. If you go before me, then I will no doubt suffer a big loss."

"Johnny Shake smiled. Malcolm offered a rare smile back then–."

'But if I go before you, than my loss will no doubt be bigga.' Johnny howled.

"The sergeant ordered the platoon back to its march through the tropical land of rotting logs, tufts of long, green, thick- bladed grass and dense jungle- like leaved plants. A patrol ordered by commanding officers. A patrol Malcolm worried about." Doc sneezed.

"God Bless you" Cal gave up.

"Ok, here they are again. Listen closely. You need to remember this after they're gone.

"Gone?"

"Yes gone, folks, adios amigo etc."

'Private McKeon. Let Private Shake and Bake take the point.'

'Sarge, I'm best there. Leave me be fer God's sake.'

'Orders, said Johnny takes the point, now. I'm keepin' my stripes, move.'

'Orders from above, heh, well they know shit. Malcolm knows best. Kept us alive all this time, always knows ten minutes before there's gunna be a fight. Prescient they call it. Hey Malcolm, Sarge is so far up my ass he could be my dentist. Damn army, damn bugs, damn VC, NVA, and Viet Nam. We headed to a fight there boy, aren't we?'

'Don't like it, Johnny. Told them before, don't like it at all. You keep yer head up, and down.'

"Malcolm, we've been pretty lucky aye, never a scratch. I ain't worried."

'Luck's got nuthin to do with it Johnny, this does.' Malcolm held his M-16 and pointed it to the field.

"They stood and followed orders. Johnny took the point. Malcolm caught Johnny's eye and winked its okay." Ten quiet minutes into the march Johnny hollered.

"So what happened next?"

"Listen in folks."

'Hey Sarge, look here a NVA-North Vietnamese Army helmet.'

'Hey Sarge, dead slope, NVA, or what's left of him, blown to hell.'

'Malcolm.'

'Yes Sir, Sergeant Sir.'

"Don't call me Sir! I work for a living. Get back up there. Check it out. Keep your helmets on. I know it's hotter than shit. I hate this goddamn, place."

'Yes SIR Sergeant Sir.'

"Malcolm wiped a bug from his GI scalped head. The only hair he had was a rectangular patch that covered the top of his head, from his forehead to halfway down the back."

'Are you shittin me? What did I just tell you, you freakin idiot? I know you're gunna get me killed. I told you, lose the Sir-Jeasus H Christ-hard enough fightin the heat, now this….be sure to take your salt pills God Dammit!'

"Jeasus this is kinda interesting?" Cal finger tipped his cheek.

"You have no idea wh– -s goi-g——" The platoon halted. Malcolm's black-laced GI boots quickly toed mucky ground pulling him to Johnny. His shirt ripped where it sweat- rotted. Humidity and heat cocktail choked simple breathing. No air- conditioning here. No fast- food. No momma, unless you called Sarge that, and that would have been a bad idea.

"Seconds later, Malcolm and Johnny knelt on one knee by the dead enemy's corpse. Helmetless, they one eye, eyeballed the soldier. Simultaneously they kept the other eye trained on the surrounding terrain."

"Salty sweat beads linked. Streamed down concave cheeks and fought their way through their jungle of scruffy beards. Lip wetting tongues caught what they could, dehydration always a serious problem."

"Musty wet reed odors filled the air. Listen up now, they are back."

"Okay" Cal spoke to his new best friend.

'Minefield,-goddamn it we're in a freakin minefield.'

'What's that private McKeon?'

'Minefield sir, minefield, I said we're in a goddamn minefield.'

'Shit. Goddamn slopes. Goddamn freakin slopes.' Sarge ducked, looked around. Malcolm looked up into the hot sky, paused, took a wet breath and without looking at him said.

'Johnny, you keep stroking your M-16 trigger with a fidgety finger someone's gunna get their head blown off.'

'Sorry Malcolm, nervous. Don't like this. Have a bad feelin.'

'No problem boy. Hey now. Is your mom special?'

'What kinda question is that? Not really sure? I guess I can say, my mama gave me my life. If I don't keep lookin around I'm afraid today I'm gunna lose it.'

"Mama, damn it are you teasing me? I want to hear that song. Give me my radio back"

"Just pay attention all. Music's coming after me. Be prepared."

"Huh?"

'Well Malcolm its kinda funny I guess. Being out here and all, I mean she spent her life protecting me, worrying and all, trying to make sure I kept mine. Now here we all are. Sittin ducks for the NVA, in a minefield, seein hell. Where's momma when we need her Malcolm, where, heh-heh?'

'Dunno? She'll be around I guess, sooner or later, today, tomorrow-sometime. I'll probably see mine before long I'm sure.'

'Yers dead, ain't she Malcolm?'

'Yep, she's gone now.'

'So how in the hell are you gonna— Ohhhh, hey damn Malcolm, don't go—'

'Hey you two shut the hell up while I try to figure this out.'

'Yes sir, sergeant sir. Yes sir. Well, the brass shoulda listened to Malcolm earlier. Wouldn't be in this mess if they listened, Malcolm always knows.'

"Malcolm sounds like a psycho."

"Shhhh all-listen in–"

'Don't call me goddamn sir, goddamn it. Do you idiots understand me? My blood pressure is high enough today, damn sun, damn zips, damn-damn-damn.'

"Johnny smiled, once a smart- ass always a smart- ass. Malcolm nodded, looking up into the blue hazy afternoon sky. His tilted head, his eyes clamped to the slits they were famous for, nose rabbit sniffed the humid air."

'Incoming.'
'What? Where? Nothin's happenin Malcolm.'
'Zips are all around. Incoming.'

"That's it! I've had it now with you. You take my radio away from me for that bullshit and now you leave me hanging? What the hell happens for God's sake?"

"Rachel, I'll stop for now and leave your audience with this. Mother, alive, around, or not, we all have one. Like most good boys, Malcolm, Johnny and Mr. Lucky loved theirs. Now some folks don't, but one all seem to love is Mother Earth, and of course her sister, Mother Nature. But, the one we all fear, the Mother of Battles. Rest well...."

"Rest well? You son-of-a bitch, you wake me up to this crap. Torture me through this god- for-saken ride to hell-land to save my sorry ass job which isn't worth two craps but all I have and —how the hell am I gonna rest well now? Now, give me... mmmmyyyy raaadio baaack... you bastard. Please."

Lightening struck. Cal remembered struggling to get up the previous morning.

Tick, tock, tick, tock,

"Rachel, they only have the beginning of it, but it's a start. Everyone needs to get up and get to work. Today's going to be a little different for your listeners. Don't forget your coffee."

"Thank you Doc, I think. Anyway, it's Monday morning everyone. Get up if you haven't. 9:30 a.m., here's Renegade."

"Oh mama, I'm in fear for my life…"

# Five

Morning sweltered. Lingering in heavy humid air, odors of rotting -yet to picked up garbage. It nauseated, and soured breakfast. The sticky grimy New York City summer's day couldn't pass fast enough.

Pete's military rock hard physique fell. Out of date double knit served his overstuffed, bulging belly well. A too short tie failed to cover gaping openings between his shirts buttons. Pear shaped Big Pete insisted the pressure he felt, touched all.

"Where the hell is he? Where the hell is Cal? That stupid son of a bitch never listens. Told him to be here by nine, no excuses."

Cal, usually late for meetings, didn't break tradition today. The elevator chimed, two old wooden doors peeled apart, he stepped out. Nervous blue gray eyes darted around at eyes peering back. Shuffling feet stumbled on his way to the meeting room. Grounded, he freed his hooked heel from the liberated strand of tattered carpet. Occasionally he shaved, and often bathed, but not today. Telltale evidence from his previous evening's goings on often carried over till the work day, a head hung in hang-over, or sliding feet-still under the influence. Sheepish runaway dogs limping home after a night's foolish pleasure presented themselves better. Big Pete stood, huffing.

"You shoulda been here an hour ago nitwit. Look, see those kids out there? Look at them."

Pete pointed-

"They all want your job, your desk, and speaking of that shithole do you have any idea where anything is on it? I bet copy is there from twenty plus years ago."

Let them freakin have it Cal thought.

"Where the hell have you been?"

"Trying to get up, some bastard changed the station on my clock radio. The oddest program was on, I think." Cal looked at the ceiling.

"WHAT? God-all-mighty, I give up." Pete ground deadline tension on end of a cheap cigar. Tobacco saliva drooled down his chin.

"Please, clean that goddamn desk up. Then get me something worth reading would ya? Today, today I said goddamn it. To—, if you weren't so damn good I'd..." Pete coughed, turned high blood pressure red. Tobacco, a nasty thing his doctors warned him about.

"You are on thin ice I tell ya, thin as paper you Sixties reject. When I was in Viet Nam, I sent men into battle. Now I have to coddle the likes of you. What the heck were you doing back then pussy boy? Hiding in school? Now get the heck outa here and do some freakin thing."

Pete's glaring eyes squinted. Coughed, ignoring covering his mouth. Jaw chewed his cigar, stomped with Marine determination to his glass cube office satisfied with his act. Witness's heads tipped to their work.

Cal's nervous right hand trembled. He slapped his hip in a beat, ground his teeth, balled a fist, and winced. Jealously, he finger tipped others work off their desks along the way he swayed his lanky frame to the temporary safety of his desk. His work lay incomplete. Partial stories a specialty.

10:20 a.m. greeted him on his blurry monitor when he started. Old passages were gouged, and replaced. Tirelessly he worked, for fifteen minutes. Took a break, wondered when this hard work would end as his head slipped from the cradle of his left palm. He struggled but failed, slowly, in a stuttering motion, it fell gently to his desk. Synchronized fluttering eyes closed pinched slits. The left cheek of his snoring head flattened to the desk in peace. A stuffy office and binge to hangover, insisted. Cal day rested in summer's heat, smelling like the night. Blood seeped from his right nostril but almost as fast as he passed out, an icy chill coated him shocking him to attention.

"Jeasus, did they fix that goddamn air-conditioning- finally?"

His drooling head lifted. An unwashed right knobby index finger swept saliva off his chin. The ridge of boney right hand knuckles wiped blood from beneath his nose. Fly- away eyebrows rose, eyelids followed. Cal struggled for complete consciousness, focused on his desk looking for his missing notes. In their place, a small-town throw-away shopper type of newspaper, anonymously delivered while in slumber-land.

Cal's hands shook. Not all the time, but on occasion. Occasion became often. He clamped them to wooden arms rests of his overworn brown leather chair. The chair was nearly as old as he was at seven dog years. He slithered in its flaking leather seat, squinted at the intruder. Limply his gray's opened more confidently.

"Aggahhh, too fast,"

Cal folded at the waist, leaned forward extending his right arm to grab the unexpected guest. He just missed his cherished paper coffee cup, precariously placed on the right edge of his desk.

Must be a mistake he thought. Cal pulled the paper to his shirt's buttons. This time he didn't miss the much needed coffee cup. The chocolate speckled rug beneath his wing tip shoes the evidence of his previous mistakes. The paper fell from his grasp to the desk. Cal pressed a bitter, "fuck," past the spaces of tanned teeth.

"Double fuck," confirmed, in case of any doubt.

An angry hang-over snapped his head and jaw ground molars.

"Goddamn son-of-a bitch."

Cal gave in to newsman curiosity, reached for the paper but this time with both hands. Holding it up he leaned back, his chair creaked. Coffee starved grays burned through, and over his drug-store reading glasses. Fumbling thumbs finger pinched its edges. He started flipping through the twenty- page shopper. One that demanded the attention of a jealous child, nothing would stop it.

Ordinarily the little free-of-charge paper, sleeved in its plastic rain gear would be thrown out without a glance. That is after it lay on a curb or a lawn for a few days. Cal smirked looking at the nothing paper filled with who cares news, and trivial information. Someone left it hoping someone would peel its skin, someone like Cal.

"Ok, where's the classifieds?" Pages parted looking for everyone's favorite, fun ads packed with items for sale, services available offered in generally insincere small boxed advertisements.

"This is crap, oops, sorry, carp I meant. I don't need a washer repairman. I certainly don't need financial planning. What finances, unless you count being broke?"

Scanning the headlines Cal's slack jaw rose to a scoffing smile. A twitching right hand slipped in his pants pocket and tickled his change. These were his good slacks. All holes stitched. Survivors of a pin-stripe suit purchased from a thrift store. The jacket's location remained unknown. Likely left on the back of a stool at some smoky saloon during an evening's outing, or, perhaps, his childhood grooming gave it to a damsel in climate distress. She would have had to have been both cold and attractive. No wonder losing the coffee angered him. Money was dear.

"Ha-ha. Some joke." Cal's bark warned those who scoffed his work and left the paper, likely from younger staff. The prank suggesting, here is where you are going, here is where your career will end. But not a head popped up.

Offense aside, curious thumbs pressed on. Cal held out hope this was not meant for him, turned the pages kicking out its seasoned haunted house aroma.

"Goddamn carp, god d..."

Cal spoiled for a fight, a bad idea in his condition. He huffed, sighed. Anxiously slid around in his cracked leather chair, rubbed his chin, rubbed his squinting grays, darted paranoid glances about the office watching who was watching him. Musty pages flipped. Sweaty right hand thumb and index finger threw pages from left to right losing the fight against the paper's absorbing cruel pull.

"Did Big Pete leave this for me? Did one of those little bastards do it for him? I'm sure they must have. Which one? You, over there," a college intern slept in her chair.

"Better not take any chances, though."

Cal was out of chances at the chance bank, and a bad risk for chance credit. He could not lose this job. No more for someone of his time and grade, old and washed up. Endure the irritations, he told himself, even if they were mosquito bites in size.

Thin pale vein- bulging hands freckled with markers of time, flipped through final pages.

"This isn't much of anything. I need this crap like I need a freakin— hey; maybe they want me to cover hay rides in New Jersey for heaven's sake."

He threw the paper on his desk. Fish-flopped to a halt, parted in the middle. He reclined watching its acrobatics. Limp eyes fluttered to soft seams, shut out harsh office lights. Subdued, he rested awaiting Big Pete, the executioner, to deliver his pink slip."

"Wait a second. What, what is that?"His eyes sprang open as though he found a much needed fifty dollar bill.

"The date, look- at- the- damn- date, idiot." Positive self-talks, never a forte'.

"It's August, heck yes, August 29, yes, but 2009, not—1995. What the Hell- HOLY CARP. Goddamn son-of-a-bitch, Jeasus H. freakin Christ, freakin ay. Tomorrow, it's fourteen — goddamn, son-of- a- bitch years ago. How the hell, what the hell, where the hell did this come from?"

His bag-of-bones chair creaked as he stood. Cal's knees creaked.

"Did someone see me? Hear me?" He looked over his shoulder

"Phew, not a soul looked up. What the H E double L L is this doing here? Today is August 28, 2009. Damn it. I think so anyway?" He checked his desk calendar. Bobbled his head yes. Dates escaped Cal from time to time. Time to time was daily.

The fight was over. He lost. Curiosity grabbed him by the throat, which coincidently happened to be the same place as his heart. Cal reached, rescued, and paged through the paper, again, from beginning to end. Nothing extraordinary banged the grays, except the date.

"Another joke, that's all. Ha-ha, you bastards. Oops, better keep it down Pete will hear."

He rolled it up, and then viciously smacked the edge of his underused desk wanting it dead.

"You've given me the handle to hate you all."

If there was somewhere else to go, he would. There wasn't. He accepted this event yet as another of the younger staff's pranks pushing his well worn buttons and he would have been correct, had they been the ones to leave it there.

Cal rapped his slaughtered desk again, and then caught the circular file only a few feet away. Holding the paper as a spear he aimed he readied to release it. The grays caught a small yellow note-sticker protruding from the second to last page. He hadn't seen it earlier. Wondered was it there before.

"Ah, maybe I missed it, no coffee and all. How could I have missed it? Odd, I didn't see it before." He figured just another daily disconnect.

"Remorsefully he pampered the paper as if guilt ridden for abusing a pet. Parental care ironed it flat with shaking palms. Delicately he peeled pages till he opened to the one tagged with the yellow sticker. A loose piece of scratch paper lay next to it scrawled on in childlike script. Cal read, Thought you would like to read this." No signature.

"Read what you say, you son- of- a- bitch." Cal shrugged in fear and looked about.

Who was it, who was tormenting him? Why? Two-handed he fist held it high, arms outstretched and stood as tall as he could. A curled pouting lip readied to ream someone.

Then, there it was. On the second to last page a small obscure story highlighted in yellow. Three short sentences that said little, about a lot, right where he found the yellow sticker and note. Jesse's ambulance service took the whole last page always.

At that moment Cal's odyssey upstate New York started. Providence, Fate, and Destiny all shook hands on it, thirty years ago. Two of the three mother's sons would meet in a storm he told me.

Thunder burped- Cal focused on the night and the road. Lightening would have none of it, and she flashed Cal back.

Cal read the–oh by-the-way, three line story reporting the battle about a ferocious gun fight in a small country bar. The article titled,

"The Mother of All Battles." Told of a blood bath which took place in Fate, a small farming community nestled at the bottom of two hills in upstate New York.It made no sense to Cal, a well-seasoned over-ripe newsman, why so little said? There must be so much more. What is it hiding? Why?

"Come on Cal think. I don't, can't remember. Why not, I wouldn't have missed this?"

Excited fingertips shed their trembles, flew tapping the keyboard.

"Any, are there any records about this, any at all? Come on, damn. There has to be. Was it was ever in real print, not a paper like this. Good newspaper writers always remember big stories, come on, boy. You remember right now."

"But it wasn't in the big papers, nor on television so how in the world did this get by me, all of us? Can't remember, did I black out that day? No, couldn't have, too big a story to miss. What happened?"

Fingers rapped the keyboard. Gray eyes strained till almost blue. Energy jacked his soul like no coffee caffeine jag ever could. His lightened step pranced and paced over the stained rug. Forgotten neurons fired. Synapses arched to fighter pilot sharpness.

"One last chance, I've got one last freakin chance to write story worth writing. This is it for sure. Too little said about something as big as this? Fourteen years ago, three lines. Heck, most obituaries say more."

Cal's heart pounded as it hadn't in years. When his damp palms grabbed for the paper again a different folded paper fell from between it pages. It fluttered to the floor. Cal picked it up and unfolded a hand-drawn map.

"Ah, a Piiirrrates maaaap, oh, where oh where am I to go?"

Charmed Cal silly smiled for every time he touched the paper, something touched him.

"Wait," he sweated, the smile fell not wanting to admit it, was the institution, far away?

"I promise, no more, no more will I miss anything. Leave me be."Solemnly, he promised

A promise unlikely kept. He would be unkindly reminded of it, if he did. Someone, something, ensured that. What couldn't be missed were the maps directions. They were clear. Prospects of what may come, electrified the schoolboy with expectations similar of pending recess.

"Damn, a story, a real honest to goodness story? Hope Big Pete goes for it?" Cal bent, gripped the entire paper in a right handed fist, stomped across the coffee-stained carpet with West Point cadet precision.

# Six

"What do you mean a vicious shooting in a bar wasn't covered? From when, what? Listen you, go get that story or pack your pictures."

"I will Pete, I will. Count on it. You bald fat tub of shit. Hope you die."

"What, what did you whisper?"

"Said I hope this is a fat story that will fly. I need a break."

"Get outa here. Go see Mother Nature, get your head clear and get the goddamn story."

Cal hang-dogged it out of Pete's glass cube, another last chance in his pocket, his last. All eyes were on him. He hid from them lost in thought, back forty years ago when a hard bodied kid twirled the sticks. Left foot worked the cymbal, the right–a bass drum. Straw, shoulder length hair broom whipped the air with every head snap. Sturdy gray eyes stayed open all night till daylight sent them to bed.

Calendar pages ripped off their pads since. Most of his rock group grew old, some didn't. Cal did, ungracefully. The only music he played now came from a clock radio begging him to wake, or a crusty car radio doing the same. Youths dreams sold out to regular income. Holstered drum sticks were swapped for pen and paper. Indulgent road managers, replaced by managers—like Big Pete. Tasked Cal left his Manhattan, East Village apartment early in the next day. His second wife just told him she had a five year plan, and he wasn't part of it.

Thunder rolled, Cal snapped back driving, self talking.

"Waaann, twoooo, a one- two—-you mad old bastard. I'll get the freakin story," Cal wrist snapped imaginary tom-tom drums. Four/four meter rock beat never left him. His arms flailed, his car veered. Knees steered. Criss-crossed hands worked the old ritual, air strike the snare drum, tap high hat cymbal. Fingers twirled sticks. Oncoming headlights took him back to a time of bright stage lights but this wasn't the big stage he never played on. Or the small ones he did. Cal dropped the sticks, grabbed the steering wheel, and just missed a screaming truck horn. Tamped frayed carpet punched free-loading dust in trampoline bounces in the air. They landed in new hiding places.

"God, that's awful. Bring back the real lights, I could sing then."

About four hours till I get there, if I get there. I'll have this song nailed by then, he thought.

"Carp, I'm almost outa gas. Thank God, Christ, Moses, Buddha, Rasputin, and the celery stalk, that damn gauge works."

The first of a few allotted lucky breaks rested ahead. His car stalled, he cranked it and it fired, sputtered. He put it neutral and coasted to the off the New York Thruway ramp. The engine quit but a wind at his back pushed him right to a pump.

"What'll it be, Bub?" she asked.

"Huh?" Cal answered.

"What—will—it—beeee? Jeasus, H, Christ almighty. Are you freakin deaf?"

"Oh, sorry… bitch."

"What's that, Bub? You're a whisperer aren't you?"

"I said pitch black out, and not sure. Not sure how far I'm goin, how much I'll need."

"Not that far, bub, but you'll need it filled."

"How the hell, do you know where I'm goin, hmmmm… missy?"

"I know. Don't worry bub. By the way, she should have dumped you."

"What did you say?" Cal raised a brow, and squinted shooting her an angry glare, from behind the safety of the driver's door partially open window.

"I said it says so, on that map, on your seat." Hanging straight black thread hair masked most of her face. Emerald green eyes lit behind the veil.

"You're not real aware are ya, bub?"

"Huh?"Cal raised his fly-away eyebrows, lowered his gray eyes to the passenger seat. There sat the map. "Oh, right. Well since you know how far, and what I'll need, just give me enough for that."

"Already done… Bub"

"How much..?"

"No charge."

"Wha–,"

"You don't listen real good either now do ya, BUB. Been taken care of, besides your gonna need that twenty in your pocket for Mother.

"Who?"

Never mind. Now listen to me, f-nut. It's getting wet out here. The storm following you, the one you been eyeing in that poor excuse for a rearview mirror, is here. Look up, right over your sorry head, now.

"Yeah, and?"

"And, and this bub. Mother Earth told Mother Nature about you, and to help you."

"Huh?"

"She's sent a couple of hitch-hikers for you to take along on your trip, been with you for awhile."

"What, who, are you high?"

"Be aware, bub. The twins, older by a minute Brother-Thunder, and temper-temper Sister-Lightning, are part of that storm. They fight like mad. Mother will have to keep score to keep order. Now, get outa here. Go finish what you started. Do what Big Pete said."

"Score, remember, what in the world? All he said was to get out of the office, go upstate, and oh yeah, get the goddamn story if I wanted to keep my desk. Also, get my head clear, get the cob webs cleared. Go see Mother Nature. Hey, how the heck do you know Big Pete?"

"Never mind what I know. It's what you— need to know that counts. Go, get you story, ask your questions, in your head-from your lips, and then listen. Listen all around, to all and especially listen to yourself. One last bit of advice, bub, keep your eyes open.... wide. That road, the one off the Thruway you're gonna go on. Well it's dark. Hidden twisty turns trick the best. Keep those grays wide open. I warn ya. This isn't the kind you're familiar with, this one's different. See ya, fuck nut." stuck in the moist air.

A gust of early warning wind, from the south, headed north. It caught her hair from behind her neck, blew it straight forward and held as if waxed tattered flag. The full moon lit her frozen silhouette as a sign-post pointing direction.

"And quit that awful singing. You're tone deaf, finish your writing. That's what you're here to do."

"Ugh" Cal pivoted his bristly face left, right, atop his chilly spine. Nicotine burnished index finger pressed a rare working power window button. He looked forward. Safely sealed inside he bravely laid his middle finger goodbye against the glass. She chuckled knowing more than he. He mashed pedal, performed a rare wheel spin. Lightening lit the sky and Cal remembered the day he found his car.

Cal found his tortured chariot, a former star slave in a rental car fleet, on a hot dusty day. The fatigued car was at the end of its trail. It sat alone on auto death row, alone. Behind it, a cyclone fence, around it, spent soda cans, beer bottles, crushed cigarette packs. On deflating soft tires, it waited, unsold and unwanted, and dust caked for a wrecker to haul it to its mercy crushing. If it were an animal a bullet would have been loaded.

Always low on funds Cal negotiated its release for a minor sum. The day he drove it off the lot a spot rain storm burst. Dust gray car morphed to blue. Shiny wet, the former beauty reminded Cal of pictures he had seen as a child of Haley's Comet majestically slicing space. Immediately he named the car the Blue Comet, or affectionately Old Blue when in the mood. After a mile or two he figured this blue comets tail that streaked behind it was from its weak engine burning oil. Cotton balls escaped out of every tear in its seats, and there were quite a few tears. So it turned out Old Blue wasn't that kind of comet. Cal reconsidered. The Blue Comet became just the Comet, or Old Blue.

Thread bare tires were replaced with better, but still used ones. Most else needed, waited, for awhile, a long while. Comet had a suspension, weak. Proudly Cal boasted about his bargain to his mechanic. After a jaunt around the block the mechanic replied —

"It has the stability of over cooked spaghetti. Turning the steering wheel should be considered more of a request then a command, a perfect death trap, perfect for you." Cal laughed. He loved Old Blue. They were a pair. Taking it anywhere rivaled thrills of amusement parks he adored. Especially if eating, smoking and playing the air drums at the same time.

"Four hours I figure to get to this cow town. Man, hope it doesn't stink too much."

As Old Blue was to Cal's requests, Cal was to Big Pete's. Commands were interpreted as requests. However this command had to be honored. He left Manhattan in the black of night that early morning. With the same physical instability of the Comet Cal pressed his 6'2" 145 pound frame, with accompanying body odor, firmly into the stained torn driver's seat with perfectly matched indentations. It gave new meaning to the term, memory seats. He slapped the accelerator, hung on for dear life.

Thunder rumbled. Cal came back and self talked.

Old Blue wobbled as the mechanic promised. Cal eyed a hiding map shuffled together with other papers on the passenger seat like playing cards. Dry coffee cups rolled over it and the circle with X marks the spot. X, Fate, a small town in upstate New York in the heart of the country, Mothers country.

"How the hell did that green eyed clown know any of that, and my singing? Hey I'm not that bad. I have to be out of my mind to do this. Why did Big Pete agree for me to get this story? He never says it's ok, but I do anyway. Probably hoped it would kill me. It may, especially if I meet any more characters like her. At least I got the nut jobs out of the way. Doubt she can be topped. Mother Nature's twins, right. Don't tell me drugs won't mess you up. Just some simpleton country bumpkins left for me."

The attendants promised storm caught him with a pounce. Comet slowed. Cal choked down his annoying singing and listened to scratchy music filtering through shredded speakers, delivered by sketchy reception. Then-

"Time for some of your news, pay close attention you need to hear–" the storm swallowed hard.

"-he weathers going to get worse, listen carefully." Returned.

"Yeah, yeah, blah, blah, listen this, listen to that. Everybody's has advice. "Hey, pay attention to your own crummy life."

Cal blinked, the road blurred. Tick, tick, tick fought for attention.

"Damn, what's broken? Not now, pleaassse." Tick, tick, tick, he looked at the dash. A sticking stuttering second- hand, on his car clock struggled. Dimly, it displayed 3:00 a.m.

"It's 1:30 a.m., good morning to all. Hope your day is starting well, or your night finishes safely, and now time for your news." The radio newsman's voice fought the static through decaying car speakers.

Cal glanced at his cars clock, again. Someone was very off. He shrugged.

"Hey, wait a sec. I had music on. That station change itself? Anyway you better get this story ole boy, or face the unemployment line, or worse."

Cal, soon to turn sixty-two looked seventy-two.

"Owwww, damn .....Damn legs, dam knees, feel like I'm ten, no twenty years older."

Fighting for his job wasn't where he thought he would be at this time in his life. But he was.

"Why the hell did I give up? Should have finished em, I'm good damn it, really good"

His abandoned dreams lay heavily in dusty stacks. Unfinished typewritten pages weightily swayed and bellied his bookcases. Cal sold out, settled for second place. Many foolishly do.

"Dam I was good-am good. What happened to her?"

Once honored, this too smart journalist hid inside a too drunk, multiple divorce shell. Emotionally left for dead he slugged it out. A numb life clung to what only remained of his soul. Crafty writing, it paid. Collaring this story would also. Fate and destiny shook hands on it, thirty years ago.

"Big Pete must have called ahead, making sure I'd get there. How'd that son-of–a-bitch know where and when I'd stop? No matter. He did. He must have." The self talker answered also.

Cal played driving games. Take the car out of gear, and see how far you could coast before stopping. A skill self taught to the self talker as a young driver with no money trying to save gas. Playfully he game showed it coasting into the next rest stop. He hunkered, looked, and worried another weirdo waited. Nature gave him courage. He ran inside to the men's room. Then out to the fast food burger bar, and a cup of light and sweet coffee. Cal shiftily shuffled out the door, girly magazine for the articles tucked under his arm, fumbling with his pants. A zipper left overlooked. At his driver door he placed his loot on the hood, hiked his pants flipped cellophane to the wind from a new pack of filterless cigarettes.

"Ok, let's get this over with. So I can get back and kiss Pete's ass. Now, where the heck is this place?" He looked at the map on the driver's seat.

"Can't see, damn it to hell."

Billows of exhaled cigarette smoke yellow tinted the Comets windows making visibility poor, his lungs worse.

"Gotta stop again, carp, I'll never get there at this pace."

Another pee, a hike of the pants, more light and sweet coffee, then with open fly Cal headed on his way, again.

"Agh-agh-agh," A mile down the road he slid Old Blue to an emergency shoulder of the road stop. Behind the yellow tints, inside the mushroom smoke cocoon, Cal howled like a dog at the moon and waved his arms. Smoldering ash from a half smoked smoke fell, to his open crotch.

"Where is this place? I want to be home. Damn it, God Damn it- tomorrow, t-o-o-o-moroow."

"Not likely" answered from out of the cars radio. Cal's eyes popped. Static irritated his ears. A long pause held, then, "that congress will pass the legislation."

Cal rolled his eyes. He exhaled, sighed.

This trip was shaping up like his unfinished manuscripts. Yet finish, he must. Or face the rudest of consequences.

"Damn, I'm never gonna get there, damn. Don't wanna go there but have to. Have to."

An uncertain right wing foot pivoted on it's heal, indecisively slipping back and forth between the brake, and accelerator peddles.

"Ok here we go." Cal mashed his teeth, then the gas pedal.

The Comet choked, gagged, stumbled and nearly stalled. Some of the dash gauges worked, some occasionally, some not at all. Red, yellow and green dash lights flickered on and off. The steering wheel twisted to the left, the car lunged forward.

"Lady Luck stay with me" Cal whispered. An appeal to someone he barely knew.

Squinting through the laminated windows he tried to see into the dark of the early eerie warm morning. Brake –gas-brake. Cal and car slowed, pulsed and surged.

"Come on, let's do this. I can't, I can't freakin wait."

Cal's story rested in Mother Nature's peaceful breast, nestled in upstate New York. He sped. Thruway mile markers blurred. The odometer spun. Resolve strengthened. So did the thickening sky that hunted him.

Light rain squeezed from the clouds dusted the windshield with a fine mist. His left eye watched through the road, his right stayed trained on the black clouds overtaking him reflected in the loose rear view mirror. A childhood memory flashed - injuns chasing covered wagon.

Chase the clouds did. Catch him they did. Thudding globs of a thickening rain dropped. It pounded his car's windshield, bulling the gentle rain away. Cal struggled to see clearly into a murky night. Being hung-over didn't help.

The map he was told to follow provided clear directions. Remarkably, Cal followed them.

I have to be outa my mind. What the heck am I doing here? He thought.

"Damn, do I turn here?" Cal said.

His right hand grabbed the map.

"Do it, now.........get there before the others get the best deals" An ad came from the radio speaker.

"Shit, I do. Damn, turn here, turn here." They skidded off the Thruway onto the off ramp in a last second maneuver.

"Ok, what now?" He clutched the aged map on its edge, disrespecting its age.

Take the one road in, Cal read. An arrow pointed the direction.

"Hey, that wasn't on the map before. Was it? Oh well?" He shook it off charging it to John Barleycorn.

The Thruway was lit. Not this slippery country road the ramp placed them on. Old Blues tires caught the roads pavement. Half a mile down the forgotten road the surface turned to dirt. Another mile, re-loved it was paved again. A hundred yards later it was forgotten again, turned back to oiled dirt, then mud. A telling series of alternating on and off's.

"Three, no maybe four hours-all I need to get this story. I'll be home in the morning."

"Doubt it," scratched from the radio, a pause and then, "the president will sign the bill."

The rain churned the dirt road it into a mud pie only a mud-er race horses would have delighted.

"I've got to remember this, write about this."Ticklish inspiration woke Cal's sleeping imagination.

"I'll start it like this. A country road, similar to the ones many have stored as their favorites. They're all right there, logged and tagged to your memory. If forgotten- they're easily remembered, if allowed. Especially when you're least expecting it, resting, alone, disarmed, in the still of a deep, dark, black, night."

"Hey, that's pretty good."

The gas attendant's forewarning held true. The road twisted. Wildly, Cal twisted the steering wheel encouraging the Comet to stay on the road, in the still of a deep, dark, black, night. The storm relentlessly pursued him. Bulleting rain drum beat pounded the hood, coated the windshield. Limp, lazy, weak wipers bowed under its weight, trying to plow the strange coating of thick gelatinous rain from windshield. Dangerous rain grew treacherous.

Desperate times dictated terms. Compelled Cal to forgo his usual evening's pint or two this night. Instead, he fought the elements on a four hour, lonely night ride. A ride perfectly suited to be joined by some companions, hitchhikers.

Boom-crack-boom... Thunder and Lightning said hello. They brought two other stowaways- whimsical thoughts and great, reminisces.

"Miss her, miss that time we had" filled Cal's sixty –two year old clogged head.

All were on board now. The usually unruly siblings -thunder and lightning- were issued strict instructions on how to behave miles earlier. She assigned each a specific job. Thunder's rumbling booms kept Cal in the present. Lightning's flashes took him back in time. A much needed metronome arrangement insisting order of the disorderly. Clever Mother-Nature, knew best. But would they obey?

Booom-ba-ba-ba boooom-bam, crack, older brother by a minute, Thunder, spoke. Granted the stage he showed off with a volley of kettle drum rumblings. Cal's right foot tapped the accelerator. Impatiently, Sister lightening huffed, waiting her turn. Dutifully, she held off her violent flashes.

"Man this is a freakin nightmare. Not sure this freakin job is worth it anymore." Cal gagged.

"What the heck, no one here to hear me anyway."

"You sure" spoke from the radio. A pause, then, "they have a chance at first place"

Cal didn't even shake his head this time.

"Ok, where the hell am, I?"

"Somewhere, on your way to the country, helped along by Mother Nature's twins." His tobacco breath answered back, the gray's rolled. Forehead sweat beaded.

Thunder's weakening rattle fluttered in Cal's ear. Sister lightning had enough. She took her shot, broke her shackles to freedom declaring independence. Jagged blinding flash of white hot electric light fired an arc scissor ripping a hole in night's darkness. Eerily, it illuminated the grooved, sloppy, muddy, road. Cal appreciated the pulse of strobe light. Then quaked looking at the freeze frame caught deer, chipmunks and snakes hiding in the forest.

Mother's ordered truce, short lived. What could be expected to happen with unruly children did. Pulsing, vibrating, punching exchanges, alternated between lightning's light and thunder's booms. The gloves were off. A pissy sibling duel competed for Mothers Natures attention. Each vibrating rumble rattled Cal's bones, but woke his soul. Each bolt of lightning's white hot current burned his tired eyes, but opened his consciousness.

Thunder bass drummed, lightening bickered back flooding the sky with a violent light. The symphony of light and beat contentiously grabbed at only Cal. His thoughts snapped to and fro. His head followed. The twin's exchanges violated Mother Nature's specific orders. Neither could be trusted. Her Governance knew she needed more control or Cal was in serious trouble.

She decided to score their turns. A ploy, hid as entertainment. At the end of Cal's trip she promised them she would tally the results. Whoever had the most points would be awarded the championship title, complete with full bragging rights, and other future benefits. They agreed, again.

The score started at even for what previously transpired. Each readied. The Comets clock ticked to 3:30.

"2:20 a.m., you still have time." A woman radio announcer's voice replaced the man's.

Who's she speaking to? Another talk show, I guess Cal wondered.

2:20 a.m. reverberated in his head. Cal thunked it, in his head. The previous hour and a half difference between his car clock's time, and the man's news-time quote narrowed to an hour and ten minutes. Cal looked at his wrist. His stopped watch showed 11:59 p.m. He shrugged.

Sneaky sister struck, threw a javelin of jagged flickering strobe spikes. The still of the dark night lit, and reflected in Cal's eyes. Wide open eyes held his mouth wide open. He didn't plan on the storm, he never planned. The Comet stabilized.

"Send an experienced journalist on such a simple task, should have been handled by a cub reporter. What a lucky break. This is surreal. If I didn't know any better I'd swear I was having flashbacks, can't be. Been forty-years since I last took LSD, sixty-nine I think, maybe seventy; hmmm seventy-one the latest I'm sure, kinda."

"Not those kin- of storms tonight frien–."

Cal's ride ate time off the car's clock. Nervous jiggling numbers spun to 3:45.

"2:45 a.m., be safe folks it's a wicked night." The newsman continued in relief of the newswoman.

Cal looked at his wrist, 11:59 p.m.

"Oh, well," he said shoulder shrugging. "Catching up?" he asked no one. "Only an hour difference now?" he answered.

It was very late, getting earlier. Dutifully, shabby Cal accelerated. The Comet groaned, Cal groaned. The spiced evening's symphony of alternating sounds, illuminations and consciousness kept him entertained. His New York City's pace gradually slowed and swapped places with the country. He sighed.

Dousing rain mixed country road dust to mud, then slush mud. Cal remembered vacationing upstate as a child. Locals closed roads with a "Washed out Road" sign on boards blocking its passage. Signs put them up after storms, not in them. All he wished for, another cup of coffeehouse coffee. Night's fog forced more squinting.

"Shit, what the hell am I doing here? Will they miss me at the bar? Wait till they find out numero three is history."

The kids rocked. Bellowing echoing deafening thunder rumbled, and shook the world beneath it. Lightening lovingly liked to synchronize with him, on occasion. Not tonight. Her bolts rested waiting their turn. Slippery country roads stayed dark. Rules were rules. Order prevailed. Older brother thunder reigned in the present. Flashy younger lightning lit the past. There would be no confusing this symphony.

Cal gripped Comet's steering wheel. The night's entertainment played on. Brother- Thunders tempest yielded some of his authority to light from a full moon peaking through the hazy storm clouds. Night's wet air filled with the moonlight. Foggy billowy haze pleased the most discriminating Werewolf. Cal, the mere mortal, wasn't.

He left his apartment wrapped in poorly patched dress pants, and a mismatched wrinkled Tattersall shirt. No tie. Tuffs of grey reached up to peek from his shirt's open neck. A drug store watch bandied around his right wrist, dead battery and all. The Comet's usually unreliable clock worked better than its radio. 4:15 a.m. blinked. Cal tuned in for the radio time. A garbled dialogue, said, "....you'd better get this right this time or you'll be back." Perhaps a woman advised, it was getting more than confusing.

"3:45" he heard for sure. Cal did the math, looked at his stopped watch, 11:59 p.m.

Blurry, sleep-deprived vision compelled repeated blinks, an old late-night traveler's stay-awake exercise. Frightened determination fought the good fight. Cal's eyes stayed wide open. His attorneys said another crash was not possible.

"We all live in a yellow submarine, a yellow submarine a yellow submarine" Cal sung out, another old trick to stay awake.

"Ah, piss is it—we all live in piss, ha- ha- ha- haaa." The gimmick worked.

Though not officially delirium, he did skirt its edges. Aged eyes that witnessed too much, strained this night in the dim light. So far so good, wicked danger dangled. Old Blue ate up the muddy road. The distance to town closed.

Time differences tightened. Road conditions worsened. Cal's historically poor driving skills raised the stakes. Retired NYC taxi cabs were in better condition than Old Blue.

"Jeasus damn it." Squinting, white knuckled Cal complained fearful of over correcting the Comets path. They wavered, and wiggled. Slid and skidded down the hazardous undulations of the rural road. Odds-on winners of an "All Over the Road" poster contest. Sneaky adrenaline raced Cal's heart. A guardian angel hovered above him.

Ten years ago he tried to get healthy. Nine-and-a-half years ago, after three different kinds of therapy, he failed. Though the techniques did not attain mental health, they made him laugh. Primal scream, the funniest of all.

"Shiiiitttt, carp, f…" Cal raged words flew out the window into the storms wind. He couldn't crash this one. Only a few chances left in the driving department his lawyers said. Unknown to Cal was that crashing was not an option tonight, even if he wanted to.

"God damn son-of- a-" he expelled. More frightened utterances smothered by the night's damp cool air. No one of this earth heard them.

Cal sleepily hung to Old Blue's mismatched color steering wheel during a rare calm. The original brown wheel broke, needed to be replaced, saving money was more important than color-coordination. All other repairs washed through identical logic. Use good enough junkyard parts when possible. Money saved was targeted for more important things, such as an evening out.

The ride settled down. Old Blue, fearful of being impounded, tracked well.

"Only a few miles left." Cal sighed.

A scowl found his face, sweat his forehead, he rolled on.

"What the Heck am I gonna find?"

Rain took a breather. The sky lit.

"BOOM," the Comet ran over a fallen tree limb. Thunder used a proxy. It counted.

The Comet veered left, Cal tipped right in a sweaty panic countering with body- English. He stamped the brakes. Hand over hand he furiously dialed the steering-wheel to the right pleading with Old Blue to comply. The four -wheel skid slowed. Cal lapsed back in time without lightning's help. Brother teased her. She was upset and downright insulted and worried that she might not be needed. Jealousy said hello, but there was a lot of work to do for her going forward. Her unexpected help was appreciated-much like thunder's use of a branch. Cal lapsed back to the previous morning.

∾

He grabbed the hand-drawn map on his desk disrespectfully smudging it with nicotine thumbs. He read aloud the incomplete words written on it. "One ro—in, two ro— out,"

"What's missing, hmmmm? Ah, I have it. One road in, and two roads out," the well known wordsmith figured.

"One road in, two roads out, hmmm, well if I'm right, and I am, maybe I'll take the other road out, because the road in obviously served both directions."

Office gossip had it Pete started typing Cal's dismissal as soon as Cal left his office.

∾

Thunder, aided by a pot hole, nearly a ditch, Cal snapped back to the present.

Early morning's daybreak hinted to the wet grass to wake. Only one treacherous mile to go, the road twisted, raised, and then lowered with subtle, floating undulations. It slumped lower into a soggy air forested glen descending on its way to Fate, still sleeping at its end.

Cal pushed the button, on-off-on-off, encouraging a fragile power driver's door window down. Damp wind whistled through the opening, carrying a melody.

"Hmhm hm hum hm ha hi hi Hiiiii RIDING THROUGH THE GLEN...hm hm......" it went on repeating itself over and over. His ear tilted toward the open window trying to make out what sounded like lyrics.

"Geezz, now where is that coming from? Elves must be in the neighborhood."

Hey, what's that? No, not the melody, something else, whistles now, here, what? He thought

Trains, riding the rails at night, cutting, zig zag patterns through the countryside's thick forest. They crossed streams, roads, anything and everything carrying local farm fresh crops.

A particularly well-known train sped over the long laddered paths this night. Black as the night she raced over the stitched paths. Wearing her camouflage, charging, she headed to the wooded glen. Cal, unaware, was only a half a mile away from where the tracks sliced across the road.

All locals knew when this late night hauler rode the rails. They stayed inside. Its metal wheels screeched on the iron tracks warning all she was loose. An out of date train, one that survived time, one an elder engineer loved. Gleefully he readied his hand. It found its favorite place. Masterfully he repeatedly pulled the whistle cord. A shrill whistling warning pierced the sleepy night "GET OUT OF MY WAY, be aware."Thick black smoke pumped its plumes into night's mist.

"GET OUT OF MY WAAAAYYYY." Again the tugged cord sent harsh warnings only preceded by her white hot headlight that lit the tracks. Lightning would have been pleased.

Cal and the train each raced to their destinations, ignorant of the other. If they crashed there could be only one victor. Well hidden slightly sunken iron rail track lay just ahead. He didn't see it. Lost in thought, he never heard the train. The flickering light sparking through the forest a mere over-tired late night hallucination No warning signs in the country or road markers, signal lights or cross arms. You just had to know, if not, then.

Cal rocketed down the road. The Comet hurdled over a small rise, lost its footing, and slid sideways. Cal finally saw the tracks, out passenger door window.

Commandingly the train charged. Heavily smoking, she was only thirty seconds from the road crossing. It would not stop. Collision was imminent if one were in the way. Finally the piercing whistle and brilliant headlamp seared Cal's brain.

Fifteen seconds from the tracks he tried to coherence the hydroplaning Comet back into control. Confused, he thought the road cut to the left.

"Wait, did it?"Sweat poured down his pasty pale forehead.

"Shit, damn it," He smashed his eyes together, once, twice.

Twelve seconds. His hands froze on to the replacement steering wheel. Cal's knee replacement, dental posts and a few other items, reminders all was not original on the driver as well. He wrenched the car left.

Ten seconds, another mistake. He yanked the wheel hard right. Old Blue's tires gripped, rumbled in complaint, slid some-not much tread.

Comet wobbled then straightened, making the thick tree lined road happy for not having to endure another crash. Its front two tires grazed the train's hidden tracks. Shoulders hunched, Cal braced for impact.

Five seconds. A final "GET OUT OF MY WAAAYYYY" deathly screamed. Magnificently the aged black smoking beauty of a locomotive followed its big bright light, exploded from its forested tunnel in a rage, right on top of them.

At minus two seconds all four of Old Blues worn tires were skidding on the other side of the iron tracks. Its dim taillights were scolded by the train's blaring angry whistle. Cal gritted his teeth.

Both wing-tips froze on a fully depressed brake pedal. Cringing Cal prayed to all deities they wouldn't roll down the grade into the road's ditch. The skid stalled the engine. He lost steering just as Old Blue's front right tire grabbed the last dirt available before going down into a drainage ditch.

Sighing, Cal relaxed his death grip on the steering wheel, but not from grinding his fright, between his weak teeth. Slits of his gray winced respectfully looking at the reflection in the rear view mirror. Tonnage of steel inertia he just missed, or just missed him. The train's engineer held the screaming whistle wide open. His omnipotent image reflected on the side of all the rumbling heard of cars passing. Locks of his loose long gray hair wind streaked behind him, the rest pinned down by his stropped engineers cap. Twisting his head his eyes grabbed Cal's, smiled persuasively at him, and then waved with an odd left hand gesture.

Change hung in the air. Certain death, graciously postponed. Had Cal passed a second later he would have been the paper's next headline.

Calmer Cal exhaled a final sigh. Refocused, and twisted the Comets key igniting it. Panic left, swapped places with adventure. They were off again still dazed from this episode. Quietly, they crept along the rest of the way, limping carefully toward town. That episode shook him so an idea came to him.

"Finally I've got a shot at real human interest story, maybe a great. Not that carp Pete assigned me."

Lightening truly re-charged, grew more self confident, sparked. Hurriedly she match lit the night, pushing brother aside. The time allowed for this ride was nearly spent.

"God, here we go." Cal floated back to the late afternoon yesterday after getting Pete's permission to travel upstate.

"Dam I hope she's up to it. I hope she is-I'll wash her, better not, mirror fell off last time, oil change? Nope, spent that money last night, maybe new wipers?" He just laughed at that one.

"Well she'll understand it's not too far. Four plus hours I guess?"

Cal left Manhattan early Friday morning, August 29th, 2009. The bank clock said 1 a.m.

"Come on baby" Twisting Old Blues key kicked the fatigued-grudging, but always dangerous, car to life. Onto the New York State Thruway they rolled, heading towards Fate, running out of gas.

Thunder toyed with sister, fired a baritone rumble. Cal snapped back to the drive.

A wind pushed the Old Blue left. Cal twisted the steering wheel right. Old Blue stabilized. Cal glanced at himself in the rear view mirror.

"Sheesh" he shook at the sight. Nature can be so unkind.

Failing eyesight worsened daily. Late night laughs didn't help. Weary prescription glasses should have been replaced years ago. That money lost to other necessities of experienced authors, professionally portion controlled Scotch and Gin drinks.

The dash clock said 4:50; the radio newsman said 4:30. Cal's watch still stuck at 11:59 p.m.

"Wondering yet?" inquired from the radio speaker.

"Hmmmmm..?" The difference in time narrowed to only twenty minutes.

Confident Cal hung onto the rocking wheel. The last portion of this part of his trip was lined by columns of the forests gate keepers. Their rank stood as soldiers protecting the wood's secrets.

The escorting storm, satisfied with its work, flickered, and spent out. Escaping moonlight lit road. The Comet's blue lost shape, bled to a fuzzy diffused oval in the final haze of the night. Descending down the final terrace of the one road in, the vessel of Cal and the Comet crept closer to town. It was still early. Even by country standards. Not-yet-awake the classic upstate New York farm town saw to it to fill his stuffy nostrils with notes of hay, manure, and dreaded rag-weed. He shook his head.

"Ugh, I knew it would stink."

He gripped his map and noticed a new squiggly line added. It noted a road leading out of town. Snake Hill Road was scrawled beneath it.

"Ah, okay I get it, two roads. Anyway I'm done with flashback road. Ha, ha, ha. No more lunatics, flashbacks. Let me get this story and get the heck" he looked up, "outa here."

"Man, I'm beat. No one in this hick town is up to talk I bet. I might as well go check that baby out. Get it out of the way, save some time, and some needless conversation with these straw chewers."

He revved Old Blue. Unappreciatively it stumbled, nearly stalled. His hand pressed the transmission lever to drive ready to launch and find the other road out when-,

"Look inside Destiny," rattled around in his head.

"Wha, where is it?" His hand slipped off the stalk pardoning the transmission. Mornings light strengthened and chased night away. Not a soul was about but the small town buzzed. A stranger was here.

Cal winced, lifted a hand quickly to his eyes shielding them from the day-breaking light. Then time checked. His cars clock blinked 5 a.m.

"5 a.m. Friday the 29th the woman's voice on the radio said. Cal looked up at the town clock in the square, 5 a.m. Avoiding eye pain from strengthening daylight he looked down at his stopped no more watch. The secondhand finally spun, but counter-clockwise, and losing five minutes. The dial displayed, 11:55 p.m.

"Carp" Cal groaned, perked up by a familiar sound.

"Whooo ahoooo, WHoooooOOOOooooOOOO," The black beauty smoking train chewed up track through the country heading toward wherever it wanted to go. Cal, mindful of his last encounter, hastened an eye-blinking look around. The whistle faded in the distance but still fiercely reminded all of its authority. Lazy cows stirred, lazier children a little later.

"Ahhh" Cal sighed.

Relieved, wide eyed, slack jaw and furry faced, he blinked through Old Blue's windshield. A football field's length away, across the dirt road bisecting town, stood a free-standing building resembling an old house.

"I don't remember seeing that. Heck, what's with this place? Better have a coffee shop here or I'll be sleeping in place."

The first part of Cal's trip ended that foggy Friday morning August 29, 2009, four hours and hundreds of miles from New York City.

Mother Earth's sister, Mother Nature, the mother Cal thought he went to see he would see. However, the mother he would meet head-on, her cousin; "The Mother of all Battles!"

# Seven

Cal thought; let's see what we have here. Ok, 5:10 a.m. Glad that's still is ticking. Now outside, good the town clock says the same 5:10 a.m. Now to my wristwatch, what? 11:45 p.m., how does that happen?

"Ten minutes more, backwards, damn."

Cal shook his head, shifted Comet to drive, closed his eyes and hoped he'd feel it move.

"Jeassuus Christ, Jeheeesus H. Freakin Christ. Come on Momma, give me the strength!"

Cal's whisper begged the God he denied for supernatural, or divine, intervention. He wasn't particular. The Comet struggled, but moved forward.

"Don't you die, don't you damn die now."Feebly, fraying gray haired arms tugged Comet's anchor heavy steering wheel. Its suspension endured too many potholes, sagged on top of balding tires crying groans, asking for mercy. The engine, jealousy not to be left out of the complaint chorus, barked a backfire. Injun quiet they weren't.

Clang, clunk, sputter, they inched nosily through town. If their arrival started stealthy, it was no more.

Half the football field distance closed, seemed like a thousand yards. The car wobbled, and shook like an-out-of balance washing machine kicking up the dry dirt road. Dust tinted Old Blue to brown.

Someone or thing listened. Cal's plea worked. Feeling confidant, Old Blue built minor momentum. Its nose targeted the curb. Cal restrained its ambition before it leapt onto the sidewalk slamming the Comet into a four wheel lockup. Cockeyed parked they were safe, and well dusted. After escaping disaster several times, he was where the map, found nearly twenty-four hours ago said to go.

Relieved Cal sat stone still, looked out the dust caked windshield. Pursed lips pursed blew an exhale, slowly. At six-two he was still a tall man. At six-three he was once taller. Tense hands clamped to the steering wheel like a shipwreck survivor would their life preserver. His rolled up sleeved, sparsely haired right arm, reached to kill the ignition. Falling forward his face pressed against the cushioned center of the steering wheel. He wept.

"What the hell am I doing here?"

"You'll find out..," a pause, static, then "tomorrow who wins." The radio man said. Cal turned the key to far.

"Bastard"

Thunder rumbled a warning poor language would not be acceptable.

9-8 brother

"Ohhhh, Ohhhh, Ahhh, Ohhhh, psycho gas attendants, crazy ride, a radio that talks back. I must be hallucinating. Man it's been a long time since I last did LSD. What next, talking cows in this hick town? "

"Thank God its day time. The goblins are gone. I'll be out of here and back at the bar by early evening." Cal leaned back, his head fell, his chin pressed to his chest.

Old Blue's engine chimed in, knocking, and running on after the ignition was twisted off. Then stumbled again, shook, and rumbled like a horse blowing through its lips. It blew a sneeze through the filthy air cleaner. Bang, a backfire completed the auto indigestion, cheap gas. Miraculously, neither Cal nor the Comet died, at least one should have. A long thunderous illuminating ride ended. The adventure just began.

"PPLleeasee, where the hell ammmmm I....?"

"I said, WHERE the GODDAMN HELL AM- FREAKIN I?"

"I'm here." He remembered, a coward dies a thousand deaths a hero but one,

"Guess I better get to it?" His hands fell from their perch on the steering wheel, landed sweaty palms down on top of his thighs.

"Ahhh" The dazed night warrior exhaled another deep sigh of relief.

The Comet rested, frustrated and jealous that Cal could still move and it couldn't. Not without hemorrhaging.

Three second-hand ticks, from Fate's town clock, drew his attention. Cal's jutting angular chin tipped upwards. Scornful eyes poked through puffy eyelid slits. He caught a glimpse of himself, in the rear view mirror. He left the city with a face showing some fine cracks of a distinguished character. During the trip they gouged deeper, and coarser.

"Daaam I hate that!"

Dawn broke through the Comet's rear window to rest warmly on his shoulders. It soothed him with welcome energy from above. A palm stroked his salt-and-pepper, five o'clock shadow, five a.m. shadow. "Ahhh," his mule burdened mind stood tough, battled confusion, regrouped and traded fatigue for excitement.

Peering through the dusty car windshield his over active imagination, held over from childhood, conjured a headless horseman galloping toward him. Worse yet, a robed, hooded Mr. Reaper leering into the safety of the car's cabin, through the passenger window.

A deathly shiver, like the chill at his desk at work, tracked his sweaty spine.

"Blubbrrrur," he shook trying to snap back to reality. Old military training kicked in. Sunken eyes widened sneaking daring, darted glances left and right. Shackles of fear crisply broke off. If metal, they would have clanged on the floorboard.

The new strength came with courage. He revisited his face in the rearview mirror, wiped the sleeper's from the corners of his eyes. As if washing his face he placed his pale thin left hand to the front of his left cheek, his right hand followed suit. With slightly bulging veins in each he swept them backwards from nose to ears, across the stubble on his cheeks, repeatedly.

"Damn, I can't focus right. Can't see, damn it"

"You will," a pause and static "get there on the..." static. Hey what the heck, the radio's off, he thought.

That fright earned another round of exercise for the optic nerves. This time with exaggerated blinks, and a knuckle rub. Opening his eyes after the sixth blink he could focus.

Directly in front of him, framed by the Comet's wiper swept arc dusty windshield, was the old building he saw across the road. A purple puffed real estate description might say," it wears a classic charmed coat of blackened weather-aged blackened cedar shakes, needs some gentle tender loving care."

The same could be said of Cal. Both were similarly dissimilar, like opposite poles drawn peculiarly to one another.

The joint, originally a house, was later converted into a local bar. Mornings rising sun lit its image. Hypnotically Cal stared.

"Was this it? Was this the place?" He shivered somehow knowing it.

Dangling from its left chain off the building's soffit hung an old wooden sign. It read, Destiny.

"Damn it is."

It sure looked like a bar, an odd one at that. Cal squinted at an unlit neon beer sign. Genesee hung in the right front window- hadn't been on in years.

"Doubt if it that works."

The sun rose showcasing a perfect day, in a perfect place, ready-made for Cal to fetch an imperfect story. One last head twisting look through the Comets cigarette smoke stained windows. Fate woke looking an ordinary country town.

First looks can be deceiving. He remembered his mom saying.

"I can't freakin believe this-is, where I'm supposed to be. This hick town and dump of a building is the place that funky newspaper sent me. Seems familiar though, have I been here before?" His mind checked all storage areas.

Calculatingly, fear punched back. Uncertainty took center stage, dominated confidence. Weakened, the building lured his catatonic mind.

He battled back. Curiosity crushed fear, leaving it lay on the floor.

Maybe I could head home tonight? He thought.

"Better get in there and see what's still around, must be cleaned up by now anyway."

Cal's left hand forcefully yanked the remaining half of the driver's doors chrome handle towards him, and then pushed the door with his shoulder. His narrow size-twelve left foot repeated its part pushing at the bottom of the mismatched door panel. Extra force ensured the creaky hinged doors compliance. Ceremoniously the door unlatched with a clunk, and sagged about an inch from the weak hinge. Cal protected himself from the door snapping back, as had been the case so many times before. Ankle scars were the proof.

Stepping out into the early morning warm country air his nose rabbit twitched scents of farm life. Four long, lanky strides and he stood between the Comet and the front of the building. His trance never left the building, till a strong wind gushed through town. Then cowardice said hello. "If I bolt now and go slow, so the Comet doesn't croak, I bet I can get home early afternoon."

The chance for a proper military about-face fled, chased by the thought of unemployment. Cal remained standing in the bars encroaching morning shadow. First sweeping over the dirt front lawn, then Cal's with salt and pepper whiskered face. His placid, ghostly white complexion cut-out contrasted against the earthy tones of the building. Defiantly he stifled fear. Yielding to a reporter's curiosity he listened to his misunderstood instinct.

The bar, once house, stood erect as lifeless rotting wood yet still arrogantly loomed two feet above a low curb. Cal stomped up onto the property. Paddling wing tips kicked up a cloud of fresh morning dust. It hadn't rained for awhile, not since last night. It was late summer, everything dried out quickly here. Combat determination pushed Cal further across the dirt lawn. He abruptly halted. Eyed it up, down, left, right, took it all in, as he was.

"Looks go both ways. Take a good look at me because I'm gonna get a better look at you, inside. You don't scare me. Think I came all this way and–" He stared at loosely flapping cedar shakes.

Ordinary building-ordinary indeed he thought fighting back.

"Not too much here." Three splintery planked steps led to a concrete floored porch. He flew up them with school boy spring. The joint wasn't Mount Everest and him no Sir Hillary. Cal never liked the cold much anyway.

"Musta been cool last night here" Both of Cal's large feet, secured in second hand rose scuffed black wing tipped shoes-complete with matching holes, rested on the porches concrete floor. The floor, the sturdiest part of the whole place, held the country night's cool, or day's blazing heat.

Cal's curiosity beat caution. Fearlessly his neck craned backwards, up-up-up way up. The peak of the raftered roof housed local, uninvited guests. Odd sort of birds hung about.

"Holy Carp, Bats." His shoulders shrugged, his mouth held agape, he twisted his head and thumbed his chin. Mental images came to him of his youth, in camp. He smiled.

"Now I'm seeing things, must be from fatigue. Shake it Cal, shake it off."No dice, different images of the past struck his eyes. The bars invited evening's guests. Ghostly they socialized on a warm summers evening. Country music played. Whisky-lies told, to each other, by each other, about almost everything. Corralled together, protected from drunkenly falling over the side by a split-wood railing. He knew without knowing the owner found the fence late at night with some friends. Rescued it, they argued, from a supposedly deserted farm. Style didn't matter. Economics did. His helpers drank for free that evening. Neighborly country living.

Cal shook. He was staring at a mess of broken tables and chairs all around the concrete floor. Evidently the Board of Health missed their visit that day. He pressed on towards the bars entrance. His frame creaked in time with his steps as he threaded his way towards the door that led inside the bar. Avoiding the splintered wood.

"Old bones don't heal well, a trip, a fall could be fatal-no one around to help." Cal tiptoed past the carnage, shin and toe kicking it out of his way. Broken bottles, bits and shards of glass decorated the floor, faux gems. Land-mines to the unsuspecting and barefoot swallowed the sun's rays then spat out their color.

Cal reached where the front door of the bar should have been. It was missing, country air-conditioning, front door removal and window opening. Only the hinges pins still threaded through them remained neatly in place on the door jamb, as if waiting the door's return. To his right, the missing door propped lengthwise against the house on its hinged edge, placed with great care for future use.

"OH, CARP, watch out boy, don't touch that." His eyes trained on door's saddle. Years earlier, he inexplicably developed an odd habit, a fear, after he came home from a long trip to Asia. He would never step on a door's saddle. Nor touch one. He couldn't remember why. Just did. It terrified him. Mustering a heap of courage, he closed his eyes and pushed his right foot through the door's opening, over the threshold landing it on the floor inside. Cal cringed. Timidly he placed his weight on his size-twelve firmly on the floor inside.

"Phew, no glass-far out." Shades of his lost sixties spoke.

Cal followed his foot and poked his crew cut head inside. He waited, hoped the fourth grade science dilating pupil trick worked in the pitch black. Slowly his eyes swallow enough light to see. His left leg followed.

"Jesus H. Christ, what the hell happened here?"

This was the battle field, he thought.

Flipped over barrel back chairs, high-backed stools, tables, blood-stained chair legs lay strewn about. The joint reeked of old beer, alcohol, cigarette and cigar smoke. Cal gagged. The bar's dank clammy interior gradually became lighter as sunlight filtered in. His old grays adjusted, the wings slid, stepping was dangerous. Foraging deeper into the room's center his shuffling his feet feared splinters, or a corpse. His heart palpitated. A lifted shoe took a cautious step. He looked down to be sure where it would land. A blood stained floor paralyzed him. He recoiled.

"Shit Goddamn it."

Sweat poured down his expressionless face catching the etched grooves. His wet shirt stuck to his ribs. It was warming up quickly this August morning. Summer's heat bullied through the vacant doorway and its cousins, two shouldering double hung windows. Nights cool ran from the charge. Daylight sent night away, reached in and spread along the inner soul of the building. Dark, thief fled home. Cal's head oscillated, took it all in, speechless till his eyes witnessed—

"What in—" No lie, there it was, the real evidence. Walls bullet riddled, gouged, hacked, and gashed.

"Jeasus, target practice, indoors, what did they have, machine guns, shotguns, bazooka's?

The rest of the joint told a different tale. Decorated in early frat house it never could have been mistaken for House beautiful.

Oversized yellowing posters of rock stars of the 1960s plastered walls. Cheaper than wall paper. Frayed and curled from age, Jimmy Hendrix, the Doors, the Rolling Stones, and the Beatles immortally covered the knotty-pine paneling. Some taped corners had lost their grip, peeled from their position allowing lighter colored wood to show. Shame it was, the gunshot holed the holy of rock.

Another wall, covered in much the same way but with photos of celebrated baseball players: Ruth, Mantle, Mays, Snyder, Koufax, Spahn, hung instead. Team pictures of the Yankees, Cardinals, Dodgers, Red Sox, Cubs, Pirates, and White Sox, hung as sacraments but this place wasn't church, by any means.

Explorer nerve pressed Cal's discovery mission. He shuffled over the dark grooved and veined planked floor. The sun rose higher outside. Morning light forcefully streamed through the front windows, crept deep inside painting the floor and walls. Dust suspended in the sun beams. The overbearing stench was overcome by his concentration.

Cal paced forward twisting left, looking left, twisting right, looking right, up and down-examining everything more closely. Holmes would have approved.

"This was some hell of a battle."

His right foot pressed down on its ball.

"Ouch, Carp" he shrieked. Something stuck him.

"Damn it. What was that? God I hope it wasn't a nail or something worse?"

Cal looked down. Something worse lay on the floor. A tooth, with a large gold filling coated with blood lay on the free form blood stained floor.

"Must have been a molar?" He bent to get a better view.

"When did I have my last tetanus shot?"

"Sorry son-of-a bitch- that musta hurt." Cal felt his heart behind his eyes.

"Ha-ha-ha," he picked up a chair.

The only whole chair left in the whole place. Set it on its four legs, as if to straighten up the place. The reflex reaction a fond reminiscence, a remnant of his mother's demand for organization. Something lost on the Comet and his desk.

Journalists think, question. His heartbeat up-ticked, sweat drops were caught in his spider-web fly away eyebrows. Imagination whirled in his head.

"What would be my lead be? Hmmm, maybe the description of the house or the spook at the gas pump, or the train-nope, lock me up for sure with that one."

Ponderous thought yielded to focus. Standing beneath the peak in the ceiling he calculated he was near the center of the building. His back to the door he looked ahead. Elevated two feet above the floor he stood on was a second level, and on it the bar itself. Twin wooden steps connected the main floor to the bar level. One set to his left, one to the right, symmetrically balanced from the center of the lower floor as little shoulders. Cal had his choice.

"Musta been a railing there "Remnant's of a wooden railing, about toddler's height, ran the distance from the top of one staircase to the other, fencing off the top level from the bottom. Most of it was missing. What remained of it and its balusters, were cracked, halved or split. Another casualty of what must've been one hellacious rumble.

"Ok now a righty's right foot first. Slowly, test their strength."His foot gently pressed on the first step of the stairs to the left. It creaked.

"No problems, ok, now the left foot." Loudly they complained but held weight.

On the upper level he quickly moved to a familiar place. En route to the bar he passed a long mysterious hallway to his left. It ran deep, disappearing into a tunnel of dark. Lacking windows it waited for the morning's sun to reach it. Cal stopped for two ticks off the second hand of his watch and studied the shaft like hall. Doors lined each wall as staggered cutouts offset from one another. He darted a frightened glance, decided it led to someplace he wasn't going but the sight injected another dose of adrenaline. Jacked his heart till it hurt, thumped and pounded. Excess excitement tensed his eyes. He pressed them tightly trying to rid it. His mouth dried- no water around.

Finger tips slightly trembled also. No amusement park funhouse could compete with this.

Three ticks later he paused with his back to the center of the bar. From his elevated perch he faced out over the lower main floor. It was then he realized the vantage point gave the tending bartender a bird's-eye view of the rest of the place, particularly the doorless front entrance.

Cal looked down at his feet, squinted. The wings stood on a checkered red and black basement style tile. Looking around he saw it covered the entire second floor. A good deal is a good deal. The tiles cost was a deal similar to the economics employed in confiscating the split-rail fence for the porch.

The distance from the front edge of the actual bar, to where Cal stood by the railing had it been when intact, covered about five feet. On step too far beyond the railing, a two foot cliff to the first floor. The second level floor curved from one staircase to the other like a quarter moon semicircle. Tables and chairs in its outer left and right wings met a similar fate as those below.

"This must've been some high-class place." Cal sarcastically muttered. Then bashfully blinked and smiled. He shouldn't have.

Darks enemy is time, and it ticked off Cal's watch. Outside the brilliant summer light heated up, wandered, and drove deeper inside. It warmed and lit the house bar's downstairs interior perfectly. Cal's watched the second hand spin backwards. Light stretched upstairs working to completely light it, except for the hall. That stayed ominously cold except for a few brave fragments of reflected light that dared to poke their pointy heads into it. New light with heat were welcome friends to Cal's aged bones and eyes, but not his nose. It woke the stench. He gagged.

Time ticked, the light pressed threatening the hallway, walls and all with light, exposing its secrets. When it completely illuminated the upstairs walls, the perforations from the lead bullets that bore holes through the pictures of deceased famous stars were clear to see. Janis Joplin, Stevie Ray Vaughan, victims. Cal winced, Lou Gehrig insulted, too. All riddled.

Why? He wondered.

"What a shame." he said.

His career took him many places, to many stories. He'd seen a lot but nothing as bad as this, nothing this violent. Everything was broken, shattered cracked or holed, nothing spared, except the chair. Outside light reached in, broke his gaze. He turned, followed it out the open front windows. Cal followed the clear line of sight to the town square. 9:00 a.m. Fate's clock told. Checking, then back to his wristwatch. It continued to tick, counterclockwise. He turned away from the light. The wings heels teetered dangerously close to floors edge. One step back and, no railing would stop him.

"Some mirror." The lure of the bars shattered mirror pulled him to safety. Only jagged shards of glass, tucked loosely into its dark wood frame, remained. Blue gray discoloration aged the glass. It wasn't much when first hung, less now. All the reflections once stored there had long since been released. Below it, shelves. Empty keepers of the spirits once sold there, except for another survivor, a bottle of brown whisky.

"Ah, writers ink. Not my brand but, for a functioning alcoholic it could be." Temptation teased a tired soul but it held fast.

Two grooved round columns, about ten inches in diameter, bookended the mirror. Their bases sat waist high pressed to the lower shelf dedicated for displaying less expensive liquor. They were pulled away a foot from the wall and stretched up to a lighted wood hood, that didn't work. No lights worked.

"Ah, must found them," Like the tiles and fencing, they didn't look like they belonged.

Cal blinked from a flash of outside light and imagined what a normal night would have been like there. Talking, laughing, arguing, drinking, crying, and remembering but eager to forget. Heat Lightening kicked, Cal shook. His inspecting head probed over the bar looking for any serviceable bottles. None, but what he did find were three black and white photographs hung one above the next, slightly hidden behind the left column. He pressed his luck lying on his belly, on top of the bars surface, spread eagled for balance.

"Man who are these folks and why the devil am I here?" The top photograph was the smallest. A side view of someone sitting in a profile position sitting a motorcycle. The front wheel of the bike was nearly to the left edge, the rear, to its right. Atop it, a fresh faced, straw haired skin and bones smiling farm boy. Squinting, Cal read "Malcolm on Victor and best friends, age 15." glued to frames lower edge.

"Hey I had one of those. Great bike, damn near killed me." Cal bit his lower lip.

Proud as a peacock Malcolm straddled a BSA 441 Victor motorcycle, a highly sought-after, single cylinder British motorcycle used for on and off road use.

Malcolm twisted at the waist toward the photographer, arms folded. He wore a big "I'm the stuff" grin.

Four of Malcolm's friends stood behind the Victor in different, kid silly, poses. Three of them, short, medium, and tall, wore open-mouth smiles and wrinkled noses. Almost innocent faces jeered at each other, their fingers pointed. The fourth, with darker complexion, drove a serious expression straight at the camera. A fifth friend took a reserved spot. She stood in the foreground, partially blocking the view of the bikes front wire wheel. Known for her knobby knees, she placed her hands on skirted boyish hips. Her smirking smile outshined the bikes chrome gleam.

A work of art preciously hung below that photo. Someone protectively screwed it to the wall through its thin frame. That same boy was in it, Malcolm. This time he sat alone, no longer fresh- faced. "Malcolm, age seventeen," was pressed to the stick on label.

"Always wanted that one of those, but had to travel abroad before I could save enough."

Malcolm sported a cheesy, immature moustache. Stoically he straddled a BSA Gold Star motorcycle, master of this powerful 500 cc single-cylinder beast. Its gleaming silver gas tank rested like a fine jewel nestled in its setting.

The Gold Star, prized possession for its lightning speed, and beauty. One also perfectly built, for raising hell on lonely country roads. Perfect for someone who liked to raise hell; perfect for Malcolm. His look hauntingly serious look seemed a reflection of some of the hell he raised.

"He's starring back, Jeassuus H. Chri—"

The last of the three photo's, on the bottom of the totem pole, was titled, "Viet Nam." Malcolm dressed in army combat uniform, gear hanging on him. An M-16 rifle rested butt-first, upside down on his right shoulder, barrel pointing behind him. His hand held the grip, finger rested ready on its trigger. A soldier's weary unshaven thin face peeked from under the helmets shadow.

Each of the three glass covered photos were cracked, unable to escape the fight. All three were cracked in exactly the same manner, top left to bottom right. The glass held secured in the frames.

"My eyes hurt, my head hurts," Cal's squints tightened. Days light grew illuminatingly brilliant. He twisted his thawing head, looking for what may have hung on the other side of the shattered mirror. The eerie tomb began to earn his respect.

"Who's that?" In the same location as the others, but on the right side of the mirror behind the other column, Cal sharpened on a large lone photograph. Peculiarly it was untouched from bullets and mayhem. The size of a modern day magazine looked as though it was just taken.

"Goddamn lucky bastard." Cal clenched a fist.

Showcased behind photo's glass was a man. He also sat on a motorcycle. A motorcycle so rare some thought it mythical. So powerful and fast, no household-brand could keep up with it. Predominately colored in rich black, but flecked with chrome accents. A meld of power, grace, and beauty machined to a work of art. Some wished it to be a myth.

Atop this bike was not Malcolm but a man Cal judged to be slightly on the wrong side of forty. Rugged stocky, about five-eight, beer paunch, bulbous nosed and a big friendly honest smile so warm Cal could not resist smiling back. He understood how pleased the man must have been. One of a few lucky ones to have that bike placed in their care. The legendary 1950 Vincent Black Shadow.

The Towns clock read 10:45 a.m., Cal's watch back ticked to 11:40 p.m.

Cal wondered what the twins score was. Time, would tell.

# Eight

"Maybe this isn't so circumstantial? Maybe this parlor tick of a place had an agent, the mysterious paper, and that Day-Glo gas attendant. Hmm that's a better lead, I like that. They'll think me insane if I write it. I'll go insane if I don't. I can't win." Fate's Town Clock gonged at irregular intervals. 10:55 a.m., Cal's watch ticked backwards, 11:35 p.m. Friday, August 29, 2009.

"This can't be by chance, can it?"

"Ahhh, NOOOPPPPE."

"Who's that, who goes there? Geezz did I just say that? I haven't said that since–. I swear no more gin." Cal snapped his head. Looked around, hoped the voice was outside of his head.

"Go to the country Cal. Get a simple story and save your sorry ass, Cal"

A simple task, get a simple story? Not so simple here. Complicated, storm clouds of doubt clouded his confidence.

"Who were they? Who the heck, where's that Vincent now. Where's this Malcolm character? If he is around, how do I meet him?" Cal scuffed the floor.

"Aghghgh, ouch-ouch- ouch, I knew I should have had those re-soled."

"I have a better chance of figuring out who shot JFK for ....sake!" Cal mumbled, scraped his foot, and picked the glass from it.

"I need to leave, now, I need to leave, I can't –can't do this.... pleaseee" On his knees on the red and black tile weeping like a newborn held by nervous new mother. It lasted a full twenty ticks.

"Likely dead by now, shoot." Cal wiped his eyes, shook his head, and pressed his shoulders soldier straight, strutted around looking as a peacock would.

"I'm on the case. Either I figure this carp out or I die here. Enough is enough." Leaning over the bar his grays swept each photo in succession. His eyes locked to theirs.

He dipped, looking around. Thought–that one, and you, over there and that one up there. Are you dead or, are you pegged in perpetuity here awaiting your soul's release?

"Well are you? Why are your photos, the chair and the bottle spared? Why they the anointed escapees, luck? Not mine, it's always out of town?"

The bar pulled him from uncomfortable comfort of the city. Seeped ever so slowly into his being, he was never so tuned in, to the country.

"If the answer posse doesn't show soon, I'll wind up back on a shrinks couch for sure."

"Wait, what was that, what was that? I heard—-yes, I heard something, or I'm mad, or both. No, I did hear something. Noise, shoe heals, shuffling soles? Yes. There it is again, shuffling feet."Cal giggled, looked to his feet and made sure.

The trance of the pictures broke when he shook his crew cut no but the debate volleyed.

"Malcolm, is it you?" Odd flavors of fear and happiness mixed.

Free, he scanned the room, no one there, not a visible soul.

Clammy skin Cal shifted worried eyes. "I must be hallucinating. Sleep deprivation, or—nooo, not that. Too many years ago, too much drink more likely. Nah couldn't be that. But I'll have to do better, or I'll be the one in those pictures."

His mind raced. The grays darted, laser locked back on all three photos. A hyper pulse ordered sweats return. He gagged on his heart.

More shuffling feet, Cal looked down at the wings. They shuffled all morning, but were firmly planted in earthly fear atop of the red and black tiles.

"I am hearing things" he shouted egging on his guest, if one was there.

"I'm just tired. Yes, that's it. But hell, I've been more tired than this. I know I heard something."

Cal had a choice to make without the aid of John Barleycorn's grip. He looked into the mirror. New color filled the cracks awarded from age.

"Darn, my blood pressure must be sky high."

Courage tranquilized him and confidently, yet gracefully, he craned his neck with the mechanical precision of a Patton tank turret seeking an enemy. It pointed to the forbidding dark hallway. There he calculated the source of the noise.

"One way in, no way out," he blustered.

"Show yourself." Someone was clever, quite the hunter, quite stealthy. Again, shuffling, scampering.

"Maybe it's just and an animal, a squirrel or chipmunk perhaps. I am in the country, after all. Oh my god, maybe a snake. There are snakes in the country, many kinds, all around." Cal's shoulders tried to cover his neck. His moving parts spun, faced the bar. He knew it was in the hallway.

Help was on the way. Morning's minutes ticked off the town clock and sunlight pressed its case through the front windows and doorless front door. It blanketed the wood planked floor. Then taffy stretched well beyond the doorway creeping into the abyss of the hallway. Every passing minute gobbled more real estate. It clawed nearer.

A flash broke the light, struck the corner of Cal's left eye like a cinder. Something lurked for only two ticks, but it was there. No classroom confessions were heard.

Physically exhausted, emotionally drained, dehydrated Cal mouthed a mousy "Damn."

"Damn, what the hell, you bastard. Show yourself."

"What, what the hell indeed," Whispered back an amused, patronizing hello.

Cal shied sensing he had been had. His torso twisted from the voice leavin his ear attached to it. Limp drooping eyes urgently sprang haunted house open. His lower jaw fell.

"Ohhhh" exhaled. Courage twisted his head, pointed a large sagging hairy left ear toward the sounds direction. It was his good ear, well better ear. Scientifically it listened seeking precise sonar blips confirming he had a visitor.

"Bats, yes must be bats."

"Oooohh, Ohhhh boooooyyyyy, and I don't mean Oh Boy."Cal knew well of his self-talk, and occasionally answering but this wasn't him.

"Not bats, not me. No not you. Not bats either, and what the hell you say? What the hell indeed, friend?" Cal turned from the bar, looked at the doorless front door.

"Not a chance there, my friend."Cal's hopes dashed, fear re-glued his knees.

"Well Friend, what- say-you? You've been blaaaaabbing since you've been here. Answer- me."

The demands volume shook the shaky frame of the perforated building. Years of dust and dirt, banked in the cracks and crevices of the old place, gave up their stash and gently parachuted to the floor.

"Oh crap, Err, Carp. I've seen this movie. I think this is where I die." Cal turned to the hall.

"What the hell, you said, ha-ha-ha." A man's voice broadcast back out of the dark.

"Yes friend, yes, what the hell you say! Or maybe what the heck, or what the devil, or wholly crap, or wholly mackerel"

Cal's right hand index finger smart-ass swung to the answers cadence. He slid to the end of the bar, tried to get a glimpse of where the sound was coming from. Something playfully darted back and forth in a zigzag, between the staggered doorways lining the hall. The days light marshaled on, eventually it would expose all. Cal and his host were on a collision course.

This passage had a soul that Cal tried to reject. The shadow-figure continued its stealthy zigzag moving closer and closer. Each movement a light-breaking ricochet of shuffling sounds.

Him, her, the unknown pressed on and came to strategic rest in the cover of the last doorway. The one closest to Cal who quivered as a wet dog in the cold would. Terror, curiosity, frustration and anger competed for his undivided prized attention.

"Uh, hello is someone there? Hello?" Cal bargained with old choirboy personality.

"Hello I said, darn it, anyone there?" Frustration spoke up.

"Hey, anyone th—?"

"Shhhhhhhhhhhhhh, shut up! Shut up! Shut up!"

More dust sifted from the rafters, decorating Cal's crew cut. His shoulders rounded, his knees buckled.

"Dam, how much of this stuff is up there?" Cal brushed off his crew cut, then rest of himself, and then more fell. "God dam rafter dandruff."

"Yes, yes, you've picked a wonderful time to call on God, you idiot. And there is quite a bit of it there, quite a bit of the pixie dust, you'll see, friend."

"Dam..."

Thunder rumbled, shook the ceiling, dust flaked. Reminded Cal of the attendants information he wondered what the twins score was.

"They always call for God when they're in a pickle. Otherwise, it's God who?"

"Who the heck are you, a spook?"

"Who am I. Who–am-I? Who the DEVIL are you?" The mysterious one's anger knifed.

"This is my house, you're in it. More precisely I'm its caretaker, its master. So, friend, who the devil are you? You little —, what was that your last girl friend called you? Ah, yes-a big fat head with a skinny little soul." Cal slipped sideways and hung onto the bar, sweat empty, fear cold. Didn't know what to do or say, out-matched, and knew it. Still no one appeared.

"How the heck did you know that?"

"Don't worry about that. Don't even think of trying to fight me. You don't have it in you. You couldn't, well better not say the walls have ears."

"How and why are you here Cal?"

"Well eh, err—uh. Geee where's the saliva."

"That's terrific. You're a writer? I suppose you're a mute also, great just great! Who sent me this moron anyway? Look you're here because you're close to failing life 101. Do you understand?"Cal's eyes watered.

"How'd you know my name?"

"Never mind that" The mysterious man's silhouette stayed a soft diffused shape within the shadows. Then, with palms and arms outstretched he pressed them into the light.

"I'll ask again. Perhaps I confused you the first time. How did you come to be here, Cal?"

"I was at my desk. I saw this paper and—"

"Let me guess. It had a note and a map, correct?"

"Well, yes, it did."

"And the map led you here, so you can write your story and save your career?"

Cal sighed, school-boy nodded, shuffled his feet.

"Why can't they ever be more creative?"

Cal twisted his eyes to the voice's direction.

The mystery stepped from the shadows. Arrogantly, he stood rail-straight in the light.

"Teh-dah, only ten feet friend,"

Cal wished it were more. Wished harder he could reach that bottle of—still on the bar shelf. It was only about 11:30 a.m. but God, he needed a drink. Gasoline would have done.

At about five-feet-eight, he stood considerably shorter than Cal, but equally lanky. His face and frame were neatly protected and well hid, under a long, black velvet hooded cape. A red sash belted his waist.

"What do you think? It's the latest. Ha-ha. " He spun around mockingly modeling it, flipped grey long hair off his shoulder, with his left hand.

"Who are you Freakin Merlin?" Cal bounced back.

"Merlin?" The building shook. Dust escaped, but less than before.

"Merlin is a recalcitrant child. Merlin my–, better not say."

The man pointed an angry long boney calloused hand index finger upwards. The sleeve of the robe fell exposing his thin left hand and parchment skinned lightly haired arm.

"Merlin sucks. I used to have him in my class. He won't amount to a thing."

With that Cal's host head flipped his hood. It flopped backwards. He shook his head, primped another hair flip.

"Show time," flew from his angular chiseled, stark-white expressionless face. Loose wavy rock-star shoulder length silver hair hung. He snapped his head; locks flopped, and settled partially over his eyes, shielding their color. Pale they were, of that, Cal was certain.

"He sucks, a little punk you had in class? Oooohh–" Cal winced as though an arrow shot him in the chest.

Oh mmmmyyyy, this was going to be different. Yes very different. Cal thought.

"Yes, yes Cal. Many people, well-hmmm, ahhh whatever you wish to call them, suck. It's my great pleasure to remind them of it also. Also, on that subject, let me be the first to offer my most insincere congratulations to you for winding up here."

"So you own this gem?" Cal's palm up hand swept the bar, mimicking the man's earlier gesture. Subordination, not something Cal's would endure forever.

"Master of all this are you?"

"Nooo, boooooyyyyy, as I said before I am Master; you don't listen very well do you?"

"So then who does own it?"

"Malcolm, Malcolm owns it. He entrusted its care to me."

"Malcolm? Hmmmm, you mean the kid in the photos?"

"Yes, quite."

"Ok, so you're not Merlin, how about the Grim Reaper? Judging from that long black robe I'd say I'm close." Cal rubbed his finger tips together.

Cal pulled a stubby pencil out from the front of his pants pocket he stole from a golf course. Then a small note pad out from his back pocket he stole from a gas stations convenience store he stopped at on the trip up. Not the typical tools of a seasoned journalist. Then again, Cal wasn't that typical. He started to write.

"Stop that, stop that, stop that. There will be plenty of time for all that"

"For what?" Cal stuffed pad and pencil in his pants pocket.

"Notes, plenty of time for that, you came here for a story didn't you?"

"Jeassuus, yes, yes I did, how did you know that?"

"First of all, friend, leave him out of it. And pronounce the name correctly. Besides, I believe there has been a book or two written about that business already, now hasn't there? And you will have yours to write. For certain, you will have yours."

"So what do I call you?" Cal forced a clenched jawed, bare toothed smile.

"MASTER will suffice."

"Oh, Thank God. I thought you were going to say Ishmael, ha-ha ha."

"What did you say? What was that I heard? I see why you are here, boooyyy. Yes, quite. You will take some work."

"So I guess you're the guy everyone says is the type that thinks outside of the box then huh?"

"Look, you little earthworm. Don't use that idiotic phrase. But since you brought it up let me explain something. No one ever thinks outside of the box."

"No one? Cal furrowed a brow.

"No, no-one. And do you want to know why my fledgling prince of darkness, hmmm?"

"Well yes, that is if you don't mind sir."

"It's because the idiots just don't know how big the damn box is. They think they're outside and they're not even out of the basement! That's why! Look up friend, look up outside. THERE'S YOUR BOX."

His words reverberated. The rafters coughed. Cal guilty dog hunkered, and then ran for safety to left wall avoiding the falling parachutes of dust. Staring from it was Jimmy Hendrix. Cal dragged a curious finger across the poster, closed in on one of the holes.

"Do not touch that. Do not touch that. Do not touch that. Do you hear me? You are not ready."

Cal, never much of an athlete, leapt backward so far, an Olympian would have been impressed.

"Buuutt I, I..."

"But nothing, you will have your chance. When you are ready, you will touch the holes I assure you. But when I say so, and the music say's so."

"What music? There's no music here."

"LOOK, look over there boy" Master laughed pointed, Cal twisted. There stood an old Wurlitzer juke box, in front of the bar. It wasn't there before.

"How the–"

"–hell did it get there? Master finished.

Thunder rolled.

"Idiot, I put it there. What did youuu think? Youuu did?" Wispy eyebrows rose.

The Wurlitzer was shot up, like the rest of the place. Its once proud glass display of 45 rpm records was cracked. Most records were missing. Those that remained, scratched, chipped or cracked. The turn table was stuck. Worse of all, it wasn't plugged in. Had it been, it still would have been useless. Earlier, Cal flipped a few ceramic, cob-web-covered light switches off and on. No electricity, no lights. The juice had been turned off for some time.

"That can't play music." Cal said. "It's all shot up. Not plugged in. And were it, and well this place has no electricity. By the way nice boots, engineers?" Cal folded his arms.

"It is shot up, true. It's not plugged in. Again, you are correct. But it needn't be. I assure you, it can and will play." Malevolent laughter iced Cal's veins. "And this place, Malcolm's place, has more electricity than, you, have, ever known"

"Ok, yeah I'm sure."

"Ok? Ok what boy?"

"OK, Sir?"

"Nooooo, no, you fool. What is my name?"

"Master."

"Do not forget it, boy."

"Yes, Sir, err well, Master Sir." Master knowingly smiled.

"What went on in here, Master? I came all the up here from New York City, in that near death experience of a car to get the story about what happened here. Can you help me?" Outside the Comets horn sounded.

"Don't ask questions of that you are not ready to know the answers."

"But, I am ready. Why I was born ready." A rare smile broke across Cal's face.

"Not what she said." Master turned to the wall.

"What? What did you say? Who she, I heard you.

"Never mind that and no friend, you are not. You are not, yet. But you will be. That I promise!" Master mastered.

"There is or was evil here." Cal stated and asked. "I can feel it."

"There are forces of evil in this world, both yours and mine, the likeness of which you have never seen." Master nodded to Cal.

"You mean like the devil?"

"That meddlesome troublemaker is a glorified amateur, a lightweight. We always know his exact location, and what the schoolboys doing." More dust.

"Meddlesome, troublemaker, school boy, hey, I didn't sign up for this." A liver spotted hand scratched his face.

"Yes, I'm afraid you did. Now before we get started go outside. Get back into the Comet, yes, I know its name—and find the other road." A hand ordered Cal not to interrupt.

"Oh you know of the note? I smudged it but figured it out anyway. It said one road in, two roads out. Pretty good, huh?"

"Marvelous. Now, go. Drive around. Find Snake Hill Road. Find the Vaughan's farm, Spirit Trail Road. Look for Heavens Hill way out in the country. It's all right out there."

"I'm tired now and need a rest." His voice softened, began to fade.

"Hey I'm not sure Old Blue can do it. Do you have a good, cheap, mechanic around?"

"I've had a talk with Comet. Come back later." Cal strained to hear his failing voice.

"But before you do make sure your, last stop, is next door at the bake shop. The wife is waiting for you. Bring me back twenty nickels. I need a rest. I'll see you later. Follow my instructions, exactly."

Cal nodded as if leaving an audience with the Pontiff. Backing away, always keeping his eyes glued to the Master. At a fair distance he slowly spun on the wings heels, and strutted towards the doorless doorway. Master smiled, waved his left hand. A unique hand wave reserved only for a select few. Index finger pressed to his middle. His fourth finger pressed to its mate the pinky. The pairs parted, between the middle finger and fourth finger, forming a vee. Thumb neatly tucked into his soft white palm.

One Road in, two Roads out, right?" Cal boldly strutted toward the doorless doorway, skipping a bit.

"Smart ass, we'll just see about that!" Master's lids slipped.

Cal's long night ride bled into a long morning. He met destiny, in Fate, head on.

The town's clock read Tuesday 12:00 p.m., Cal's watch receded to11:30 p.m…still August 29, 2009.

"Three mother's sons, two would meet—-" followed Cal to the door.

# Nine

Cal's toes stopped an inch before the doorless front doors saddle. Got to go, got to go out there but Cal's courageous thoughts lacked action. Master nodded in faked sleep. He hid in a permanent shadow on the main floor reserved just for him and company. All knowing he benevolently offered Cal encouragement. His finger twisted sending a cool whistling breeze to goose bump and stroked Cal's back. Cal eyed the saddle.

"We won't be touching that, nope, nooo we won't. Okie dok, here I go."

Cal raised his right leg, bent at the knee, and jammed it through the doors opening. A big wing foot led the way. Once it surely cleared the saddle he securely set down on the concrete floor of the patio. The other leg followed. Two breathes later both excited feet stood flat footed on the dirt front lawn.

Late morning sun greeted rubbery legs still numb from their long ride. Cal knew of his newspapers circulation better than his own. He basked in feeling victorious. Relaxing, pain soothing warmth yielded his body's numbness, but was no help otherwise. Hard to understand what he had seen thus far.

Lazy benign country life unexpectedly turned the tables. Last evenings, and early mornings events, tamed his arrogance. Time and change moved quickly here. Cal slowed. He also blinked, a lot. It was a poor habit, but a good marker. Telling of when he was nervous, or confused, or both.

From the dirt lawns vantage point Cal stared. Then blinked, at the Comet he unsurely sought as sanctuary. The wings betrayed his authority. With a mind of their own they kicked up the dust. Cal stood a foot from Old Blue. If Old Blue were human it would have shuddered, starring back at him.

I'll quit, leave, make something up, they'll never know, he thought. Quitting wasn't in the cards. Not for Cal, and certainly not for the Comet. Their die was cast and Master smiled. He knew something Cal didn't. Thoughts in these parts weren't safe.

In a soldier brave move Cal broke from the Comets appeal, made a quick sharp left turn. To his left he toed pat an ally reminiscent of the hall the feared earlier. It led to who knew where. Narrow and deep, it parted the house bar and a row of elevated western style stores. Before he climbed the ten wooden stairs he stopped, thought and watched. The town woke. A very small town that a local once said, had thirteen people been in the bar, one of them would have been a stranger.

To his right, yards across Fate's main dirt road sat the town square. A large clay pot sized bell hung above the town's monument that honored all the fallen war heroes from the area. The names etched in bronze, were listed in descending order. Recent battles on top, fallen heroes of the American Revolution on bottom. When struck the bells clang vibrated eerily. Resonating ground trembling vibrations echoed throughout the entire county. The sign at the bottom of it instructed it rang only when a new name was added.

Confident Cal pressed on, right leg up a stair, then left. Creaky wooden stairs warned. After the tenth he stood on top of a wooden walkway matched to the rest of the place.

He chucked a left. Swaggering wing tips stepped over the doors saddle carrying him into the bake shop. Someone was working behind the glass display. A busty woman thickly built. Not brand new, but with motherly charm. Her smock well dusted in white flour.

"Yes?" She peered over the case.

"Good morning! Do you have twenty nickels for the meter?" Cal tight lipped smiled.

"Ha-ha-ha, yes your meter is running. I do have twenty nickels. However, you, do, not. Nor will you." Motherly charm school just closed.

A once soft, white angelic round face, tensed. Squinting brown eyes glared. Her reddish blonde head snapped backward, hairnet attached.

"Ah, err, sorry. I was told to come in here. The man next door said he was your husband. The man in the old, shot-up bar." Cal back peddled.

"I know what you were told. Do you think you're the only one who's passed this way, for heaven's sake? You're going to be a challenge aren't you? Look, Cal, you have a problem already. You don't listen, you never listen."

"Whoa, wha–, what do you mean?"

"What, were you told?"

Cal thumbed his cheek.

"What were you told, son. What were you told?" She smiled and blinked.

"He told me, uh, Master he called himself told —"

"He is Master. As far as your other comment goes let me advise you of this. He, is, my, husband. For a very, very, very long time also, as I am his wife, are we clear on that?" She finished placing baked goods in the display case.

"Yes, yes, sorry. Ok the Master, err Master instructed me to go outside, get in my car–"

"The Comet–" she interrupted.

Cal stroked a stuck throat.

"Yes dear boy, the Commmmet, I know."

How the hell does she know–? I give up, he thought.

"No more of that or you'll rattle the sky forever. Well let that one go, for now."

"No more of what?"

"Watch your P's and Q's mister, and your damn, hells and so forth around here."

"Ok, jes—, oops"

"You'll figure it out all right. Now, go–" Her arms folded.

"—Find the road out of town—"

"–One road in, two roads out, yes?" Cal beamed and raised his eyebrows.

"Dear boy, go. But, be sure to stop by here–."

"-and get twenty nickels, before I go back in the bar to learn what happened in there. Sounds like a school cafeteria plan to me." Cal looked outside.

"And, you decided what, before?

"Toooo, get the nickels, first?" Cal stroked his face.

"Now, my less than quick study, do as you are told. Snake Hill Road is outside to your left. You can find your left can't you?"Three flour dusted stubby fingers pointed at him.

"Maybe, if you would have listened to the messenger's messages during your life, maybe, no guarantee, but just maybe you wouldn't be here. Come back later for the nickels."

Shamed, Cal avoided eye contact. His spanked child's head slipped an inch with each of her words till his chin pressed to his chest.

Can't tick her off, that's a bad idea, he thought.

"Yes mum." He spun around. Walking away Cal gestured good-bye partially raising his right arm.

"God, I hope its starts." Eagerly Cal sought the safety of the Comet's familiar surroundings, such as they were. He toed toward the door. He couldn't see her. Had he, he would have been greeted with a smile and her waving her left hand, index and middle finger pressed together, the same for the fourth and pinky, the pairs split apart forming a vee. Her thumb folded to her flour dusted palm. It was a bake shop.

Into the hot August sun Cal's pace broke into a trot. He headed for the Comet. 12:30 p.m. ticked on the town clock.

"If I listened to who, who told me whaaa, Big fat head, skinny–?"

It was an awful lot to remember for one day. Especially a day that just began.

"I need to get this on freakin paper before I forget."

Cal snapped the remainder of the Comets broken outside door handle.

Something's missing he thought. No noise. The usual chorus of rusty clunky sounds, absent. The door opened smoothly, happily as new. He lightly tugged it. Effortlessly, it fit back into place with new car precision.

"Ah" was replaced with "Hmmmm." Unusual occurrences were becoming, usual.

"Did the trip kill it? Man I don't know if I should be hitting the key. Maybe let a mec-a-nic check her out. Hey, what did Master mean he had a talk with Blue? Anyway, here goes. Come on baby. Please, dear God, one time, just one more time. You've had a fair rest. I'll fix you up, when we get back, if we get back, I promise." His fingers should have been crossed.

Comets key was so worn a screwdriver could have been its copy. Cal slapped it into the steering wheels ignition lock. With closed eyes he pled as an alter–boy to the heavens he disowned. Twisted, dash lights lit. Twisted more, dash lights turned off. Cal's eyes opened wide then. "Hey, I think they're supposed to do that?"

Twisted more, cringed, "Vroom." The usual medley of mechanical complaints sung to a whirring, whining, knocking rhythm, absent.

"Damn."

"Uh-oh, sorry, sorry." Thunder rattled.

Cal exercised his forehead, adjusted the floppy rearview with only minor success.

"Hmmmm- one road innnn and two roads oout, we'll see aboooout that. Bam, Bam." Losing control of his air drumstick he air slapped the sleeping steering wheel. The horn chirped, the town clock answered back. Cal shook his head. "Fantasyland, I'll title the article."

"Well I know the one road into town would certainly lead us out." He paused, thought and continued his dubious conversation with Old Blue.

"So, better do as they say. Find that Snake Hill Road, my guess the other road out. Shouldn't be too tough, this wasn't as tricky as a pirates treasure map, was it?" The Comet backfired.

Thin pale lips turned up. Cal placed transmission in reverse, held his breath. Dutifully his dubious chariot backed up. He pushed the gear stalk into drive. Comets front wheels cut the dust coming out of the zig-zag three point turn. They lunged forward with renewed life, or outright fear. Either way they had the energy. Cal hustled out of town toward Snake Hill Road.

The Comet clock received no mercy. Dimly it read 1:00 p.m. the Town clock said good-bye, 1:00 p.m.; Cal's watch, 11:25 p.m. still moving, counter.

# Ten

Summer in the country toasted the dirt road to corn flake crisp. Cal seated in his memory seat looked out freshly washed car windows Master must have had a hand in. Farms and cows hung on the country's rolling hills like Christmas ornaments. Failed farms rightfully collapsed fading their red.

"Not bad, not too bad at all, beats the stench of the city. That's for sure."

Hills and pastures of rich black earth grew the dew covered grass at night. Some animals yawned. Some stretched. Some did both. The heat sat the smarter over-fed livestock. The clever the elders didn't budge, contently idle in the barn. They would be fed whether they moved, or not. Yet some did. Lazily they lounged on warm sun-drenched hills under cloud shadow-shade. The adventuresome ones, the younger's, often escaped and made their way to the road, even Snake Hill Road. A weak spot in the fence and off they were looking for greener pastures. Some made it across the road. Some didn't and remained as reminders of the price of risk as roadside statues.

"Ahhh," Cal inhaled humid country air through the vents.

Toasted big air was packed with notes of cow manure, hay and grain. Plump pigs, cackling chickens, were regulars. Goateed goats complained and, of course what would farm country be without a snake, or two? Particularly a large, some thought, mythical snake.

One, only the local's spoke of in private. They said it lived atop of Snake Hill Road.

Cal leisurely followed Snake Hill Road toward it, pairing the rich farmland. A country road other innocent sightseers rolled across in their chariots, traveling tea time slow. It pulsed in size and construction. Mostly black top, but occasionally oiled. Single lanes quickly became doubles, and then without warning back again. Not much warning of hazards in these parts, none at times. Things changed quickly here. Complicating matters were neatly packed tall mature corn stalks, alternating with forested land yet cleared. Visibility suffered. The crisp orderly rows of motherly corn stalks grew large man tall. At their peak they shrouded those within their midst. Heavy sagging limbs held silk wrapped babies, awaiting adoption. Plucked friends hid in silos.

Cal traveled the all American storybook scene. One Norman Rockwell would be jealous of. A scene composed of normal, familiar and usual items, and some not.

"Man this isn't too bad, pretty cool…"

"Sun feels dam good on these old tired bones."

Cal and the Comet rolled on their way. Comet's rebirth brushed off by Cal as yet another minor miracle. He had seen so much today. Any more awakening would be no more than a slight finger jab. Car and master- master and car, educated by Mother on how to precisely follow instructions temporarily unified as one. Effortlessly they rolled in country road dust toward their destination.

"This is getting boring, one road in two roads out, yeah right." Cal spat. The window wasn't down. "Aggahhh–"

The dust thinned when Old Blue's aching tires hit a part of the road recently oiled. No need to spend money on tar when you have oil to be rid of, locals agreed. Yankee thrift ruled the day.

Streaming sun through Blues windshield worked Cal over. He yawned, groaned. Fought his eyes closing and wondered what the big deal was. Why was Master, Mother and the map insistent he see this, travel this way? Arthritis and a well understood headache made things worse. Cal jaw stretched his gummy salt and pepper face battling the suns seduction. Brown stained fingers with complimenting with swollen knuckles, loosely hung over the top of the replacement steering wheel. Tasked, Cal stayed the course, in a creaking Comet.

"Dam it's hot, hotter than Millie's kitchen" Who Millie was he didn't know, or care. But it sounded like something someone would say, in the country.

Something else he didn't care about, air-conditioning. Hadn't worked from the first day Cal owned the car. Didn't need it he thought at the time. A bargaining chip to negotiate a price lower was more important. Cal self talked and self-argued. He would fix it sometime later, when the funds showed up. Sometime never came. Saloon keepers campaigned better places for that money. Air conditioning yielded to mental conditioning.

Cal owned many Junkers in his day. As a teenager most of his cars, and there were many, had no air conditioner at all much less a broken one. Yet he loved to impress his friends with his new toy, wordsmithing, an early indication of a future career. He coined the term, faux a/c, or, just turn on the fan.

Cal patted Comets dash like a favorite pets head. It was the dog days of summer after all. Two boney fingers impulsively reached for and snapped switched the AC switch. He waited for a weary fan to build speed. Arthritis was everywhere. The car signaled peak speed was reached when the worn out and out of balance fan, noisily clanged from its blades smacking against its metal housing.

"Darn, no noise. It's broken, just what I need." Cal's grinding teeth wore on waiting for the confirmation of the fans death. Double checking he stuck two finger tips in one of the cracked dash's vents.

"Christ almighty. Its cold, cold damn, yeah babahheeeee." The fan spun new car quiet muscling cold air out of dash's air vents.

"Cold air—daaaaam—Whoaaaaa," Meat locker cold fought its way through broken sticky vents housed in a cracked, faded, pencil and pen pin cushioned dash. Sleepiness blew off Cal, landed in the back seat.

"Cool, Real cool, ha, ha, ha."

Will wonders never cease? This place is really different he thought. This country was nothing of his knowing. But so far, he had little to complain about.

"Add cold air on a hot day to some good music, and you're close to perfection."

Since the beginning of the Comets and Cal's union the radio worked poorly but wasn't nearly as bad as the air conditioning. The Comets radio aged to a crackling mess. The speakers frayed from volume abuse of bluesy rock music. Poor reception plagued its function as well, even in the city.

"Well there my friend when it goes bad, it goes bad." Frustration bounced back and got the better of Cal. Occasionally he spoke a disparaging comment to the Comet. One often recycled from when Cal received it from the verbal abuse of a Big Pete encounter. Comet took it in stride.

"I'm a little confused. Maybe local news will help me get my bearings."

A prejudice finger snapped the radio on.

"The price of corn today on the futures market— Lots of issues to be solved" Cal cocked his head. No rain or too much of it?

"Look up once in awhile." scratched out.

"Huh?"

The radio sounded bad because he didn't want to hear the farm report. However the sound was excellent. No scratchiness, no crackling. A strong signal jammed the little radio with perfect clarity. Cal didn't even blink.

"Man let me change this, any music?"

A boney right hand index finger pressed everyone's favorite button. The radio must have attended a healing tent service. A much loved station broadcasted his favorite bluesy rock music, clear as a bell, all the way from New York City. At home he couldn't receive that station clearly.

Now, this was home. Concert hall sound rang out. Old Blue's radio sang to the heavens.

"Renegade," the classic Styx song blasted about Mamma and the law. Cal pressed another button. Different station, same song, then again, and again. Same result.

Cal mouthed the lyrics always a syllable, word, or phrase behind. Faking it never stopped him before, wouldn't stop him now. Fearlessly he sang out loud, bobbed his head to the rhythmic pulsing beat.

His grays squinted deep in thought reviewing the welcome surprises, not from the brilliant sun. These tantalizing moments were just the beginning of electrifying country seasoning.

"I'm not wanted, am I? Is this a story really worth chasing?" a tormenting question curled his lips.

The radio station changed, "We all have to do this from time to time," and then the farmer being interviewed went on about crops.

"Ah, ha, ha, ha," Cal shook, swept the rear view mirror. Spat a small laugh at his craggy face, and then howled. It echoed in the cars cabin until finally muffled by a muffling torn headliner. Cal and the Comet bucked rolled and bounced down the dusty trail. Cal lowered the passenger side window down half way when he left town, never expecting the air to work. He forgot to close it. Some of that thunderous school boy laughter, not swallowed by the headliner, leaked. Out the window, danced in the wind and blew to all nearby to hear. All nearby to hear, took notice. Cal sped on.

Ten fence posts ahead, on the right, a few grazing cows lazily stood close to the roadside as the fence allowed. They lifted their heads. The hair on their chins was courteously primped by the wire. They watched the dust ball Comet, hurtle toward them.

Cal slowed as he closed the distance between them and himself. He stopped, twisted his head to the right. Looked directly at them and childishly screamed an "ahahahhhahha." Two ticks of his wristwatch later his grays went wide eyed.

"What in the world? Did they just smile back?" He snapped his neck from right to left in a double take, wiped his face. Looked forward and–

"Ok baby let's see just how healthy you are?" The accelerator slapped the floor. Comet leapt like a switched stallion. Front tires sliced the oiled dirt funneling a rooster tail of gravel and stone against the inner wheel wells. The hard dirt plume rapped a snare drum riveting beat. A drum beat bragging about new found health. Cal smiled, raised his hands and practiced a drum roll of his own. He could still play if he wanted, he knew it. He knew if the Comet were alive it would be smiling as well.

"Jeeze, I can't believe how spry you are?" Cal petted its dash.

Cal and Comet rocked to music while threading through an idyllic "Made in America" landscape, as if chased by the cops after a 1920's bank job gone bad. Two amigos played with their new toy, rejuvenation.

Three miles from Fates center flat pastures rolled up to hills. The base of Snake Hill started in a gradual incline, progressed in a steep angle as the hill rose. Snake Hill was a towering hill. Most would categorize as a small mountain. Cal reached its base full of various momentums. Effortlessly they climbed the ramping road. At its crest they stopped, and parked on the shoulder. The revived driver's door smoothly opened. Cal winced while scraping the wings over the gravel. Stood in front of the car, faced forward partially blocking the Comets view. It was then he knew what the fuss was about.

"I've seen hell. Now I've seen Heavens door." Cal's reverent watery eyed head tipped, standing in Mother Nature's cathedral. Ahead of him, a sweeping valley rolled down and out from atop Snake Hill as if ocean waves surged to shore. Pastures dotted with mounds of swollen hills were perfected for cows and horses grazing, children raising mischief, and, a few other special purposes. The view reached the end of the world.

"Ah. Ah ah," Cal gasped. The breathtaking, dramatic, serene scene ended when Cal looked straight down at the road that led down the other side. There, a worrisome sight, a steep winding serpentine road twisted in sharp angles, almost to the bottom.

Seductive, notorious, and wicked Snake Hill Road so named for its curving turns, not a snake. Though some thought it should be otherwise. Historic, in the early 1700's it bore a straight line from top to bottom causing a dangerous slope. Heavy wagons laden with cargo from the local farmers, or munitions for the revolution often lost control traveling it. Crashes were plentiful. Nothing was done till a wagon owned by the local mayor crashed. Shortly there-after an enlightened local community redesigned it. Adding turns it was thought, would slow travel but stabilize the passersby's loads, a good trade and it did for most. Heat lightening struck, the bar photo of Malcolm flashed.

"Gee Whiz, I think I'm acrophobic." Cal held his breath, looked down Snake Hill. The sloping twisty road apportioned the mountain in two unequal parts. Had they been they could have called it Peach Mountain. The smaller right half remained wholly untouched, unmanicured. Rough, sparsely forested, it descended steeply to the bottom. The left half, infinite in size, was rolling grazing pasture land. Like its cousin it descended steeply at first, then more gradually. Finally its flow completely released creating miles of fields of flat pastures at the bottom of the decline, like a spent wave crashing to shore. .

Cal squinted down Snake Hill's twists, noticed the road straighten out about fifty yards from the bottom and disappeared into a pot belly circle its base.

"Wonder where that goes?" Cal looked to his right. A criss-crossed arrowed white sign pointed in two directions. The one pointing straight was labeled; Vaughan's farm road. It hid on the other side of a swale framing the pot belly and was swallowed by the forest. Though the Fowlers owned it now all knew it as the Vaughan's. Land ownership changed more slowly in these parts than minds, only when necessary and often uncomfortably.

The other sign pointed left. Spirit Trail Road connected to the pot belly. Heading away it sliced the flattened valley in two parts. Each border framed in eclectic fencing of wire, split rail, and missing split rail. With fair eyesight and a good squint Cal followed Spirit Trail Road to its meandering end, miles away. There it disappeared around a big hill that loomed into the clouds, miles off in the distance. Heavens Hill the sign noted after Spirit Trail Road.

Seduced, Cal warmly stayed in his trance. Gently blinking, unfettered, he looked downward at the road before him. Pointing his finger he counted the roads cut hard slashes left and right. Seven, maybe eight hard angled turns till it rolled to the bottom.

There were lots of twists in these parts, he thought.

Heat lightening said hello.

"You have a big fat head and a skinny little soul!" flashed.

"What the heck did that mean? Look up? I am. It's a nice day big deal. Ok a fabulous day. What in the world was that creepy old dude talking about?"

A car's wheels drummed over the crest of the hill passing him on his left. The rumbling brought him back.

Cal followed the car all the way down through the turns and into its final descent down the last steep straight slope, empting into the pot belly.

"Where are my binoculars?" I know I have them." Cal shot to the back of Blue, opened the trunk. There they were, next to his rifle case. He closed the trunk and ran back to the front of the car. Raised the glasses and focused on something he didn't see before. Something the car drew his attention to. There, to the left of the pot belly stood a bevy of weeping willows behind a split rail fence. Fencing the bar owners must have missed. The willows were a well know landmark to all in the area. Well known as guardians. They ringed an inner circle pond with their weeping willowy whip like branches, shielding it in a cocoon. A pond frequented by grazing livestock, until local devils showed up.

The car slowly turned left out of the pot belly, around the willows bearing warriors weapons. It connected to the final leg of road out of town, Spirit Trail Road. Named it was thought for the troops of the revolution which passed this way once on their way to glory. The driver raised a left hand waving good-bye. Cal pulled his eyes away from the binoculars.

Daytime was beautiful. Night would be less so. It was getting late. Cal looked at Old Blues clock, 6:00 p.m. His watch, 11:20 p.m., soon the soft smoky clouds that hung in a big blue sky would evaporate. Hot but comfortable, Cal sighed. Inside the Comet Cal's eyes locked on Spirit Trail Road following it as far as he could to the hill.

"What was behind the hill, Heaven Hill?" He had no instructions to go there. He would have to wait to see where it disappeared to. The Comet fired up. Cal put it in gear, looked to his left making sure nothing else there before turning around.

"What the he–? Nothing here at all, no body, no animules, no nutin. That grass was untouched. Stood straight up when I first got here. Pasture tall. Now it's trampled. Nothing, I heard nothing, saw nothing, no cattle to be seen. No beings at all. Jeasus, I can't tell anyone this." His forehead sweat beaded.

An overactive thyroid hallucination, he figured, hoped and dismissed the mysterious trampling as a minor question. Time wound down. Summer's sun peaked, late afternoon shadows cast passed.

Night hurried in. If Cal stayed he would have been treated to hear the corn grow in the night and watch the brilliant firefly dance in the sky, but he couldn't. Safe inside old unreliable, Cal shook his head wondering what in world he saw today; cows smiling, grass trampling, cars rejuvenation. Heat lightening blinked some guiding light.

Cal's first day of class started pleasantly. It wouldn't last. He hustled back to town. The nickels were waiting.

# Eleven

"I'm late. If I tick this guy off I'm——. Maybe I, I, I should just should leave. Go home. That view seemed familiar. Never been but seemed like I knew it. Man, I've got to see what's with this joint but–." Cal kept glancing in a bobbing rearview mirror. Night's dark curtain fell behind him. He drove into dying light diming the farm land. His open driver's window demanded the air sampled. His nose tweaked, sniffed musky thick air that could describe to a blind person where they were.

By the time they snuck into town, night crashed. Cal's right index finger quick-spun the steering wheel. The Comet skid and came to rest nose first. Mother's bake shop rose directly ahead. The Comets dash clock read 7 p.m., the town clock 7 p.m. Cal's renewed life wristwatch spun, backwards, 11:10 p.m.

"Excuse me friend." Cal excused himself to the Comet with a borrowed phrase of Master.

He rushed to the shop eager to tell Mother what he saw. Palpable excitement pulsed his tried eyes, nearly forgot stores doors saddle but phobia did its job. Cal halted. Double foot hopped it. Ran two steps and stopped in a skid, near fall, right in front of the counter.

He flashed his corn white and yellow teeth, waited. Master's missus, Mother hen, stood by the register decorated in her signature, flour dusted smock.

"Come closer, Cal. He's waiting." Her pointing fingertip curled.

"Waiting? Thought I was on time? Of course no one said when to be back but–"

"Yes, waiting"

"For how long, I didn't know there was a schedule?"

"He's been waiting for you for years, and well, for years Cal." Cal recoiled. His eyes rolled in mock surprise.

"Now, let's see. Twenty nickels is–"

"– a dollar where I come from" Cal grinned.

"Well, you don't come from here, now do you?"

Cal stammered, "No. Ah, no I don't."

Fearful grays shifted, avoiding contact. Her eyes with arched exaggerated left eyebrow never left him. She wrinkled face to a questioning pose, tucked he chin.

"Twenty dollars son, they're twenty to you."

"Twenty dollars, hey that's a dollar a nickel." He started negotiating.

"I can add, yes, I know bright boy."

"That's ridiculous."

"Hardly, did you think that gas station attendant was kidding about needing that twenty you have?"

"Son, these are not ordinary nickels, you need them. Look at the transom above the door."

"What about it?"

"Do you see word Charity written anywhere?"

"No." "Look, Mother, all I have left is twenty dollars. I need it to get me home."

"On the front window perhaps,"

"Nooo," He stared at his feet. "Damn, ah ha-ha."

Boom, thunder was serious.

"I warned you about swearing."

"Yes, I know, sorry. But I just noticed I had on a blue, and a black sock."

"That doesn't matter here, son. Watch what you say and to whom you say it. All is heard, all is known, except for you."

"Ok, but if I give my twenty–"

"Let's see it!"

He shoved a hand into his right pants pocket, and felt around for his last loose bill. Somewhere in there it hid tangled amongst the coffee-house change dropped in yesterday.

Ah, got it. Uh oh, did I stuff my note pad in my front pocket?

"Nooo you didn't."

"How do you know?" Cal swallowed hard, forgetting the mind-reading parlor trick.

"Well, what do you have there?"

Cal opened his hand. Absent the single twenty he put in his pocket last night. It hid somewhere amongst the fifty others like it. All folded neatly together in a family meeting, wrapped by a lone rubber band. Stone-faced, hand shaking, his head jostled looking at Mother. She heckled a laugh, winked. Cal's well practiced knees buckled.

"Give me the top one, son. The rest are yours."

"Thank you."

"Now here are your nickels. You must take them from me."

Mother extended her left arm, cupped palm up and rolled it over. Cal held his outstretched right hand open palm below hers. As her wrist twisted she poured them from the side of her palm. One by one they fell, like slot machines winnings without the bells. Twenty of them, all brand new, brand new mint condition Indian Head nickels. They hadn't been minted since 1938.

Cal's stirred the shiny coins with his left index finger examining his purchase, financed by Mother Bank. He knew something about coin collecting as a childhood hobby. He could not believe his eyes.

"Still think they're expensive?" Smiling brown eyes telegraphed a dare. Cal feverish shook his head no.

"It's not what you think that makes them valuable son. Forget their age, condition and those things. Yes, they are quite real if you are thinking otherwise. But no, it's not what they are, it's what they do. Now be off, he's waiting, and you're welcome. Your mother taught you to be thankful and polite, didn't she?"

Cal couldn't look up tramped in brilliance of the new 1938 coins.

"Thank you," softly escaped his lips, caught a wispy wind. Mother broke a smile.

The nickels, wrapped in his fist were gently stuffed into his right pants pocket. His newly found paper wealth was held tighter in his left hand and pocket. Which pocket held the greater wealth he wondered? Wrinkling his nose, shaking his graying short haired head, Cal shuffled past the empty once morning full display cases. Before he went on his way out of the store he stopped, and glanced over a short curtain that stretched from the end of the last case to the wall behind it making sure no one was hiding back there pulling strings or something, then looked up at the transom.

"It should say Charity up there. It should."

She laughed. Mothers always know. Cal looked out the door before crossing the saddle.

I wonder. Was that the only other road out of this dumpy town? He wondered.

"Be polite," reached his abused ears. "And yes, son, it is"

Cal's shoulders shrugged. Twisting his head sharply to the left jutted his chin. His grays squinted.

"Daaaaa– I didn't say it, I didn't, I didn't."

"By the way Cal, what did you think?"

"Think?"

"Of your little trip today," Cal raised two open beggar's palms.

Waving her floury hands, she smiled and shooed. "You're late, get in there, he's waiting!"

8:30 p.m. Town Clock time. 11 p.m., Cal's watch lost another ten minutes. Still August 29, 2009. Two would meet buzzed like a mosquito near his left ear.

# TWELVE

The last of this summer day's twilight held off night, for a few more minutes. Then dark shooed its rival cousin away. Cal looked at the moonlit town through the bakery window. Grasping his newfound wealth he schoolboy skipped out the Mother's bakery shops front door onto the splintery wooden walkway—careful to miss the saddle! Light footedly he gnome-like danced toward the bar, remarkably as instructed. Fate's clock ticked forward, his watch lost more time.

Following Master's instructions, still a work in progress but following Mother's mattered. And hers were clear. He trembled at the bars doorless entrance. Peering inside it stayed dark, hollow, but magnetic. Soon he would see, light would banish the darkness.

The previous night and day's events replayed in Cal's mind while he decided what to do.

"Am I out of my-ever–loving gourd? I could hit the road with the cash, pay some bills. Make up the story. Heck wouldn't be the first time." He gnawed out from behind his chapped lips.

"Still time to cut and run. Done that before, I don't need this anyway no one will believe this stupid story. And what kind of story is it anyway? Who knows, maybe this is a bad dream or better yet, I'm dead."

"Noooooonsense," A Zeus bellow roared rattling splinters from the dry-rotting door frame. Cal shook, collapsed forward through the doorway as a drunk. Both feet floated over the saddle. He brushed himself off and regained his balance. A well practiced maneuver.

"Get in here, boy, before immediately before the light is completely gone." Master lurked within the interiors shadows.

"The moon is leaving. Soon it will be the darkest night of your life. Do not resist your instructions."

Cal's heart thumped. Courage engaged. His throat dried. "It's too dark in here, I can't see a thing."

"From darkness, you will find light, my friend."

"There's no electricity in this dump. Nothing gets past me." Cal's bravado would prove an unappreciated remembrance.

"Really, nothing gets past you? Nothing, eh, well, we'll see. We will see."

Master slipped from his shadowy womb hiding place. A convenient sliver of moonlight lit him menacingly tall, taller than Cal remembered. Master held court, preacher-style from the second level in front of the bar. His right leg crossed his left. A black engineer boot toe pointed, barely touched the floor. "Come, come, a lot to do. Fetch the chair you righted before. Bring it here."

"What if I don't?"Cal folded his arms.

"Well, you could leave. Return to the existence you sucked in, and suffer." At least now you have paper money, you get to keep that. But I will require the nickels back. They do not leave ever, much too valuable."

Master's head turned, the corners of his slit eyes he never broke contact.

"What will it be? Time's wasting, and you are wasting my time."

"Think I'm outa here actually. Thanks for the dough. What am I a child?"

"We are all children of the universe, boy. Off with you then. Go to that magical island you've dreamt about, gooooo."

"Well, I just want to go somewhere away, from here."

"And there, and there, and there." Master chanted. "It's not where your body is, friend. It's where your head's at."

Cal laughed, countered. "My head would be happier on an island!"Cal laughed, fencing.

"Touché,"

"I meant, your mind, now be a good boy and do as you're told."

"Ok, Ok here's the damn chair." Thunder rumbled.

"Where do you want it? You stinky old goat," Cal twisted toward the doorless front door.

"What's that?

"Nothing sir."

"Put it over there, where Jimmy was. He's away for awhile. Yes, put it there with its back to the wall."

Cal foot shoved the chair across the floor. Its back came to a gentle rest, neatly in place, right where the Master wanted. He brushed his hands together satisfied with himself.

"Now, I'm out of this haunted house and heading back to the city. I am also keeping the nickels. How do you like that?"

Cal strategically paused for a second with a playground smirk.

"I'm kidding, got ya."

"No friend. Now get in the chair."

"No."

"Yes."

"I will not. What kind of freakin power do you think you have? You can't make me, and what kind of shoes are those anyway for a Halloween spook to wear, gee—" Before the last syllable escaped Cal was air mailed across the floor and punishingly slammed to the chair.

"I see your point, Ok, I will." He shook the birds from circling his head.

Master brushed his hands together. Cal gulped, straightened up, and sat electrocution rigid curiously close to where he before wanted to touch the bullet hole in the Jimmy Hendrix poster. The posters of rock stars were replaced. Sixties muscle cars and motorcycles hung in their place. Things changed quick as a flicked light switch around here.

"If we're going to have this dance, then let's have it boy."

This place gets stranger by the minute. Cal thought.

"You have no idea."

"Great more parlor tricks, now I don't have any private thoughts."

"No, no you don't. No you don't." Master rubbed it in.

The bars interior held pitch black. Cal repeated the morning's eye exercise.

"That won't be necessary," Master, standing in front of the bar wrapped his celestial silhouette in soft gauze light.

"The bullet hole, you wished to touch before. Do you still? Well, speak up."

"I did, yes. But you—"

"—before, my friend, you knew nothing of this place. That was then. Today you went to the top of Snake Hill. Now, shall we say, you have a flavor of Fate. Are you prepared to know more?" Master curled his cupped left hand. When he unraveled it his fingers pointed toward the bullet holes.

"So I ask you again, friend. Do you want to know more?"

"Do I really have a choice?"

"No. I was just being polite."

"Man you have issues."

"At my age boy, you have to have accumulated something. If it's issues, then so be it."

"Know this, Cal. The time you spend on this trip, from its beginning till the time you arrive back home, if you arrive, will be a fortnight and four. Touch whichever hole you wish, it matters not. Use your left hand only. Grip the chair's arm rest with the right."

"A fortnight and one equal fifteen days. I'll be here fourteen more days from today?"

"So you can add."

"Is there a test afterward?"

"A question and answer period of sort. Now I ask you, do you want your story?"

"Yes."

"Then you must know Malcolm's story. Are you ready?"

Cal submissively nodded.

"Do it. Touch it."

Cal's left palm smacked the wall. He couldn't see the wall facing away from it. It blindly glided over aged glossed posters. Memories of his BSA Victor flashed, and the picture Malcolm was in with his friends.

The Victor, a 1960's single cylinder on and off road motorcycle, born of an English company named BSA. BSA stood for Birmingham Small Arms. It was founded in 1861, in the gun quarter of Birmingham, England, by fourteen gunsmiths. Successful suppliers of guns to the British government during the Crimean War, but the gun trade fell. They branched out into other enterprises, bicycles, autos, auto engines and such. By 1909 they were making motorcycles. BSA acquired a competitor, Triumph motorcycles, in 1951 and became the largest motorcycle manufacturer in the world. The Victor, one of their most successful exports, became prized by motorcycle aficionados.

"Touch it!"

Cal's fingers spider walked, he curled his bottom lip over his top. An index finger found a torn piece of the poster. Cal stroked it.

"Now, now I said."

Cal closed his eyes, jammed his finger with cellophane popping force as far as it could go. The hole shrank, tightened around his middle knuckle deep finger. Cal tried to retrieve it, he pulled back. Too late, only amputation could have freed him. His trapped finger tethered him to the wall, right through his Victor's iconic half chrome, half yellow, red labeled gas tank.

"Hey, hey, what's —" High voltage electricity bolted from behind the wall through the hole, into Cal's finger wire. He panicked. His neck tensed, twisted right, body twisted left. Prey caught in a trap. A trap that dealt a sting reserved for a death row inmate from "Old Sparky." His head rapped repeatedly against the wall with a drummer's rhythmical beat. The commotion would wake up anything asleep. Cal hung on. Veins in his hands and neck bulged, pulsed, swelled then shrank. Both grays blinked wide open in amazement, and then momentarily slammed closed shielding the fright. Charged wings toe danced till exhaustion. They stopped flat-footed pressing firmly on the red and black tile hoping to find safety in the cellar. Cal's free right hand, the one he was instructed to hold the chairs right arm rest tightly with, held it tightly in a white knuckled death grip and cancelled his arthritis.

The torture seemed to go on for an eternity. In reality, twenty seconds. With the prescribed twenty spent, the switch that turned it on now shut it off. Retreating electricity receded from the wall, as quickly as it struck. Cal's contorted face and clenched teeth, relaxed. He slumped in the chair, panting. Both legs outstretched, locked at the knees and crossed at the ankles. His one free arm beggars palm up. Battered he rested his head against the wall with continuing labored breathing. Orientation was almost over.

"No electricity? You think so now? Do you? You smug little—" Master held his breath. Mother was watching.

Master pranced in a dance exclusively reserved for newbie's. His feet shuffled front and back. Slid right and then left. Arms bent at the elbows carried soft fists that swung back and forth coordinated in opposite directions of his feet. The black hooded robe flowed in unison.

"Noooooooo electricity, huh, are you quite sure? He sang and strutted around in front of the bar whistling. Indifferently he examined his left hands nails, bit a cuticle, and spat it out.

Mother glared a strong suggestion, he stop.

Cal struggled, un-amused. However his feelings didn't matter, Master's did. After all it was his place, or at least his to be, Master.

"At least now they will work."

"What will work Master?"

"The coins, they must be charged to work!"

"Oh? Surrre, the coins need to be charged of course" Cal pulled his cheeks up to a clown smile.

"And I'm the extension cord that helped that. Didn't I?"

"I suppose in a manner of speaking. Give me one. We, we, we, will, will, will, use, use, use, more, as you feel more coooommmmfortable." The room echoed.

"More, later,"

"Yes yes-more about that later, flip me one—you need to stay there."

"Well I can't remove my finger anyway?"

"Yes, quite, you will in a second. Now flip me one with your right hand. I said we'll go slowly at first, only one to start, just one, for now my boy."

Cal dug deep into his right pocket. The coins warmed to the touch. As told, he flipped one. Master shagged it in a left hand, backhanded, major league baseball catch. "He'll like that."

"Who?"

"Never mind for now."

Master strolled over to the shot up Wurlitzer and deposited the coin in the slot.

"Hey, you just wasted my nickel. That thing will nev–."

Master waved him off. Click clack, Clikity·clack. The rare coin slid into and down the chute, triggering and tripping all the ingenious mechanics inside.

Whirr-r. The old shot-up juke sprang to life. Model 1015-Bubbler had a curved arched top. Tubes of multicolored pink and yellow lights ran up the sides meeting nearly at the machines top, capped a decorative chrome band. A jeweled red medallion acted as crown. She was beautiful.

In its youth, teenagers looked into the machine through its convex glass, watching it pluck and play records. Chrome, latticed metal work formed the diamond shapes of the grill that protected the speaker. A dark wood insert filled in the rest of the bubbler's face finishing its brilliant look.

Two flashes of light on far wall caught Cal's eye. His head snapped. One word next to another blinked in the stealthy darkness.

A sign, he wondered?

"Yes, light from dark." Master answered.

Cal sighed, squinted. Twenty years, projected in brilliant neon blue.

"Twenty years, wha-? Hey, Master–" He was gone. The wall, and bubbler lights, perfect decoy's for a Masterful escape. He pressed a selection on the juke box before he slipped off to sit in his personal shadow on the lower floor. Cal sat alone, both listened to the lyrics.

Cal's eyes watered. Thought what next? What in the world is next?

"Yoooooouuuullll, Seeeeee, Boooooyyyyy!!!"

"Yes son. You will see and don't mind Master. He's found the writer's ink. The two of you need to take a break. Come back to this in five minutes. Not a minute before-not a minute after. Do you both understand me? I'll hold things right as they are till you return."

"Of course- me love" Master bowed.

"Yes Mother." Cal looked at his watch, 10:40 p.m. Tuesday, August 29, 2009. He calculated what time it would be in five minutes backwards. Outside the town clock dimly read11:00 p.m.

# Thirteen

Cal blinked, again, and again. Watched the time, Fates town clock ticked forward five minute's to 11:05 p.m. His watch lost five, 10:35 p.m. but still Tuesday August 29, 2009.

"Well, that's that, times up." Cal shook his crew cut, blinked, and then raised his brows smiling.

"Yes son." Mother looked at Master.

Cal blinked, and blinked and then blinked some more.

"Listen," Master looked at the juke.

The theme from "A Summer Place" filtered through the Wurlitzer's chrome grill. Movie music of violin strings serenaded, soothed.

"Haven't heard that in years," Cal flexed his hands, chewed remaining tension from his jaw. His ears grabbed all they could. What a welcome surprise. Music, from a simpler, long-ago time.

"Music, friend, binds us all. Places, times, events, no matter my age, or young, as you are." Cal stared at the juke, tipped his head toward Master's whisper.

"Yes friend.... Yess...." Master nodded.

"Your time with us will be marked by it. I promise, I warn." Master muffled a chuckle within his black cape.

"Where were you when you first heard this song, Cal? Think Cal, remember. We all know where we were, how we were, what we were when the music played. Don't we? Have you traveled this way before

Cal? Some lessons come easy, some, hard. Don't fight it Cal. Let it take you."

Uh, lesson?

"Yes son!" Mother nodded.

"For heaven's sake, shit, goddamn it. Am I ever allowed private thoughts? Anyway, where I need to go? I'm here.

"Ah, the boy has teeth."

The boy?

"Yes, the boy. Now, my young man-"

"-Young man? Listen, old man, I am sick of your snide —."

"—let's remember the question I've asked you before, shall we, boy?"

Mother twisted her choked down smile referee head.

"Before I release you from your stare, are you ready to proceed?"

"Yes."

Cal's chin tipped up. Master laughed, admired his left hands twirling index finger. Cal blinked once to wet his eyes, another to scrub terror from them. When the blur cleared, the bar was alive.

Night-time bustled as if nothing bad had ever happened. Nothing broken, no bullet holes, chairs and tables stood where they should. Tobacco smoke thickly clouded the air, twined with scents of beer, liquor. All perfumed the knotty pine walls. Musical laughter grew loud. Little lies were squashed by bigger ones. Local's only this night, nine in all in all including the bartender.

The farm hands usually wore suits of worn faded bib coveralls. Some sported freshly laundered tee shirts and jeans. Element over-exposed, cracked leathery skin matched the wear on their boots. Hard lives started early, chewed all day at the hard work earned simple pleasures of shots and beers. Later, modest, protective wives came around to make sure Pa got home okay. Morning came fast. The unfiltered cigarette a boy's club allowed few exceptions.

Two women, Mary, fit, tall, sturdily built, but not fat, came occasionally. That occasion, when Destiny was open. Her beau left her years ago. Said he had some work to do for the State, would take him at least three to five years to finish. She waited the full five, and then ten. Poor girl, time passed her by, but alcohol wouldn't. What she lacked in beauty, she gained in brains. Taught herself French,

Spanish, started Russian during her wait. Dad left her a few bucks. She traveled when she closed the only dress shop in town.

There weren't many of those in the county. Feed and tractor places were better- suited enterprises up there. When she'd return from a trip she reopened the dress store. Matron Mary, as the locals called her behind her back, could be found in shops back room. Big brown eyes on riveted on a book. Her medium complexion hid from sight behind a Dickens novel. Auburn hair properly pulled into a bun. A well groomed proper woman, who wished not to be, and thanks dad she knew more about pistols then most men.

Cal moved. No one looked. He stomped his feet and again no one stirred. "I'm invisible, ahahahhhahha. I can be voyeur." Sammie the bartender greeted Mary. He seemed familiar to Cal, but couldn't place it.

"What'll it be?" Sammie's hoarse voice laughed. Mary's tonic and gin waited in front of her favorite stool, on the left corner of the bar.

Sammie was an infant when his father was killed. No one knew how, or why, except his mom. She wouldn't talk about the incident at the bank, but did become very protective. Still her smothering couldn't stop a severe childhood illness that left him always pale, and five feet two. His friends, including his best friend Malcolm, affectionately teased him nick-naming him, runt. He stood as tall as he could in the crowd of boys jeering at one another in the haunting motorcycle photo. Malcolm treated Sammie as kin.

Sammie's size, wavy brown hair, and round facial features crafted a safe dutiful son, but no less a boy. Nature's hormonal sleight-of-hand encouraged a rebel. He resisted Mother's overly protective smothering. One afternoon he set out to prove himself, rise above his short stature atop Snake Hill Road. The stunt was so dangerous Napoleon would have taken notice. Malcolm's Band of Brothers, all in the picture, were playing Race with the Devil that day. Desperate to show them up, Sammie's heart, and courage, coupled with little sense. The accident on the wire fence ripped his throat, forever affecting his voice. Likely, that event saved him from a trip to Asia, and much more.

Cal counted the patrons, nine souls all together now.

If there were ten there would have been a stranger in town Cal thought, smiled a chuckle.

"There are ten, friend." Master said. "Count again."

Cal groaned, looked at Master, and pointed his finger to his own chest. The hole finally released its choke-hold on his finger. His clenched jaw relaxed. He eased it from the wall fearful of its condition. Numbness yielded to feeling buzzing back to it, albeit slowly. No visible scars, burns, or marks. No electricity indeed Cal playfully thought. He sighed.

Cal's head fully cleared. He eavesdropped. Soaked up a blend of garbled bar-talk of psst, psst sss, I know I know. I haven't seen him either but he, over there he has. The last seductive notes of "A Summers Place," vanished.

"Hey, they can't see me. I'm invisible, anonymous, and irrelevant."

Nine heads turned, stare right at him.

"Uh oh," Cal gulped. How can I get out of here, he thought?

"Silly, you don't. Not now, but eventually it'll be fine, eventually." Mother looked away.

"Oooooooo Booyyy." Cal shook his head.

"Yes boy, yes indeed." Master never missed an opportunity.

The whispering crowd at the bar nominated an ambassador to speak.

"Excuse me, wheeerre iiis hheee, Sir?" Matron Mary sang in a church choir soprano voice.

"Where is who?" Cal pushed back.

"Malcolm of course," Farmer Vaughn, a huge, boulder moving farm-strong balding man in overalls, with a deep bass voice, chimed in.

Mary explained. "Malcolm, he owns this place. Left us many years ago, haven't seen him since."

"Well, how the heck would I know?" Cal's tenor voice answered.

"Because you were sent here to tell us," Sammie's scratchy, somewhere between a soprano and alto, said.

"No I wasn't! I came here err, Big Pete sent me here to get a newspaper story."

"So tell it, then." Farmer Vaughn's bass said.

"Ugh-how can I tell you something I don't k—?" The pause held for a minute-seemed like an hour. Master coughed.

I can tell you when he was young. Cal spoke; open palms faced the floor held tightly to his waist.

All nine tipped their left ears toward Cal. If there a campfire Cal would have been the old man spinning scary stories to kids. However, his listeners were not children, the story, not a yarn.

Great now I'm a medium. What's next floating around the room? God, Cal thought.

"Leave him out of it." The soprano, bass and Sammie chimed in, and then snickered.

"You'll rule at some time. Mind yourself till then." Master left the shadows, arms folded.

"Okay." Cal looked away, wet his lips.

"Another nickel, now," The Wurlitzer needed to be fed. Master insisted background music play. No Wurlitzer, no story. Cal dispensed nickels to Master like a kid with a Pez dispenser. Master edge spun another coin down the chute. It slipped slithered and rattled its way to its end, finally clanking with the others in the coin cup. Well fed, it plucked another record from its nest. A summoned bluesy tune played, complete with a guitar whining about lost love.

Cal moved close to the railing above the lower floor at Master's finger point direction. His weathered audience sat on bar stools. All eyes and ears looked at teach Cal.

"It's yours to know, yours to tell, they're allll, yours, now." Master coughed.

"Okay, here's what I know."

His listener's nodded encouragement. A single outburst pressed Cal. It set him back. He fought back, regained courage and continued stumbling and stuttered as badly as the Comet would when trying to start in the dead of winter. Anger stirred. His hard headed head fired.

This fellow Malkie-,

"–Malcolm, Malcolm, only his mother could call him Malkie. Do you understand?"Bass, Soprano, and Sammie's squeaky voice chorused in forceful unison.

"Malcolm only, never use that name again."

"Uh, uh yes. Sorry, dunno where that came from, sorry."

Cal swearing at God would have brought a gentler response. Memories flashed of a dreadfully unprepared schoolboy, standing in front of class, fearful the paper he was reading would be discovered for the plagiarism it was.

Sheepishly he returned to his task. His poise, fear-rattled. He took the lead, as in a clumsy school play. His role began as it had for all of the previous guests of the bar. That passed though the doorless front door. All players knew their roles, Master, the director of course. Mother the Sergeant at arms. Master coughed.

Malcolm Derrick McKeon, born in 1948 from the union of his immigrant Irish father Sean, and his American mother Margaret, mainly of Scottish and Sioux descent.

Unrehearsed, emotionless, the text book account had no style. Cal squinted, looked around the room curious if his audience still were watching.

Keeerrrapp, he thought. They chuckled.

Master coughed.

They lived modestly. Something people in upstate New York called it back then.

~

"Ah, ad- libbing, how refreshing..." Master whispered to Mother.

"Yes, we know," Farmer Vaughan's resonating bass blurted.

All laughed facing one another. Frustrated, Cal glared, Master coughed.

~

Farmer Vaughan and family owned the largest dairy farm in the area. It covered all of land of Snake Hill Road, Spirit Trail Road and beyond. Tragedy put it up for sale. Eventually Fowlers took title, and still own it. Farmer Vaughan used a big bass voice ordering his hands around. He stood six foot three, two hundred and eighty pounds. He may have been heavier at times depending on what he had to eat. A lot was his favorite meal. He never showed bad temper. Good thing, he could crush an opponent with a single swipe of his sledge hammer hands. He did once, but that was the war. The only hair left on his head wrapped around the sides. Puffy eyes that saw too much were puffier than they should have been, hiding something in his bloated face. Coveralls covered him, often shirtless underneath. His locks of gray chest hair poked out free.

~

Farmer Vaughan sat unmoved listening to Cal's recital. He wore his Sunday best. Clean coveralls and a blue tee shirt. Master coughed.

~

Malcolm's father, Sean, wasn't a farmer but a very fine mechanic. He was in charge of all the farm equipment that the Vaughan Dairy farm relied on, a huge responsibility.

Farmer Vaughan knowingly nodded at Cal. Cal saw Master was about to cough, started.

Sean, lean in his youth, morphed to portly, Father Time's usual swap. Hard work, harder drinking, over exposure to nature's elements, helped cast his ruddy complexion. He inherited his dad's protruding bulbous nose, road-mapped with fine broken spider web blood vessels.

Cal's grays toured the room. Confident he had them in the palms of two shaking hands Cal's writing skills broke out of fear prison. A sharpened tongue twisted to a fine, fine point. Emboldened, Cal spat words with machine-gun succession. Master coughed and sneezed.

Sean's bulldog, boxy head, still had the cover of straw blonde hair. Flecks of gray marked time, hands exercised by mechanics tools muscled to clamps. Shaking them flirted could be a mistake. Fingers were stained in tan, brown and blue hues. Reminders of the years he worked his trade, the cigarettes he smoked. Sean, the county's brilliant machinist, could make anything, from nothing.

"Okay, okay, but where is Maalcoolmmm?" An alto voice sang back.

Cal snapped in the direction. Cold gray eyes grabbed her blues.

"When I'm done you will know. Not a minute before, nor a minute after. Do you have a problem with that?"

Mother cackled a chuckle. The questioner, disciplined and dismissed, sulked in her chair publically spanked.

She was known as Reddy Red, and always ready for a fight. Red sported well coiffed store bought red hair. It mated nicely to her pasty, white freckled complexion, and green eyes. A buxom, Rubens built woman. Self painted in harlot makeup. She always carried a weapon, her signature sharp alto voice. Once there were only eight regulars in the bar, until one day. She showed up one day and joined Mary as the other regular woman. Reddy was not a life-long resident of Fate, but an import. Thought to hail from New York City, she never admitted to it. The others didn't know for sure but it seemed like she was running from someone, a husband maybe. She bought the old small farm house a few miles out of town. Unlike her counterpart the Matron, Reddy was tough talking, good with men but not guns. She lived there in contradiction to her mouth, quietly, in early retirement. The other regulars were all envious. Retirement in those parts didn't come with a watch, usually a headstone. Cal stood. He kept a deathly stare at the patrons, now converted to members of his class. Their roles irrevocably reversed.

"You can take the boy out of New York City but not the New York City out of the boy, at least not for long now can you?" Master couldn't leave it alone.

"I don't need your help, sir! I am quite able to handle this myself, thank you."

"Oh my, the boy's teeth are longer, stronger and sharper now, aren't they Mother?" Master played hide and seek safely from the shadows.

"Yes, he's already grown my dear, and in such a short time. Best you go on without being so smug young man. You have no idea of the waters that lay ahead. You just might need a friend or two."Mother broke in to the light out from the shadow. She walked at Cal wagging a finger, gently scolding him. She whistled. Cal started.

Margaret, Malcolm's mother, willowy, lean, and narrow girlish hips. She glided with warm informality and class. Long straight jet black hair framed chiseled, angular facial features detailed as if Audubon drew her himself. Knowing dark brown eyes contrasted against a misplaced stark white complexion. She stood a unique mixture of Sioux American Indian, and Scottish. As her years added, her weight never did. Margaret was a reluctant beneficiary of her Presbyterian mother school teacher. Improperly used or pronounced words were immediate interruptions. The tradition continued with Malcolm. Sean was another matter. Her father she hardly knew. He never came back from his government-sponsored trip to Europe.

Malcolm carried more of mom's physical being than dad's bulk. The both had pale complexions. Pencil thin facial features mimicked hers. He shot up in height, quickly for his age. The physical sameness of Malcolm and mother ended their similarities. Malcolm honored dad. Sandy blonde hair, two blue eyes his behind puffy slits and a personality craving fun.

"Who whoa, whoa, do weeeee neeeed allll of this?" Master raised his upper lip like a horse about to whinny.

"You bet, sit down."

Spanked, Master slipped in his chair. Mother howled. A gleeful class harmonized a chorus of laughs.

"Hey, hey, hey, hey, hey, where is this going?" Bar fly voices spoke up, winked in Masters direction.

Cal held up a stop hand. "Wait my friends, just you wait, but you may not like it."

"Marshall on Teach, Marshall on." Master coughed.

Sean and Malcolm, different in appearance yet so similar when dusk faltered and the stars lit evening's ceiling. Mutual mania took hold in the cool evening air. It fed childish minds. Minds that could, and would, reach back seeking governance for what only they could understand.

Brightly the class listened. Flashes of light blinked. A neon-sign hung over the bar, presumed broken lit to, Whines and Spirits.

"Ha, these rubes don't know how to spell."

"Ah, but they doooo, boy, they do. Best be careful. Watch your ground. What you speak will appear, light will come from the dark."

"Ground below, will appear, light from dark?" Cal frowned at the riddles. Mother whistled.

Sean and Margaret's union was hardly a match made in heaven. Strong drink, stronger words sparked furious fights. If it wasn't so scary to watch it might have been funny, Malcolm often said. Spirited passionate people, full of spirits will do that. Yet never a night did they sleep apart.

Sean loved an occasional evening card game. Tuesday occasionally. One card evening Margaret grub staked her beloved to a twenty with the usual warning of when to be home. Sean ventured off. The players told half truths, half lies and complete lies, about sex, money or sporting success.

Pop, Pop, Pop– Cal's head snapped. Masters words prophetic. Flashes of light lit, will appear, on the far wall. A spotlight beam bore down from the rafters, partially struck Cal. He winced, threw his arm up to protect sore eyes. The beam completed its mission splaying diffused light softly on a cleared area of the wooden lower floor, illuminating Sean and his buddies all at their card table. Cal's students looked at him, then to the scene. Cal's questioning look looked back at them, then the card players. The card players play, played. All eavesdropped.

Bob Richards boasted, "I remember, I banged the Hubbard girl. Tuesday morning, late May of 67, shot three pheasant that afternoon."

His buddy, Dean, said, "Was that before, or after, you and I got outa Mrs. Twiton's English class you bull shit artist."

"Well, maybe it was the afternoon?"Richards covered up.

Dean added, "And maybe you're as full of it as you always have been. Now play your cards. I have to get home before I don't have one. Like you Romeo. How's the ex, anyway?"

Five card players, ten wet eyes. Two others in the other room fixed sandwiches. Then all faded. Cal took the reins. The card player's images thickened then disappeared. Master coughed.

The evening wore on. Old jokes were told, older whisky swallowed. The games lasted hours. The members of the liars club either won a few dollars or lost a few. No matter either way, just usual and customary fun. Sean, drunk or not, always knew when to leave. After a long weaving way home, down moonlit dirt roads, he arrived, with a crash, through the front screen door. Momentum carried him to a marionettes collapse, at the bottom of the stairs that led to the bedrooms. He made it, with only a few minutes to spare. Sean was concerned with jeopardizing future permission. Margaret was relieved to see he returned, and in one piece. Her ex army boxer got into fights now and again.

After a slap-stick struggle Margaret managed to sit her card playing, somewhat drunk husband, on the front edge of their marital bed. The dry, aged frame creaked, but held firm. Margaret looked around. Sean's condition, not the example she wanted her precious to witness, but it was futile. Sean liked to spin around dancing to imaginary music.

"Come 'er Maggie" he'd grab her. She worried he'd lose his balance, crush whatever, wherever. Losses of any size, income or belongings, were difficult to recover from. Like the time he sent an antique lamp to the glue farm. Undressing Sean made sense. Love at work, fear of loss. Margaret took no more chances.

One dam fool is enough in here today, Margaret complained. Sean weaved. Well relaxed he slobbered. John Barleycorn, the elixir of conversation, he added as if a self assured trial attorney. The last intelligible thing he said that evening disappeared in to the night air. Sean fell backwards, flopped to a motionless crucifix. Margaret wrestled with the snoring lummox, removed his work overalls.

"Where's Malcolm," filled the bar from the doorless front door. Cal seethed but had his court. The room ceded power to him. No one, no one, would take it from him.

The tenor, an older man, stood in the doorway dressed in a shiny sharkskin suit. Professional manicure, receding styled grey framed his ears. An overly groomed a poster child for Wall Street.

"I knew him," accented slightly faux British.

I Imagine I met Malcolm many years ago, in New York City, by a statue."

The bar crowd, alto, bass, and soprano, Sammie and tenor Cal, all fired a unanimous shush. Sulking, the new guy walked over and joined the choir: Matron Mary, Sammie, Farmer Vaughn, Reddy Red, and newbie, nicknamed Mr. I Imagine. Each, would eventually solo. Master whistled.

Margaret, Cal paused, exhaling bull like through his flared nostrils, glaring at the new visitor. The visitor's eyes would not return the favor, shifting left to right. He started-

Routinely Margaret cleared Sean's pockets hoping to recover any of the seed money she gave him to do card battle with. Sean, a decided lefty, southpaw always stashed his day's fortune in his front left pocket. A habit his father taught him to reduce the possibility of being pick-pocketed. Not many pick-pockets in the Dairy farm country, but old habits die hard.

The years together taught Margaret where to start looking. Her fingers slithered past the grease crusted pocket. She felt something, deeper down. A sock she thought or some fabric of some sort. It bulged. She knew it wasn't his—Anyway she tugged it out of the pocket and it was a sock, but not his. Her heart pounded? Was he was having an affair. She laughingly dismissed that as soon as it entered her mind.

"Who would want him? Oh, a stuffed man's argyle sock. What a relief." She pried it open with a slim dry hand. Pulled out money, yea, he didn't lose.

"Oh my heavens," A sizeable wad, some slipped out her grasp, dropped like autumn leaves to the floor. The rest remained folded organized with the larger bills on the bottom, smaller bills on top. All faced the same way. Sean's for certain. Christmas would be good this year. Barely breathing she claimed the fallen bills. It was a lot, nine hundred dollars of a lot. Her heart wouldn't slow.

This was sizable money these days, in these parts. Sean broke the bank. It was a run in cards like no other ever, in that county. A run so good it almost seemed wicked. So embarrassing the losing participants never admitted to it, or spoke of it. Her eyes watered looking at him. Her wounded conquering knight saved the castle from the invaders. Quickly she found a temporary place to hide her good fortune.

"Anyone need a break?" Cal looked nose down, around. Not a peep peeped. Mother coughed.

Sean woke wracked with his favorite headache and cousins, dry mouth and foul breath. A fogged memory nudged him. Anxiously, he dug deep into his pockets faintly recalling a perhaps good fortune. John Barleycorn numbed most things, his memory included. Panicked, he clawed through the depths of his coveralls pockets again, and again. Sean stood sad but furious with himself. He just knew he'd lost his opportunity to squander a windfall spoiling the love of his life. In the past, meager winnings were frittered away on Malcolm. This time, Margaret got the edge, a large one.

Cal stopped, interrupted by a flash of light illuminating the floor for two ticks. He palm swept his hand over his wet face, went on. Master coughed.

~

"Maaaggrett, did you happin to see any thin of unuuuusual portion in me pants there love?'

"Sean, there hasn't been anything of unusual portion in your pants since I've known you darling."

Sean reddened redder than a pile of summer beets at a farmers market. He pursed his lips disgusted he somehow dreamt his good fortune or worse yet, lost it on the way home. He would not bring it up again, swore off drinking for the fifth time that month. It was only the 20th. Ample time left for 10 more vows.

Margaret had a plan for the money. First, she had to make a deposit of it into the 1st Bank for Savings of the Good Earth behind the barn. After Sean dressed and left for work, Margaret armed herself with deposit slips, pick and shovel. Leaving nothing to chance, she looked around corners before walking around the back of the barn. At the X on the ground, only she knew of, she dug. Her personal safe deposit box, an old tin can, nestled about a foot deep in the dry earth's crust. There she hid the money with her other savings. The deposits added up. Sean's windfall gave her enough money to get what she wanted, something special but not for her.

~

"Thirty seconds everyone." Cal sat muttering. "How do I know this? The sixties have to have healed by now?" He batted crooked eyes.

Tight smiled he slouched in the chair, arms outstretched, legs smugly crossed. Thirty ticks ticked. The flock huddled, whispered. Guiltily they looked back and forth at Cal as busy bodies do at church socials. He rose, strutted, almost a peacock way. The King bellowed to his court.

"Break's over."

“Ah look at him ma darling.” Master and Mother emerged from their shadows stealth.

Cal nodded to them. With an elevated chin he glanced at the chorus, nodded. A stomach twinge reminded him this was serious. Turned up, pursed lips hid worry; he coughed, smiled at a surprised Master, who shook his head no.

~

The McKeon home was a four bedroom farm house too big for this modest sized family. Margaret’s inheritance was home never the less. The leaking roof Sean promised to get to, last year. Clanging pipes would wait also.

“I’ll get to it in the early Sat morning darlin,” he’d say. Of course he had to be up Saturday morning to fulfill that hollow promise.

Margaret’s new found wealth might have been spent wisely on the house. She had other plans. Her love loved machinery, particularly motorcycles. He owned a few, more than a few.

Buy em cheap Margaret, I always buys em cheap ya know lass. From someone who dun’t maintains them ya know, he tried to oversell her knowing smile. The ones he loved needed care. English made. BSA’S and Triumphs.

~

“Where’s Malcolm?” Tenor Mr. I sang out.

“Sit down.” the chorus overwhelmed him.

The guitar playing from the last record Master plucked hit a long sultry whining note.

“You’ll all get your turns to talk. But only if I say so, and you wish to.” Cal harnessed the unruly class.

“Oh my,” chuckled from the shadows.

“We’ve created a monster it would appear, Mother.”

“Shut up you old pompous, pedantic, and pontificating prick.” Cal-counter-punched.

Masters mouth hung, eyes widened. A howl of his haunting laughter echoed in harmony with Mothers.

"Oh my, oh my how unappreciative. Was that a twenty dollar phrase my dear?"

"Ten would be quite right, I do believe no more than ten." Mother always knew, pointed to Cal, whistled.

~

Sean, a heavy smoker, developed a raspy relentless cough. A cough Margaret knew would not go away. Margaret's uncle's died from a similar cough, as did Sean's father. They both felt a heavy weight in both of their aging hearts. Unspoken, but not unfelt. Inevitable, Malcolm's father followed in his own father's footsteps, but not before a new member to the McKeon household arrived in 1961. That year Vincent arrived.

It wasn't a younger brother or cousin for thirteen year old Malcolm. It was a motorcycle. Not just any motorcycle. An English motorcycle that muscled extraordinary power, and speed. One, Sean the brilliant mechanic only dreamt of riding, at its astonishing hundred-and thirty mile per hour plus speed. To ride one was a dream, come true. To own one, bliss. Time was short. Margaret contacted her brother- in-law, Michael, in Ireland. She asked him to act as agent for her purchase and shipment to the States of the motorbike. That's what she's would call it, a motorbike, with a monstrous 998 cc engine.

"I'll have nuthin to do with them English limey bastards" Michael argued into the black phone.

Long distance calls from the states were expensive. Margaret quickly explained the situation. The days of Sean McKeon were numbered. A groan slipped from Michael's lips followed by a deafening silence, followed by his cough. Margaret heard the rap of the dangling telephone receiver hitting against the pub wall. Tears leaked out of the corners of his experienced eyes. The ten tick pause felt like an hour. Michael took another drag, picked up the receiver. His voice emotionally cracked pledging and all assistance. The 1950 Vincent Black Shadow was timely shipped to the states.

~

"Time's up, time's up." Master slipped from his shadowy home. He strolled, imitating a surly pompous Elizabethan Stage actor. Snickering, he reminded all that looked at him who really was in charge. Master turned, panned all their faces and—

"Parting is such sweet sorrow dear people. Come back later. Cal's tired. He'll pick up where he left off. I assure you." Master snapped two favorite, long boney stick fingers. A dry branch cracking turned all, except Cal, to smoky mists. The mists streamed through bullet holes in the bars walls. Cal flew backwards, landed in his chair with arms outstretched and eyes shut. Master hovered.

"Cal, are you there boy, Cal?"

Dreamy eyes limped open. Everything was as it was when he first got there—a mess.

"Wha–what now?"

"Quite enough for one day I think friend, quite enough, correct, Mother?"

Mother stood below them on the main level. Her back was ten feet from the doorless front door. Night traded places with dawn. Early morning's light lit a new hard farm day, and backlit Mother's silhouette.

"Yes yes, quite enough. Very good days work indeed. You've met your friends. Well most all are, but one. Be watchful of the Judas. And oh my, you know how to run classes now don't you? Master likes your style. Count on many more classes. Light comes from the dark. Speak, listen, observe. Answers will come. You will get your story. You're on your way, it's just the beginning. Now it's time you're on your way, to rest. Time here is not what you are accustomed to. It comes and goes more quickly. Tomorrow will be here soon." She spun around, faced the doorless front door and marched toward it. Her left, black clog mashed the doors saddle with a thud. Cal winced. She twisted backward toward Cal. Caught his sneaking eye, smiled and disappeared.

The Wurlitzer's speaker moaned final blues guitars cords. The last note lingered until swallowed by morning's heavy mist seeping inside. The Wurlitzer shut off, returned to the condition the first time Cal saw it. Over stressed eyes pinched looking for escape.

"No, not there," Master caught Cal.

"Man, this not going to be easy."

"No, it isn't. You've made a good start, friend. From now on you will experience a veritable multitude of multiplicities. Multiplicities, multiply difficult."

Cal hung his head reminded his thoughts were not his own. Master pointed his overused boney finger toward a dark corner of the bar. Dim light hazily exposed an old, Victorian style, heavily stained, crushed red velvet couch trimmed in dark wood. It wasn't there before. Thankfully, freshly laundered white sheets, and a robin's egg blue summers blanket, were neatly folded in squares resting on the middle seat cushion.

"There, you sleep there. Now blink twice." Master coughed.

Cal blinked once, the room spun. He blinked the instructed second time. Under the blue blanket he gagged, cringed, gulped, calmed, and said "Mine enemies in life, brothers in death."

Then fell fast asleep. The town clock read Wednesday 2:00 a.m., Cal's watch ticked backward, Tuesday 10 p.m., August 29, 2009. Brother thunder led.

Master whispered, "Sleep well my Prince, three Mothers sons–"

# Fourteen

He never wore a watch–that worked. The one on his wrist spun flawlessly as he snored lying on the red velvet stained couch, counter-clockwise. Tuesday, 9:30 p.m., August 29, 2009. The town's clock argued, 12:55 p.m., Wednesday, August 30th, 2009.

"Ahhaawwahhww" Hippo mouthed Cal, stretched his jaw. The beginning of his second day foggily started.

"What the he–," Like wakin up in jail and not knowin how or why ya got there, worse yet, afraid to. Okay feet, do your stuff." hissed through clamped teeth.

Cal sprung to his feet, stood on a leg, fell to a knee. Stood again, this time urgently he shoved his legs in his pants. His nose pressed to his sleeve.

"Hey, this shirt looks clean. What's going on here?"

"Hmmmm" Stained fingers rubbed his forested chin. He couldn't remember taking his clothes off. Not uncommon, but he had no excuse now, he hadn't had a drink. Anxious feet, clad in the wings shuffled. The confidently sprang light footedly looking around. Well lit from the days summers sun Cal saw no one around. No Master, Mother, no Bar Flies. The bar was torn up.

"Hmmm, half full glasses of writer's ink, right where the Bar Fly's left them." Writer's ink, writer's ink, what Cal's literature professor called it.

"Someone left in a hurry. Someone smart." Chuckling, he twisted his head back toward his couch bed. The sheet and blanket were folded.

"Oh boy, how the heck, some service." Cal looked around waiting for an answer. Hoping he wouldn't get one.

"Yes quite, boy, the best of service."

"Thanks, now I remember, Mr. Master or whoever—"

"-whomever, friend, I believe it is. No matter, go see Mother. Get something to eat. You need to drive around a bit. She'll tell you."

Eat? Now that sounded good. Cal hustled heel toe, heel toe to the doorless front door and leapt over the doors saddle. Heel toed across the concrete porch, missed the stairs to the dirt lawn. Dusting off his knees Cal looked around, straightened up. Kicking up the dust the wings made it in three ticks to the walk. Panted, Cal snapped a left, flew past the ally, and chimp climbed the stairs to the wooden walkway. He looked inside, there she was. Both feet hopped the bakery's door saddle. He raced to the counter. Skidding to a halt in front of the register Cal's mock twelve year old self beamed with surly confidence.

"Why, Good Morning Mother."

"Good morning yourself, good afternoon you mean?"Mother stood covered in pixie dust flour, correcting Cal.

"Coffee?"

"That'd be great, thank you Mother."

"We don't have any!"

"Whaaa–?" Cal's head tilted sideways.

"We have something better, a tea, of sorts."

Cal looked to the ceiling, pursed his lips and twisted his chin towards his right shoulder.

"I should have known, should ha–."

"–Yes, yes, you should have known." Her thunderous laughter soothed him.

Cal grabbed the paper cup of hot something Mother handed him. Then some fresh baked rolls, stuffed with something he was afraid to ask about.

"The cloth wrapping the rolls has your instructions for today. Do not lose it."

Cal spun, scooted, and slid to a halt in front of the door. Double toe, he jumped over the saddle. His faithful chariot, the Comet, waited.

He parked on the side of the road neatly in his old tire tracks. Atop Snake Hill Road he sat in his trusty traveling companion. Serene, gazing at the valley below, it hadn't rained in awhile. Tire tracks from the heavy lumbering farm equipment-tractors-harvesters–and produce haulers, trucks, grooved the dirt road when wet. Dry weather froze their crusty claw impressions in the road bed. Dry roads meant dry fields. Rain was needed, and soon.

A summer rainstorm could strike furiously. When it did, torrents of water rushed down the roadbeds washing away most of the tire impressions. Rain grew everything here very quickly, even the rocks seemingly when the flash floods exposed the rounded tops of sunken boulders, their little elf bald heads rising up from the ground. Hit a big enough bump you lost traction, and in the ditch you went, if you were lucky. Sometimes a well intentioned driver didn't hit them. Yet an overreaction, a swerve left or right, same result. Tractors and harvesters suffered. Trucks hauling produce, worse. But, the occasional automobile, or, less frequent motorcycle, the absolute worst.

Maintaining the road was a chore, expensive also. So ordinarily it wasn't. Live with it, the prevailing attitude. Once in awhile a road crew, decked in blaze orange, inexpensively patched it. A gift provided from the state. Crops had to get to market. Snake Hill Road couldn't stop that, but slow commerce, it could. Demon of a road it was. Cal sat absorbed in the days light, and country history woven in its rays.

Local folklore believed this fiend road had a guardian watching from the ditches. No one knew who the attendant was for sure. No one ever saw, for certain. Had they, they would not say. Something of a child's imagination, argued by those who never saw it, Malcolm would.

Cal's awareness grew on his second trip. Time flew. It turned late early. No time for a motherly consult today. His watch was of no assistance in this country. The cars clock synced with the towns clock. Time to get back they advised. 7:00 p.m. August 30, 2009.

Cal skidded to his seat, slapped his hand along the wall, found the first available bullet hole and the noose tightened. His eyes rolled back. A taunting slight smile curled up his hollow cheeks.

"Cocky little bastard," peeved Master. Then looked up with his arms outstretched, palms open, waiting. Fidgeting, he impatiently looked over at Cal. Cal's smile left, but not the one on Master. Someone dialed up the juice.

"Aghaghaghhaaaaghhh." Cal slammed against the wall in near death electrocution.

Another nickel paid for shot down the chute. Proper payment for the record plucked from its nest. The needle missed its mark. Skidding across the vinyl 45, scratching Nat King Cole's "Those Lazy Crazy Hazy Days of Summer," a screeeeech wailed out of the big speaker.

Master lethally glared at the Wurlitzer. Lights flickered apologetically, and recued the needle arm. Nat's voice filled the air.

"Thank you, I haven't thought about that song in years," Cal said "Takes me back."

"Marks time boy, marks time. Connects the dots, some would say." Master smiled.

Cal looked around. The Bar Fly's were back and ready. Master snickered. Mother's elbow found Master's rib. Then light came from dark. Soft hazy light lit the first floor wooden dance area as last time. Sean, Margaret, Malcolm and a big wooden crate were wrapped in the light.

Mother whistled.

Margaret made certain Christmas came early for Sean. He hugged and kissed her more than their wedding night. His crowbar wedged and pried Michael's Irish crating. Wood splintered, flew everywhere as if hit by a truck. Sean finished in a flash. There it was, mostly assembled, the Vincent Black Shadow. Sean's Vincent Black Shadow.

Sean's nicotine stained teeth schoolboy beamed at Margaret. He couldn't prove it, but knew. Wasting no time he bolted on the handle bars removed for shipping, and few other items. A column of sweat darkened the middle of the back of his blue work shirt. No matter, excited Sean poured gas into the black gas tank. Forehead sweat fell on the paint. Sean wiped it as fast as it fell while looking down at his black motorcycle boots heal, on the chrome kick start lever. He stood with his leg balancing on the kick start. In one swift surging move, all of his might pressed it toward earth. Not so much as a slight engine rumble alerted the world the Vincent was alive. Again, he tried. His leg kicked down, no dice. Once more, over and over, again and again futilely he tried kick start the Vincent to life.

Temperamental, Sean said excusing failure. The hand assembled all black monster proved difficult. Margaret laughed noting their similarities. All things mechanical can have their way, and he needed to learn the Vincent's.

Not supposed to be like this. Sean's said, block head shook, ash flew. The truth he never could admit, he wasn't all that familiar with this little bit of manmade thunder and lightning,

God dammit, must be something wrong with it. Frustration peaked.

I'm going inside. You'll figure your cherished toy out. Margaret spun toward the house. Her laughing words floated with wind down the wide dirt path that connected the barn to the kitchen. Black sensible shoes kicked up the dust of the long dry, grow nothing patch of dirt she named, Shepherd's Walk. A gust of wind trailed her dress behind her. The closing kitchen screen door just missed.

I'll fix you, I will fer sure. Sean wrestled the Vincent into a stall in the barn. No stall had ever held a horse like this.

Malcolm followed Sean. Sean propped the bike up on its stand. Malcolm eyeballed the Vincent standing poised, proud, and powerful. The fine race horse beckoned anyone next to it, take me for a ride. Malcolm was close, but too young. The virile machine was detailed in sparse, but crisp gleaming chrome. It accentuated the almost, all black bike. Malcolm's daze was tethered to chrome bouncing light off the single pod speedometer, prominently fixed in front of the handle bars. The King of Motorcycles, an understated magnificent sight, from any angle, had him.

Malcolm—what are you doing in there? Margaret always seemed to know where he was. The wind floated he gentle voice from her kitchen. It flew across the barren path of lifeless poisoned earth of Shepherd's Walk, to the barn. The path couldn't grow a thing, Sean saw to it. Dumping engine oil, and other machinery fluids on it, will do that.

Keeps the weeds down, yup—less to care for. Sean argued.

Malcolm, well tuned to Margaret, as most boys are to their mothers, heard her as if she were right next to him.

Stay away from that machine, Malkie. You know what your daddy said. She's too much, for most, especially a young boy. Margaret used Malkie addressing Malcolm on certain casual times. But if she said Malcolm, then that could mean trouble.

His wide eyes, in a wondrous stare, never left the image while slowly back stepping out of the horse stall where Sean penned his prized ponies.

Malcolm git back in da stall. You need a beatin. Sean ordered.

No, No dad-I didn't touch it. Malcolm begged.

You'll learn yer lesson. I warned ya, don't go lookin fer trouble-it'll find ya fer sure.

Outside the wind slammed the barn door to an uneven clunked close. A whips crack ripped the air.

AHHHAAA... Owwww..! Malcolm screamed, at thud was heard.

Margaret toe sprinted from the kitchen, screaming waving her hands.

Don't you touch that boy Sean—don't you dare or I'll be touching you, and NOT the way that's kind –Not in any way kind.

Cries and moans came from Malcolm's lungs. They lashed out, again, and again. Panting, Margaret rushed in. Malcolm lay face up, on some hay in one of the many unused stalls. She stopped in her tracks, her hands to her chest, one on top of the other and screamed.

Sean McKeon what have you done –what in the world have you done?

Ohhhwww, Malcolm moaned.

Sean turned away from her, his head hung. Margaret threw herself to Malcolm, held his head, cupped his face, and scanned his body assessing the damage.

Good—no blood—no bruises. She pondered the situation again looking him up then back down again.

Where does it hurt son—tell mommy where?

Whaaaaa ahhh Haaaa hah ha….. Ahhh hah hahhhaaaa. Malcolm couldn't contain himself.

Sean shrieked. His cough corked it.

Margaret sat confused, for a second, and then got it. Malcolm held his sides, wet his pants a little. The great put, on a great success. Mother Margaret its victim.

Sean loved teasing her. His way to saying he loved her. Margaret sat on her rear, pursed lips, squinting daring brown eyes and frown wrinkled forehead calculated retribution.

As most old barns are, they always seem to have old things in it. An upright splintering support post, holding up the loft, had a nail placed squarely in the center of it. On it hung an old rusty toothed sickle. Malcolm, sensing trouble, smartly fled.

Margaret stood, dusted her dress off of the hay. Casually she slipped to her left shaking her head, feigning a humorous smile and chuckle. Sean looked at her and held out his arms offering a tender lovin I'm sorry embrace. Before she reached him she broke to the sickle, grabbed it by its wooden handle. With the blade held up high she pointed it, toward Sean. He froze. Who wouldn't?

Sean unfroze, stuttered a clumsy mispronounced apology. Backing up he held pleading hands out stretched. "Darlin, think about what you are doing." He kept back-peddling, turned, and fled like a race horse breaking from its gate. Margaret gave chase. Not far, but far enough to see the old man run as he hadn't in years. Laughing, she lowered the sickle blade to the hay on the barn floor. From a distance Malcolm sheepishly looked at her and they laughed in unison.

Sean finally stopped running. He wheezed and hid behind the barn, began to cough, spat out some blood. He never told Margaret of the incident. She knew anyway."

The song ran out, another nickel met its coin chute fate. The lighted dance floor went dark for a moment, "Father and Son," by Cat Stevens played.

"Don't say it any of you, I know it's out of time sequence, recorded after many others. But anything can happen here, anything, and for good reasons." Master finished.

The class of Bar Flies hung on every word, raising and lowering their heads in agreement with Master. Cal stared at the scene, "Bobble Heads," he said.

"Quite, now carry on Master said. The light will come from the dark." He coughed.

That evening, instead of going to the usual card game Sean stayed at home. He would be missed for sure. Secretly his card cronies plotted their revenge. But Sean had some reading to do. After an evening's review of the Vincent's manual, he became well enough acquainted with the beast to get him in trouble. And trouble it was.

Early morning came quickly. Sean excited as never before, headed to the barn. The gleaming menacing Vincent stood motionless in its stall. Sean moved behind it, imagined himself wrapped around its fury. The road disappearing under its wheels at a sizzling clip, road divider lines, where there were some, disappearing as well. Today would be the day. The day the devil and hell reunited. Heaven help the county.

Sean returned to enjoy his morning coffee with Margaret. They sat at the kitchen table next to one another. Malcolm charged into the kitchen, wide-eyed.

"Dad will she fire up–will she?–Let's go get her going–lets go NOW! Pleeasssssszzzee..."

Sean smiled his famous twinkling eyes. Nodding yes he held up his right hand indicating to wait a few minutes. His catcher's mitt left hand rested on Margaret's. Stroking it he looked at her. Margaret stopped him and intertwined her delicate slender long fingers with his two toned stubby ones. Sean wondered, but never asked Margaret, how she got the money to purchase the Vincent. He knew, and she knew he knew. She smiled, then turned her chiseled face away from his not wanting to give up the secret so easily, a secret which gave her the greatest of pleasure.

Thump, thump, thump. Rrrrrrrrr rararara then thump, thump, thump, thump. Again—thump, thump buuurummmmm. Thump thump thump-sssssssss. This time we've got her Malcolm, this time we've got her for sure.

"Malcolm she's a fine, fine, beast- can ya hear me lad—can ya?"

"Yeah, yeah dad, barely though it's loud, but neat."

"Yes she is boy—yes she is and she gunna get louder in a sec son –in a sec."

They both saddled up. Sean wrapped his hands to the grips. Malcolm climbed on behind him, feet resting on the foot pegs, arms around Dad's waist.

Malcolm remembered the jolt backward, when they first took off, his entire life. He was hooked, on motorcycles. Sean's DNA flowed within him. Holding on for dear life his young fingers dug into his dad's belly, his thumbs hooked under his Sean's thick black belt. Wiry 5'6", boney, and legged body clamped to the seat. Fear, glee and holy hell raced through Malcolm's mind and Sean's soul. Malcolm's eyes watered from the wind whipping his loose straw hair into them.

Sean's right hand twisted the throttle. The Vincent swallowed its breakfast, burnt remnants spat out the tail pipes making beautiful motorcycle organ pipes music.

"Dad, ahahahah," Malcolm screamed. His face morphed into jack-o-lanterns. Sean chuckled.

"Hang on. Tell yer mom and we're both sunk."

"Don't worry dad, don't worry. Let her rip."

Rip they did. The tread of the tires shook hands with the road. They tore on.

"Hang on lad, hang on. We're gonna race the bastard devil himself, hang on."

The Vincent wasn't Herculean, but Babe Ruthian.

Malcolm rode perfectly on the back of the soulful machine leaning, as instructed before, in the same direction his dad did. Sean slung the fine thoroughbred bike through its paces. They flew down the one road out of town. Sean alternated banking the bike left and right through the roads curves. Often leaning it over so far, scraping the pegs on the ground. The sound warned him and he straightened it back up, snapped the throttle. Malcolm day dreamed of riding it alone. An unexpected bump snapped him out of it inspiring a fearful scream of rollercoaster laughter.

Let it rip, Sean remembered Malcolm's words. He opened the throttle. The Speedo would, couldn't lie. The Vincent shot through sixty, seventy, at eighty she just cruised. Most bikes of the day would be huffing. Faster and faster they went. The engine droned on taking them right through eighty-five to ninety. They pulled the wind behind them bowing the wheat grass in their wake. A tempest, they were.

At one hundred, the Vincent hardly broke a sweat. Sean's distorted face howled.

"Malcolm, Malcolm she'll be yours someday, if I dun't kill us first."

Storm clouds chased them. Sean cut his way through the dying light. The Vincent ran so strongly that if it could talk it would have said…Is that all you have?

Unexplained high whining guitar notes combed through the woods. It filled Sean and Malcolm's heads, pumped their souls. They hit a bump, wobbled, sense snapped into Sean's mind.

What if I wreck? A bad notion, too much fear could be dangerous, too little, a certainty.

Slowly Sean's right hand relaxed allowing the twisted throttle to reverse. They slowed, very slowly—no jerky motions here.

"Smooth," Sean instructed Malcolm.

"Always, always smooth. Keep control."

"This magnificent Black speedster is fit for one of gods best Angel's." Sean said laughingly.

"Who Dad, Who..?"

When they left the stall the bike's jet black tank had only factory emblems and identification on it. Sean looked down. Somewhere through the run, he thought likely by the guitar note forest, "Winters Eve" scripted itself in silver grey by a feather's brush, on both sides of the tank.

"This is my winter's eve Malcolm, my Winters Eve. It'll be yers someday son-yers."

"Whaaaa…?"

"You'll see boy-you will see, best gittin home now, mommas waitin.

The Vincent throttled down to a steady 30. They turned up the hilly dirt drive back to the farm. Everything in that area hung onto, or around, a hill, except for the stretch locals called Spirit Trail Road. It began as a soft left curve from the bottom of Snake Hill Road, where the weeping willows ringed Vaughn's pond. From there, it rolled out flat for miles till it disappearing behind Heavens Hill.

That year was nineteen sixty-one, nearly sixty-two. As the storm that chased them home abated, another storm in Southeast Asia began to brew.

"Go to black," Master instructed. "You, Bobble Heads. Turn to smoke, be off through your holes. Go giggle behind the walls. Cal, to bed, there on your red velvet couch, tomorrow will be here soon with a new day.......and night."

The Town clock struck, Thursday, 3:00 a.m. August 31, 2009. Cal's' watch ticked backward, 8:00 p.m. Tuesday August 29, 2009.

Two would meet in a storm, and one was brewing—-

# Fifteen

"Seriously, this is serious. I sweat more than I drink, I see and hear things I can't possibly see or hear, and know things I have no way of knowing." Cal's trip to the seductive, tranquil hilltop of Snake Hill Road bared its teeth. Cal and Old Blue slid, wobbled and bounced back to the safety of home, Destiny, early.

Before Comets tire dust could settle, Cal sprinted over the dirt lawn. He leapt over the doorless front doors saddle.

"Uhhhhuah, uh-ahhhhhaa" he huffed, wheezed. Successfully two wing tip soles slid to his chair. Shiny pants pressed it the wood seat. Tobacco stained fingers stroked the side of his salt and pepper sideways tilted face. Smug as ever he waited. Fingers drumming the chairs arm rest. Master, black boot strolled in, purposefully and unapologetically, late.

"Routine forty seven,"

"Whaaa- on earth do you mean, boy?"

"Usual procedure for this situation, that is." Cal answered.

Master smiled, bent his head with a pondering nod. He sensed a change, a new, improved, emerging energized Cal.

Wonder if he thinks I'm losing my authority, control, Master thought. His head cocked, he finger flipped his locks. Perhaps his disinterest in today's charge is–. Noooo, he's not there yet. We'll just see about that, Master resolved.

ZZZZZZZZZAPPP,

After the charge Cal nonchalantly exhaled, flapping his rubber lips. He flipped a nickel to Master. The buffalo rolled on its edge down the chute, racing to its friends sleeping in the Wurlitzer's coin cup hostile. Well fed the juke brilliantly lit.New York City's famed theatre district would have noticed. Master's choice plucked. Notes flew forward from behind the big chrome grate. A drum pounding, horn blowing, furious dance beat took the air. It rocked the house. The bobble heads tapped, then stomped their feet, smiling and nodding knowing assurances to each other. Mother stepped from the shadow, coughed, and finger pointed to Cal to carry on.

Cal rose. Just as he was about to speak, "Where's Maaaaaaalcolm," harmonized. All, soprano, alto, tenor, bass and Sammie joined in clumsy mutiny.

"I don't know where the hell he is, or who he is." Cal smacked the bar. "But I hope to hell he shows up soon. I have some dam questions of my own."

"I know, I'm keeping track of Brother's and Sister's score." Mother said.

Master barred old teeth.

"I have to write this story, get it done soon or I'm screwed." Cal reminded himself.

The bobbles sat down after Teachers spanking. Master smiled at Cal. Cal sat down, sighed, relaxed his chest, and proceeded. His eyes glazed just a little this time. Hazy light lit the floor. It burned brighter as time went on. Cal spoke from his seat.

The last day of school began for Malcolm's eight grade class. His tolerant teacher stood at her desk dutiful to do as she was trained, educating the local youths. No easy task.

Warm air from the early afternoon, June day, bulged through the classroom windows. The early breath of summer's sleepy air, Margaret called it. Malcolm sat in the back row, lost once again in his best subject, a friendly daydream. He always earned straight A's in a subject that competed with his teacher's words. Adventure beckoned his soul. It lay out there somewhere, outside the schools bricks and mortar, and oversized windows. He needn't look too far. Nature had it adventure find him.

Where was that dismissal bell, he wondered, ending this school year? Malcolm's gaze broke from the great outdoors and presented a smiling face toward the teacher. Blackboard behind her, his teacher counted the minutes in a final appeal about poetry. He fidgeted, spun this time toward another escape, the classrooms door. Solid dark wood on the bottom, nine, three by three, small wood divided panes of glass on top. Malcolm lapsed again starring through the doors glass panes. He knew the schedule, one of the principals couriers would disrupt teacher delivering a notice from the principal. A cherished job reserved for students, unlike Malcolm. Good report card students. His next door farm neighbor, Stephanie Vaughn, was. Her family owned the farm where Malcolm's dad worked as a mechanic. Next door often meant many acres, if not miles away. Year after year, Malcolm looked forward Stephanie's visits. They broke the monotony, a teacher's monotony, particularly on topics he couldn't care less about. Like literature.

Today, as usual, Malcolm saw his favorite courier's smiling face approaching the classroom, through the door's glass panes. She had her rounds to make. Malcolm had his dreams to dream. He never paid much more than friendly attention to her. She was a gangly girl. Played with and became as much of one of the boys as the boys were.

"They was almost kin," her father Farmer Vaughn often joked.

"If I'd known you'd been this much of a boy, I'd named ya Tom." He teased.

That's the way all the boys had seen her."

Farmer Vaughn smiled. His puffy eyes leaked. Mary glared at Cal, took Farmer Vaughn's arm. Master whistled.

Malcolm ticked off time of another usual day. Then it happened, change. It came quickly in here and at the most unexpected of times.

Today change struck Malcolm while he innocently sat in his usual dreamy gaze. The usual fleeting, mischievous eye contact routinely exchanged by Malcolm and Stephanie changed. Malcolm felt as though he crash-landed from outer space. Mother Nature gave no fair warning. Puberty sprung', all's fair in love and war.

The usual image of a five-foot-nothing, freckled, blue eyed, black haired girl seized his heart. It was spring of 1963. Malcolm would never ever look at Stephanie Vaughn the same way again. Tom was gone.

"Malcolm, Malcolm," the teacher said. "So what do you think the author meant by that?" She asked as if Malcolm hung on every word of hers. His classroom performance at its best could be qualified as, disinterested. Today, however, he landed on Mars.

"Uh, uh, well….."

"I'll reread the passage, and you tell me what you think he meant.

"Ok, what do you think Malcolm?"

"Well, uh, hmmm." The teacher shouldn't have bothered.

Since the Stephanie sighting he hadn't a clue about question, nor himself. This was new territory, serious new territory. An infallible ability for fake impromptu participations vanished. He was stuck.

"Malcolm what do you think the author meant by that?" His teacher persisted.

Malcolm squirmed and then blurted…

"I guess, well, what he said. I guess that's what he meant. Otherwise, why write it?"

His trademark grin beamed as he spun his head left to right, seeking approval from his classmates. He pulled a rabbit out of his pants, somehow, but he did. The classroom screamed. Summer time laughter ricocheted. The teachers head sank. No one could get mad at Malcolm."

"Swiinng loooowww sweeeet chaaariootttt…." Cal's head snapped and glared into the dark space. Master howled. Cal pointed his finger, and then wagged it in the direction the interruption came from.

“Let me, finish.”Cal protested.

“Tsk, Tsk, and move on with it b–” Master.

“–I’m trying to you i…”

“Owwww, okay, okay, I’ll stop!!” Master yelped. Mother wasn’t amused.

“You two boys stop, stop this instant!”

The Bobble Heads were choking they laughed so hard. If laughter were money they would had five million at their feet.

“Go on Cal!” Mother coughed.

“Malcolm, don’t you see the symbolism? His teacher asked. He’s trying to tell us something using symbolism.”

“You mean like a sign, or sumptin? No, I don’t understand. Why don’t he just say it?”

“Doesn’t,” she sighed. His schoolmates suppressed their howls, to a dull roar.

Malcolm’s answers were serious, as were the teacher’s. The bell rang saving everyone, especially the teacher.

“Have a good summer. Class dismissed,” she shouted, sat, and took a deep breath. She looked out the window at the sky, smiled. Malcolm taught her some things.

The kids stampeded from the classrooms screaming carnival screams. Recklessly elbows and legs nudged and tangled fighting toward the door in cramped hallways. Finally they funneled through the schools wooden, double outside doors, into the warm outside. Laughing, pushing, and jabbing they mocked and finger wagged at each other. Books were punched out of best friend’s hands. Girl’s ponytails used as horse reigns, then quickly released, by boys and girls alike. It was the happiest of mob scenes.

Earlier that morning Malcolm, and those who his mother called his band of dark angels, leapt off their bicycles before coming to a stop. Their bikes gyroscopically rolled, but missed their mark, crashed off the slotted bike rack, bounced to the ground, and slid to a stop. Pedals clawing the ground served as anchors. Dust was everywhere.

Malcolm, and his friends, pigeon-toe raced across the black playground to retrieve their abandoned bikes.

"They were all good lads. Typical young boys, erect more than safe." Sean said.

"Let's go," Malcolm shouted, climbing onto his bike's seat.

"Let's go to Snake hill, the great race is on. Race with the devil is on."

Master fed the juke a new nickel. It triggered the release of the theme from Peter Gun.

Dun, Dun, Dun, dun, Dun, Dun, Dun, Din, dun, dun, Dun, din, dun, din, Dun, Din rang out. The powerful rhythmic resonating horn section stirred Cal, Mother whistled.

Malcolm arrived first, at the top of Snake Hill Road, his plan ready. His boyish, falsely innocent face lit up looking downward at the valley. His heart quickly beat. Dry-mouthed, he imagined flying down the steep hill on his bicycle, twisting through each curve of the serpentine dirt road that partitioned the farmland in sections. This was never an easy or safe race. Today's was worse, much worse. Last evening's much-needed, torrential rain bore into the road. Fine snaking crevices cut into its crust, a heavenly compliment to the road's name. Impressions stamped by the dinosaur rubber cleats of the farm's tractors tires complicated matters even worse. Truly, it was a dangerous mess, perfectly suited for Malcolm's vision for the afternoon's event.

Stephanie's family owned the two abutting farm fields.

"We know, we know, we know." Annoyed Bobbles sarcastically spoke up.

Cal glared—Master whistled.

~

The roads path cut the hill in two parcels becoming one side of each parcels borders. Dairy farmers needed grazing grass. Malcolm looked down the rolling hill parcel to his left. Standing tall grass covered it for as far as the eye could see. He stopped smiling when his eyes focused on a small pond, at the bottom of the road, hiding within the protective weeping willows. Large weeping willows, drooping with heavy thin vein like vine branches. Some touched the ground. That marked the finish line.

That was the larger field, the left filed. Malcolm twisted his head to the right. Partially forested the narrow parcel measured only about fifteen acres from top to bottom. Gradually sloping downward, it eventually declined in a steeper drop finally rolling flat near its bottom. Makeshift drainage ditches used mainly as hiding places for creatures wishing not to be seen, shouldered the road. Both sides were fenced with the barbed wire, tacked to wooden splintering posts. Wire, Sammie found out about last year.

~

"Hey, didn't we hear this already? What's he up to?" The Bobbles muttered looking at each other. Master started to clear his throat, Cal noticed.

~

The bottom of Snake Hill Road pot-bellied then curved left. If a rider were to go straight at the bottom, he would run right into the tree shielded, Vaughn farm road. After the turn, the road turn–

~

"Haaay we hoid all this" raspy alto voice Reddy Red.

"Well, listen to it again, it's important, make sure you see it. Be sure you do." Cal scolded. Mother faked a whistle.

After the turn the roads name became Spirit Trail Road. Safer than wire but occasionally stolen split-rail fencing incompletely tried to contain the land. It walled in the cattle it, out most intruders, but not all. The road rolled out flat for the length of the flat grazing land. It went for miles pairing grazing land on both sides.

Spirit Trail Road, thought by the elders of the area, was named for the Patriots who traveled it fighting in the Revolution. No one could remember or say for sure. Many miles down Spirit Trail Road, on its right side, stood a hill. The road disappeared behind its back. There the view ended from atop Snake Hill Road. Locals called it Heavens Hill.

During the daytime, a casual passerby might be entertained by the sight of cattle grazing. Occasionally a calf was seen stuck out of its mother's womb, like a trailer. It's eventual delivery certainly quite a sight. Lots of sights there of interest if one looked deeply.

Malcolm stared at the end of school for the year's celebratory tranquil peaceful scene. The view that day from atop that hill stayed with Malcolm forever serving as a welcome hiding place in the most difficult of times. There were none better. But as always the peace would be broken. The rest of Malcolm's company of boy's, intent on mischief, headed to the top of the long winding Snake Hill Road on fat tired bicycles.

"Hey Malcolm here we come Malcolm." His day dream broke. He leisurely turned. All four of his boy band- of- brothers, were at different stages climbing the hill.

"Come on boys," Malcolm shouted. He hooked and pulled his hand toward himself. One by one they arrived.

"Malcolm—can we get em this time –let's get em, no prisoners." Georgie huffed.

"You betcha,"

Little Georgie, Georgie the Tank they liked to call him, typically the first to be there, or anywhere, they had to be. He wasn't that little, about five-feet-six, and still growing. Everyone had a nickname. Georgie loved mechanical things. Most thought when he went in the army, he might be with a tank battalion, knowing he was always ready for a fight. He took his place to Malcolm's left, squinting Scottish decent, tense eyes. He and Sali competed with each other for the best at horsemanship.

Sali, an acknowledged boy of few words, followed. He seemed a bit more tense than usual.

Generally quiet, subdued, but he loved entrances. Flashing piercing brown eyes directed muscular build, crowned with curly black hair. A long neck, long arms, and oversized hands were properly mated to a fierce temper. Schoolyard fights he won. Whether Georgie the Tank liked it or not Sali also won the rights to the best horseman label. He always stood tall in the saddle. Today he stood tall on Malcolm's right. Sali fought the fights Hank started.

Hank loved to pretend fence with swords. Hank the sword was Malcolm's regal first friend, without question his best friend. Showy, bold, tall for his age at five-ten, he strutted around as if the natural leader of the boy-band of brothers but knew Malcolm was. He claimed his family's last spot behind three other Hanks preceding him, in his warrior family. Any fight brought to him he fought, and finished. If there were none around, he'd pick one. He liked long odds against him so he could show off. Light brown hair crowned his placid expression. A perfect background for his thin, sharp edged, face. A pleasant face for the most part till he barred slightly parted front teeth. His sharp blue eyes gleaming terror froze those who gazed into it. Finally his lean wiry frame casually arrived atop the hill, quite unworried. Nothing would happen without him. Boldly he shoulder forced his way between Georgie and Malcolm.

Slow Sammie followed Hanks arrival.

He wasn't all there, locals would say. Something happened at birth. Thin-boned, slightly built Sammie had a sickly complexion. Most thought him a terrific friend. To save the rest, he would have thrown himself on a hand-grenade.

"Me, me, let—me—ugh- in Sali, let me in damn it," he begged. Sammie used his head as a wedge, squeezed between Sali and Malcolm waists. Sammie the runt, brave, always hoarse.

They stood in a straight line, shoulder-to-shoulder. Georgie the Tank, Hank the Sword, Malcolm whom only his mother could call Malkie, Sammie the runt and Sali the horseman.

~

The bobbles chorused "Heeeyyyy, you can't say–." Mother waved them off, coughed.

~

All five held their bicycles by their bars to their right. They walled off the road. Five boys as close as brothers could be, all who would dared come. Chores, the others used as excuses. Fear more likely the real reason, and rightfully so. They all knew of the race, and wanted no part of it. But these five would always lead the pack, now before and beyond.

Before the Great race with the devil could begin, preparation was needed. Bicycles needed to become, motorcycles. Baseball cards were strategically fastened to the bikes' frames with moms clipped clothing pins. Positioning was critical, the wire spokes needed to just clip it enough when it spun.

It was the cheapest way to turn an ordinary, rusting, somewhat bent bicycle, into a pretend motorcycle. Mom wouldn't mind about the pins. If she did, it would be just one more item on a long list to answer to.

"Throw me a pin would ya," Malcolm ordered.

Sali reached in a bag of them freshly liberated from his backyard clothesline.

"Closer," Malcolm parented. "Sammie, pin it closer. So the spokes hit it better and it won't fall off.

Sammie's bike rested upside down on its seat and handlebars in preparation for its conversion.

"Clip, Ooookaaay, good. Now bend it a little," Georgie, Malcolm supervised offering help on how to do it correctly.

"Okay, damn, are you sure it's okay to do this to Mickey Mantle," Georgie said.

"Yeah, we have others. Anyway, we can always clip a pack, or two, from the Hudson's store," Hank chimed in. "I'm sure we'll find more of the Mick but if not, well if not there then we always have Sammie's collection he added."

"Sammie's not quite right in the head, easy prey he is. You gotta look after him Malcolm, my Dad always said. So that's not happenin. If my mom ever found out, well, plus it just ain't right, but I'd take yours in a sec ya jerk." Malcolm laughed.

Their bikes rested on their backs like Thanksgiving Day turkeys.

"Let's test em," Georgie said,

He spun his back wheel — Bbbbbddddduuddddudubbdd.

"Hmmm, pretty good," Georgie said. Now for the front-Bbbbdddbbbdbdbuubbb, same noise, a good noise. Georgie smiled.

"Wow, sounds just like just like your Dads Vincent,"

"Ah—, yeah sure Sali. Just like it." Malcolm smirked.

"Just like it, IIIII'm suuuure." Hank butted in.

It wasn't close at all. Malcolm heard the Vincent more than once. Close up-very close up, in the barn or while riding on its back as his Dad slung the bike through its paces. A fine Thoroughbred race horse it was.

The riders flipped their dotted with crusting rust, bikes, over, stood them upright. Their seats were usually loose and the brakes weak. When their brakes failed, their sneakers or farm boots, linked to rubbery knobby kneed legs, sufficed as drag. They worried not. Attitude's that really kept the others away.

They called it the Race with the Devil. One boy would be selected to be the devil by drawing straws—there was a lot of straw around those parts. The shortest straw won, or lost, depending on one's perspective. Whoever it was became the day's Devil. He started riding down the hill first. The others waited till a ten count signaled their start. The object, catch the Devil. The head start should have given the Devil a good lead, but some people can't count, intentionally. Often ten became eight. Good enough if the pursuers were eager, and not particularly trustworthy. Most of them counted to eight. The fun started when and if they caught up to the Devil.

The winner of the short lot this time was Malcolm. Positioned in the middle of the pack, he strictly adhered to the loosely held rules. Sali stood, bike in hand, to Malcolm's far right. He waited quietly, intensely, focusing as a great warrior. His serious brown eyes locked on the pitched Snake Hill Road.

To Malcolm's immediate right stood little Sammie. Sammie need shepherding and no one was better than Sali to do that. Sali kept him to his left, reducing the chance of his interference.

On Malcolm's immediate left was Hank, who pushed Georgie aside earlier. Little Georgie power play wedged himself back between Malcolm and Hank.

"Hey, who are you pushing?" Hank bawled out at him. "You little shit," he went on.

"Little huh, we'll see." Georgie was fired up.

He liked to be next to Malcolm. They all did, but for different reasons. Malcolm was magic.

"Ready to go, ready to go, are all your guys ready to gooo?" Malcolm barked, his heart pumped

"Ready?" Malcolm asked looking right at Sammie the runt and Sali the horseman.

"Yep, born ready," they chorused.

"Ready?" Malcolm said looking to his left at little Georgie the Tank and Hank the Sword.

"Ready," they said, shoving each other back and forth.

"Are you all ready lads?" Malcolm asked one more time to all, facing down the steep serpentine road as if a dress rehearsal.

"Readdyyy," they all screamed. All except for Sali, he knew of the carnage that lay ahead.

Malcolm's mouth opened wide. Spirit and recklessness harnessed together. The riders anxiously fidgeted like thoroughbreds in their gates ready to race. Malcolm screamed....

"CHAAARGEEEE," blew past his often inflamed tonsils, out to heaven.

"CHARGE LADS—CHARGE,"

Malcolm pushed off. His bicycles balding tires tried to hold the dusty road.

"Charge of the light brigade boy's, let's go Gunga Din." Malcolm's voice faded streaming behind him, taunting his brothers. Lines were often stolen from movies often watched. Sometimes they made sense, often not. Today was no different. Malcolm was off.

Waiting on the hill Hank ordered Sammie count to ten. Hank was also smart. If anyone challenged the count-and Sammie made the call, well no one would argue-he wasn't all there, clever Hank. Sammie was a little more there than thought, though. He whistled while presumably counting, allowing Malcolm more time. Hank shouted at him and glared.

Ten, Sammie whispered dipping his head with a guilty a sheepish smile.

"Whaaaa," Hank screamed.

"Ten," Sammie said. A little louder this time, a full smirk on his face.

Nearly fifteen seconds had actually passed. Wildly whooping, and screaming they all leapt forward pushing their legs downward on cocked bike peddles. If they caught up to you, if they caught up to the devil, the battle would begin. Malcolm was flying.

Downhill racers they were—not skiers—in the winter, yes—but now their bike tires caught the grooves of the road, and when their tires left the groove the bikes were air borne. The riders fought to regain control, and regain ground. Farm work boots worked the ground. Dragging their feet saved them from falling. The bikes were loose, flipped left-right—more boot sole worn down, Pa was gunna be pissed.

The baseball cards did their job—pouring out faux motorcycle melody.

Some cards were liberated by mishaps. Those lucky few glided in the dust clouds kicked up by the motorcycle rustlers. If someone's front wheel struck an elf rock sticking its head out of the roads surface it may be a problem. That is if rim bent, and locked up. Then the rear tire would buck like a bronco. Georgie didn't care, he never used brakes, never knew how to stop, Hank or Sali either, but Sammie did. Today his front tire struck a rut, it bent. In a panic he squeezed his front brake. He left his perch catapulting forward, over the handlebars, airborne and landed on his back. A short slide down the road stopped, he laid as a helpless upside down turtle. Sammie scrambled, got back on his bike.

The mob continued howling at an absent moon. No risk now, none, but come sun down that would be different.

"Who cares, we're all gonna probably die in a war anyway," Hank always said.

"Bringing in the sheeeaavves, bringing in da Sheaaaves, we..... OOOwwwwwwww," Cal looked at the shadow, snorted, raised and lowered his eyebrows, twice. Mother interrupted Master's interruption with a well placed finger. He coughed, Cal smiled.

Fresh faced terrorizing kids streaked down the hill. Faster, furiously, each well known turn mastered with ease. One boy ahead of the other, and then the next in the grandest of race's to be sure. Screams of fear and delight, anger and joy filled the bright light and heavy summer day farm odor air. Pushing and shoving, they tried to catch today's devil, Malcolm. No human heard them, except for themselves. Wild Injuns they were called. Wild they were, some did have Indian blood in them but that wasn't the issue, they were just kids. Fearless, reckless, waiting for the world to anoint them warrior kings.

The group heralded their charge screaming each other's names, beckoning each other to look at them slide their steeds to the left and right. More tumbled. Torn pants, laughter, blood trickling from scrapes on bare arms, or leg wounds. Facial wounds usually required all to stop, usually, but not always. Because this group, this band was omnipotent. Nothing serious could happen to them ever, except for one. And Malcolm always seemed to be that one.

Then it happened. They caught him. Malcolm missed a turn and his bike scooted for a few yards without him. The band of brothers reached into the top pockets of their blue jean coveralls to fetch their weapons generously provided by the weeping willows from the banks of the pond at the bottom of the hill.

Vein thin willow branches, stripped of leaves and sheaths, made perfect stinging whips. And whip they did, the enemy, the devil, Malcolm. He yielded they didn't care. Why waste such a wonderful charge? Turning on each other, they laughed and lashed each other.

Malcolm seized the chance. Hopped on his bicycle and sped off. The others followed in pursuit. His attackers slid and twisted to the right, left, chased and tried to reach him with the taste of a branch.

"Charge,—you asses." He taunted his friends, safely out of reach.

Whip and sting, the order of the day, Malcolm, your friend next to you, no matter. War is hell.

Plenty of time, do some stinging damage. Hank the best friend said.

All five, apart, halfway down the hill. They stopped for a five ticks of truce. Looked down the remainder of the hill where Spirit Trail Road was born of Snake Hill Road. The boy's hoped destiny.

"Malcolm, watch out." Georgie the protector yelled.

Sali crept slyly toward Malcolm. A well executed sneak attack, whip, whip, whip.....

"Owwww—ow—ow, ow," Malcolm's eyes watered.

Over and over Sali stung Malcolm, laughing mercilessly. Wild, fierce, Sali was as inexplicable as the wicked storms that struck Spirit Trail Road and Heavens Hill without warning. From another time some parents joked. He retreated almost as quickly.

Malcolm lost his concentration. His bike slipped. He couldn't regain balance. Down he crashed, very down, very hard down. So down, so fast, he slid, rolled and tumbled fifteen memorable yards over the rocky rutted hill road. On his back, front, side, till he stopped. He lay fortunately face-up starfish spread, caked in the dirt. Dazed, he tried to get up, but fell. His vision twisted the landscape. It wobbled, and then cleared.

What's that, he questioned, a drummer boys drum beats, here? Coming in and out of focus Revolutionary soldiers, in ragged bloody uniforms walked marched past. More drum beats, more ghostly soldiers, walking dead marched past. A pale, flag carrying soldier ran past trying to catch up to his position, pointed his flag forward. He called to Malcolm.

"Lieutenant Malcolm, quickly sir." With a haunting smile he offered Malcolm his hand. Malcolm reached to touch his. Interrupting images, voices, alternated between then and now. Malcolm struggled to get up. The flag bearer partially faded. Malcolm wobbled and fell back to the ground.

"Malcolm, get up, quickly." Georgie offered Malcolm his hand. The rest of the flag bearer dissolved. Back into the present Malcolm heard, are you ok buddy are ya.

Malcolm let his head clear for five ticks. Then rage raged. Georgie saw this look before, stepped out of the way.

"You son-of-a-bitch, what the hell are you doing?" Malcolm sharp tongued out at Sali.

Stoned faced Sali stared back. Sali felt no fear. He just caused it.

"Kiss my ass Malcolm. Remember what you said in front of Stephanie Vaughn yesterday, you shit?"

The stars that danced around Malcolm's head, some were packing to leave. He regained his full balance, stood. "Yeah, yeah, so what," he answered?

"You told her I loved her, you asshole."

"But you do."

"So freakin what? I didn't want you to tell her."

"Well, too late." Malcolm laughed.

Truth was, Malcolm himself fell to cupid's arrow that very day, but he wouldn't admit it. They all would, eventually. Of course, the pickens were slim in that part of the country. All of them were battling puberty and losing. Stephanie was the bell of the ball. She wouldn't find out about Malcolm's feelings, right away.

Sali's fierce brown eyes held rage and pain. He leapt onto his Arabian Steed of a bicycle and regained the charge. Malcolm did the same, chasing him this time. They sped on down bleeding from their knee scraps. The rest of the mob followed, shoving, hooting and whipping.

Lightning flashed, lit the bars windows.

Big Fat head, what the hell does that mean? Cal wondered.

"You'll find out son, now move along," Mother coughed, Cal flinched.

No one died. They reached the bottom of the road, came to a rest at Vaughn's Farm pond. They were packed with youth, not much else, but it was just their beginning. The gang of boys ditched their bikes, in the drainage ditch. Often snakes like to cool themselves there. They were harmless snakes for the most part, black snakes, not very large. But they could be a problem from time to time.

Stealthily they wormed their way through the combination of wire and weathered splintering rail fences, or climbed over them. A boy's size, strength and ability decided the tactic. All of them climbed the pastures hill, slowly creeping to within a close distance of unsuspecting grazing cows. Race with the devil finished, onto a new adventure. Georgie, always hard to hold back, arrived first, at the usual rendezvous point. Winded, he panted sitting half way up a small hill in the pasture. Olive complexion Sali competed. A very brave against all odds leader, a few ticks later he shoved Georgie. Kingly Hank, stuck with helping Sammie, third and fourth. Malcolm was the last in, first to get hurt.

"Ahhhchooo, sorry," Master apologized shaking his locks. Cal glared. He knew an attention getter when he heard one. But respected the clever Master, and nodded a smile. Master whistled.

Sali hollered, let's get the infidels. The rest snapped their heads toward Sali. Quizzically they looked at him.

"What the hell is an infidel?" Hank laughed.

Sali shrugged and muttered something he thought he heard somewhere.

The battle with the cows, for control of the pasture began. Unfortunately for the cows, they didn't know they were in for a fight.

Stephanie heard the boy's cries coming down Snake Hill. She came running out of her house road across Snake Hill Road, past the fence, and onto the field. Cow manure and hay scents filled the air.

"Maaaalllccolooom, what in the hell do you think you're doing, Malcolm?" Stephanie yelled at the top of her lungs. Then chased them all, especially Malcolm the ring leader.

"Chasin Sunbeams," Malcolm shouted back, from a safe distance.

"Chasin Sunbeams," he echoed, smiling, pointing to the sun.

Sunbeam was Stephanie's pet cow. She knew what Sunbeam he chasing.

Her best, and only school shoes, clawed at the muddy field grass toward the crest of the hill. The boys scattered, Malcolm and Hank stayed together racing away, jeering.

"Ha aha, ha, ha," taunted.

Each laugh stung, there would be a penalty. Then the boys bent over and shook their skinny butts at her. Today was just another episode of quarrels between Malcolm and the girl next door. It wouldn't be the last. Cupid would see to it.

"Malcolm, I'm gonna get you."

Stephanie raced after them, pressing the pursuit. She was faster than most but catching them would be a challenge, not impossible. Frustration and anger fueled he resolve with every step she had to take. Huffing rage reddened her face, her freckles disappeared. The finishing touch of her determination, cat slit eyes.

She stopped. The boys stopped, and continued their heckling assault. She scanned her farmland, found what she was looking for. A rock, a perfect rock, perfect for throwing. Anger became exorcised.

Stephanie's Granddad had a short stint playing minor league baseball. He pitched and made sure his granddaughter could throw as well. She remembered her lessons. Arm position— hip rotation-leg drive. She was a lefty. Strategically she braced her right foot against an embedded rock substituting for a pitcher's mound's rubber. She pushed off forward.

Stephanie, always a good student, would have made grandpa proud. The tomboy showed up in a nick of time, wheeling and throwing the rock as if it were the last pitch of the final game of the World Series. The stone left her left hands finger tips. Whistling, it carved a path through the humid late summer's day's air. Malcolm watched her but never worried. He allowed her come close enough knowing she didn't have his boys baseball ability. He turned his back, he didn't know about granddad. The rock found its mark. Square in the back it hit him. The major league pitcher sent a message to all, don't crowd the plate. Malcolm went down—a familiar position for him as often the local baseball field found Malcolm that way, in Right Field on his back, suffering from one of his many mishaps. Usually from valiantly crashing into an outfield fence, trying to snatch a ball from going out of the field. He never succeeded. The spectators, mostly the player's family members, loved the entertainment. They didn't get a chance to go to the circus much. The games would have to do, and Malcolm was a one boy clown act. He smiled, loving the center ring. Jesse the ambulance service was always close to the field, ready to pick him up. Jesse came shortly to fetch Malcolm from the hill.

"Tonight was a good night Mother wasn't it?

"Yes, yes, he's moving along but it's going to get tougher. Put him to bed please I have to get back to the shop. It's late, you know how quickly it goes here; I'm not sure if we can get this done? That storm will be here, he will be here! Look at his watch."

Cal's arm limply fell. His sleeve rose exposing his wrist as Master carried him to bed. Cal's watch continued ticking counter-clock wise. 6:30 p.m. August 29, 2009. Master looked, cockily smirked, nodded all will be ok.

"Lost a full hour but says he has about three or so hours til–"

"– I don't care, I'm not sure, move it along," Mother said convinced.

The class of dismissed bobble heads vaporized, with the one exception, Matron Mary. She daggered eyed at Cal. Then took Farmer Vaughn's arm and left together through the same hole. Something was up.

Three Mothers son's, two would meet reverberated from behind the walls.

# Sixteen

Something was, up. Comet's clock ticked to 6 p.m. Friday, September 1 and Big Fat Head, with his ssskiiiinny little soul, rolled to town. Cal lifted his wrist, 6 p.m., Tuesday, August 29, 2009. In front of Destiny he tilted his head, and exhaled replaying today's tour. Things were changing, fast. He needed less and less time there. Too bad, he loved soaking it up there.

He ditched Mothers bake shop stop. Awkward arm and legs raced to the bar's porch trying to catch a quick daydream. Solitude was best there. Not the dragon, Master. Big Fat Head leaned against the fencing on a cleared part of porches concrete floor, craned up at the blue ocean above the hills. His head swiveled in soft tight slow circles picking up the sounds of the day, crickets harmonizing serenading chatter. Three hours were stolen. Fleeting daylight swapped places with dusk, dusk with nightfall. Time to go inside, the town clock minute-hand stuttered to 9:00 p.m., Friday, September 1, 2009. Cal looked at his wrist, 5:50 p.m., Tuesday, August 29, 2009. Boom, boom, boom, thudded inside.

He looked in. Marching band music pumped from the Wurlitzer. Blaring notes broke the peace of a still bar, flew past the doorless front door and raised hell shaking night awake. Lazy bugs scattered from the porch light, combined in a swarm and spun to tight black thread. The Corkscrewing thread raced across the backdrop of a bright full moon, and then disappeared in the black. They knew better. Cal didn't.

"Come in, friend, come on in. Please, come, make yourself at home."

Cal never looked down stepping over the doors saddle. He looked second level. Master held a staff, paraded around as a military band major. John Phillip Sousa would have been impressed.

"Aghagh aghhahah," Cal couldn't hold it in. Doubled over watching Master dance, snapping his head left, then right, then forward.

"Come up bu, bu, darn, boooy." Master's voice sounded different.

God I hate being called boy, Cal thought.

"Yes I know," Master giggled.

"Damn!"

Mother made note, thunder rumbled.

"Might as well, say it out loud. No secrets here, are there?"

"Nope, none, boy," his jackal laugh reverberated throughout.

"Hey, how did you get that to play?" Cal asked. "I'm the one with the nickels."

Master paused, looked, and locked eyes with Cal's. His lower lip extended beyond its upper mate, and curled over it. Cal nodded an, I understand.

"Now, here, come boy, here. Come up here, times a waistin."

Cal turned his back to Master, headed to the right staircase and the red-and-black tile upper floor. Something heavy fell with a thud. Cal looked to his right. Master was gone. The wings slapped their way to the second level.

It was a sight, the great Master on his rear. He looked up. His elbows supported him. One eye wide open raised his fly away, sparse grey eyebrow hairs. They pointed in every direction, caught some of the pixie dust that loosened and parachuted from the ceiling. Destiny had a lot of dust, ashes to ashes and all that. Master partially open the closed eye, squinted a leer.

"Help me up. Get me up, boooy." He ordered, shaking his shaky head. His arm clawed the air looking for something to grab onto.

Behind Master, Cal hooked his two arms through his. He stood and hauled an air light Master to his two shuffling feet. Cal thought the weight of an Angel?

"Get me over to my piano."

"What piano?"

"That one, right there," Masters boney finger pointed while genuflecting a bow at its location.

Cal shook his head. He knew better than to ask. Master walked as a blind man toward the piano hooked to Cal's arm.

Familiar, what's that I smell, Cal thought?

"Hey, that's booze. You're drunk."

"Yes, yes I am. And you're not. Tsk, tsk. Now get me to the piano. I want to play."

"You play, you play the piano?"

"Did I stutter? Yes, I play. But if I couldn't, I could fake it as you know my friend. Plenty of electricity in here now, isn't there? More than enough to plug it in. Let it play itself. No need. Malcolm taught me, he played."

"Hey wait a sec, pianos don't get plu–."

"–Are you forgetting? Boy! Anything can happen in here, anything, at, all! Now help me to my seat. We must move this along. You have work to do tonight, more to learn. They're waiting. They must know where Malcolm is. You're their only chance"

"Who is, waiting?"

Master whipped his head backward, tight lipped smiled. Cal helped him to the piano seat.

"You are an old bastard aren't you?"

"Well, you know my boy, when you get older you can become eccentric. No one really cares. In fact it's preferable. And yes son, yes, yes. I am old, quite old by your standards, not others. So, to you that is bad news for me. Good news for you, for compared to me you are still quite young"

Cal beamed.

"Hoooowwwever, the good news for me is I have made it this far. The bad news for you is, you haven't."

"Aiieeeeeiee,"cackled. Master's heinous laughter rattled the rafters. His lower jaw dropped extended fully. Dust sprinkled. Some landed on his protruding tongue.

"Ugh, feh, yuck," Master wiped his tongue with a flapping cape's arm.

Cal's mouth gaped, out dueled. Sober or drunk, Master prevailed. He slid behind the piano and finger struck the out of tune keys.

"Ding ting dunnnn," Mis-struck keys grated. "Isn't music wonderful? Shouldn't life be more like it, more like music, great self indulgent rhythms with charitable lyrics?"

"Yeah, yeah, whatever you say. Hey, can I get a drink?"

"No. A clear head you need. Clear it must be." Master slipped attempting to stand during the reprimand. Wisely, he wobbly legged sat.

"Music, Art, Literature, gifts of the universe to you, humans. Keeps you sane, isn't it? Moves you, motivates, and propels you. Imagine a world without them? Heavens, and by the way, why do so few of you ever look up, down here?"

Cal thought, shook his head, he did lose touch. Master slid off the piano bench, tried to stand again. His legs bent. Failing him he twisted, folded, and fell to a knee. Stabilizing pontoons of outstretched arms with face up open palms alternated in up and down pulses. Gradually, he weakly rose.

"God Dam it, you know this alcohol is a marvelous lubricant of one's jaw." Master flipped his hood off.

"I heard a politician say that once," Cal said.

"Politician, not me, you must be kidding. Harrumph the Mooches."

"They're not all mooches, I've known quite a few very good ones."

"No, they're all not mooches. Some are just simple panderers." Master comically bantered,

"Yes, yes, you've know a few. How long have you been around hmm, my friend? How long have I? You think I may have known one or two?

No answer worth hearing could be uttered. Cal stood silent.

"Change of subject," Cal said.

"I win again, I winnnnnninin, again."

"Stop that." Mother scolded from the cover of the shadow.

He looked over his shoulder. A wobbly peacock, chest puffed, failing not slurring, paraded around the room.

"Listen, can we have a heart to heart? How much more of this I can handle? I should ride that one road in right the hell out of here. Forget the other damn road, forget the damn story. I find another job"

"My my, now you watch your language. You both give me a pain, and an awfully large amount to add up. Yes, one heck of a score, so far, I have to leave. Master will carry on."

"Mother, what's the twins score anyway?"

"Never mind that, and Mother also. It's too late. No one can stop it now. You are bound to finish up after the first time you placed your finger in the hole."

"Bound, by what? I didn't sign up for anything. I'm not bound by anything."

"Yes, you are, I am afraid. Clearly says so, in your contract."

"What contract? I didn't si–"

"–Right here, third paragraph," Master pulled a scrolled document from inside his cloak. Rolled it out, pointed to the clause.

"Well I didn't sign anyt–"

Master tapped Cal's signature at the bottom of the page. Cal's head jabbed toward the signature.

"Ugh, should have known. When did I–"

"–Never mind, not important, don't worry. It gets worse." Master chortled slurred words.

"But then it improves, then worse, then better-until–"

"–Yeah, yeah, I know. Worse, but I haven't seen better, yet."

"No? Come, let's dance. You need the practice."

"Why? Hey, I'm not dancing with you."

"Not like that, you idiot, Zorba it. Suck the marrow out of the bone of life, my friend.

Your lights will dim, before you know it. Where is your soul? Pay your respects for life. Men and women died here, but a child was born."

Cal cringed, raised his arms, and faced Master who raised his. The dancers snapped synchronized fingers, and danced. Cal forgot all, became Anthony Quinn as Zorba the Greek, dancing barefooted in the sand. Great fun while it lasted. Cal looked at Masters Finger. It pointed up. Master weakened, fell. His cloak kicked up.

"What's that?" Cal helped Master to his feet, looked at something quite peculiar covering his leg under his cloak.

Are those pajamas boy's pajamas? Cal doubted his tired eyes.

"Blue ones covered with pictures of rocket ships, stars and planets. What the h-" Cal started to accuse Master, but then thought better.

"Yes, son, paint your own canvas. Live your own life. Get done what you are here to do, before they suck the air out of your lungs. Stay away from the plum bishops. Avoid all self pity, as it is without a doubt, the grim reaper of happiness."

"Yeah, well, thanks for the seminar but listen, I'm just a reporter; I don't make up the news."

"Really, well, throughout, your, life, I think you've made quite a bit of news. Quite a bit."

"Okay, so, why am I here?"

"Why do you think?

"To learn about this place, get the story of what happened here, this shoot out and this guy Malcolm and by the way there was no mention of him in that paper. Where is he? I can't be here forever you know. Besides those haunts are getting on my bloody nerves with all that, where's Malcolm jazz. Wish I could smoke away. All I've done is, suffer. Am I about to be transformed into something?"

"No, No, this isn't about something you become. It is about something, heavens, you are. You think you being here an accident, a hiccup of luck? Good or bad?"

The riddles tormented Cal. Master knew it, loved it.

"Sometimes friend, that's how you learn to be aware. If you were before, maybe you won't have to suffer so much."

"Aware of what, do you mean I should have been more charitable? I'm lost? I'm not an uncharitable person, does that count?"

"Yes, of course, a great deal. As you know you, can't give charity away now can you?

Cal's eyes popped. "I, ah, I I've heard that before."

"Yes you have. Yes, yes my boy. So, you have been listening, sometimes, after all now haven't you?"

"A friend of mine, use to say it. Actually, more like an acquaintance. Didn't know him all that long but remembered that."

"No kidding?" Master darted a look.

"What am I to learn here? The truth about what actually happened here? I just don't have forever. Bartender's livelihoods are depending on me."

"There are many levels of truths my friend. It depends. And no, you do not have forever."

"Okay riddle man. Like boring philosophers, blah, blah, blah? Quiet lives of some bull. Well educated, truth-sayers. Hey I like that line. I'll have to remember it. Get it, not soothsayers but truth– well never mind."

Master looked down his nose. "That's true boy, but if you only memorize or regurgitate facts, then no. The fact gatherers, they're the brilliant ones friend. Think, what are you? Now I must leave."

The conversation quieted, to father-son. Master index finger twirled his silver grey locks.

"Don't worry so much. You mortals have excessive needs and demands for order. Oddly, it causes the chaos you seek to avoid. You can't stop killing one another. Your governments can't, your religions can't, imagine if–"

"....Imagine, John Lennon, great song." Cal looked down

"Yes, yes, that it is! He's a fine man."

"You knew him?" Cal's ears perked.

"Knew? Oh, yes, a favorite of all. His time unexpectedly cut short, a very expensive disappointment."

"Record sales, money?"

"No, not money, how do you measure loss boy? Be aware. Now, Jimmy, he can be much more difficult.

"Jimmy?"

Master pointed to a poster. "Yes, Jimmy my boy, Hendrix. Hendrix, he's a little more trouble. To answer your next question, I know, them all."

"No,"

"Did I stutter, again, my boy? Yes, I know him."

"Who else did you know, know rather, whatever, who?"

"ALL of them! All you wonder about. Lennon, Hendrix, Morrison, Janis Joplin, Elvis, Buddy Holly, the big Bopper, Stevie Ray, and few other folks, you don't."

"Like?"

"You mean, as in. As in, Mozart, Beethoven, Schubert, Bach, Brahms, I can't name them all, but I know them all, and they all know, me."

"Whoa. Wowy, cool."

"Yes him also."

"Him?"

"Yes him, Zappa, Frank Zappa "Wowy Zowy" Mothers of Invention Zappa. I'm late and must go. Remember memories are just that, memories. Live in the present, look forward to the future. You should have some left. People come into your life for a reason. Be aware, of the messengers. Be aware before the fog of heaven comes and gently takes your last mortal breath, as it embraces your immortal soul. Get done what you are here to do. Now, go title your, I's. Get class started."

"Ok, I'll see you in a bit."

"No, you won't. I have to go fishing now. Mother will help you with the next class."

"What, fishing. Now- at this time of night-where, how?"

Master sturdily stood up. His coloring dulled, diffusing into ghostly smoke, morphing into a translucent figure. Taffy stretching to a height twice his usual he could have inspected the dust in the rafters. He shrank back. Rolled his head backward till his hood fell off, leaving his grey locks hanging downward. Bent over backwards, in a trance, he turned his palms turned upwards to the heavens and waved his arms mimicking a conductor directing the symphony. The Wurlitzer seized the opportunity, came to life. The famed conductor Mr. Fielder would have been proud, the 1812 overture played. Master's sorcery peeled apart the bars roof at its very peak garage door style. Outside, a rich deep blue-black sky held sugar crystals of brilliant gem quality, multicolored lights.

"Hey, I don't remember seeing that before?" Cal said.

The roof thing seemed expected these days. The light show was different. Wind pushed through the doorless front doorway. Streaming upwards it funneled through the roof in a twister violently bowing the shaky walls and rafters.

Master concentrated looking, up, out, waiting, till a more furious wind cork screwed. Following that, another surged. This one tightened the loose winds curls to a vibrating licorice twists. Three ticks later, another forceful stream of warm summer's night air encircled Master in a shroud. Heat lightening lit the sky. Mother added points.

"Up there! They're all, up there." Masters finger, his favorite, pointed out from his hiding place within the twister to the heavenly body above.

"I'm going fishing there, with the Crimson Walker of the Grand Nebula."

A final wind streamed through the bar, spun Masters Cocoon as a possession and rocket blasted all through the roof. The blur streaked like a Comet leaving a sparkling dust trail of brimstone behind, and then disappeared. The roof folded back to its place with a clunk.

Dust hustled from the rattling rafter's splintering wood. It swirled and spun in a wild whipping whirlwind keeping beat to the shaking walls, making the bars interior a Christmas glass ball snow scene. Cal squinted, could hardly see through it.

"Who the hell is he, where the hell he is?"

Sister flashed, the sky lit. Pitch black of the night disappeared in the County's largest lightening storm in months. It lit the inside of the bar.

Cal looked out the window at Fate's lit Town clock. 10:30 p.m. Friday, September 1, 2009. His watch, stuck on Tuesday, moved back a little 5:40 p.m. August 29, 2009

Mother strolled in whistling. "Class anyone?"

# SEVENTEEN

"Sit down. We haven't all night, have we?"

"Yes, err No, well whatever Mother. Hang on a sec. Everyone's in a rush in this, good excuse for an amusement park fun house."

Cal obediently sped to the chair. Slapped the wall, slid it till the index finger found the dreaded portal, held his breath.

"Here we go, and I've got to know."

Delicately he probed the hole as if a bare bulb socket. It was one of sorts. Illumination came from the hangman noose tight grip.

"Heeeyyyy, what's this? Nothing, feel hardly anything."

Theatrically, he cringed, faked a body twist. What would happen? The nickels, those shiny beautiful Buffalo Head nickels needed to be charged. Cal mocked the episode. Wiggled, mashed his teeth, faked terror.

Mother's index finger circled. The current increased. Cal snapped off the end of his chairs right armrest. Likely weakened from prior visitors, or perhaps Cal's physical strength once thought long gone, was perhaps, not.

"Oh my, what will we do now? Master will have to come up with some–."

Before her last syllable was lost in the night's mist, the chairs broken arm, knitted. Mother and Cal craned their heads toward the ceiling, and then smiled at each other. Long distances couldn't keep him out of it.

"Throw one to me son, quickly, throw one to me."

Cal flipped the nickel, made a poor toss. Mother snagged it before it fell to the floor with a behind the back catch that outclassed Master's.

"Heeeyyyy, what gives here? Everyone's an ex big leaguer, a fan?"

"You think it's only for men, silly boy? Yes we all like baseball. It's perfectly, imperfect you know. Consider hitting, a series of failures interrupted by an occasional success."

"Yes, I know." Cal remembered his fumbling days on the field as a young boy, wishing them back.

"You remember Mickey, don't you?"

"Mickey, as in Mantle, we'll sure I do. Why?"

"Yes, of course, silly."

"Wait a second don't te–."

Mother smiled. "You'll be pleased to know, I think, we know allll. Now that Babe, George Herman, he's a handful I'll tell you."

"Ruth, Babe Ruth, wholly cow." Cal's arms limply fell to his sides.

"Yes dear boy, Babe Ruth. That child never really ever grew up. Similar what I have in front of me I'd say."

Cal beamed. Then his head sank till his chin pressed to his chest. Ten ticks passed, he was lost in imagination, wide eyed starring at the floor.

"Jeeze, I thought I was catchin on to these folks or whatever they a–."

"–Not even close, son."

"Dammmmn," slipped. Cal lifted his head.

Thuuuunnnnder rumbled a comment in cadence. Style counts!

Mother slotted the nickel. It slithered and rattled through the Wurlitzer's coin steeplechase. Ready boys and girls, you'd better be ready the coins journey musically announced to the Wurlitzer's records. Finally it crashed, into its awaiting family in the collection cup.

Who'd be the lucky one picked to set the mood, this time, Cal wondered.

Dum, dum dumm, dumm, dummm, dum, baaaaaaaaaa ba, ba baa b bbababababab dad a de da...The theme from Peter Gun rocked again.

Bobble Heads attentively sat nodding approval. Good thing also. The alternative would be a class nodding out. Matron kept dagger eyes on Cal, clinging to Farmer Vaughn. The crowd grew by two men, who snuck in overnight. A tall one, a shorter stockier one, and both recently divorced. Mid forties, both got to keep their golf clubs and summer homes. Class fattened up.

The walls grip released, Cal shook his finger. Stood from his chair and moccasin quiet crept toward the newbie's, and eavesdropped.

"Look, there are always two sides to a divorce." The stocky one said.

"Yeah, I know. Homicide and suicide," The taller answered.

If laughter converted into money, five million dollars would lie at all their feet.

"Listen up," the short one said. "I have a good idea. Say I marry your ex-wife, you mine. We each stop paying alimony, right?"

"Well, Yeeeah, I guess so?" the tall one answered scrunching his forehead.

"And if we divorce them shortly after, we can't possibly have a big bill to pay, right? See, we're done, we're out of it. It's perfect I tell you." The tall one spat out his drink.

"Hmmmm, you're a devious one. It just may work. With my luck I'll like your ex and stay married. It's not like their lining up for me anyway. Besides my ex, mother of my children, nah never do that to mother, mother of my children. That's worth a lot."

"Mother, hmmmm, yep, guess you're right. Heck of a plan though wasn't it?" The shorter one howled, threw a shot glass to his lips, sent more oil to work.

Reds throaty alto barked. The devious operation cancelled. They all talked sports. Great lies were told till interrupted. The flickering neon sign on the right wall abounded. POP- POP- POP A few words lit. Difficult to read, Cal walked closer to the wall. They grew brighter as he approached. They weren't positioned next to one another, like the others. More light from the dark Cal thought.

Throw, off, safe bowlines lit. Cal scratched his head.

"Hey you, where's Malcolm?" harmonized.

"Hush. Nurse your drinks and listen. He'll be here eventually. I've been assured."

Using a teacher's prerogative, a lie, he silenced them. He had no assurance of anything, from anybody. When, and if, Malcolm would show, no one knew. Not he anyway. Master probably knew, Mother certainly, but they weren't talking. Not yet. Cal hoped they would soon before an angry mob took him to the gallows, and the Comet to the crusher. Anything seemed possible here, most likely was.

"Don't worry, heee'llll be there, guaranteed, he'll be there. But youuu, maaaay, not, like, it," echoed from a long distance.

The room looked around, fell silent, Master went back to fishing. Cal shook his head, fidgeted in his chair Courage raced quickly this time. Something changed.

"Now listen all. I only have a short time. This night's speeding by. The town clock says its 11PM already. You know that before the dawn I will, and you will, be gone. So listen up."

The Bobbles spun on their stools, faced him. Attentive as first grade students, staring at their teacher first thing in the morning on their first day in school, dressed in their best. The music played in the background as the previous sessions, all- night- long. The spot light lit the lower floor. Caught some of Cal. Mother whistled.

Margaret walked out of the kitchen to the middle of Shepherds Walk fifteen-foot wide dirt walkway. The stretching connected to the barn. Sean regularly dumped used motor oil on it, mostly from his bikes and cars. "Keeps the dust down, he'd say."

Gracefully, elegant Margaret tilted her head. Her long jet black hair released, hung straight down, pointing to earth. A once bright sky windily dimmed. Yellow tulips rooted beside the kitchen door nodded in the from the advancing storms breezy calling card. They were the only plant life that grew around Shepherds Walk.

Storm clouds danced back and forth. Menacingly they sped up, turned forbiddingly black, fast forwarded toward Margaret with no hesitation. She saw many sky's like it before but knew this unique from others. It stirred and energized her soul. Goose bumped her skin. Glazed eyes winced. Malcolm wasn't home. Softly she pressed her lips together, looked skyward, nodded. Today began the beginning of change. Mothers always know.

Cal looked at the ghost tale, campfire faces, hung on the bobbles. Their mouths gaped in O's, eyes wide. He heard Master's cough, squinted.

They ditched their bikes by the pond. Malcolm and Hank jumped, yelled, and kicked their feet over the valleys sparse grass heading up Snake Hill. Manure and hay stained the air. Forced to stop once, to huff and wheeze, close to where many battle of the cows started. Their pony legs, slashed by what was left of the tall grasses sharp edge, continued on. Summer bright pale blue sky tinted with the yellow cast of the sun, grew dim. Boys bent on fun, at the expense of trouble, without a care in the world, wildly laughed, didn't notice. They weren't engineers. Foolishly they ran up the hill, pulling a kite, hoping for its flight. Mostly it dragged behind, bouncing off the ground. Occasionally, slight wind whipped mercifully took the battered sail skyward, streamed it behind them for only a few ticks. The just wasn't enough wind, yet.

Trouble making, skinny scrapped legs, hinged to bony knees, driven by lion hearts pushed their T-shirts and shorts to the crest of the mountain. Malcolm and Hank looked skyward from atop the peak of the hill. They saw the changed sky. War clouds in the distance torpedoing toward them. They'd seen many before. They didn't know what Margaret did.

Sneak clouds deceived the boys, moving, stopping and moving again. Unaware and unimpressed, the boy's paid mild attention.

"Hey, Malcolm, we're gonna get a little wet huh?"

"Get a lot wet I think, so what?"

"Well, I don't give a crap Malcolm. Let's get this bird to fly. Lest we'll have enough wind now."

Once more glance up, a scoffing look by both, they ran looking for the wind, looking for them. Run they did, burning through their daily allotment of the stuff that energizes demons. The kite flew, once in awhile, but mostly dragged. So battered, if human, it would have wished its self merciful death.

Malcolm and Hank, Hank and Malcolm, bound together, inseparable irresponsible polar opposites, continued laughing, jeering and heckling the clouds, stabbing the sky with their middle fingers. They ran until all the bologna sandwiches were spent, and then they'd run some more.

"You don't bother me and Malcolm, you bag of hot air. You can't do anything to us. We are killers.

"Yeah, get lost fat boy." Malcolm snubbed the widening black zeppelin cloud. It moved directly at him.

Charged boys need charging. They breathed deeply, inhaling the storms energized air. Delighted they were when the kite caught another lost breeze. But this breeze, had family. The kite flew. High as the line that stripped off its holder would allow. Bird high, preying bird high it soared. Victoriously proud with their success their arms flailed, hurrah. Hank's unmarred hands flip-flopped back and forth, then raised and pointed to the dark sky provoking it to fight. Irreverence fearlessly, and foolishly mocking nature's force. Two laughing, secure in their immortality ran, danced and jumped spinning nearly to flight. Change was coming, without coins. The sky alerted all, its shade turned to coffee.

Storms initial introduction was warning of fine mist. Minutes later, it tired. Shed its tame youth, turned on a gentle rain, rain danced with its cousin, wind in a seemingly ordinary alliance. Obliviously the boys stretched their legs with great pride, and greater contempt. Reckless, but the kite soared. The heavens had enough, opened up. Storms smaller drops, swallowed by larger ones that grew to the size of large pearls. If struck by one, they stung like glass beads. Summer's warm gentle rain turned fierce.

The boys missed a lot. In particularly, one large cloud, miles in the distance, high up in the heavens. It tracked Malcolm and Hank as any good hunter would prey. Steadily, it steadfastly descended gradually falling as a zeppelin would to earth. Once grey, it spun to black.

It had a long memory. This, the parent of the one the elf's earlier jeered at, and middle finger pointed to.

The partial band of brothers also mistakenly pointed at this one and daringly laughed at it.

"Rain, rain ha-ha, I'm Hank, that's Malcolm now go suck an egg." Hank loved to pick fights but Sali wasn't there to win it.

Un-offended, the undaunted cloud continued shadowing the boys into the afternoon. Tired, the winded boys rested, looked up, started to be concerned. This odd cloud wasn't anything they had seen before. It slipped lower. The ground below the tracker painted a dark blotch shadow that streaked across the valley toward them. The hunters were hunted.

"Golly," in unison. Finally they noticed.

"Bout four football fields, Malcolm, I figure. Four long, Jeasus." Hank choked.

"Oh boy Hank, we'd best get the hell outa here."

But the mass locked on them. Though they tried to move they couldn't. It had them. Their innocence, influenced by adventure, colored with recklessness, left. Sense and sobriety took over. The show just began.

This peculiar cloud could morph its shape at will mesmerizing all who dared look. Its image burned in retinas. Closing in, it purposefully stalled about a half a football field from them. The vessel of atmospheric moisture split in two. Each part shaped into a seven-story smoky chalice. Each chalice tipped over toward each other ever so slowly. Rain water gushed in two large streaming rivers with waterfall force. They pounded earth with a gift, sent from one of heavens most reliable messengers, Mother Nature.

"Skinny little soul, what the heck," Cal reverted to old habits. He couldn't shake it.

"Yes boy, yes. It changes though, we hope," echoed in the distance.

"Hey, go catch something, would ya. I have work, to do here." Master, whistled all the way from—-

~

The dousing quickened. Five fingers of a Zeus's light flashed, raising the storms stakes.

"Don't worry, Hank. I've seen this before. It'll be over in a few minutes, fer sure."

The storm wasn't listening. Water cascaded quicker, heavier, and endlessly. Fistfuls of thunder joined in.

Malcolm's optimism faded. The boys once lightly wet mischievous faces, were now soaked. Prays for it to end went unheard. Soaked tee shirts clung to their skin like plastic wrap. Worry fought arrogance, and won. Together they retreated, running from the rain down the hill toward their bikes, looking backwards over their shoulders. Smug faces chiseled in arrogance, turned. Stunned frightened ones, eyes held wide open leaking fear their replacement. They thought they could outrun the heavens wrath, they were wrong. Spent, the misty chalice shapes reunited with each other and formed one, single large black cloud. Heavens messenger had a message to deliver. Today it was.

Volleys of thunder shook the county warning all, stay away. This wasn't any of their business. Vicious flashes of strobe light cut the dark. The boy's feet barely touched the ground.

The pearl sized drops linked together forming great wavering chains. The chains twisted into red, blue, yellow and green spinning helixes of pencil thin DNA like ribbons. One thread of black ran lengthwise amongst them. What a designer. Whoever made these was the same designer who sent them to stalk their prey, Malcolm and Hank.

Blinded by the dark, the rain, petrified by the lightening, they cried. Desperately, they begged to be home. The storm wouldn't hear of it. Winds raced with greater force. Thunder beat the drum. The threaded rain punished them, stopped going straight down, twisted sideways hovering and snaking a tall mans height above the curves of the ground below. Malcolm and Hank looked for a place to hide. Not today, destiny spoke, lightening confirmed.

The stalled threads of colorful rain found its targets, caught them within the shadowy mass. They speared the boy's young bodies, in the face, torsos, thighs and feet. The ribbons tightened. Fine piano and guitar wire sized it penetrated harmlessly through the boys, leaving slight stinging sensations. Zeus's light hit the wire rain.

Shear panic drove them down Sun Beams Mountain. Alternating pumping arms moved as fast as they could go. Their feet followed. Rain turned ribbons, turned fine thread like wires pursued them. Hank slipped, fell, got up. Screamed for Malcolm's help but Malcolm had his own problems. He fell again. A sharp edged rock sliced his rib cage, tore his shirt. It changed color.

Malcolm fell, tumbled thirty feet. Along the way three sharp stones cut him, once on his right calf, and on his right bicep what there was of it. A big gouge tore his left thigh. The two bloody wet messes, the hunters turned hunted, yielded. This battle the warriors lost to their pursuers. They fell to their knees, rolled on their sides, curled into fetal positions lying in the mud like future fossils.

Middle spearing fingers of contempt, that once jabbed at the skies were now silenced and fearfully joined other fingers to form palm cups. Cups clamped to their faces. The anointment had only twenty ticks to go. The piano wire rain receded, and returned to normal. The storm backed away. It was he it wanted, found, Malcolm. For one brief moment, time stood still. They lay defenseless, embedded in the hill they terrorized.

Frightened, huddled in fetal positions, sunlight returned, defrosted them. Gradually Hank and Malcolm stiffly uncurled, uncertain the storm left. Unglued from the mud the boys limped home pedaling. Not a word was spoken. Hank was in bad shape. Wounded, but not as mortally as Malcolm, much of the storm targeted him. Malcolm was in different shape. The color in his eyes paled, the glint, fainter more detached, quiet. Neither would be the same. Not to each other, nor anyone. The changes changed slowly, at first. Progressing as time passed, Malcolm especially. Jesse the ambulance lost its best customer.

At home Margaret had a hot bath waiting. They always know. Malcolm cried out after soaking for a few minutes. Sean ran into the bathroom, stopped, felt Malcolm's tearing eyed head.

"The flu," Sean questioned. Malcolm's temperature climbed the thermometer scale.

Malcolm, punished, slumped in the tub shaking, trembling, and cold, sitting in warm water. Sean frightened. He got up to make the call. Jesse needed to get him to the hospital. Malcolm mumbled. Sean could barely make it out.

"What, what is it son? What are you saying boy?"

Dispassionately Margaret watched from her lean against the bathroom door jamb. Her stark ghost white skin always contrasted against Malcolm's. In the tub she saw his skin paled to her haunting shade, and his eyes lost Dads blue deep hue, paling to near blue-gray.

The room was lit by soft light of the full moon, pushing its way through distorting sagging glass of the old farm house window. Malcolm's molten, eerie image, hazily sulked in the tubs water. The tub water turned pink.

"They're coming," Malcolm told.

"Who's coming son?"

"They're coming to get them Dad."

"Who, what, He's getting crazy-listen to him." Sean pleaded to Margaret.

"The black capes, they're coming to take them home."

"Who, Who?" Sean pressed his pursing lips.

"The boys, on the battle field, they're coming to take them home, to their mom's.

"He's sick. We've got to get him to–."

Margaret calmly raised her left hand, fingers split in a vee, and thumb tucked to her palm.

She gestured to Sean, hold on. Her knowing look convinced him. Malcolm, trancelike continued in the light.

"The dark angels are coming, to get them." Malcolm repeated.

"Who, who?" Sean angered.

"The boys over there, in that foreign land, they're streaking in to get them. Wrap 'em up, take them home, in their black capes."

Sean was stunned. Mother Margaret wasn't. The rain found its mark, done its job. It set in. A hospital visit missed. Malcolm slumped to sleep in bed. He talked in his sleep, reciting something, Sean couldn't make out entirely. Margaret could, wouldn't say.

"The horsemen came a riding, riding to the glen, four horsemen came a riding to–." Malcolm fell asleep to his new world. In the morning he woke, without a scratch.

POP- POP, "from now," neon lit up on the wall. More light from dark. The stunned class silently hung on every word. Motionless, they sat till the music finished. One by one, stiffly, they slowly rose off their stools looking at each other bewildered. They thought they knew the entire story. Last of the music held in the air for a few ticks. Farmer Vaughn, a glaring Matron, Mary, Mr. I, and finally Sammie smoked through their holes before the last notes ended. The Wurlitzer clicked off.

Cal flexed wobbly legs. Stood, nearly fell, forward, grabbed Mothers hand. With closed eyes Cal blindly followed her. His crushed red velvet Victorian couch waited. Before the blue blanket covered him he was fast asleep. Tonight's episode was a milestone. How far away could the other Mother's Son, be?

Today was Saturday morning, 3:45 a.m. September 2, 2009. Cal's watch ticked, in reverse to 5:30 p.m., still Tuesday, August 29, 2009. Mother looked up adding up the kids score. Darted alarmed eyes, tilted her head, listened, and then sniffed the air. A new storm was on its way.

# EIGHTEEN

"Tsk, tsk, tsk, you took your plaid shorts? It's too cold this time of year for them."

"I'm fine Mother, not that bad. How's he doing?"

"Coming along, coming along, there have been easier ones." Mother's strict eyes closed.

Saturday evening snuck into town. The town clock ticked to 9 p.m. Cal's watch lost only five minutes, 5:25 p.m. Still Tuesday, August 29, 2009. Cal strolled in.

"The wall, the wall Cal, we must move ahead. Time's against us."

"Yeeees Maam." Cal banged around, flipped Mother a charged nickel.

She spun it on its rattling trip down the mechanism till ski jumped to rest with its friends. Wurlitzer's happy lights brightly smiled. Its needle carved the records grooves. Hiss, pop, pop, pop the record said hello waking all not paying attention. Sammie's drooling head lifted, nodded all's well. What in their world would they hear worry, hung on their faces.

Ah, Etta James, "At Last."In unison class tilted their heads left, and right. Bobble head metronomes fell under its spell.

"Malcolm? Who's Malcolm?" Mr. I's tenor voice joked. No one new showed up today to cause a stir so he did.

"I feel it." Matron said "Love is in the air, isn't it?"

Light from the dark lit the bar floor. Mother whistled–

~

Rules were rules. Everyone had to play no matter how desperate the situation. Malcolm's team was in a desperate situation and that included Malcolm. He hadn't played, yet. Ordinarily the game would have been decided by this late inning. Adding a dash of Malcolm meant little consequence. Not today.

~

"Hey, that's not a love story. It's baseball story. What's with all the baseball stuff?" Sammie rasped.

"Shut up," fatigued Cal lashed. "Sit down before I make you listen to Mr. I Imagine pontificate for an hour on a subject of his choice. Would you like that?"

"Heeeyyyy," Mr. I Imagine protested.

Mr. I Imagine, so named for when purposely spoken to, a rare occurrence, he always responded with, "We'll I Imagine that– "delivered with a hint of faux English accent.

"–Just get back to it, will you, Heavens." Red extinguished Mr. I's forthcoming rant, looking at Cal.

"Going military on us huh? Be kind," Echoed from above. Long distance worked well.

Bass, tenor, alto, soprano, and Sammie gulped in orderly rapid succession. On the verge of losing control Cal looked at Mother. She held two fingers to her lips about to whistle. He shook her off and started–

~

The fans knew him as funny Malcolm for his circus-act sloppy play. The coach knew Malcolm as a player with a good heart, but weak skills. Coach also knew right handed batters from the opposing team were coming up to bat and likely would crush the ball to left field off his marginal pitcher. Malcolm was protectively banished to right. The coach prayed.

The opposition was the best team in the League. They had last-licks, a better than good hitter stood at the plate. Malcolm's team stood their positions, uncharacteristically ahead by three runs, in the bottom of the last inning. The opposing teams players paced in their dugout, anxious to get at it.

Malcolm's team star pitcher, ordinary on his best days, was taken out with a sore arm. A boy with a fresh arm and even less ability his replacement. He proceeded to make a game of it, allowed the other team to erase all but one of the three run lead. Somehow he did manage to find two outs, loaded the bases doing so. A base hit with runners moving on the pitch surely would tie, or win the game. Malcolm's play could be as much of an asset to the opposition at times as he was to his own team if you relied on his arm throwing someone out, much less putting away a lazy fly ball.

"Crack of the bat, everyone's going on the crack of the bat. Let's go, two outs, come on let's go, go, go we can win this." The opposing coach hollered, clapping encouragement.

Malcolm's coach sagged watching his team's lead, evaporate. He threw his clipboard sensing their chance for a miracle win, lost. Wished Malcolm was drinking soda in the dugout but rules were rules. Everyone played, no matter what and if a player took the field you were stuck with him till the inning was over, unless hurt. Malcolm stayed in. The hope was he'd get hurt. He could, and would regularly.

Players, coaches, fans, people passing by, all had a desperate dire feeling. Two outs, down by only one run, bases loaded. The opposing team's coach pinch hit for a righty hitter with a lefty. A very good lefty, the county's best.

"Hit the ball as hard and as far as you can toward Malcolm." The coach whispered. The boy smirked and nodded.

Picking on Malcolm may have been cruel but made sense. The batter wiggled his toes, dug up batter's box. It hadn't rained in awhile. It looked like an overused horseshoe pit. Two minutes passed and the count stood full, three balls and two strikes. A legendary baseball dream fantasy, batting in last game of the World Series filled the batters head.

The next pitch had to be a strike. If not, the pitcher would walk in the third base runner and tie the game. Malcolm's team's pitcher didn't have his command, he never had it. Every day he pitched was an adventure. He looked in at his terrified catcher's pudgy face, and threw the ball right at it. A remarkable perfect strike the lefty batter remarkably, didn't hit, but crushed. High in the air it flew toward its intended victim, Malcolm. The runners watched it fly, and then took off not waiting for it to come down from the clouds. The crowd of players and biased family fans froze watching it soar, hoping it went foul. His coach turned away. The team, regardless of religions, prayed.

Malcolm tracked it to his left, then right, wavered. Professionally he held his glove up shielding his eyes from the setting late afternoon sun. Girls held their breath watching the screaming white sphere fly toward the eight foot green wooden wall behind Malcolm. Jesse the Ambulance's advertisement hung on it. Malcolm backpedaled. His glove up and pocket open, still tracking the balls flight. Something he wasn't particularly good at. The ball was going to beat him and he knew it. He turned to his left and flew with his old playmate, reckless, with complete disregard toward the wall.

The runner on third streaked home. The runner from second screamed rounding third and wildly leapt in celebration along the way. Awkward Malcolm, refusing to give up, leapt into the air and slammed his back into the green wall. A frightening crackling wood splintering noise would be later recounted at family dinners for years to come. Malcolm fell like an untied scarecrow. What heart. His eyes shut right after looking back at the Jesse the Ambulances destroyed wobbling sign. He lay semiconscious, on his back, dazed. No sign of the ball. It must have left the field. He gave it his all, no one could fault him.

"We won, yippee" victorious, mean spirited screams shouted from the other team's dugout. The keepers of Snake Hill Road slithered and hissed.

The umpire jogged out circling his hand indicating a home run and to check and see if Jesse would or wouldn't be needed. Compassionate worried fans and his team's player's raced him there. Jesse started the ambulance spun its rear wheels, and bounced over the outfield toward their favorite customer, counting their money. All arrived together, stood in a circle around him.

"Is he alive?" Someone whispered. Malcolm's foot twitched, his trademark smile spread across his face. He held up his glove. There it was, neatly wrapped in Rawlings leather, there was the ball. What a catch.

"He caught it. He caught the dam ball, gaaaammee over." The umpire bellowed.

"Malcolm won the game?" His coach asked.

Malcolm shooed the hoverers with a swipe of his glove hand, rose to his knees. Angels dancing around his head cleared. Whoops, hollers and thunderous applause, thirty fans applause roused the birds nesting in the scoreboard from their afternoon nap. Both sides were amazed. The other team hang dogged their heads. When they stopped kicking the dirt they congratulated him. Back-slapping and applause all for him, the likes he had never heard. Never worried Margaret never budged. She watched from her usual position in the splintering green stands.

Yes, things were changing. Jesse sped away. Their best customer, a most treasured resource, turned them away for the first time. Soon they would be in serious financial trouble.

Margaret and Sean conferred. In honor of Malcolm's great success the kids could have barbecue and a sleepover. All were invited, but previous plans had been made. Only Malcolm's closest accepted the invitation for his much deserved hero worship night, including Stephanie.

Hot dogs, burgers, fresh corn, homemade ice cream served for–.

~

"Hey, where's Malkie," Interrupted.

The class held their breath. Pursed their lips in an O uttering, "OOoooooooooo."

Cal's eyes opened, and then snake silted to a lethal squint at the offender. Interrupting was a capital offense, calling Malcolm Malkie, well–.

"Malcolm, Malcolm," Master's protégé shouted with a finger point at Mr. I Imagine. "Now, shut, up. He'll be here, but let me hear one more out-burst from you, or anyone else, just one and we're finished. Do not let me hear a one."

Cal sat listening to Master's hyena laughter.

"Well dear, we've created a monster don't you think?"

"Yes, my, how quickly they grow." Mother confirmed whisper chuckling.

Cal shook it off, glared toward the shadow on the floor, looking to make eye contact with the Master but to no avail. Master and Missus toyed with him. He cleared his throat, started to speak, stopped, and then started again. "By the way—you'll each get your fifteen seconds of fame to tell what you must. That is if you want, err, if I want you to, and I do. So be prepared." Cal threatened.

"OOooooooooo," Bass, soprano, tenor, and alto, groaned together. Mary's soprano was agonizingly harsh.

The Bobbles pursed their lips forming tight O's. Cal's mind reloaded. Etta sang the final lyrics. Another nickel slid down the coin chute. Mother winked. Tommy Edwards sang, All in the Game. Master coughed.

Night fell. Well fed, the kid's shooting star shot through the kitchens back door. Malcolm led. Moon-light mixed with star-light and detailed the warm moist summer sky. The kids didn't look up much. Stephanie did. Felt she had a special connection.

A weak creaky barn door closed behind them. Flaring nostrils and snooping minds checked out the horseless stables. In their shorts and tee's the six elf's, Hank, Sammie, Georgie, Sali, Malcolm and her ladyship, all five foot of her, crept inside. Stephanie proudly announced herself as five- foot and a half but it was of no matter. Everything grew in the summer. Stories and the kids did also. Stephanie grew also, but in different ways than the boys. Her Mom made sure she stayed a lady. New garments issued, Mother issued, ones boys would not see.

"Hey guys, over here, over here. Come now before my Dad comes. Come on-over here." Malcolm the ring leader, and today's center of the universe, pressed them into service.

"Help me with this bench. Come on Sali you're stronger than any of us." Malcolm hooked his arm beckoning them to him.

"Kings don't do slave labor." Sali uttered smirking.

"Yeah, well if this, king doesn't help, he won't see it. Get it." Malcolm barked back. Sali stood overcoming the weight of the last of two hamburgers.

Three horse stall's were closed, and locked. From a standing position one could not see inside them but, if you were on a bench you could look over. Sali, Malcolm, Hank and little Georgie dragged an old, thick-heavy, wobbly solid wood bench to one of the stalls walls. Sammie watched, laughing. Though long enough it was unsure if strong enough. The kids didn't think about that much.

One, two, three, four, five and Sammie, climbed aboard popping their heads over the top, having a look. Sammie tip-toed. There it was. The newest addition to Malcolm's family, courtesy of a lucky night and a cagy resourceful wife with a loving heart, and a helpful brother.

"Malcolm what is it?"

"My dad's Vincent, Steph, his Vincent motorcycle."

"It's amazing, Malcolm."

"Yeah, I know. He calls it his Winters Eve."

"Why?"

"Dunno, said I would sometime, maybe. Mom says that if my Daddy was a jeweler it would be his Hope Diamond."

"What's a hope diamond, Malcolm?" Sammie sorely asked.

"Dunno, named after Bob Hope maybe?" Malcolm shrugged.

~

Bobble heads mouths hung open listening to Cal describe the scene and watch it come to life under the spotlight. Mary handed a paper to Cal. "Time you learn more about that black monster Sean was perched on in the photo." Cal read it aloud.

"Only eighteen hundred Vincent Black Shadows were manufactured. All hand assembled. Sean's came from a long line of pedigreed motorcycles. Many technological advances argued the finest ever made to that point. The Vincent, painted mostly black, no one really knew why. Some argued for looks. Some thought otherwise. Whatever the reason it contrasted distinctly from others heavily chromed issued by other manufactures.

Beauty is in the eye of the beholder. Many viewed the Vincent, with its few flecks of chrome accents, as just that. It wasn't just looks that made it unique. The builders wanted a bike that could be ridden by injured combat servicemen. Only two fingers needed to operate the clutch. Maintenance was much easier also than anything at the time. At the heart of it was its 998 cc engine, quite large at the time. The label HRD proudly mounted on the bike stood for Howard Raymond Davies. A young British flying officer during World War 1 that was shot down over Germany in 1917. Imprisoned, he dreamt about building the perfect motorcycle. After the war he and E.J Massey built the H.R.D. Stylish, but so advanced they set the standard for motorcycles throughout the 1930's.

In 1928, a schoolboy named Phillip Vincent left Cambridge University. With backing from his cattle ranching family he acquired the trademark, good will etc, of the company for five-hundred British pounds. Quickly he renamed the company the Vincent HRD co. Ltd. Later the HRD was dropped, too similar to Harley Davidson. Vincent produced many different production bikes. They evolved over the years. Each one was better, faster, than their predecessors because of technology."

"Eeeeeeenough-enough about the damn motorcycle,"

"Shut-up Red, by the way, nice lipstick, you workin the streets tonight?" Cal hated interruptions. The crowd roared, except one. Cal started reading again…

"One of the Black Shadow's predecessors, the Vincent HRD Black Lighting, set a new US national motorcycle land speed record of 150.313 mph on September, 13, 1948. It was on a cool Monday morning when Rollie Free, wearing only a Speedo bathing and a helmet, to limit weight and resistance, successfully took the prize from Harley Davidson establishing the pedigree of the Vincent motorcycle." Mother whistled, Cal got back to the barn.

Sean's Black Shadow beauty was a stock bike. It could exceed 125 mph. Stunning performances for the time. No one else was close. Sean knew them all being great fan. He wanted the King. Margaret saw fit her king, got his. Time grew shorter by the day.

"Ok we've got to get to sleep –they'll be out here soon." Malcolm ordered.

The kids jumped off the bench competing for the best distance. Sammie no fear, won. Make shift beds of sleeping bags, pillows and hay sufficed. Some climbed in, some lay on top. A quick pillow fight or two, and that, was that. Malcolm and Stephanie lay side by side. Sali wondered how that happened.

"Fix my pillow Malcolm." She said.

Malcolm took it from her as he had so many times before at sleepovers, pretended to fluff it, fix it she called it, and then instead of putting it under her head he put it over her face pretending to smother her. Tonight was no different except Malcolm carried on too long.

"You're smothering me, Malcolm. Stop, stop." Stephanie muffled her plea from beneath the deathly pillow.

Malcolm continued, then realized.

"Sorry, sorry, don't know-"His hands shook. Said he didn't know what got over him and re-fluffed her pillow in an apology. Smiling, she laid her head on it.

~

"OOoooooooooo" the class harmonized perfectly.

~

The barn door opened. Sean walked in, Margaret in hand. He spied the bench, motioned to Margaret. Softly they laughed not to wanting to wake the fake-sleeping kids with their eyes mashed together, noses wrinkled and mismatched teeth. Out the couple went -back to the house. All partiers fell asleep, but two. Malcolm and Stephanie rolled on their sides looking at one another as they never had. Feeling safe, Malcolm boldly inched closer. Each had their first kiss from someone who wasn't a family member, right on pillow soft lips. Malcolm thought it the fourth of July. Stephanie stayed composed. She fell asleep, Malcolm couldn't. He stared at her for what seemed like hours watching her breathe. Ten minutes later the lateness of the evening stole the moment, he fell asleep.

Stephanie woke an hour later, held her head in pain. It went away as she stared at Malcolm, and watched him breathe. Fair is fair. Then off to sleep. Morning marched. Malcolm had a lot of praise to manage. His sleeping angel had to help him through it.

Gauzy light on the dance floor faded, as did the images held in it. The Wurlitzer whimpered final heartfelt notes and lyrics. Fell silent. Cal limply slouched. His chin pressed to his chest.

"Mother, please go get him. He's done." Master requested from afar as you don't tell Mother anything.

She led exhausted Cal to the Red Velvet couch. Its sticky cushions stayed covered by the freshly laundered sheet. Foul odors of the bar stung his nose. Too tired to complain he fell fast asleep hugging one of the cushions. Master was on his way back. Things were going smoothly, too smoothly. It was 2 a.m. Sunday, September 3. Cal's watch back ticked to 5:20 p.m., still Tuesday, August 29. Mother added the score.

# Nineteen

"Hello Mother."

She shuffled her feet, wrung her hands. Cal turned his head away.

"Do you know, now, son. Do you understand? It's all around you, in you, always."

What was she talking about? He pondered that he never considered, thought before answering. Two right hand finger tips tickled a light scratch of his left forested cheek.

"Oh," he quaked. Neurons fired sparking a synaptic furry. A seventh-grade party memory struck.

"Not sure whatcha mean there, Mother?" Cal played dumb. Her stricter eyes locked to his.

His porous memory gave him up.

"None," Mother blurted. "Nooo secrets son, now tell me, what you know."

"Carp," wide frightened eyes dog darted around the room. No escape.

"Damn, oh sorry damn it, oh not again hey I'm-"

Thunder rumbled. Mother looked outside touching her fingertips to one another.

"Soooo, I guess this is the deal. I get beat up in Destiny. Then I get to think about it, and then tested? Things could be worse I guess. Geezz, I wish I had you guys when I was in Grad school."

"Yes, quite right my son. Now you've got it, and, by-the-way, maybe you did?" Mother chuckled

"Got what, did what?"

"Never mind that now. The answers you need are coming."

Answers huh? I need to get this story and get outa Dodge. What other questions? Cal wondered.

Thunder.

Hey, I didn't say it. Wanted to but didn't. Don't count that he thought.

Mother whispered. "Yes, answers. Think, who else do you know that can read your mind? And, no, I won't count that."

"Master and okay, I like games."

"Another can."

"Really, who Mother?"

"You'll know eventually."

"Okay, mind games huh, game on lady." He laughed. She didn't.

"Look, I never had any questions that I knew of, except the one figuring out what the heck happened in that garbage-dump of a bar."

"You haven't?"

"Well maybe more than one. I need to know the what, how, who and why of that mess over there. Write it and save my job. That's all I know."

Mother muttered, "Yes, hmmmm."

"What's the trick, what's with all the, magic?"

"The magic is yours. Answers to your questions are already here. Find them. You've been told, many times already, son."

"I've, been what? Told what? I haven't been told a thing."

"I beg to differ. You've been told quite a bit, and quite a lot. Is this is all chance? We know you've wondered, don't try to hide it."

"I suppose. Still I don't know what happened here and need to."

"By the end of your time here you will. We must move along. Quickly the sand pours. It gets late early here you know? How are the nickels holding up?" Mother brushed her hands of flour.

"Fine I guess? I have a few left."

Cal stuffed a hand in a linty pocket. Pulled them out, and counted. All twenty were still there.

"Heyyyyyy, what's goin on here?"

Mother chuckled. The clock in the town square ticked to 8:30 p.m., gonged.

"Time for you to go, we'll talk more. Remember listen, listen carefully. Had you before, you may not be here. Listen, it comes to you, from you, places, or people you might not know, or expect, perhaps even like."

"Like Master?" Cal laughed.

"Yes, even him. Especially listen very carefully to someone very, very, very, close to you. Now be gone. He's back, waiting and a hungry bear."

Cal left the shop scratching a thinning crew cut. "Who the hell is close to me, that I trust?"

Thunder rolled. Mother added thinking if nothing was done soon they'd reach basketball numbers.

"Riddles, you're all crazy. Anyway time for the evenings, festivities." Cal shook his hung head, leather slapped the dirt lawn, slipped climbing the steps, tried again, marched toward the doorless front door. He stood for four ticks. Night's darkness fell behind him with the grace of an old theatre's regal curtain closing the show. A forceful smelly breeze pressed at his back, encouraged him inside. Someone felt neglected.

"You have to be a little bit crazy to keep from going completely, INSANE."Masters echoing howl, rocked the rafters, blasted Cal's overgrown face.

Pixie dust parachuted to the wood floor. Cal blew over the saddle. He skidded to his chair, sat, and waited for instructions to start his electrocution thrill ride. Master walked in. Impolitely he nodded hurrying to his position in the shadow, pissy. Everyone knew.

Cal's finger hooked a portal. He twisted. Wings happy toed tapped, sole slapped, and heal kicked the floor. Fallen pixie dust bounced off the floor and danced in streaming moonlight.

Shocked, exhausted, Cal quietly sat as a martini stirred, not shaken. Master wryly peered over drug store specks, sarcastically smiled. He had perfect eagle vision they said, those he replaced but how else should a Master look?

"Thaaaaa nickel, quickly!"

Night's wall charge charged everything and everything ached. Stiff knees were exceeded only by stiffer hands, the only things to get stiff on him these days.

Carp, feels like the flu for Pete's sake. Hey, wonder how he's doing. Cal thought, Master laughed.

If the flu, Cal hoped it would deliver him out of this place. Master shook his head no. Grimacing an annoyed contorted faced Cal struggled to pull his finger from the wood socket.

"Carp, splinters," Out of one portal, into another, Cal hastily stuffed his sore hand in his pants pocket.

Master caught Cal's flip in style, hurriedly hustled to the juke box and finger spun the nickel down the chute. The Wurlitzer woke. Colors glowed, but were not vibrantly as before. It had discretion to change as it saw fit and it did tonight. Frankincense perfumed the air. Mother noticed.

"Ah. Ah hah, she knows." Master looked at Mother.

Wurlitzer knew. How? A better question, but know it did. Somber browns flecked with red, thin piped with black coursed in its lights. Cal's brow wrinkled. Quizzically he looked at the great sound machine.

"Funeral colors, oh no." gasped from his dry lips.

Mellow classical music grooved from a brittle plastic record. Oboe's leaked melodramatic notes, soulful violins whined together, wrenching hearts, preparing all fourteen. Fourteen bar patrons, including the bar fly bobble heads, all sadly anticipating Cal's words. Mother coughed, Master whistled territorially staring at her. Cal started-

Sixteen year-old Malcolm watched his father worsen. Sean could no longer work. A strong minded weak bodied man, fought death.

"OOOoooooooooooooo" Bobble's voices collided.

Dismayed Bobble heads bowed to their chests. Mary parked her attitude, blew her nose. The light on the lower floor reluctantly showed. Farmer Vaughn covered his face with massive hands. His double chin tipped, touched a salt and pepper chest showing a balding head. Rarely, did he wear tee shirts. But always wore blue jean bib coveralls, and clunky brown rubber farmer boots. Cal waited for the characters to thicken in the light. Mother looked at Master. Master humbly nodded. She whistled.

Malcolm grew strong. Steadily he grabbed a man of the house's responsibility. Sean weakened, struggled against the tide but was forced to yield. Margaret outwardly kept a cheerful attitude, wept when alone knowing her best friend hovered at deaths door. Normally she could fix things. This she could not. Her heavy heart ached. The best mothering in the world could do nothing.

Sean's illness strengthened, he weakened. Once very clever he succumbed to just, clever enough. He waited for his opportunity one afternoon. Malcolm and Margaret went to town, left him home to rest. Ill, or not, Sean never liked to listen much. Had he, he might not have been ill but too late for that. Not too late to ignore loving orders to rest however. The little rest he had charged him enough to wobbly climb from bed. With a grace of a scarecrow in a windstorm, he dressed. Too loose overalls were well matched to his gaunt boney face. Pale blue eyes showed little life hiding in recessed hollows. Occasionally, his famous charming twinkle twinkled. Today was such an occasion.

Out the back door and into Shepherds Walk. He stopped and looked directly at the afternoon sun, smiled and then grimaced. His body reminded him time was short. The pills didn't work very well anymore. Doses of two became four. Addiction was of no concern. He couldn't drink, but with this stuff, he didn't miss it.

Loose boots caught the bottoms of looser overalls. Sean nearly tripped mounting the Vincent. He prepped it to start. Prayed it'd easily. It hadn't been exercised in awhile and he had little strength to strongly argue.

"Help me God, I'm seein you soon," he pleaded. Up on the bikes foot pegs he stood. Grip the handle bars by their ends. Twist the throttle, feed this hungry baby. Almost ready, pull the kick-start lever out with his foot.

A nub of a work boot-heal caught its rightful place. Sean's right foot applied pressure. He weighed fifty less from months earlier. With all of his remaining might, weight, and prayers, he shoved. The engine fluttered, but failed. Sean panted, rested hang dogged, then up again. This time using heaven issued strength. No go. He sagged forward over the gas tank, arms stretched out, inhaling the gas tank fumes, defeated.

Pain pills plagued his memory. Heavenly intervention filled his nostrils.

"Damn hell, switch the fuel petcock open boy, she's starving, he said aloud."

Happy bobbles nodded to each other. Cal smiled, Mother nodded to Master, who coughed.

Sean reached for the closed fuel petcock valve, twisted it open. Gas slid quickly down the fuel lines to the carburetor of nearly 1000cc monstrous engine. Weak, he struggled on encouraged. Faded blue eyes sparked.

BBbbuudummpp –Buupmmd. The Vincent's thumping twinkled Sean's eyes, renewed his optimism, and rewarded him with strength. Skin and bones temporality strengthened to wire and steel. His right hand feathered the throttle. The engine's music pulsed, grew stronger, Sean didn't.

"No reverse on motorcycles son. Got ta back em in, park em rear wheels against the stalls wall makes getting away easier. "He mocked his own words said to Malcolm.

Bright sunlight mercifully drove warming rays to his blood. It helped enough to ride. And ride, he did. With a head full of pain medicine, and a heart full of nonsense, he lit out through the stalls door passed the rickety barn door, across Shepherd's Walk, and bounced down the dirt farm road in a cloud of dust to main road. It was all he could do to hang on.

Hang on he would, twist the throttle he would. Ten mph shot to forty, forty played tag with eighty. He held the speed steady racing the wind. Old skills carried the day threading the country roads essess in fine jockey mastery. Sean's face froze in a grin. Fearlessly he showed off. Hoped Mother Nature was taking notes knowing soon he would return to her. Thoughts of a crash came and left, and only for the sake of his beloved bike. "I'll take ya with me," Sean screamed into the face distorting wind. They disappeared in a cloud of dust.

Hours later, locals coming home from town approached the Vincent propped up on its stand along the side of Spirit Trail Road. No sign of its well known rider. They stopped. A few yards off the road, in a lightly forested area, Sean sat peacefully, resting, against the base of an old oak. They quietly approached not wanting to wake him as his head slumped in a Huck Finn afternoon cap nap. The cigarette he smoked burned to his tobacco stained fingers in a ceremonial symbolic gesture. It extinguished itself, as it had done to him. A faint trickle of blood leaked from a corner of his mouth. It curled down an etched groove to his chin, leapt off it signing its name on his shirt.

Clever to his end, Sean saw fit to place the undamaged Vincent with great care on its stand alongside of the road he so often conquered knowing it'd draw attention. A perfect position for the tow truck to come fetch it as he knew it would have to be. Sean loved his bikes.

"They was members of da family, like children," he'd declare. Margaret argued he was one himself. His wake, a one day affair was held two days later, between two and four. Margaret and Malcolm thought a few people would show. They were wrong. The funeral home overflowed. It could have been a wake, or a class reunion and a wedding combined. Wife and son had no idea the affection people had for him. Friends, family came from near and far, including his brother Michael from Ireland, and his cough. Most knew Sean as a mechanical genius with a decidedly warped sense of humor. A few months earlier, aware of his fate, he decided to save some, "unlucky bastard," he'd say, the trouble of writing his eulogy. So he wrote one, for himself.

"Open upon my death. Malcolm to read and be a man," was scrawled on the front of an envelope containing his self-written eulogy. Like the Vincent, purposefully left to be seen.

Wet eyed Malcolm stood before the crowd packing the parlor's main room. The wings were shoulder to shoulder and the crowd flowed outside through accommodating open white double-doors. His father's open casket rested behind him, slightly to the left, surrounded by reeking over-bearing sympathy flowers. Funny sight to see Malcolm and Mother Margaret whispered to each other earlier. The crowd wouldn't know it but Sean when alive was allergic. Someone sneezed. Margaret and Malcolm snickered a laugh wondering.

Malcolm followed Sean's instruction and began to read his words.

"These are my dad's words, not mine. If he were here, he'd do a much better job of telling you all what he wanted to say. But, you're stuck with me. Bear with me, please." Malcolm cleared his throat, started.

"Folks, when I was alive I was always happy to go to a funeral, pay my respects and give thanks I wasn't the featured person. There was also no doubt of the profound affection I had for the deceased. There was also no doubt of the profound loss, and pain, their passing meant to me. But, now it is me laying here, and I must tell you, there is no doubt the pain and loss you might feel now, doesn't even come close to mine."

A note from Sean to Malcolm said for Malcolm to pause there, look up, and smile after reading that passage. He did as only he could. The mourners chuckled as Sean intended. Malcolm continued.

"Now I know most of you are here to pay your respects. Be honorable, kind citizens and support my loving ex-wife."

Margaret's head shot up. Then she got it, they all did. A roar of laughter was heard for miles it would seem. Malcolm went on.

"Deal's up, baby. Till death do us part, I'm a free man." Malcolm went on.

The crowd roared with a second burst of laughter. Malcolm continued.

"And as for the rest of you that are here wondering I'm really dead, well, I am. That's that, and you will too be someday. So watch yourself. I'm watchin you."

Nervous glances and guilty smiles were exchanged, Malcolm pressed ahead enjoying Sean's desired result.

"Now, one little bit of business. If you owed me any money, and you know who ya are, please give it to my beloved wife. Cash, no checks, that means you Jimmy! Now, if I owed you money, just come see me and I'll get if for you."

The rooms exploded. Tears of laughter and sorrow merged. Some ran to the bathroom or risked permanently embarrassment. Small towns have big ears. Everyone knew a lot about everyone else.

It went on like that for 20 minutes. Sean always knew how to make people happy, even in death. The funeral became legend at that moment and Sean immortalized.

Malcolm finished. The minister brought things back to solemn. Mourners sang two hymns. Margaret played a song on the piano– a favorite of Sean's. They assumed it would be Danny Boy.

"Another nickel"

Cal flung it. Master caught it major league style.

"You play?"

Master tightened his lips, looked back at him. The juke broadcast a tenor singing Danny Boy. Mother whistled.

The next day the burial finished with a short prayer Margaret wrote weeks earlier. Malcolm was again to be the proxy of his parents bidding. Standing by the suspended casket an old memory flashed. Malcolm couldn't hold back the smile. The crowd whispered what was so funny? If he told them they would have laughed in spite of themselves.

Malcolm remembered the time the three of them were in church one Sunday, at a christening. Sean had a few beforehand. After awhile he grew tired and pretty bored with the proceedings. Frustrated, hungry and somewhat....well drunk, he unknowingly uttered

"Abra Kadabra, Alakazam, make this kid a Christian, as fast as you can." Mucous landed on Malcolm's smiling lip, Margaret's elbow found Sean's rib.

Malcolm choked back the smile and started.

"And the Angels waited for you in the shadows. Sent gently to take your last mortal breath and embrace your eternal soul. The end of this life danced in sweet surrender. When it was time they wrapped you in a soft cloak and walked with you through Shepherd's walk. The place of renewed ground, where the fog is heaven coming to you.

In the coming winter, the new, fallen snow will blanket you in the good earth. Warm you as much as the sun, embrace you as a mother's arm does her child, and shield you from all harm. Welcome the mist. Rejoice in the tingling touch of its season. All will last but a moment, just one brief, tender moment as the guardians shepherd your soul."

The mourner's wept.

Danny Boy ended. Weeping bobble heads finally understood. Malcolm was to become who he must, go through what he must. They swept away knowing more. Drained, Cal went to sleep. Tonight's quest to find Malcolm and learn what happened that day in the bar, ended.

"Things, was rooolin." Sean would say.

The town clock ticked to 3 a.m., Monday September the 4th, 2009. Cal's watch did as well, in reverse. 5:10 p.m. Tuesday August 29, 2009. Mother sat in the shadows muttering about how hard it was to keep score.

# TWENTY

Master whistled.

~

Tim, with his pinkish skin did the best he could. Filling in wasn't easy. "Different as thunder and lightning they were," Margaret said. Sean could fix anything mechanical. Tried to teach Malcolm, but wasn't in him. "Other abilities, other talent's," Margaret use to soothe. She knew, only too well.

Margaret's older brother, Tim, a retired soldier, came from a lineage of soldiers, accomplished horseman, hunters, and lethal marksmen. He could not replace Sean. Didn't try, wasn't meant to. Malcolm needed to learn something's Sean never could teach him.

"One heck of a shot he is," all said about Tim. Army snipers required talent, discipline and training. He left his mark. Locals came to Tim wanting him to teach their kids how to.

"You want him, or her, to pick a hair off a bug's ass, at thousand yards?" Tim asked, saving the parents the trouble of a stumbling request.

If Tim thought you had the talent, he would provide the training, as long as you were willing to pay the price. Training was tough. None stood up to it; they tried, but the talent pool was not so good, except for one.

Malcolm changed. On a cold afternoon he dropped his bicycle with, baseball cards clothespin attached it in hay in the barn, for good. Sean's BSA 441 Victor was his own. His toy guns lay in his toy chest, swapped for the real ones Uncle Tim taught him to use.

"Teeeeeeedious, what in this world does this have to do with anything?"

"Shut up you old goat. You'll see, you, will, see. Keep your eyes on the floor. You will see."

"I will, and do see. Do you, friend? Remember your past, live in present, look forward to the future."

"What does that have to do with anything? All I get is riddles, you old bastard."

"Old bastard is it then, hmm boy? You will see, yes. You will see." Master doubled over. His hood flipped over his head of long locks.

Cal maneuvered reading himself to lunge. Mother intervened, held Master by his cloak. Sad faced Bobbles handed their bets back to one another.

"Set up again? This is getting ridiculous. Am I ever going to win?" Cal gritted his teeth.

Master poked his head out from the shadow, bottom lip curled over his top. Smiling a ruby colored carnival clown smile. Forcefully he pulled his lower jaw down making a suction smacking noise.

"UH, that would be a no." Master childishly skipped in and out of the shadows.

Cal fell, grabbed his chairs arm and crawled in it. Stretched legs crossed at the ankles. Arms draped over the chairs arms. For the first time since he arrived at Fate he was too fatigued to go on.

Show time but I'm out of gas, Cal worried. "I need help," he whispered. "Okay all, now's your shot, your time to cough up what you know."

Cal stood as if he found the writers ink. His mostly seamed shut eyes directed an extended hand with upturned curled palm and pointed to Farmer. He pulled his arm back toward himself beckoning Farmer forward.

"Come here, front and center. Farmer Vaughn, you're on." Cal remembered college drama class.

Startled, nervous Farmer shook his head, no. Drool flew. Others ducked, Reddy wiped.

"Nnnnnohh, I,I,I, I'm ill p-p-prepared to ra-ra-run the class."

"Come on, you can do it. It's easy." Others harmonized encouragement.

"Come, my good man. Everyone has to help now. I think it, you say it," Cal sighed, slipping to his chair.

Farmer nodded. He panicky stood, fixed the straps of his overalls and then heel thudded his work boots directly in front of the class. Master coughed. Facing the others, he broke his silence.

Days became weeks, weeks months. Tim honed Malcolm's skills. He succeeded in horsemanship, better as a hunter, but excelled at his place, marksmanship. The county now had two to be feared.

Time moved on, the world changed. A storm in Southeast Asia raged torrentially. Styles changed. A smudge of facial hair grew above Malcolm's upper lip. His hair grew shoulder length he wore in a ponytail. Mom said it was okay. Dad wouldn't. Tim called him a girl, ruffled Malcolm. He grabbed for his rifle. Tim went for his. Malcolm looked, thought better and put it back in the kitchen corner. Margaret laughed. Watching them remembered her of the day in the barn when she thought Sean whipped Malcolm. The days over mothering him were over. She knew it was coming the morning when Malcolm and Hank climbed the hill with the kite. Greater forces stepped in.

I remember one day Malcolm stopped his occasional mischief, firing flaming arrows into my barn. We think Hank was really to blame though. Stephanie did like to brag to us how Malcolm showed off around her. She said once he put lighter fluid in his mouth, and then spat it out across a lit cigarette lighter flame becoming a human flame thrower. Nuts I'd call him. She'd twinkle, laugh. Even made him do it for me to prove he did it. I shook my head. This was my daughter's boyfriend? Another time she proudly announced Georgie, and Malcolm, had stopped cherry bomb fishing in the pond by the willows. I sighed, and worried what was going on.

We knew Malcolm had the best relationship with his mom. He'd ask her a question, sometimes about life and she's answer in French Stephanie told us.

"Vous trouverez votre raison d'être... Cherchez-le, C'est là..."You will find your reason for being. Look for it. It is there. She'd answer

Malcolm scratched his prickly chin repeating, votre raison d'être. Home schooled French lessons a handed down gift from Margaret's mom.

"Ooooooooooooooooo" The bobbles harmonized waking from their daytime naps behind the wall. Farmer glared, Mother laughed. He continued.

Knee high stalks of corn started their climb to the sky. Malcolm stretched also the summer of 1964. He grew alright, in many ways, we saw him a lot around the house. He shunned the smaller Victor motorcycle for Sean's BSA Gold Star. Who wouldn't have? When he wasn't showing off, spinning its wheels for Stephanie, we watched him terrorize Spirit Trail Road. Came natural, in his blood after all, Tim told us.

That picture of him sitting on the Gold Star, hanging on the wall next to the bars mirror, was taken days after the swap. The Victor came back into his life, later. Good transportation in a crowded place.

Malcolm told my daughter Stephanie one day Tim took him aside. He said Tim told him about his and Mom's side of the family. Margaret never spoke of them. He said there's something you should know about them. It'll help you know, who they are, and who you are. Malcolm concentrated, stroked his bottom lip with three finger tips from his left hand. His eyes grabbed Tim's. It was scary. There, all of you Bobbles, Cal also. See them, on the floor. Watch them on the floor.

"Malcolm, you come from a long line of fighters. Not boxers and such, though they all could, and would and by the way your daddy was a pretty good one. But on our side, we were the warriors, the soldiers. Back a long, long ways, in their homelands, and in this new land. One of your Great Grand Daddy's fought in the American Revolution. Said he was a drummer boy for a short while at first. Then he lied. They gave him a gun, and he took to shooting naturally. Marched all over the country, and never got hurt. His kids, theirs, all in some war ever since. Till then no one got killed. Now your Grand Daddy, my and moms dad, never came home from where they sent him. But they never found his body either. So, we just figured he liked it there, and stayed." Malcolm thought about it, got it and laughed saying, "yeah that school teacher Grandma musta made him nuts." Tim howled.

"Eeee-nough, my heavens, you fatigue me to no end my friend." Master sauced around.

"He's getting to it," Cal blindly answered, waving his arms, mocking Master.

"Ssshhhh" said the alto.

"Ssshhhh," the tenor.

"Ssshhhh," the soprano chimed in.

"Ssshhhh," Sammie added.

"All, of you, listen. Do not mistake my kindness, and generosity, for stupidity. That would be a serious mistake." Master wagged his favorite pointy index finger. The Bobbles hunkered.

"I said, he'll get to it." Maestro Cal raised his hands and nudged Farmer.

The Barfly Bobbles watched mute quiet, the last thing they needed was to be drawn in to this exchange. Especially knowing Master most probably hadn't eaten.

"A nickel please. Another nickel—music cannot stop—quickly now quuiiccckkkly."

Sleepily, Cal robotically flung one. Master spun it on its edge. It rattled rolling down the chute. Wurlitzer plucked a bluesy, sad ballad. The crowd sighed. Mother whistled. Farmer continued.

"On a rainy day I, I, I...."

Farmer stammered, coughed, folded at his waist. His eyes welled. Mary toed to his rescue, caught his trembling left hand in hers. As a blind man he walked with her, weeping. The bar flies shrouded him. The surrounding misty cocoon, parted. Farmer sat alone, wet eyed, sighing, but feeling better. Family counts.

Maestro Cal nodded to Sammie. Sammie leapt over his rightful place behind the bar screaming show time. Facing the crowd the spotlight lit him in his brown, sleeveless criss cross patterned tattered sweater. No one knew why he wore it in the summer.

Sammie, the new authority demanded their full attention. His finger took attendance while his smiling face spun left, and then right. The harsh light from the spot brightened the floor, made him wince. Sammie's adjusting eyes widened. Master whistled.

The Vaughn family's pickup truck rolled down Snake Hill Road on a rainy Sunday afternoon in 1965. Farmer Vaughn drove. Mrs. Vaughn sat by his side, snuggled between him and Stephanie, who sat squished against the passenger door, door handle jabbing her in the ribs. She daydreamed about Malcolm through the trucks windshield near Sunbeams hill. No seat belts, or air bags but the truck did have a metal dash. The road was a wet sloppy mud slide mess. The trucks wipers squeaked back and forth.

Sister lightning threw a jolting bolt. One likely borrowed from Zeus. It ripped the sky white, shook earth and struck a one large oak bordering the right side of Snake Hill Road as you descended. The tree split in the middle. Gutted, it elliptically spun a few times falling toward the road. Farmer Vaughn's right eye caught the action. Instinctively he veered away from where he guessed it would fall.

Crack, it smacked the road. The shattered trunk exploded. Limbs and bark flew. A cloud of chipped wood and debris filled the air shielding Farmer Vaughn's vision. He didn't see the smooth heads of the elf rocks, exposed by the rain, and the ruts from the dinosaur treads. Too much for the old trucks suspension she flipped. They rolled over three times down the hill. Farmer, and his wife, heads rapped together. Hers found the metal dash. Farmer's banged the unpadded steering wheel. The rear view mirror snapped off and fell to the floor. Like marionettes dancing their arms and legs flailed. Blood speckled the interior.

Finally, after skidding on the trucks roof for a length, they came to rest in a ditch. Upside down, turkey style, like so many before all four wheels spun. Threatening smoke warned spewing out from the under the engine hood. Neighbors traveling behind them saw all, slapped their truck into park and raced.

The three were alive, but hurt. Farmer Vaughn, the luckiest, with minor cuts and scrapes. His missus suffered worse. She took out the rear view mirror. Plastic surgery would be needed. Stephanie wasn't cut, didn't bleed, but wasn't conscious. Jesse the ambulance made some money that day.

Days later Mrs. Vaughn was discharged from the hospital. She joined her husband who stayed only over night. Stephanie lay unconsciousness, internal bleeding. The Doc's did what they could do. All anyone could do now was hope. The Vaughn's visited daily. Malcolm and Margaret did as well. During visiting hours each of the four went into her room, one at a time, and spoke to her as if she was awake. Weeks passed.

On a Saturday, late afternoon, thunder rolled into the county. Margaret, stood in Shepherd's Walk, looked up, winced. She grabbed Malcolm. They raced in their old pick up to the hospital. Mr. and Mrs. Vaughn, with their pale stark faces, were just leaving. Passing each other Margaret nodded, and they, gently back. Nothing was said. Margaret went in Stephanie's room first. She lay there, thinner than ever, her breathing labored. Margaret bent and whispered in Stephanie's ear. Then stood and watched. Stephanie lay still offering no response. Margaret waited another minute, nothing. She looked out the hospital room window. Then back at Stephanie. Margaret turned board stiff. Her eyes widened, her head sank in a bow and nodded looking outside.

Margaret gracefully walked to the waiting room to see Malcolm. He sat waiting his turn, a magazine white knuckled clutched. She bent. Perfume filled his nostrils dampening some of the hospitals caustic disinfectant aroma.

"Time to say good-bye," she said.

"Sssheee wants you to, fix her pillow."

Margaret's heart pounded. She didn't know about the fix my pillow game he and Stephanie played but felt danger. Malcolm's eyelids parted. Stiff legged he shuffled his farm boots across the white tile floor. Wearing a man's stone face he opened Stephanie's hospital room's large oak door. It snapped closed with a crisp metallic latch clack, and a wooden crack. He kissed her for a last time, fixed her pillow. Her legs kicked once, twice. A minute later he walked out, cold, wet eyed, pale as a ghost. The eerie stare on his face never seemed to go away. Her funeral was in few days.

Sammie was balling, and exhausted. Closed eyed Maestro Cal waved his hand for him to go. Limply his legs carried him back behind the bar with his folded head.

That night came to an early end. All bobble's sulked, grief stricken. They didn't know. Not even Farmer. Master was heard sniffling. Inconsolable Farmer begged to be forgiven crying over and over again....There was nothing I could do, nothing I could do.

Puffiness, around his eyes, flattened. Raspy Reddy Red stood at his side doing what she could. Matron glared. Cal went to bed wishing for a drink, thinking this was getting tougher, saying, "Where the h–, is this Malcolm?"

"Closer, much closer Son." Master said.

The town clock ticked to 1:30 a.m., Tuesday, September 5. Cal's confused watch said Tuesday also, but 5 p.m., August 29, 2009

# Twenty-One

Afternoon wind woke. Loose dirt spun to mini twisters and skidded like tops across the dry town road and dirt lawn. Cal stood on the concrete porch floor looking out, readying himself for his trip to Snake Hill Roads mountain top.

"Don't you go anywhere yet mister. You stay put." Mother came running out of the shop hollering across the alleyway.

"If you wwwwish to, you may pass on your trip today." Stuttering, she offered Cal a hall pass.

He pressed his lips together.

"Kinda like em Mother, gives me a chance to think, and flirt with that winking cow out there."

Mother laughed, wriggled her shoulder in it's a "your call" move.

Cal stuffed Old Blue's key in his pants right front pocket, then powdered the wings with dust from his stroll. He stretched out on a small patch of dry uncut grass about thirty yards from the town square, in a treed area. Restless, he squiggled to get a clear view of the sky. Interlocking fingers wove his hands together in a cradle that supported his head. He looked out into the great wide ocean above. Sun's rays blanketed him, warmed aching bones, and lost him in space. A light chest sank. Exhaling, he sighed, and then turned his attention to the town square with the town bell. Next to the clock, it hung above the monument in tribute to fallen soldiers. It rang only when a new name chiseled to its face. Consciousness yielded to daydreams, and a simple childhood pleasure of cloud, picture gazing.

"There's one, and another. Ha, ha, that one looks like a bust of Lincoln. Hey, that looks like that smartass cow."

The day streaked by. Early evening sun dipped. Cal pressed his knees into service. Strolling back toward the bake shop he swiped a nervous glance at the town's time piece. The hands spun to 6:30 p.m. Tuesday, September 5, 2009. His backward ticking wristwatch disagreed, 4:55 p.m., Tuesday, August 29, 2009. Cal shook his head, and two skipped to a sprint.

Neat counted. He twisted left, right, stretching to brush straw grass off his back with reclaimed limberness. Most fell off his arms, sides and pants before he skipped over the bakery's door saddle.

"How's the Pixie Dust?"

Mother didn't laugh. Absent, her warm, sparklingly smile. In its place, a chest covered in flour, fiery seriousness etched in her eyes.

She nodded once toward a lonely chair sitting in a corner. Taken as more than a suggestion, concerned curious wide eyed Cal slid in it.

"My turn," Mother said. "My turn to tell you, part of the story you seek. We won't need the coins here."

"But Mas—"

"–Never mind him."

Cal remembered his mom. Nodded, whatever you say in a grin. He squirmed in his seat awaiting torture. Mother began-

"One Sunday, morning brought a gray sky. Malcolm's cleverness bordered on deviousness from time to time. Today figured to be one of those times, gray sky or not. His secret plan, set weeks ago, hatched.

Part one, a fake sick ploy, always a legitimate excuse from church. The ever elusive, hard to disprove, convenient stomach ache the feigned illness. Margaret took the bait. Knew he had a lot of church since Stephanie's burial. That Sunday Church would be an all day affair, Baptism day, with the usual boring cookout afterwards. Margaret feared an older Malcolm might take a page out of his father's book regarding baptisms, without being drunk. She granted him the pass he wanted, on a day that gave him the time he needed.

He lay on the couch carrying the fake sick act on the outside, gleeful on the inside. Mom and Uncle Tim would be gone for hours.

His mind raced. Mother Margaret gave Malcolm one last, distrustful, look.

"Stay put Malkie. No going out. No friends, no nuthin." Intentional poor grammar used to make a point, Mothers point.

"Ohhhh" sales jobbed from his lips. He held his stomach.

Curled up he poured it on from his position on the green and brown flower patterned worn tattered couch. It's stuffing escaping. Not too much to keep them home though. He nodded a final fake wince completing the compelling last act of his one boy play.

"I'm too weak. Don't worry about that mom." His eye lids fluttered closed.

"Hmmmmm," intuition spoke. She knew her son. Knew him a con artist at times but let he doubts go. Shook her head, and pushed the green kitchen screen door open.

Tim waited for her in the pickup with the engine running. He bellowed "get moving, quickly. We're late." The two drove down the dirt farm road in the old white Ford F150 pickup. A dirt driveway, that hadn't been oiled since the passing of Sean. The truck bounced. Its rear wheels hopped kicking up clouds of dust. The passenger side front wheel's silver baby moon hub cap was missing. Probably in a ditch somewhere thanks to road rut, or an elf's head. Malcolm listened to them drive away but stayed put, just in case.

Off to church on the newly asphalt paved two lane country road. It bordered their property in the front. Some of the road paving was done. Some wasn't. The parts not completed were left with ruts and oiled dirt, as paving a very slow process in those parts. Late morning sun chased gray skies that Sunday. It also baked the partially completed new road surface. Pungent odor unmistakably reminded everyone country life was changing, forever, and so was Malcolm.

"Catching up with the city folks," Margaret remembered Sean chuckling, flashing glinting eyes.

"We'll be all caught up soon," she said sitting in the passenger seat, looking out the window at the sky.

"Huh?" Tim said.

"Never mind," she held up her hand.

Use to be the bar only had twelve in it at the max. If there was tirteen den a stranger was in town. Margaret broke out laughing remembering that one.

"Huh? Whaaa–," Tim said.

"Hey Tim, you notice how the town's grown?"

"I guess. Mostly city folks I think. Head count at the bar grew."

Malcolm sat up anxious as the school boy he was. Part one of his plan was a complete success. He listened, waiting. Then waited some more being sure they didn't double back.

"Dad caught me that way."

He had two things he could do, wrestled with both. Dig out the nudie magazine of Sean's he found hid in the barn or, an adventure. He figured he had time for both, but the magazine would come out later.

Time ticked. Malcolm sat up ready to go, ready to grow into manhood, without dad. Plus it just seemed like fun. He stretched, reached for his new jeans properly crumpled on the floor. On they went. Chore boots laced. A prized Gene Autry Cowboy shirt tucked in, pearl like buttons snapped closed. Never fancy Malcolm loved cowboy shirts, and bowling shirts. You have to like something. It was an appropriate uniform in deed.

He flew across the living room floor, knocked into a table. The lamp wobbled. He grabbed it in a- nick- of- time. Speed built through the swinging door into the very country kitchen aiming toward the screen back door. He flipped unhooked hook hanging on the green screened kitchen door, pushed one foot between the door and frame. A skill well choreographed on his way late for school. A misplaced finger missed its mark. The screen door's screen earned another hole. Malcolm withdrew his finger from the punctured screens new wound. He twirled dragging his other foot outside, elbow held tight to his body.

Boyish legs matched to booted feet, leapt, stretched, and clawed lifeless dusty dirt. Why Margaret called it Shepherd's walk remained a mystery. The distance to the barn closed in a cloud of Shepherds dust. Right handedly he grabbed the handle and dragged the cranky barn door open. Malcolm shot inside. In front of the entrance to the horse stall he came to a shuddering halt. The bedroom of the Vincent!

"Respect—respect her," dad taught.

"She's a beauty, we know. Not to be careless with. At times, a beast not from here," he went on.

Malcolm's chest swelled with held air. He went into the stall. Winters Eve stood proud on its stand poised, ready for action with its next rider. If it could have whinnied it would have showing off its jet black fuel tank, detailed with gleaming wisps of chrome. Winters Eve titled on it in feathery whitish gray script on both sides of the tank. Ferocious, menacing, it beckoned anyone to come closer for a better look. Malcolm was anyone. He mentally rehearsed starting it for weeks earlier. In its aura he lapsed in a daydream remembering Dads lessons how to—.

"Malcolm lad, this is for this. This is for fuel–, and that is–." So it went on. He knew everything about this bike there was to know. Everything, except what it would be like riding it himself.

"It can be a tough job to get her to start on cold marnings Malcolm, typical woman." Sean added cowardly looking around making sure Margaret wasn't in ear shot. He never decided whether Winters Eve was male or female flip flopping between nominations. It made no difference.

Over and over Malcolm replayed dad's tutelage about the making and development of this motorcycle, and its mechanics. Gear shift here—front brake there—rear brake there—clutch here. Kick start-lights.

"The gents started the company—well they were a couple of lad's–." Malcolm remembered Sean's speech. That was then but now, was now, Malcolm spoke aloud.

Malcolm was right where he shouldn't have been. Dad was gone, temptation too great. Rightfully his now he justified, but justice had nothing to do with it. Bring on the apple.

Malcolm's heart furiously pumped. Adrenaline drilled all the way to his finger tips. He stood closer along side of the Vincent. His right hand, his pitching hand he called it, he never pitched much but liked the idea, pressed palm down flat in the middle of the large single seat. Overloaded trembling fingers tapped the fuel tank. Pressure mounted. He thought his eyes would pop. "You could almost feel the engines horses stomping their hooves, and whinnying as you got close to it," Sean told Malkie one day with a twinkled wink.

~

"Malcolm, Malcolm, Malcolm," the Bobble Heads, tenors, alto, soprano, bass's and Sammie shouted in unison from inside the bars walls.

"Only his mother, Margaret could call him Malkie! A mother's right!" They added.

Mother turned from Cal. Glared out the door. The uninvited chorus behind the bars walls went eerily quiet. Whispered stuttering replaced harmony. They remembered who they interrupted. Mother knew something, about mothers, and their rights. She turned to Cal and went on.

~

Some fear set in, but would Maaaaalllllcolm—- Mother paused, looked around.

—.honorable son of Margaret and Sean, tempt fate? A good boy overall, but had a laser where some had a gleam. He loved television westerns. Started horse-back riding early and became skillful, just not as good as Sali, or Georgie. Like a cowboy climbing on a horse Malcolm gripped the Vincent's gleaming chrome handle bars. Left hand- left grip, right hand gripped the right throttle grip. His left foot pressed on the left foot rest peg and he threw his right leg over Dads dream. He sat on the wide black seat, released the left grip and left hand petted the fuel tank.

"Maybe today my friend, maybe today," he spoke out loud. Then his right hand gently twisted the throttle.

"Yes maybe today, maybe today," He said imagining the wind in his face. He thought Dad won't mind, if I try to start it. The Vincent, the one Sean called Winters Eve. Always off limits without his presence. Dad wasn't around. So with some very bad reasoning Malcolm pressed on. Press on the kick-start he must. Definitely today fired in his soul. Let's see now, where was that carburetor primer? Ah here it is he remembered. His pitching hand delicate fingers gently pressed the small fuel tickler, some called the bulb. It force fed fuel to the carburetor.

"Switch on." Malcolm mimicked lines pilots barked out in the old WWII war movies.

The Vincent, the Victor and the Gold Star, were always backed into the stall. In case, of a need, for a quick getaway Sean would fun. Meaning, get fast out before Mom could stop him. As a result, the first thing anyone saw when first entering the stall was the Vincent's large gleaming headlight.

Upright on the seat Malcolm leaned looking at the large speedometer fastened in front of the handle bars. He remembered the few lessons Sean gave him on how the starting routine went. Malcolm was a very quick study in class, that wasn't about the use of symbolism in literature.

"I'm tired Cal. It's dark now." Mothers face unusually strained. Cal wrinkled his brow thinking it didn't seem too bad of a story. She nodded towards the door.

"Finish it inside. You'll finish it inside. I'm tired now. Maybe I'll see you later. By the way a white dove had been hanging around the McKeon's farm."

Cal winced, cocked his head. On his way he saw the town clock, 8:30 p.m., Tuesday, September 5, 2009. His wristwatch barely moved, 4:54 p.m., Tuesday, August 29, 2009. He raced, over the saddle and backbone pounded in his chair. Master tapped his shoe. Someone stole his thunder, and he had no say in it, at all.

"Nickel quickly."

Cal's hand slid, found the first hole, finger probed through the gas tank of a 441 Victor. A hangman's noose tightened. It hurt shutting off the blood. The walls energy flowed. Cal, up to it for a moment, frightened, resisted. Twenty ticks ticked. When it was all over he sat straight leg spread eagled, sprawled in the low backed wooden chair. The tips of his wings pointed skyward, still covered with the leftover dry grass of the town square.

The nickel bought a rock piece featuring a raspy guitar. The spot lit the floor. All bobbles were back from their rest, but embarrassed for interrupting Mother. Attentively they waited. Curious opened wide, wanting to learn more. Fidgety mouths wanted to tell more. Mother coughed. Cal stood.

The Vincent thumped, vibrated, and then stalled. Unspent fuel turned into thick black smoke pouring out of its tail pipes.

"Over choked, she was over choked," Malcolm remembered his dad telling him if he saw that.

Malcolm adjusted the choke. The Vincent thanked him with a vibrating purr. The exhaust corrected its color. Malcolm pulled in the clutch; toe pressed the gear lever and right hand feathered some throttle. Forcing his will he gradually let the clutch lever slip from his left finger tips. The engine and transmission shook hands. Malcolm, alone atop the Vincent for the first time, shot past the stalls gate, out of the barn and blurred down the farm road in a trail of dust. Dirt and gravel rooster tailed behind them. The farm road was covered in record time. He hung on for dear life, a junior jockey riding a fine race horse. He made an unsure left and sped off down the country road.

In the three minutes it took for him to reach the county road he knew. This was going to be different. The other two bikes sat dejected on their stands. The Vincent's power was not a well guarded secret. Any rider was immediately advised of throttle misuse. Sean added a few of his special touches. It ran better than new, and a lot faster.

Inexperience showed. Malcolm unsteadily rode. The Vincent wobbled, pulled left and then drifted right as if a horse wishing to throw its rider. His balance was off. A minor throttle mistake could be dangerous. His heart pumped. Smartly, he stopped and put his quaking feet to the ground. Composure lacked. He remembered Tim's horseback riding lessons, one very important one in particular. Never let the horse control you. Riders must take control.

Dad's taught gently, squeeze this. Press this hard—twist the throttle, let off. Malcolm siphoned some air. Holding it, he looked at the sky, then back down at the Speedo. He took off. This time in a divine moment as if he were born to it. Perfectly balanced he confidently pushed his steed past the half mile marker of the stinking paved country road on his way to the top of Snake Hill Road. Speed built, trees blurred. No one recently rode anything this fast past them. Not since Sean. Malcolm lost track of time and speed. He didn't know it at the time but he blew past Sean's best time ever. Recklessly he rode a mighty jockey at breakneck speeds. Guitar whines filtered through the forest encouraging him, pressing him to quickly morph into the man he needed to be. Mother Nature ordained he shed his innocence. Plans were made for him.

Wind wildly whistled. Malcolm's ears flapped. He reached a patch of forest on his right. The recurring melody heard first when pummeled by the storm with Hank, followed him warmed his ears. The lyrics were clearer. "Four horsemen came—"

Then silence.

Malcolm thought no hands would be fun. He hit a bump. Re-thought it, hands were an absolute necessity. Man and motorcycle, one with the universe, sped on their way to the top of Snake Hill. Winter's Eve needle- threaded, knowing exactly where to go, when to slow, and when to go full bore.

"Lean a little more in the turns, son," came to him. He thought the Vincent schooled him.

I can do it, he thought.

Tire flesh gripped fresh laid asphalt. The Vincent flew. Grinning, Malcolm hung on. Not a moment of this thrill ride to be missed. The bike lay left in the soft twists of the road, and then right as it bent right. The stretch had had some of the best essess a rider could ask for. Down the straightaway he cracked the throttle. The wind whipped his eyes to tears of joy.

The engine spun the chain hooked to the back wheel. The back tire pressed, and dug. The Vincent squatted, and then forcefully climbed the Snake Hill Roads steep incline. At its peak Malcolm's left hand clamped the clutch lever disengaging the transmission from the engine. His right pulled the right lever applying the front brake. The Vincent's engine sang in a baritone rumble eagerly awaiting its next command. Malcolm faced the valley that took my heart. He straddled the bike where the gas tank met the seat. Leaning forward he could barely hold the bike steady with worn work boot toes scraping the ground.

Malcolm panted. He rested for ten ticks looking out over the Valley. Then in one of his trademark daydreams he imagined he and his band of brothers playing race with the devil, the battle of the cows, and leaked the only tears allowed thinking about Stephanie. He remembered Stephanie's well tossed rock, their first kiss. His lips pursed a smile. The last day in the hospital room bubbled up and then he turned stone cold.

Malcolm toe pushed the Vincent forward as he had done so many times on his bicycle. But, this was no bicycle. They headed down Snake Hill Road's winding turns. The Vincent's weight, power, torque and thrust were very difficult to control. First turn, an easy soft left. Next, a twisting right turn that hooked back into a tighter left. After three of each, the turns stabilized. Malcolm, cautiously and gracefully negotiated each hook of the road he knew so well. No quaking, tipping or wobbling. Smooth and steady, Sean taught him well.

Confidence is earned and Malcolm earned his. He pushed the bike. The front wheel cocked sharply sliding it through the turns. A technique he learned atop his bicycle. The rear wheel skidded and dragged behind him. When they changed directions, Malcolm, the seasoned racer, cocked the front tire in the other direction. A lot of mass to control, but control it he did, as if born to it.

Conditions worsened. Mud caked grooves left from the dinosaur machines hopped the bikes wheels. The front was bad, the rear was worse. Farm boot soles slapped the ground, steadying his path as they slid through the twisty turns. Dirt and gravel flew. Malcolm hung on. Kept the bike on the ground but began to struggle. Hang on, only two turns left before straight to potbelly bottom Malcolm thought. He sensed success. Smiling he thought of dangling his feet in the pond, a rest, and more memories revisited.

A quick right, then, only a few yards dead ahead a large black branch from nowhere lay across the road. It wasn't there five ticks ago. Malcolm blinked. The branch moved. Not a branch but the legendary watcher of the hill. The notorious mythical fire-hose thick black snake folklore said lived there.

The Vincent's front tire struck the fat snake, it coiled in raging helix, the front wheel pointed skyward. The rear-wheel hopped as if a purposeful bouncing wheelie stunt. Malcolm hung on. Airborne the bike pranced for five ticks, the engine screamed. Malcolm had been on horses when the reared up on their hind legs. This was nothing like that. The rear chrome wire wheel regained its grip on the road. Malcolm hands stayed fastened to the handle bar grips. Until that point Malcolm made a few mistakes.

That run of luck was over. He made one, a big one. His right hand held tightly to the right grip on the handle bar. It is also the throttle. When the Vincent landed from its brief flight Malcolm jarred. He held the grip, the throttle, too tightly. Accidentally he twisted it, wide open. You might as well have switched a fine stallion. All of the Vincent's horses released. Malcolm tried to hang on, but a loose bike, and a racing engine, equaled a bad combination.

Sunbeam, Stephanie's prized pet cow, watched the circus act from behind the fence. You couldn't be sure whether she was happy or sad about the sight. Malcolm and company did torment them so. The Vincent torque twisted left, and then right as if a young bronco was being broke. Malcolm valiantly tried to correct the behavior but to no avail. Rearing again, Winters Eve stood on its back wheel prancing, and then started to wobble in a poor elliptical spin.

Malcolm floated in and out of consciousness in the mayhem. He saw himself atop a horse, dressed in a revolutionary soldiers officers clothing, holding the reigns of a falling gunshot horse, his boot caught in the stirrup.

He snapped back. The bike crashed to the mud caked road, fishtailed and lay over, slid skid, and bounced on one side. Then flipped to the other and tumbled, crashing down the hill. The uncontrolled engine raced to sure seizure. Confused, Malcolm wasn't sure what was dying. Was it the whinnying screams of a horse, or the bikes runaway engine? They harmonized so. Instinctively his chore boots looked for the ground as the momentum slowed. Sad he ruined Dad's third love he tearfully tried to hold the bike up. To no avail and visions of Sean being furious raced through his head. How was he ever going to explain this?

In the final slide the rear wheel toothed chain sprocket grabbed Malcolm's jean pant leg, pinched the material between the chain and itself. Malcolm was clamped to the bike, like the baseball cards, or a mouse by its wire jailer. The Vincent spun, Malcolm with it. Centrifugal force whipped the great amusement park ride, but no one here was amused. Each spin forcefully flung each in opposite directions. The Vincent's proud beautiful headlight caught an elf head. Glass flew. The chrome bezel that held it in place mangled, as if aluminum foil.

The twister crash ended. The Vincent's runaway engine raced to a stumbling halt. A glass, metal and flesh crumb trail lay in aftermath. It was the worst of dances. Skin on the inside of Malcolm's left ankle was now, and forever, tattooed by the red hot exhaust pipe leaving its indelible mark. The Vincent lay scraped, bent, and crumpled. Its beauty dismissed. The handle bars faced the opposite direction of the bent wire front wheel. Malcolm drifted in and out of consciousness. In dreamland he walked in a path of lush gardens. Flanking his sides were crepe myrtles, oleanders. Flowers petals showered him in their colors. Semi-consciousness returned. He looked around. World War II jeeps, tanks and armored vehicles passed him by in his daze. Men shouted to him to get up. Get back in the ranks. Pinned to the bike he lay in the same ditch that stopped the Vaughn's truck. His eyes fluttered. This time his stomach ached– for real. It was a terrible bloody accident.

The keeper of the hill—the big black snake –slithered quickly towards its prey. Malcolm was in his worst of all predicaments. Dazed, damaged and trapped to the bike, a partial cripple unable to move, or defend. The clever snake pursued, manipulated into the ditch. A ditch well hidden, hardly anyone would see, and rarely a passerby that time of day.

Helpless, he awaited for what he thought was his deserved, fate. The snake closed to within a few yards, mouth open, fangs bared and protruding. It lunged. One fang caught the heavy denim jean, piercing it, slightly penetrating his leg. Venom started to flow. The new resident at the farm, a white dove, flew like a hawk towards the scene. The big black snake released its fang sensing danger and an approaching foe. The dove couldn't win this battle but could distract the snake. A taunting strategy was battle on.

The suicidal bird, dive-bomb dove bulleting at the snake. Bravely, the puff of white pecked, and then darted off. It circled back for another assault. The snake, the watcher of the hill, tired. It had enough, paused, coiled and waited. The serpent, like a loose fire hose, lunged at the dove in flight. Missing, it angrily waited for a second chance. The next attack would not come from the dove. The hissing angry snake didn't see the large hawk high above. It watched the scene below, waited, circled with talons razor sharp, and readied.

Malcolm made a big mistake that day. The culprit snake did as well. Last seen the snake fled, the Hawk after it in hot pursuit, talons barred, grabbing, slashing and clawing at it. Terrified, the bully devil snake slithered into the tall hiding grass. It must have been panting.

Malcolm's luck finally improved. Farmer and Mrs. Vaughn were just coming home from the church Malcolm should have been at. They saw the carnage. Jesse the Ambulance was not quite out of business yet. Anyone seeing him in the ditch would have thought the undertaker would have her work cut out for her.

He squinted trying to open them. Everything seemed to be white, bright white but no tunnel. A hospitals look. That's where Jesse carried what remained of his teen body. Pant-less, covered in blood from top to bottom, Malcolm looked like a well used paint can. The Vincent's teeth left chewing its rider's pants.

Uncle Tim worried Margaret couldn't take losing both of them. If so, she'd cry for the rest of her numbered days. A certain waste of such a young innocent life was spent recklessly in one afternoon of poor judgment. It happens. But it wasn't to be. Malcolm had things to do.

What was left of the Vincent, Sean's Winters Eve, was tow truck retrieved with collected severed parts. Unceremoniously, Margaret had it placed back into the stall it shot out of only a few short hours ago. There it stayed, bent and broken in its stall. A tomb locked shut.

The bobbles nodded to each other in amazement, then smoked into their holes. A grinning Master filed his nails feigning disinterest. The music shut off. The light on the floor went to black. Cal fell over but before he hit the floor, Mother and Master grabbed him by his arms. They looked at each other nodding now was the time. They flew him to bed. He curled in a ball.

Master leaned over Cal, and whispered–.

"A classic star doth ye search for, in rhyme, on Earth and Heaven. Father, mine enemies thrice struck. Mine entrails slashed. Whilst I lay stuck, in this bloody bog, slain but yet to perish, on fragments of parchments my reed pen with bloods ink etch final words, waiting. I pray that by day's end, I may find all that's hidden within ye. Darkness creeps amongst thine dead. Weak and cold I grow.

Heaven, I beseech ye. Hear mine plea. Almighty God, mercifully blow the wind, let the reeds whistles call your dark Angles to this field of glory.

Come, fetch me, and mine twelve enemies in life, brothers in death, imperfect souls.

Amen"

Master backed away. The clock in the square said it was early Wednesday morning September 6, and struck 2:30 a.m., Cal's watch ticked to 4:30 p.m., still Tuesday, August the 29, 2009.

"I know that, where's it from, I know that. Shakespeare?"

"No, but yes, of course you know where from. Sleep my Prince. Breathe in deeply the night air, and it will come to you. It blows in the wind. We'll talk in the bakeshop later."

# Twenty-Two

"Hey, watch it. Be careful would ya. What's that all about anyway?"Cal ducked, right forearm shielding his face, backpedaling. Master had a gun, in fact, two.

"Don't worry me boy. They can't fire, yet."

"Look, Master, you know this place has more trap doors than an amusement park's Fun House. Strange stuff happens here all the time, what if they did go off, hmmm? What then?"

"They will son, oh but they will. Stick em up. Bang, ha, ha."

"I've had just about enough you crazy old coot."

They all did, Mother knew it. "I think you boys need some time off, actually, a night off.

Master quickly shook yes, Cal declined.

"Charge on, charge on I must get to the bottom of this and get back. Big Pete's waiting. I have to have this story, soon."

Master gruffed, threw his boney hands at the ceiling. Hands of the town clock sun dialed around its face. Cal was correct to refuse Mothers offer. Time was of the essence. Maestro had a plan.

Cal sat. Wizard wall worked an intravenous charge. He yawned, tilted questioning look mocking Master, and blew him a kiss from pursed lips. Master nodded as if calling a truce, and slid a charged nickel in the coin slot. It rolled down the chute rattling on its crisp edge, to its awaiting fate.

"Clunk"

"Heeeyyyy, where's the jingle-chingle? No noise, no coins, where the hell did they disappear to." The Bobbles harmonized.

The coins family was gone, kidnapped, robbed from the Wurlitzer's poor box. There could be only one suspect. Cal thought that dirty bastard. He did it, I'm sure he's the coin grave robber. Is nothing sacred around here?

Master guiltily bobbled, and wrinkled his forehead in feigned innocence. All eighteen accusing eyes glared. Defiantly he stared back. His fist tightly gripped the loot stuffed in his pocket in a weak attempt to suffocate their jingling cries for freedom. For someone so bright, he could be so dumb. He pulled his hand out. In shrugged momentary embarrassment he parted wrinkled lips. Then whispered through bared clenched teeth something not repeatable, at Cal. Hostel darting eyes looked over flaring nostrils. Humiliation took back seat to, perturbed. Master ground his teeth muttering. Forcefully he spun each stolen nickel, one by one, in rapid succession down the chute, back home. Cal peacock sat on his chair smiling ear-to-ear counting the coins as they dropped. All clunked together in song. The happy family of Indian Heads reunited.

Cal slouched in his chair. Closed his eyes, nodded, and waved his baton at Reddy Red to come forward. Maestro raised his baton.

"Pick up, the ball. Let's roll." Cal labored as his conductor right hand slashed the air. He enjoyed his new role.

Master seethed. Sullied by his petty crime he angrily he fed the Wurlitzer a new nickel.

All along the Watch Tower, a Bob Dylan song covered by Jimmy Hendrix, played. Master, was a big fan. Mother whistled.

"Ah cha hacouh haw," Reddy cleared her raspy smoker's voice, stood and spoke.

Malcolm graduated from high school in 1966. He tried his hand at a various jobs available in the area after. Farming and mechanical work mostly. Turned out for the son of a mechanic that lived on a farm he wasn't much good at either. But that was all there really was to do in those parts.

"Matron might need some help, in the dress shop."

"Not funny Mom."

Malcolm didn't find that funny, languished for the next few years deciding to everyone a favor. He quit the jobs he wasn't good at for something he was, smoking pot.

The Viet Nam War ate young men back then. Georgie, Hank and Sali enlisted. Away they went to South East Asia where they all always deep down knew, they would wind up. It was their natural destiny. Born to it, grew up playing it. Widow Margaret held her only son back. Reluctantly he agreed not to enlist. If called, that would be something else. Three of the five were in, one was out, and Sammie. He fought to go but was too damaged. Classified unfit to serve he too loitered around Fate, helped out where he could. His mother couldn't have been more pleased.

Time passed. Expectedly Hank came home in 1968. His mother couldn't stop crying as they shoveled the last of the dirt. Georgie followed a year later. Rested close to Hank but no one heard from Sali. He was always a little different, cagey. Malcolm figured he was ok for sure.

"My time Mom, we all had a deal, it's my time."

"Go see some of this country, first, Malcolm."

"Start with New York City, not far. I think it'll be over soon anyway. Sali will be back before you know it." The debate lasted for months. Malcolm came to her on a dreary Saturday night.

"Big new place for Rock n Roll down there Mom. Call it the Fillmore, something. Maybe I'll get a job there? Fillmore East, in New York City, that's it."

He loved music, knew that all the current Rock n Roll Gods, and future legends, all passed through the Fillmore West in California. Margaret sighed. Malcolm figured for awhile the war would wait.

"You earned it Malkie, go see some of the world, and go have some fun. Memories are important."

A week later he jumped on the BSA Victor. Margaret waved her blessing good-bye to him as he and his back-pack rode off. She worried it'd only be a temporary stay. Glad he left she prayed every day, the storm in East Asia blew out. If not, she knew he'd awaken for sure. It was June of 1969.

Her prayers were unheeded. South East Asia roared to a fiery storm ragging out of control.

~

"OOoooooooooo" bass, soprano, tenor and raspy Sammie's voice, harmonized. Reds alto was thankfully missing.

Master scowled. Gruffly his arms flailed, gestured, taunted and finger jabbed at everyone. He was still more than a little peeved about the coin incident. Some thought he found a new bottle of writer's ink. He smelled medicinal. Cal gave him a, really, look. Then finger pointed to Reddy to continue. Master coughed.

~

Malcolm lived in the New York City for the next year. Usually, well always, he slept late. Night work as an usher at the Fillmore kept him up late into the early morning. On a too early afternoon he woke to a phone ringing. The bill was barely paid so it rang this month anyway. Mother Margaret held the receiver on the other end.

"Malkie, they found Sali, he'll be home in a few days, joining up with Hank and George."

Malcolm shoulder slid down the door jamb.

"I have to make a call."

"No."

"We agreed, we all agreed. It's my turn now, I'm the last one. I always knew. So did you."

"Nooo." Sniffled in protest.

Sighing, said finally she understood. Knew this day would come from that first day looking up into the sky. He awoke. Warrior DNA traveled time, wouldn't be denied. Gently she hung up the wet receiver.

Malcolm's limp hand gripped the phone white knuckle tight. The deep dark stare he tried to lose, hardened. Tight jawed, he slammed the phone. Plans set long ago hatched. He had things to do.

~

"Bah, Blah, Blah,"

"Shut it you old prick"

Master needed a lot of attention. Writers ink the indulgent one. Cal didn't want to hear it.

"OWWWW," came from the shadows. Masters tantrum went silent. Mothers intervening, punctuating elbow saw to it. Disciplined Master sat still as stone on a stool, in the shadows.

"POP, POP, POP" Disappointed, discover, catch. All lit on the neon sign. The blanks started to fill in. More light from dark.

Mother held two fingers to her mouth, Cal waved. Red looked up from starring at the floor and started.

~

"I'm leavin soon, guys. What I have to do. Been set but when I'm done with that I know what I want to do." Malcolm turned around and walked away. A copy of J.D. Salinger's -The Catcher in the Rye – was stuffed into the right back pocket of his blue jeans.

Two nights later was Malcolm's last in Manhattan's East Village. He wanted to savior a part of the city he grew to love before heading home. His roommate buddies all agreed, one last time, as a tribe, off to Central Park. Ordinarily they went under the cover of darkness and under the influence when they didn't have work. Or, sometimes, before they went to work, at the Big Show, at the Fillmore.

Malcolm's last day in town, before he worked his last concert at the Fillmore, he and his friends rode the rails. Perched themselves at a favorite spot on top of the Big Rock. The best place to smoke some pot, and overlook the terrain. Cops were easily seen. Good looking girls also but the best of the views lay almost at their feet. There, a cage, in the Zoo. Big Rocks vantage point offered all sitting on it. A perfect view for the show not many knew of. Malcolm, his, two buddies, and one pretty curly red headed girl all three boys liked, but were too shy to approach, thought this the best free entertainment in the city. This is if you were clever, and didn't get too close.

The cage housed monkeys, one large odd looking creature in particular, an Orangutan. One so clever the boys named him "OTCO," short, for Orangutan the Clever One or O for short. The group basked in the sun making much needed vitamin D. Strict night life had its downsides. All were use to working shows but not this one. They waited elevated and high, for it to start.

It did as always with the same opening. The audience filled open areas in front. Parents paraded pushing overfed, plump legged toddlers stuffed into strollers. They nagged, cried and pointed to O's cage. Summer heat, unchanged diapers provoked tantrums. Parents waited, hoping and sweating in the summer's swelter he'd come out of his cave.

One thing O was more of than being clever, being lazy. Eventually the crowds begging buzzing noise irritated him to action. He dragged out of his cave and perched on a rock in the middle, closer to the crowd. All could see him. He had a perfect view of them. Leaned closely toward his building viewers, flopped around, and twisted his head so his left ear directly faced the crowd. Taunts, ridicules and jeering fingers pointed and poked mocking the dumb beast. Great fun made at his innocent hairy bizarre face.

Lazy O didn't like to waste his celebrity efforts. When enough became enough, and the crowd swelled to a decent size, he held court. He leapt from his stump. Ridiculed, he strutted around the perimeter of his cage, close to the black iron bars that walled him in to safety. He always seemed to know when the crowd stood five deep. The kids wondered if he could count. After the quick appraisal the hairy clown returned to center stage, even closer. The clever lazy one made sure not to take his eyes off crowd. He spun his head following the curvature of the cage while gently lowering his red butt to the ground and barred his teeth. As the crowd grew so did the torments, laughing at his meek appearance. They pointed, jeered. Terribly unfair, but O took it all in stride. He watched sitting as a multicolored funny looking, fat and saggy beast. Heat angry kids with their stay at home moms, and or dads, nanny's, or occasional out of work or hooky playing parents, obnoxiously pushed and squeezed to get a better look. O flaunted the attention. Gave them what they wanted, funny faces, nose picking, and other orifice probing.

Good weather especially packed his area. A building crowd pressure packed the limited semi-circular space. At five deep it was hard to get a good view, at six, nearly impossible. At seven, school was out for the summer. Unhappy kids screamed and threw food. Cereal, grapes and potato chips flew. Some landed in O's cage much to his delight. A baby's milk bottle flew irretrievably into the cage. O looked at it.

Insistent Mothers led the charge. Dad's jungle challenged O from the safety outside of the bars. Pebbles tried to get his attention, often did hitting him. He snapped his shaggy face. Thankfully kids quieted when the ice cream vendor came around. Mom held their balloons. Malcolm and friends sat up on the rock. They had seen this show before, the visitors hadn't.

O passively took it all in waiting till the large seven-deep crowd was well sucked in, with no ability to quickly escape the subway style pressure. Dreamily, he wagged his head back and forth, scanning the crowd. They quieted. Wondered what he was up to. He looked at them. Barred bad brown teeth in a joker smile, craned his head completely to his left, stopped and puffed his cheeks. Some people though it cute, some strange, some rightfully wondered is this a good thing?

All the time O was outside he was preparing a gift, for them. Fat and hairy, his multicolored head delivered it twisting from his far left to his far right spraying all with profuse amounts of spit. Fire hose volumes of O's phlegm and saliva spewed past his bubbling flapping lips precisely striking its targets.

The jeering instantly stopped. O wouldn't. One pass wasn't enough, three maybe. He didn't want anyone to feel left out. It was perfect. The best part of that particular afternoon came in the aftermath. Jeering adults switched to screaming, like unhappy school yard children. Adults shoved, pushed, and rudely forearmed each other trying to escape. The dense crowd wouldn't dissolve fast enough. Men cursed wiping their faces. Shocked women cursed. The kids loved it. Rebellion starts early and they were on his side. Their previous screams of anger turned to ones of joy. Malcolm and his friends, friends of O, howled from safety, stoned. The hysteria was hysterical.

O leapt on and off his centered perch. Monkey ran around the perimeter of the cage in a ranting screeching rage. His arms flailed his hands, spanked the air, picked up the baby bottle and sucked on the nipple. Spat out the formula smiling a wet smile, and threw the bottle back to where it came from. One of the mocking fathers headed to the eye doctor.

OTCO stopped. Unrolled his arms and his fingers scrapped the ground. His mouth opened to a giant O. He screamed it was his time to mock, his time to jeer. If he spoke English, mothers would have covered their kid's ears. The crowd dispersed to their four corners feeling defiled, took with them a lasting memory.

Malcolm's friends left. He stood. A little dizzy. Stoned, Malcolm's tapestry pant legs dragged against the rock. He brushed himself off. A rare smile curled watching remnants of the crowd flee. It looked like a scene from B sci-fi film.

As they walked away his friends shout-

"Hey Malcolm, are you holdin?" Malcolm stopped, paused, looked at them, then checked his pockets, shrugged his shoulders in a no, I don't have any pot.

Off the rock he slid, on his butt, wearing out what was left of those favorite pants. It wouldn't matter. Clothing style was going to change, free of charge.

He never wore a watch but always knew what time it was. Malcolm was late. Work started in a few hours. Wiry legs broke the park's 59th street perimeter, a word he'd get to know better. Streaking over the concrete to the subways steps, the corner of his left eye caught a glimpse of a man lost in thought looking at a very large statue. Malcolm sneaker skidded to a halt. This was an unusual, even for New York. Curious, he approached wondering why. No one ever seemed to pay attention to those statues. Thousands passed by daily and most, if not all, never offered the slightest glance of care or awareness.

"Hey, what are you lookin at Mister?"

A shabby bum spoke. Maybe a drunk or junkie, he smelled like a urinal.

"You never know about people sometimes," Malcolm remembered Mother Margaret's schooling.

"A victorious soldier proudly atop of his horse, what about that son?" What could have been taken for a drunk or junkie spoke. Gaunt, thin and unshaven, wrapped in a mis-buttoned stained white shirt his education spoke louder than his words.

"Huh, what do you mean mister, err sir."

The stranger delivered detailed a brief lecture about the towering statue. Bored, Malcolm went to leave. His feet wouldn't. So he listened to the explanation about who the warrior was, what his accomplishments were, and what it all meant. The stranger's diction, vocabulary and grammar dazzled. Margaret's mother would have her equal. A peculiar bit of chance this serendipitous meeting.

"Most people walk by. Say eighty to ninety percent I guess. They never even look at it. They have no idea who these people were, or care." The stranger pointed to the statues figure never taking his eyes off it.

"Celebrated, accomplishers of great things, and yet, only few know who they are.Look at this statue boy, what do you see." Still he wouldn't break his line of sight.

"The statue, that's all. Why?"

"Look closely son, what do you see? Tell Me."

"Ain't nuthin but old dirty statue sir, why?"

"Yes, yes, old statue, dirty old statues of people who accomplished great things and for the most part, forgotten. But there is one thing that you haven't noticed, be aware son."

"Whaat-"

"Closer boy, come closer. Keep looking, what do you see?"

"Nuthin more Sir, just like old dirty statues, dirty disgusting statues." He sighed, the stranger sighed.

"Quite right, quite right, But what is oooooonnnn, all of these statues?"

Malcolm wasn't in the mood, went to leave, the man shook his head. Malcolm stayed but being stoned didn't help.

"Look, mister, the only things I notice is most em have pigeon shit all over them."

"Yes my boy, pigeon shit. There's fame for you, pigeon shit. Don't let them cover you with pigeon shit boy. Be aware boy. Don't let them cover you with pigeon shit." That was the last thing Malcolm heard him say. The whistling stranger turned, walked away finger combing his hair without once looking squarely at him.

A few hours later Malcolm worked his last night at the Fillmore. The band played more loudly than usual, rocking the house more than usual. Electric guitars whined. Thudding pounding rhythmic drumbeats and bass guitar notes kept the bands musical time. Some notes found their way to the forest, and the jungle. Even the numb were touched. LSD had a hand in that. Audience and staff joined together playing air guitars.

Behind the last row of cheap seats on the top level hid a large spot light. They called the Super Trooper. It poked through the wall like well hidden cannon shooting its tracer like laser wand of light to the stage floor. The light wiggled and waggled paint brushing the audience of dancing possessed gnomes.

Shadows cast on over-aged fabric coated walls. It was ok, all ok. The smoke that filled the air gave all its permission. Malcolm left the concert before the last guitar note was plucked. Encores took the night deep into the morning. He had a long journey.

Malcolm hit the road on the Victor backpacked with all his valuable belongings hanging behind him. Urgently, he rode through the night. He had to be on time this time. Sali was home. His service was scheduled for the late morning.

He cracked Fate's border and continued directly to the cemetery. There he slid his bike to a halt, planted a foot on wet cemetery muddy grass, propped it on its stand just in time. They were just about to start. Sweating, panting, Malcolm pushed through the crowd wedging himself next to his Mother. Sammie stood on her other side. The only two left. Malcolm clasped her left hand. A letter to Malcolm from the Army held tightly crumpled in her right. There they were, all in a row, as they all knew they would be.

No priest or minister was present. Sali always said his family was different. A religious man of some kind was there. Speaking funny Malcolm thought. When he finished a beautiful military ceremony followed complete with bugle bugling, and folding the flag draped over his coffin. Sali's pale mother stood stoic and calm. It hadn't set in yet. Malcolm shed his first tear since Stephanie's internment. When the service was complete he said a private good bye, stopped to say hello to Stephanie, Hank and Georgie, and Dad. He grabbed the Victor's handlebars and rode.

Only Sammie would be left behind. Unfit they thought. He would not be part of this battle.

"I wanted to go—they wouldn't let me-I should be there, I should – we were brothers." Sammie's head hung down from behind the bar. Master coughed, Cal nodded, Red continued—

"Malkie, the farm's too big. Dad's gone, well, money is a problem and-"

She left out recently she lost balance, several times, fell and saw the doctor.

"For heaven's sake, this is soo depressing, all the time, my, my."

"Owwww," Mother weighed in.

Reddy smiled taunting Master. Farmer Vaughn was beside himself. Mary was quiet. Sammie stood stone still but couldn't hold it. His impish face twisted to a smile.

"I want, to see, Malcolm."

Cal held his index finger to his lips. Nodded he understood. Mother whistled, Cal raised his hand instructing Red to continue.......

Margaret told Malcolm she had come to an agreement with the Vaughn's. The house, barn and twenty acres would be spared. The money cleared up a lot of debts, and then some.

"Malcolm, the bar in town is for sale. I think we should buy it. Something I can manage. Dad always liked it after all and someday it'll be all yours."

She went on about how it might be fun to own. Especially since Sean had spent a fair amount of his time, and their money, there. Honored, his picture hung to the right of the bar mirror on the Vincent, as well as Malcolm's to its left.

"Maybe we can get even?"

"Doubt it." Malcolm laughed.

"Anyway, sooner–" she paused and took a deep breath—"or later it'll be yours."

"We keep the Barn?"

"That will never change Malcolm, not as long as I'm alive."

Malcolm paused, remembered Sean tinkering on his bikes, especially the Vincent. It still rested broken, boarded up, and untouched since Malcolm's wreck sealed its fate.

Margaret smiled remembering the day Malcolm and Sean fooled her into thinking Sean was beating Malcolm.

"Thank god a haaaapy moment, at last. OOOWWWWWWW."

Mother nodded it won't happen again and to continue.

Malcolm, and the BSA Victor, spent the next two days of 1970's summer riding around town saying his goodbyes. His final stop, a sacred place where he spent so much happy time mired in mediocrity, one great miracle aside. Margaret drove Malcolm to the train station the next day.

"You know, it's in my blood mom."

Margaret placed her hand over her heart, nodded.

"What I'm born to do, we were born to. We had a pact."

She didn't answer. They drove past Destiny cutting through the center of town. The town clock and monument to fallen heroes with the bell that hung above it that rang only when someone died in battle on their left. Malcolm daydreamed. Wondered what the weather would be like there. Hot and sticky always he later learned. The farms new resident, the white dove, flew along side of them on Malcolm's passenger side, window high. Gave Malcolm a well wisher good luck nod, and then flew off.

Three months later, on the other side of the world in hell, Malcolm received notice Margaret passed from a brain tumor she knew she had, and he didn't.

Early morning, Thursday, September 7, 2009, came without a warning. The town clock ticked to 3:45 a.m. Cal's watch ticked backwards to 4:15 p.m. Tuesday, August 29, 2009. Mother knew the twins score but wouldn't say.

Red fainted. Morning light started to bleach the night. The juke went silent, dark as did the super trooper and the floor. Cal hit the sheets on the Red crushed velvet couch. Sammie and company left, sullen, wondering when Malcolm would show. Things were going to get hot.

# Twenty-Three

"My favorite trustees ready?" Cal asked in a nod as he slid from his charged chair.

"Yup" The bass bellowed.

"Uh huh" Wouldn't be left out, belted the baritone.

"Yeppers" Scratchily screeched.

"Wadda ya think" Alto added.

"Hurummpf" Soprano soured.

"Hmmmm," Cal still didn't understand it.

Matron was still upset, about something no one knew.

Cal slid the wings walking around, acting Monk-like in deep contemplation.

"I've decided"

"Decided what?"Chorused.

"Today, err tonight. You all will have your moments in fame, if you haven't already. I grant you all, part time rule."

Master scuffed the floor.

"NOOOO, we don't want to,"

A nickel rolled. Bobble's nodded with tilted ears at the juke.

"Clunk, clink" confirmed the family reunion. Master's guilty eyes hid starring at the floor.

The Wurlitzer dished, Feel like I'm Fixin to Die (Rag), by Country Joe and the Fish. Cal strolled, paused, violently jackknifed opened folded arms. If he were metal, they would have clicked a switch blades warning snap.

Cal rolled open a balled fist, snapped his drumstick fingers, cautioned attention, and then gently pointed at the Bobbles.

"Who's the lucky one today?" His devilish grin whispered.

The Bobbles looked left, right, slid backward away whispering, snickering and bickering with each other.

"Guess I should be," Reddy chirped.

"No me, I'll do it," Farmer bellied.

"No MEEEE I should be," Mr. I the pontificator quaked with an uncharacteristic wobble.

Encouraged by their bravery Cal allowed the flock fight. He sat and finally intervened.

"You there- Mr. I Imagine-before your lovely orange, err, red headed friend puts you away for good, again, get up here." Again, where the heck did that come from Cal wondered.

"Yes- again-oh magical one," Master confirmed.

"Yes, again," Reddy giggled.

Mr. I Imagine smoothly slipped off his stool, in well rehearsed move. He spun in a tight right. Faced the mirror, straightened his red diagonally striped tie. Swallowed a mighty belt of his favorite Gin—free gin. Stood ready to serve, oiled up.

"Cuhuhu–"

"Sorry, frog in my throat."

Obnoxious to a fault the group tried to censure as it the only prohibition he could follow. He liked his gin.

"Hue caw, hue caw" Phlegm flew. Others ducked, some imperfectly nor fast enough. OTCO would have been proud. Mr. I strutted to the broken banister separating the second level from the first, his back to the class. Turned around, faced his furious mates still wiping his gift from wrinkled, lemon sucking faces. They glared. Pompous knew no side.

"Ha, ha- ha," Entertained, Cal sat down. Amused, he waved his Maestro's baton. Master whistled. Mr. I. started.

To say the war was unpopular would be the same as saying the Titanic had a little leak.

"Whaaaat did you say?" Orangey Red- Reddy Red, leapt off her chair, freshly sharpened pencil in hand.

Jeassuus, anything can happen in here Cal thought snapping his feet heel first, whoa.

"MMMhmmm" Master agreed.

Reddy Red turned Pirate Red. Dagger in hand she chased Mr. I. Smartly he fled out the doorless front door into the sanctuary of the night's black. One bar stool seat sat empty for the rest of the evening.

"I'll tell ya all, if ya need to know. I'll tell ya, and the right way without that idiot's embelliments." Red seized power.

"He's hardly an idiot, though pompous as the night is long, and its EMBELLISHMENTS" Cal corrected, tapping the back of his head against the wall.

"Embelliments, or embellishments so who cares mister?"

She was retired. Cal wasn't. Who knew better?

The Bobbles nominated Reddy Red, she was always ready for a fight, and her hair, always kinda Red.

"Anyone have a problem with me? Well?" The pugilist challenged.

The bobbles eyes darted all over, but never forward.

"Now pay attention cause this where the dots get connected. Do ya understand?"

The bobble noggins nodded and wobbled, up, down, and side to side. Mr. I safely hunkered down outside on the porch by the door jamb of the doorless front door. Bravely, he curled his head slightly inside. His cheek pressed tightly halfway down on the door jam. He couldn't miss this. Out of the corner of her eye she saw, motioned quickly to him. He flew backwards. Master coughed. The light lit the floor. Gloating, she chuckled and then spoke.

Malcolm never lost a fight after that frightful day on the hill. Ya hear? He always seemed to know ten- minutes before a fight there was going to be one. A pretty good edge I'd say. Anyways several months passed since he landed, in country, they called it. This pretty new soldier came age old seasoned to Viet Nam in late April. Malcolm would turn 21 in a month.

On a normal, sweltering hot, humid, buggy day, this mother's son's platoon marched to base camp through the God forsaken hell hole. Orders seemed always to be the same. Until that particular minute of that particular day, all they killed were bugs. The enemy would have to wait. The next day the platoon hung around camp.

"I want you to move forward, here. Right freaking here," barked the lieutenant.

He pointed to the map.

"Sir, that's perfect for a trap sir," Malcolm said pointing. "Can't go that way it'll be bad news sir."

"A trap, who said there's a trap there?" Red faced the officer pissed back mashing his unlit saliva soaked cigar.

"Intel said the damn area is secure, dam it. So if Intel sez its secure then we go. You got it?"

"Sir, they're wrong. I'm certain they're wrong and it's, you go, unless you're planning on coming." Mother's grammar lessons learned well.

"I don't give a holy crap what you think punk. And watch that lip. If I didn't need the best shot in the company, you'd be locked away."

"You mean best shot in the whole freakin Army," Johnny Shake said.

"Look you frakin idiots, who's in charge here? I am, see. I'm in freakin charge and if I say you go then you go." His arms waved about and face reddened. "I'm in control, I'm in control. Just how in the name of hell do you know there's a trap there anyway private?"

Malcolm looked at the sky.

"Just do Sir. Feel it in my bones. Yep, feel it Sir—they're there. The fights gunna be before we get to the objective Sir, heavy casualties."

"Feel it in yer bones huh? Well you're gonna feel something in your bones if you don't get the hell outta here, and get movin. Intel said you're wrong. Now I want you to go take the point. No hiding for you, you son-of –a bitch. Sarge will have you drop back after awhile. No runnin for you."

"Wouldn't think of it sir, I'll take point all day if you want."

"Let me know when you get there."

"Yes Sir." Sarge stood looking up.

The platoon fought the push back of the high grass. Thick brush edged the field's sides. Rustling wind that followed whipped through the grass, encouraging them forward. Malcolm heard the tune he heard the night after that day on the hill. It whistled..........

"Four horsemen came a riding, riding through the glen—.

–to kill—- in the end" was all he could hear. This time more clearly.

After Johnny found the NVA helmet the nervously confident platoon pushed forward with rifles gripped loosely watching their step. Land mines were around. Malcolm looked around. Made his call for incoming, attack imminent, but nothing happened.

"Maybe you're loosin yer touch Malcolm," Johnny joked. He forgot Malcolm always knew ten minutes before.

"Look sharp men. Look sharp."

The men quizzically looked at him, eye questioning what he was saying.

"Sarge, let Malcolm take control." Johnny knew better, who knew better.

They all listened to Malcolm, all except the Lieutenant. No sign of trouble around yet though. Wide open clear field.

"No sign of NVA or VC, cept that NVA helmet," Johnny laughed teasing.

"Keep looking, they're here, I think. Keep lookin Johnny."

"Hey, you two shut the hell up."

"Yes Sir Sergeant Sir. You hear Johnny?"

"I did Malcolm, Yes Sir Sergeant."

"Do not call me Sir you two idiots. I work for a living."

"That helmet's an omen Malcolm, isn't it? You know damn-it, you always know."

"Zips all around, Innn coming—Innn coming—-"

"Where, Malcolm? Where? Nothin's happening, you said that before?"

"IIIIInnnnn Cooommmm–"

"Damn-it to hell Malcolm, whe—"

Ten ticks of deathly quiet ticked off time forever.

Boooom—, boom, boom. Dirt, rock and grass sprayed, taking bodies with it. The mortar attack started. The platoon, a sitting duck, just as Malcolm warned.

Sssssssszump-Sssssssssssszzzump-Whhhirrrrrrrrrrrrrrr

Whizzing bullets deathly spun boring their way through thick afternoon air at the hunkered soldiers. They came from, everywhere.

"Down, get down," Sarge screamed.

The ballet of a combat ambush commenced. The one Intel said wasn't there. The boys and men were shot at from both flanks in a NVA turkey shoot.

Well hid, the camouflaged enemy popped out of high grass. Whizzing bullets stung stunned soldier's arms, legs, heads, and necks. It wasn't Custer's last stand, but wasn't much better. Stealthy, the death delivering enemy deliberately advanced. The platoon broke, ran to cover wherever they could. There wasn't much, except for the higher grass.

"Get down-get down Johnny, down, stay put."

Johnny Shake broke for better cover. It clicked when he stepped on it. He heard it, looked at Malcolm. Malcolm screamed, broke toward Johnny.

"Don't move, don't move Johnny, I can—-."

Too late, Malcolm's feet froze refusing to step on a board in front of him. He fell forward and violently shook in a fetal position. Airborne debris rained.

High grass hid the well placed mine field. The NVA applied pressure from two sides pinching Malcolm's platoon. Johnny was heading home. The rest scattered, crept on their knees. Getting shot, or blown up would ruin the day.

Some panicked. Bodies flew. Malcolm gritted his teeth wishing the lieutenant and Intel was there listening to the painful cries for a medic and fading haunting calls to their mothers. Time stood still it that late afternoon.

Malcolm was a brave soldier, but not an idiot.

Red paused. Her voice rose. She craned her head toward the door. Mr. I Imagines head slumped. Mother was about to cough. Red continued.

Malcolm lay in a muddy hole tucked in a fetal position, similar to that fateful day on the mountain with Hank. He wished he was home. But he was home, his new home, Vietnam. Rolling and slithering he maneuvered behind a low embankment, squatted, and tucked his chin into his neck. M-16 tucked to his chest. The odds were against him in the first of his two Mother of all battles.

Panting, kneeling in sweat-soaked clothes, sticking to the mud, he watched the battle. It seemed like it went on forever, but it just began. Cries from wounded unattended soldiers competed with gun fire. Some tried to escape. They were cut down in target practice from a well prepared enemy.

Stephanie's memory raced through Malcolm's. Parent's deaths, explainable, expected as that was the order of things. Stephanie's death wasn't. No comfort came from religion, or friends. Maybe an enemy's bullet would. Malcolm stood, called out to his platoon to regroup. They lay scattered about the field out positioned, and out manned by a clever enemy.

Fury raged. Gun fire bolted. Solely he charged an attacking, startled enemy. Uncles Tim's lessons paid off. Messages floated home alerting the mothers of the dead enemy.

The advancing enemy returned fire. It found its mark. Bullets tore Malcolm on his forearm, shoulder, neck and right leg. Searing pain crippled him, he fell. Tried to stand, fell again. On the ground he reloaded, waited, and watched the enemy zig-zag through the high grass. Heaven sent wind parted grass providing a vee window. Enough light for him to see them but them, not him. He rested his M-16 on his left leg, and waited.

I'll get a few before they get me, he thought. Uncle Tim will be pleased, maybe a few Grandpas also.

Hold your fire, Uncle Tim used to tell him. Hold your fire till you have your shot. You have the advantage. You're a better shot. Patiently Malcolm waited. The NVA weren't close enough yet. Malcolm's eyes squinted down the rifles sight, past the flowering.....

~

"Where have all the flowers gone, long tiiiime...."

"Shut up you old fart." Cal jabbed his dagger baton arm at Master.

"Have you any respect?" Cal was hot.

"Oh, but I do my friend. A deep abiding reverence in fact as I've lost so many."

"Come-on you overstuffed wind bag. I know what you're doing. You think you're so clever manipulating the conversation. And by the way, your vocabulary isn't what you think it is so why, don't- you- just, go over there and do something worthwhile"

"Worthwhile? Like what boooy?"

"Like going into your shadow and farting. Let out some of the hot air you're stuffed with."

The Bobbles screeeeaaamed... Thunderous applause rattled the roof. Dust strapped on their parachutes. Thunder gained ground, Mother thumb-added.

"And find Malcolm would you before I do something drastic!" Cal warned.

The Bobbles gave Cal a standing ovation.

"Ah, but you are doing something drastic my boy, you are...."

Cal's head slumped, wagged back and forth. Limply he raised his arm. Mother hushed Master's cough. Red started again.

~

Malcolm looked at the late afternoon sun. Waiting for the creeping creepers his eyes shrunk to his famous bunker slits. They filtered out the glare. Poised, the professional executioner took precise careful aim, and fired. Two enemies fell, then three. Stunned, the NVA covered in the high grass. One popped up rifle ready. He fell backward, an M-16 round found his head. Another angry challenger made a foolish mistake. Ten dead, but they kept coming. Malcolm held his position. Two other survivors from his platoon joined him. One wounded, both frightened. They both stood and fired. Their fear left for good.

All from his platoon were dead, except himself. Secrecy no longer an option Malcolm's fire gave the enemy his position. Born a killer he fired at will breaking Uncle Tim's rule, shoot and move. The enemy stopped advancing, regrouped, and pressed on directly toward their lone remaining assailant.

During the lull Malcolm reloaded. The pause reminded him he was wounded, and losing blood. Grimacing, he fell to his knees and rolled to his side. Malcolm lay in the grass, breathing through his nose, awaiting a fateful bayonet, or bullet. Or perhaps both.

A brilliant windy sky quickly sped clouds over him as fast as that day on the hill with Hank. Furiously it whipped and bent tall grass, and jungle brush. The tropics were hard to explain.

Clothing soaked in his life wrapped his body. The brutally hot day couldn't help. He shivered listening to the wind playing a familiar sound.

"Wwwwheeeesshhhhhh whh... Ffffthh TH... Ffffiiiit fooorrwhislll...Foooorrr horsemen cccaammee a rriiidinding, riding thooough the whheewwggleen–" Eerie notes carried on the winds wings whistling it through the brush.

Malcolm rolled, kneeled. He twisted his salty sweat covered blood splattered head towards the very late afternoon sky, aimed. Peaceful calm returned knowing he physically would no longer be of this earth. Margaret knew he wasn't long ago.

Enemy boots trampled the grass with a warning crunch. Malcolm's ears perked listening to his executioners pant legs brushed together. Deaths stench hung in the heavy moist air. Malcolm lay ready. Someone was going with him.

Cold sweat magnetically clamped the straw grass to his face. Nature's natural camouflage covered him, head to toe. Uncle Tim warned him it was always a bad idea to take one's eyes off an enemy. A familiar noise pulled his eyes to the sky. The hawk! The dam hawk was there. It circled three times then left. The enemy happily noticed also as the hawk gave up Malcolm's exact position. Ten ticks later they unhappily heard distant whirring whipping thunder. U.S. helicopter rotors chased away the winds ominous melody.

Two synchronized cobra helicopter gunships broke over a small mountain top. Vicious props thudded. Fading bright sunlight backlit them, casted their shadows. Shadows advising all below, their grim reaper was at hand. Triggers pulled, perfectly mounted mini guns deathly spat lead trimming the hiding grass. The hunters, now the hunted, fled.

Took off for the hills, Tim would say.

Their lives replaced concern about Malcolm's. The fast ones, and first ones, escaped seeing hell. The slower ones were shredded. Shot in the back, and front. They screamed in different languages, but offered the same message. They had mothers. They fell. Those that hid in the high grass made equally fatal mistakes. Goodbye messages to mom, goodbye messages to Dad.

How all this started didn't matter to the soldiers. All that did, staying alive. As far for its end, well it never seems to end. For these unlucky souls there was no escape. It ended for them that day. Lifeless, punctured, motionless, wrapped in their uniforms, soaked in their life resting silently waiting. Hard to tell if it only the tall grass being chopped and floating in the humid wind. Or, mixtures of flesh and bone blended into swirling mini-twisters spinning away in black magic streaks toward the clouds, flown home by the dark angels. The whipping wind left as quickly as it had arrived. Malcolm lay in the grass looking skyward saved for the moment. Exhausted, tense, bleeding, as Uncle Tim taught, M-16 in hand.

A hundred and twenty ticks ticked. Certain he was alone Malcolm wobbled to his feet. He looked for safety. Four baseball base path lengths from him was a local hut village. He didn't remember it, but there it stood. It repopulated after the battle. Hard to trust anyone, enemy hid everywhere. Malcolm gimped toward it.

Bodies of innocent villagers, caught in the crossfire, laid as discarded twisted tangled marionettes in the mud and grass. Survivors, men women children, and some children carrying their children stood over their dead. Sad, not stunned. The young earned field promotions to adulthood. The puppeteer's follies made it certain graves were dug.

"Ohhhh the puppeteers are they, hmmmm. Whoooooo, are these bastards the puppeteers?" Master lurked in the shadows as a shepherd watching his student teacher, teach.

"So my dear Maaaadammm, who are these puppeteers?"

Cal howled. Reddy Red slowly twisted. Her furious red faced head glared at Master. Then realized she was lord over-seer of Mr. I Imagine, only. Here, she was out of her league.

"Well, did, I, stutter?" Master provoked her with a finger point.

"I-I-I-I'm…. not really sure sir. I need some water."

"Stop whispering, speak-up. You're not sure did you say? Not sure? You've gone out of your way to peak——-eeeveryone's curiosity and you're not sure??"

From his shadow he strolled into the light. Curtsying with outstretched rising arms, his cape rose. He looked like a bat.

"What about these bastards? Who aaaaaare they? Are they the merchants of death, the sinister deliverer's of the innocent, the power hungry, the vicious trail bosses of Nations. Well? Are they control freaks, sons-of-bitches, pious deceptors, or perhaps, some that just never sucked their Mothers tit long enough? I demand to know, now. Expose them all." Master grew tall in his rage.

"You—-you just did, sir. You just did." Reds gentle cadence surprised all.

Master paused, tilted his head. Gray lockets fell to the side in his ceremonial pose. Two fingers pressed against his old man's soft cheek.

"Yes, quite," he accepted the answer, pressed his lips together into a protruding mock kiss.

"Go on." he instructed.

Cal, left out the exchange entirely, lost some clout. The Bobbles wrung their hands, snickered. Hoping for a fight between he and

Master their betting money came out. Matron was gleeful. Master turned his back to all. He strutted back into the shadow but, before he disappeared he twisted his head over his shoulder looking back at Cal. He knowingly nodded. Master loved pushing his buttons. The Bobbles stuffed their cash back into their pockets.

"Eh hem, excuse me."

"Yes?" Master backed out of the shadow into the light. His head slightly turned, feigning interest.

"Yes? You have something to saayy. Boy?"

"Well, eh hem, Siiiiir. You forgot something, something important."

"Oh? Now what would that be then my boooyyy," ricocheted, reverberated, and echoed. The rafters shook freeing more dust.

"OOOOoooooooooooooooooo—-," Master's yes men and women droned wet dog shaking the dust off. However, loyalty wasn't a word in their lexicon. They favored whoever was ahead, applying choruses of appreciations accordingly.

"Yes, yes I do," Cal coolly said regaining some authority.

"Go on boy." Master nodded.

"Never mind, what's the point?" Cal huffed. Master looked at him. Read his mind and nodded.

"Hmmmmm, yes indeed, quite right, you are quite right. We'll add them also, to Reds list.. After all it's usually a cover up anyway." Master laughed disappearing into his shadowy home.

"Continuuuuuue- please—" Master whistled.

Red obeyed. Something she wasn't particularly good at.

~

Malcolm's strength improved, a friendly hawks right. He continued limping. At much closer range he saw a young girl. Maybe 12-13. Standing upright she wore a much too big for her hand me down sun dress. So well worn, and torn, it was more sun than dress, but it covered what it had to.

~

"Pay close attention here-" Red insisted, looked around.

The Bobble Heads, heads, bobbled up and down. So did Cal's.

Clap, Clap, Clap–" Mother coughed-

The young Vietnamese girl stood cautiously still looking around, fearful the battle would begin anew. The front row witness had painters brush jet black hair. It hung straight down, some that cupped her yellow hued face matched perfectly to black slit eye liner drawn eyes but she wore no cosmetics. One of the tropics pets, a flying insect, pestered her. A reflex hand slapped at it, struck her face, broke her catatonic trance. Looking down she slowly moved her bare feet up and down in their gluey mud bath.

Two of the NVA soldiers that escaped the mini gun visit, slipped out from their heavily overgrown brush hiding place. They walked into the village, and toward her. Malcolm didn't know much about love. He did know their intentions. No more young mothers were necessary. His raison d'être commenced, it planned so long ago.

Steadily, stealthily, he raised his weapon.

"Steady, Steeeaaaddyyyyyy," he heard Uncle Tim's words.

Picaowww, Picaowww two shots flew, one head shot true. That soldier was down, out, and going home. The other shot just missed the other who smartly disappeared into the brush.

The girl's toes kneaded the blood mud pie, relieved that the NVA's attention had been drawn from her, to Malcolm. The inside of her thighs were wet. The enemy soldier Malcolm missed had a job to do. Professionally, he circled back cleverly working his way toward Malcolm's position. Indian blooded Malcolm kept low when playing war as a kid with his band of brothers and did so here. The NVA soldier searched. Malcolm, remembering Tim's lessons, moved. He knew his adversary would come back. They were both professionals.

He couldn't see Malcolm, Malcolm couldn't see him either, but both could hear. The usual telltale air went deafeningly quiet. Both hearts painfully beat.

Wind stirred, parted grass. "Hey, Hey" in English and Vietnamese was screamed. Too late and too close to use guns. Hand to hand combat.

"Ooooooooooooooooooooooooo"—the class harmonized. Master was stopped by Mother from coughing.

Malcolm threw the soldier on his back. Held a knife high over his head and forced it down with both hands against the soldiers defending arms. They rolled on their sides. Then over, and over, exchanging positions. Warrior DNA charged. Minutes ticked, seemed like hours. The stronger NVA soldier wrestled Malcolm on his back, turned his dagger toward Malcolm's chest. Malcolm almost welcomed it.

"AH, awaiting the peaceful liberation that comes from deaths embrace." Master added.

An interrupted Red, well accustomed to interruptions, went on without help.

An image flashed in Malcolm's mind. The monument, the one erected in the center of his home town honoring him and his other friends lost in the war. He cringed remembering his teacher by Central Park.

"Pigeon shit, ugh."

The scream startled the soldier. His opponent was talking to him in battle. This wasn't to be. He had no idea what Malcolm said. Inspired Malcolm momentarily rejuvenated, took the element of surprise and continued fighting. Two grimace faced combatants gripped, grabbed and gouged at each other. Valiantly they carried on. Each determined to win. Malcolm's rejuvenation yielded to his great blood loss. Energy failed. Pigeons couldn't carry this day.

The sharp bloodied pointed tip of his opponent knife's blade held high over his head. Malcolm resisted with little strength. The dagger's blade quivered in the soldier's hand as he pressed. Malcolm looked up to the heavens for comfort. Awaiting his fate, there it was again.

That dam Hawk is here again he thought.

"God dammit I can't even die in freakin peace."

The NVA soldier, a quick study, wouldn't be distracted this time by Malcolm's ramblings. Too bad he didn't know English. Had he, he would have seen the feathered missile streaking to earth, at him, razor sharp talons barred.

By the time a flash of light from the bird's flight hit the corner of the soldier's eye it was too late. He threw his hands up as if about to be in a head on auto accident. Fearfully he waved them fending off the talons. No training prepared him for this type of assault. Confused, panicked, he fought off the bird's repeated assaults. His hands were sliced open and bled. The hawk retreated. He sighed, happy he protected his face. Malcolm lay below. He raised his dagger again over Malcolm.

Five shots rang out from a Russian made AK47. The NVA soldiers head split open like a watermelon dropped from a building. As he fell, blood, bone, skin and hair flew in the air, everywhere, some splattered Malcolm. He couldn't see from his position where the shots came from and who fired them, but whoever it was knew how to fire a rifle. Malcolm knew the sound of an enemy weapon but why? Another mother had a bad day. If she didn't know already she would soon. They all often seemed to know before the official message came.

Malcolm weakly laid on his back. He touched his cheek, it wasn't sweat but blood. In the confusion he never felt the soldier's dagger hit him. When it slipped from the soldiers hands it was free to do what it wanted. It wanted to strike Malcolm, in the face slicing him from the corner of his right eye down his cheek to just above the corner of his mouth leaving him a lasting memory of the day. The carving bled terribly.

Malcolm looked into the ocean blue sky for the hawk. It was gone. He turned his head to his right. The young girl he went to save was standing next to him holding hot barreled Ak47. Her innocence forever lost some time ago. A flash of white streaked behind her. A few white feathers floated. She screamed in Vietnamese. Malcolm figured he was next. More and more she screamed, tamped her bare feet and threw the weapon into the bloody mud.

~

"Oooooooooooooooooo" the bobbles lost their appetite.

"Eh," Jealous Matron acted unmoved. Mother whistled-Red continued-

~

The girl calmed down, picked up her weapon, squatted at Malcolm's side. A US Army medi-vac helicopter landed to pick up the dead and injured. Medics came to get Malcolm with supporting soldiers. Weapons aimed at the girl. Wide eyed she jabbered in Vietnamese on the wrong end of a gun. Malcolm, busy fighting blood loss, laid semi conscious but caught a glimpse, angered, and energized.

Stop, stop, he signaled with his hand.

"Wait a sec guys…I know this guy," said Hank Barstead. He came from the same county upstate New York that Malcolm did. Crew cut, straight white teeth, green eyes- his dad was the county sheriff so he knew Malcolm well.

"Malcolm McKeon, is that you? Jeasus H. fucking Christ I shoulda known only you coulda survived a mess like this. What the fuck are you doing here? They said you went off to school, wanted to be a–"

The copter noise drowned him out as they stretchered him. Malcolm nodded with a faint smile. Then weakly muttered in his ear-

"Get the girl-get her outa here."

The soldiers shook their heads no.

"Malcolm, Jesse can't pick your sorry ass up out here, we're the only game in town so now listen–"Hank looked around.

"Put me down then." Malcolm gasped.

Twenty ticks later they were all on the copter. The medic tended to Malcolm's wounds. Tien sat next to him on the blood pooled floor holding Malcolm's IV. Delirious, he looked at her, filterless cigarette stuck to his bottom lip. He said-

"If you get to heaven before I go to hell, say hello." He passed out as the copter banked.

Tien got to the states escaping the rest of the Viet Nam War, but would never escape that day. The horrors sealed her fate, on to medical school. Malcolm survived. Brought home three trophies from the war, his scar, a thousand yard stare, and Tien's safety.

"Ah, his Raison d'être," mouthed Farmer.

Spent Ready Red's blood shot eyes shifted to Cal's, then to the couch, and then pleadingly back to Cal.

They said I've done mine and his I dese—

Cal, cut her off with a, don't even think about it baton wave.

"Go back to where you came from. Back behind those walls," he dismissed her.

Matron grunted and grabbed Farmers arm. Mr. I Imagine snuck in. They all smoked through their holes. The lit floor flickered out. It was early Friday morning when Country Joes song finished.

4:00 a.m. September 8, 2009, so said the town clock and the Comets ticker. Time marched on Cal's watch also, backwards 4:00 p.m. Tuesday, August the 29, 2009.

Cal walked unassisted to the Red Velvet couch but wearing a wrinkled forehead. His concentrating face pointed his right ear in the direction of Master and Mothers shadowy corner. A new strange noise tapped from within. "When are the two going to meet?" came out.

# Twenty-Four

"To-to-to-night—may-b-, b-b, e-e-e, a little de, de, different." Stuttering wasn't a good sign. Her busy darting eyes dashing, worse.

"What.... In, in, in the -woo, woo wooorld- could be so different?" Cal mocked.

Mother's face red ballooned—-.

"—HAhAHAHAHHA, every freakin day around here is different. So, why so red, Mother?"

"So what you say, Mr. Big Fat Head?"Master's voice unnecessarily came to her defense.

"Hey look you old bat I was speaking to Mother. I'm freakin done with this, all of this, all of this spooky hocus-pocus crap." Cal's shoulders rounded. "Sorry, sorry for the cusses. Yeah I know they go against me. Who cares, I don't know what's real anymore anyway. Who are you? Who am I? Where the heck is Malcolm? Why is the bar all shot up? No freakin anybody is telling me nuthin."

"Oh, no one has told you anything? Who are we, you? Where is Malcolm, is it? Why is the bar all shot up? You haven't been told anything yet? Is that correct sir?" Mother winked a brown eye.

Cal's legs buckled, dropped sideways and hit the floor confused tired wishing for an early trip to the red couch.

"You poor, poor, boy, we'll just have to do a little something about that, tonight. Get in here, now. The pistols want to see you."

"Oh carp," Cal rose on unsure feet. Straightened his jackknifed torso, and shuffled the well worn wingtips across Mothers bake shop splintering wood floor. He just missed the doors saddle board stopping flat footed to a glued halt.

"Phew," Mother stared back at him with eyes that turned to coal, absent their twinkle.

He blinked, faced forward looking out into the rich black night and two foot hopped over the doors saddle. Things changed quickly in Fate, even Cal. His new home, no longer the forbidding place it was of just a few days earlier. Cocky Cal fired up the wings movie star style, toe dancing to his seat.

Along the wall, found a hole in waist of Hendrix. Wham, Old Sparky was back. Mercilessly a tooth crushing tourniquet grip grabbed his finger. The tip swelled to the size of an Italian sausage. The pair was well rested. Unprovoked under entertained thunder and lightning chimed in. Their cacophony of combative pounding bellowing thunderous rumbles, and electrifying strobe pulses shook the bars walls. The bobbles panicked, listening to the storm. Tried to stay put but fled to their stools once shaken from their resting places. Tonight was going to be, different. Mother knew.

Mother counted the best she could with her index fingers. Their score headed higher, sibling rivalry continued. Flashing light punched Brother Thunder and cast shadowy silhouettes of the just woken Bobbles against the walls. They froze, but their silhouettes didn't. Was this the end they worried, Cal's end? Each palm clasped their hands to the sides of their faces and lowered their jaws to mouths of innocent O's.

Cal twisted, turned, and desperately tried to escape the teeth grinding pain. His face squished to a squatty, wrinkled, sagging mess and jaw stretched as wide as it could go. The wings joined the show slamming against the floor fighting the pain, and dancing to the electrical surges. On, off, ON, off.

"Now boy, nooow, throw me a nickel." Master admired his shinny nails on his left hand purposefully taunting Cal.

Throws? You're a stupid bastard Cal thought, wrinkling his nose.

"Oh my," Master snickered.

Cal couldn't comply, the walls shock, too great. An odd ally, Matron Mary, raced to his side in a moment of gentle weakness. She shoved her hand into Cal's lint filled pants pocket. Her scorched fingers flung it. It missed her mark flying twenty feet to its ricochet off the wall.

"EEEEEEE," the soprano screamed.

"Ohhhh," Farmer tried to collect it, but collapsed.

Mother walked in. Calmly plucked a shiny new nickel from Cal's pocket, slid it in the slot, pirouetted brushing her hands together and walked back to her shadowy home. Master's glare scornfully tracked her. She stopped, turned and glared back. Everyone's eyes were on them.

This is my act, stay out of it, Master thought. A little territorial are we, Mother mind answered. Loud cackling broke the silence. Everyone laughing looked around, except Cal. He was still busy trying to extract his sausage finger from the hole.

The noise of shuffling feet stilled the good humor of the day. Bobbles, Master, and Mother snapped their heads toward one another, then where it came from.

Some Enchanted Evening, from the play South Pacific, melted through the Wurlitzer's grill. The soothing music played over the new sounds and muffled it.

"Waa, whaaa, wheerree am I?" Cal sloppily straightened up after snapping his finger out of the walls socket. He shook his head, blinked sharpening his eyesight. Heard the noise and pointed an ear to Mother's and Master's shadow home. It stopped.

All Bobble sat on their perches, waiting. Electrified Farmer and Mary nervously wiggled around, almost fell had not Sammie reached over the bar and grabbed them.

"Are ya all right now son? Reddy Red rhetorically asked. Cal unconvincingly nodded. Then fell back into his seat. After a few more try's he rubber legged stood.

"I wish Malcolm was here. He really needs to be home. We'll play Race with the devil." Cal winked adding to Sammie's plea.

All the bobbles heads nodded yes. Then, in dismay, shook them sideways looking down at the tiled floor. Indications were this was never going to happen. Smirking Master gleefully shook his head in agreement.

Thunder cracked filling the room with enough amperage to make children flee to their mother's breast, and dogs howl from under couches. Again and again it carried. Lightening answered, pushed back so hard she turned night to day for 15 ticks.

The stunned frightened class never saw the outside lit, sought the refuge of the wall protecting pale eyes.

"We can't get nutin dun today." Sammie said.

"I wish he was here. I'd give him a piece of my—" Reddy Red shot off her mouth as she flew back in. It'd turn out that's all she could shoot.

Another huge volley of lightning and thunder pretzel twisted together in unusual, perfect, sibling unity. The storm, directly above them, flashed, flickered and blinked on and off. It strobe lit the bars interior. Jimmy and Mickey appeared to move. Cal partially squinted, but his curiosity overwhelmed.

Lightning exposed something hidden from Cal thus far. Blue, an odd eerie deep blue color painted on part of the bar's knotty pine paneling wall. It spread over five boards at a height of three feet from the floor. From an eleven o'clock starting position it windshield wiper swept a blue arc to the right down to the floor. From there it bled at the base of the wall out on the floor thickly drying in a free form kidney shape. It blinked in and out as sister furiously fought for respectability. Then, a final furious charge completely lit the bars interior including Master and Mothers hiding spot.

Master pressed his nose into his left shoulder and elevated pointing arm as a sharpshooter would a rifle. Long boney finger tips sighted to his once shadow protected home. Its permanent shadow erased.

"An open house all" he grinned.

The bobbles and Cal twisted frightened heads toward the area following Master's fingers instructions. They screamed.

"Close your eyes!" alto.

"Close your eyes!" soprano.

"Close your eyes!" tenors.

"OPEN YOUR EYES!" bass.

"Gulp" Sammie.

No one ever invited them here before. All quivering eyes opened.

"Ahhh, ahhh, ahhh, the soprano shrieked.

"Aaahhhhhh, alto also.

"Whoaaaaa," bass boomed.

"I- I- I- I- I- I," tenor told.

"Yyyeeaaaaaa," Sammie's raspy voice rivaled thunder, shook heaven and earth, the rafters, and the tile floor. He leapt over the top of the bar, and froze in motion in the light.

"There, there he is, there he is," Master pointed.

"Booom, aghhahah, crackkkk, eieeeee, boommmm, crackkk, ahhahh, hahagh" Master howled at the night, synchronizing in time with Lightening. Mother answered back with Thunder.

Cal cowered.

"Maalcoolmmm," Reddy sang.

"Himmm," Mr. I agreed.

"Maaalllccolm," Sammie barked.

"Maaalllccolm," rumbled from Farmers whisper.

"Maaaaallllcolm," Mary joined the chorus.

There he was standing next to Mother. He'd been in the shadows all the time, watching, and listening.

"Boom," Dust fell.

Cal held his ears, wilted under the deafening artillery noise. Lightning splattered light off and on. The bobble heads moaned to the pulses of Thunders melody and lightning's strobes. Malcolm flickered, on and off. There, then gone, there again and then gone again, frightening, electrifying, terrorizing. Much needed rain wrung from the sky, struck the building's roof, driving a hard drumming beat.

Sammie's eyeliner red eyes watered. Red, for the first time, had nothing to say. Farmer Vaughn, unsure, squinted. Then his melancholy took a hike, replaced by joy remembering the past. Matron quietly sat. Cat like she looked over at Cal, screamed at Malcolm "you Mother's son." Cal stood from his cower, stared at Malcolm as if a ghost. Malcolm did the same at him.

Cal lost. His legs gave out, slumped in his chair. Master looked at him, and then loosely waved his arm. A flash of lightening later Cal sat covered in a purple hooded robe. Crowned with a tall pointy hat ringed with stars around its border, and held a real Maestro's baton in his right hand. The new sorcerer's apprentice looked over at Matron, waved his baton.... The spot light hit the lower floor of the bar. Mother whistled. Matron rose.

Malcolm physically healed after he came home from the war. Went anywhere a motorcycle saddle tramp wanted to go. Bounced at bars, rode the barrel at carnivals, and worked construction jobs all over from Boston to California. Two of his better jobs were in the West Coast, checking tickets at baseball games and Halibut fishing. A tumble weed in wind traveling everywhere he had to go to protect his charge, Tien.

She never knew it but he was always around. Making certain no harm came her way. The shadow game went on for years until graduation day ensured her safety from those who would harm her, and dismissed Malcolm. From afar, on a hill, Malcolm watched the end of Tien's University life commence.

Tien, a brilliant student graduated with her doctorate in biochemistry. Viet Nam bound her to Malcolm for all time. Now, all time was up. She was heading out of California, alone, off to chase her raison d'être, cancer research.

At ceremonies end Malcolm jumped on his BSA Gold Star. A non filtered cigarette pinched tightly in his mouth, dark sunglasses as goggles. He headed home to Fate.

The third stop light leaving town turned red. The Gold Star's engine happily thumped, vibrated and leaked oil at rest, a family tradition. The engines noise was gradually overruled by an unpredicted wind. It kicked up on the calm day.

"Four Horsemen came a riding, riding thru the glen. Four horse–."

Malcolm heard what only he could, but hadn't in some time. It came in on the winds wings on this hot California day. The traffic light held red longer than it should, too long. His nose twitched. Thunder from another motorcycle, a fat black one, drowned out the winds words. On Malcolm's right he saw the rider. He wore a long gray dust coat and dark glasses that hid his eyes. Then another, a red one skidded to a stop on his left, same coat, same glasses. A white motorcycle, with an eye blinding bright white headlight and a rider dressed the same stopped inches behind him. Malcolm was sealed off except in front. The light held red. Finally, a pale rider dressed the same leapt in front of him. The light turned green, but there wasn't anywhere he could go. The invading bikes engines revved in angry unison. Malcolm usually knew ten minutes before a fight there was going to be one. He didn't see this coming. Who were these riders?

Army combat training, Uncle Tim's training, and Malcolm's instincts were his allies. However, his greatest though was being a child of the clouds. He couldn't out run them. The white bike rider crept up and jammed Malcolm's bikes back fender. Malcolm snapped his head. Then the rider on his left, the red bike rider, swung a hammer. Malcolm barely escaped its blow. The rider on his right, the black bike, pulled a long dagger from a sheath strapped to his waist. He sliced at Malcolm, caught his arm. Slashed it open, it healed.

Malcolm fought back wondering how his stealthy assailants possessed such an advantage. The pale bike rider in the front kept him pinned in. The others continued attacking. Malcolm, ducked, swayed. He was in trouble for the first time in a long time. The hammer and knife repeatedly swung and slashed at him. More cuts opened, red flowed then sealed. Malcolm cut the wheel of the BSA, tried to thread through an opening. The pale rider cut him off. The white rider kept slamming into the back fender of Malcolm's BSA Gold Star, jolting him forward.

Tien's protection completed he'd go out in a fight-to the death. A tire bar strapped to his bike for just such an emergency lay ready. The bikes on the left and right sandwiched him blocking him from it. It looked bleak. In the darkening sky a racing the hawk made Malcolm laugh. He thought this bird must know superman.

"Hahahahahaha" harmonized.

"Shhush, we have to get out of here sometime. It sounds far-fetched I know, but it's true, I assure you!" Master walked away nodding to Mary.

"Oooooooooooooooooooo,"

Master whistled–

The hawk bared sharpened talons bullet streaking at its targets. The riders had Malcolm's keen senses. Before the hawk reached them they smartly fled like school boys after breaking the neighbor's window. The tails of their dust coats riding in the wind behind them.

"Baseball references, again?" Cal the sorcerer noted. He shook his head, waved the baton at Matron.

"Shush," Mother.

"Hahahahaha," Bobble heads nodded in agreement.

"Shusssshhhhh, he has more to do." Master, Mother and Cal chimed.

"OOOOoooooooooooooooooo" Mr. I.

"Oooooooooooooooooooo" Red.

"Oooooooooooooooooooo" Sammie.

Farmer and Mary were busy looking at each other. Love was in the air. Mary continued, Master's eyes sprang open being ignored.

Four possessed villains ran from one bird, an old one at that. As fast as they could their bikes raged nosily down the boulevard and out of sight. The bird motherly circled. Time was short. Time, for Malcolm to come home, he'd been gone longer than twenty as Farmer Vaughn would say. Over twenty years.

"Ha ha ah ha," Farmer Vaughn looked around for confirmation. Mary winked, Master hurriedly coughed —

Malcolm made it home a week later on a sunny mid-afternoon day. On his way to his farm house he passed the Little League field. A game was on. The bikes brakes clamped. Malcolm slapped his left black booted foot on the ground, pivoted the Gold Star back around. He stopped. Put her on its stand. The usual oil leak did. Malcolm gave it a casual look for three ticks on his way to three levels of wooden splintery faded green stands. The late summer picture-perfect day-started to set. Half the field baked in sun, the other in shade. A hard to pick up the balls flight off the bat, nightmare. Malcolm remembered his coach coaching. Seemed it always was hard for Malcolm to pick up the ball no matter what, except for that day. That put a smile on his face.

Dark green well cared for grass was two shades. A soft blue sky held a few cotton candy white clouds. A perfect seventy eight degrees gently blew across his rugged face. A better greeting to him than if a band was there. He match lit his unfiltered cigarette. Pushed battered legs straight out to the bench seat on the level below him. Exhaled slowly and for a moment, all was right with the world.

An hour quickly ticked. Casually he looked up at the sky. It had been awhile since he was home. He still knew the area, and the time of day well. Night rushed. He needed to get home, and soon.

The familiar shriek of the umpire's call shouted. Girls in the stands watched the boys. They giggled coyly staring at their favorites, acting as if they didn't care. The boys acted like they didn't see the girls as they hit doubles and took double takes with cat like smiles. Malcolm remembered Stephanie doing the same when he was lost in space, banished to right field.

"Steeeeeeeeeeeeee rike 3," the ump rang him up, called the batter out looking at the third strike.

Dinner was waitin. The ump was hungry. A boy about 12, furious at the call threw his helmet and bat to the ground. Stormed off stiff legged in a mock goose step to the dugout to receive another reprimand from coach about getting called out looking. Malcolm smiled. Some things never change. He took a deep drag.

The game was over. Someone won, someone lost. On his way to the farm house Malcolm stopped to visit Margaret, Sean, Stephanie, Hank, Sali and George. Sullen, he instinctively rode to the family farmhouse wondering if anyone put his statue in the town commons. Or worse yet etched his name on the town monument.

Malcolm quickly filled out after that day on the hill with Hank. Sinewy muscle rapidly clung to his tall, bright eyed mischievous reckless youth's body. Mother Nature knew best. He left town fit. Twenty plus passed since anyone up there had seen him. He arrived home thinner, still about 6'2'. His tall frame wore poorly to his forties, often looked sixty, at times older especially when his skeleton creaked. Parts rubbin, Sean used to say.

Malcolm woke every morning at 0500 hrs. Holding himself erect in the early morning was a struggle and about all he could keep erect. In the bathroom he studied his reflection in the distorted, cracked medicine cabinet mirror. It told the story better than most. While scratching his bare rear, faded pale blue eyes stared back in his reflection.

Like a great photographer, the mirrors image perfectly caught his well worn body. Tufts of grey chest hair centered in a pocket. Sagging chest muscle held together by sinew. A daily ritual that daily made him, wince.

"You can't lie to your own eyes," he confirmed to himself.

Experienced eyes they were. Puffy slits pinned deeply in their sockets. Nature's way shielding his windows from the days light, and the night's fears. They were well matched well to the rest of his angular face, including a lengthening narrow nose that protruded to a rounded point. Thin generally pursed lips spoke only when absolutely necessary. The thick sandy straw hair of his youth turned thin, receded. What remained of it was flecked with grey threads, completing an aged distinguished image.

The impolite, but honest mirror carefully pointed out the most striking detail this face. A pronounced scar that drew stares from the most well-mannered. Its curved mark started just below the outer most corner of his right eye. Hugging the curve of his right cheek it carved straight down to the corner of his lip as a less than subtle reminder of his travels. It bulged when he rarely smiled. Pale placid skin served as the background for his hollow look. The mirror showed him what he looked like. Not who he was. He was of course, a warrior.

"OOOooooooooooooooo," The bobbles moaned.

Master was speechless. Mother whistled, Mary proceeded—

Malcolm finished shaving. Early morning summer sunlight filled the bathroom waking an agonizing soul. It was coming. He knew it. Warrior DNA always did. He fought the light. His eyes winced, shielding penetration. Crash, Malcolm ducked. Puffy eyes forced open. Stealthily, he tiptoed into the living room, Injun quiet, careful not to break a branch. Urine reeked. Gallagher, an inherited fat surly cat pompously sat, surlier than Cal, licking his paws.

"Ahahahahahh," hummed the Bobbles.

"IIIEeeee Hahahahahaha" Master chortled.

"Ha ha, ha," Mother chimed in.

"UUHhhhh Ohhhh," Cal groaned. His baton drum stick fell to the floor. Master started to cough—

Tuffs of white fur perched on his chest as a priest's medallion. His regal-gray coat its backdrop. Gallagher loved to primp. As reigning king of this houses jungle his attitude was, if something broke, toooo bad. The front paws he tasted had eight claws on each. Polydactyl's normally proved to be formidable opponents in the open fields. Not him. Not the spastic. Malcolm the warrior laughed watching his incapable cat chase taunting prey in the yard. He could stalk, and pounce. He wasn't good though. Prey played him. Let him get close, then scamper off running, or flying, or just casually walking away. How embarrassing but the farm needed amusement. Malcolm needed amusement. Gallagher provided.

"How the hell, did I get the only spastic cat in the county?"

Gallagher came from one of the many litter's of the neighbor's cat. Penelope gave new meaning to the term, Cathouse. Regrettably bags of mews were heard all too often at the local lake. There wasn't enough money to support unwanted offspring. Unfit, incapable, should have drowned funny Gallagher escaped his sure fate. Someone rightfully figured Malcolm needed him to provide a few ticks laughter.

Malcolm surveyed Gallagher's damage. He fought flash-back battle scenes. Today's land mine, a broken wine glass left on the table from last evening, lay on the floor. Sometimes it was a plate. Malcolm knew never to leave expensive things around with this klutz of a cat. What a pair, Malcolm and Gallagher. Could they have been more different?

His neck hairs relaxed. Malcolm went to the kitchen. Electric can opener whirring was music to Gallagher's ears. He wouldn't starve. Not today. Malcolm fumbled spooning Gallagher's meal. Gallagher showed appreciation rubbing against Malcolm's ankle scar. A scar he earned the first day he rode the Vincent alone. Hot exhaust pipes will do that, crashes for certain.

Malcolm, adjusting to home, recognized the bar he entrusted Sammie to care for while he was away, needed help. Regulars were few twenty plus ago. Since, city folk bought summer places. The area and customers grew. Soon, the town became a great getaway for prosperous city escapees and poor Sammie could barely keep up. Original locals liked some of the new additions. Not many though. Especially one's with attitudes. But all liked their money. Prosperity spread. Some farmer's became merchants, community leaders and then prosperous politicians.

"Just then, just then" Farmer Vaughn woke. A nominal amount of saliva trickled from his thin lipped mouth. Feebly he wiped it away using the back of a trembling left hand.

"I had a dream Malcolm was back and——" Farmer slobbered, coming to his senses.

All looked, at Cal first, then at the exposed corner where Malcolm stood moments ago. He disappeared.

Friday night ended Saturday morning, 4 a.m. September 9, 2009. It was a very different night. Mother knew it. The bullet holes knew it. Masters pistols knew it, but said nothing, yet.

The light on the floor flickered out. Last notes of the enchanted evening's music died in the air. Bobbles smoked home. Cal hit the couch mumbling about the story he had to write. His arm flopped; 3:45 p.m. Tuesday, August 29, 2009. Fifteen more minutes lost. Tomorrow night couldn't come quickly enough. Time was running out.

# Twenty-Five

Cal liked the color. He stood regally dressed in his purple hooded robe, grimaced, mashed upper and lower jaws.

"Mmmmy turn—-my turn I say."

Reluctantly he nodded approval to Mr. I.

"Heaven Foibid-noooooooooo." Rasped the alto Red.

Mr. I, beamed, stood. Farmer twisted his head, stroked his face wishing he could be dismissed.

"Hehhehehe" giddy Mary's soprano sang a hyena's laugh.

"Ohhhh, boooyyy, this should to be fun." Sarcastic Sammie dry throated.

Master spun two nickels down the chute. One chased the other. A country tune sang a plea for mercy. The light lit the Destiny's stage floor. Outside, the town clock ticked to 9:00 p.m. Saturday, September 9, 2009. Cal glanced at a defying wristwatch. Tuesday, 3:40 p.m. August 29, 2009. Mother just looked, Mr. I started—

"All the regulars were there."

The bobbles giggled intentionally tormenting Mr. I. Third grade was in session.

"Shhhhhush," Red-faced Mr. I weighed in with O protruding mouth, looked at Master, he at Mother who chirped a cough.

~

Destiny's after work scene didn't differ from most other bars. Men and women, old, young, and tweeners, fought for their space. The young were mostly stone hard fit. Their elders, absent youthful shapes were no less strong. Careers of hard farm work saw to it. Some had full heads of hair. Some were relegated honorary cousins of the elf rocks. All were alcohol relaxed. They talked, joked, laughed and argued about most everything, most of the time. Those were the locals.

~

"Giggles," from the Bobbles interrupted, pressing Mr. I's torture. They must have found Masters Writers ink.

"Shhush you morons,"Iiiiiii haaaave mmmmy tale to tell! I imagine you don't understand the Kings English then now, doooo yoooou."

"Shut up you Pedantic Prick," Reddy Reds alliterative alto tongue wouldn't stay sheathed.

"Hmmm-pedantic, Mother that's plagiarism, is it not? Should be a twenty for that, but two will do wouldn't you say?"

"Maybe, but five I think is better. Yes, five."

Mr. I Imagines eyes darted warning glances. He paused, waiting for comments but the admonished quietly sat mashing their lips. He continued with no instruction.

~

Conversations of little significance grew to passionate debates.

~

"ZZZZZZZZZZZZZZZZzzzzzzzz," Farmer Vaughn cast his vote.

"Wake up, wake up right now. You were all there. You saw. You were all there."

Farmer woke, wiped drool from the corner of the left side of his mouth, blinked a few times, two finger saluted Mr. I to continue. Master sighed, coughed.

~

Malcolm stood in front of the bar. A lingering thousand yard stayed well hidden behind deep recesses of no sale eyes.

~

"Mother, oh my. How mellow dramatic. Who is he talking about?" Master couldn't help himself, Mother yawned, it was good enough.

~

On dark, black stormy summer country nights when heavens voice slapped thunderous clattering raps on the bar's roof, Malcolm flashed back to artillery fire, or motorcycles.

~

"Speak English would you, the moment indeed. For Heaven's sake, English, please?"

"Yes Matron, quite, the moment. Something you don't have much more of either. Be aware. He isn't making up the news, just reporting. Ok?" Master defended

"Well I never—"

"I doubt there is much, you never, madam."

Her virtue in question, Matron slumped. Mother held two to her mouth—Mr. I continued, smiling———-

~

The quiet, at home citizen, Malcolm, over-thought. He snatched thoughts of the past watching the present. At the bar his eeeeyes—-

~

Mr. I paused. Looked around, continued.........

~

—flashed about. He hardly spoke.

~

Destiny, a quiet, peaceful, fun place which never had a fight. No one dared. Malcolm's well earned reputation founded in truth, and legend the reason. A warrior hidden in a good boy, groomed, turned angel of death. The puppeteers knew him well.

~

"Ohhh the puppeteers, the puppeteers, the puppeteers—can't you ever get off of that?"

Cal rolled his eyes at Master, shook his head no Mr. I wouldn't. His hood fell. All hoped Master and Mr. I to mix it up in an outright riot. The entertainment would be welcome. Cal looked at the Bobbles with a "what are you kidding me," face. Then silly with laughter, doubled over. He hadn't laughed that hard in years. More his chains fell, his weight lessened. Mother shook her head fearing a verbal blood bath, whistled. Mr. I Imagine struck back-

~

Trust funds and power needed to be protected. Present day, past days, or anything in between. Different names, places. Always the same game, same rules, same outcome, same, innocence lost, forever. Cheated from feeling the sting of cupid's arrow, but not lead rain.

His eloquent delivery stunned. Master slowly backed away repeating a knowing nod, coughed. Then glared at the other onlookers with a, don't interrupt him hollow eyed stare. Mr. I continued-

Images of corpses, especially children's all broken, shot up, and mangled hid behind his slit eyes. Grieving mothers, fathers carrying lifeless, limbless children over muddy trails, all buried deep inside. He had no permission for tears, but all the rage he wanted. It burned coal hot for the real power hidden behind thrones.

Each hour, of each day home, he fought bubbles of guilt. They could not be allowed to break their barriers. The sweet fun Malcolm, taken by the clouds, made killer agent, and it wasn't over. He knew it.

The recitation was a hit. Water leaked from all eyes. Master nodded knowingly to Cal. Cal understood Master intentionally provoked Mr. I knowing only he could deliver that he sought with the reverence and eloquence it deserved.

Spent Mr. I Imagine could not continue. The channeling finished him. His pleading eyes locked with Cal's. Cal turned, looked at Matron Mary. She stood, Mother coughed—

During his long train ride from the city he emboldened himself with whisky mouth from the several he had. The well educated, wealthy, minor puppeteer walked drunk into Destiny. Evening fell but not Malcolm's eyes.

"Get me my drink this instant my good man and I'll reward you handsomely." The showman pulled a plump right hand from his well tailored high- grade woolen pants pocket. A packet of highly numbered bills were pinched together by a gold monogrammed money clip. The dapper man un-pinched a few, held them in his fingers high over his head, and released them. Like autumn leaves they fell to the veined, dark stained gouged bar surface.

"Buy them a drink. Buy them all a drink," he bellowed as he examined his company. Malcolm's angry eyes shifted, teeth clenched. He didn't like this man, not at all. He knew him somehow, not personally, but knew him.

A whisky conversation broke out about war. Usually bad bar talk. The portly train rider, a practicing blowhard braggart, stood swaying, unsightly sweaty. He let all know his feelings.

"What do you know of such things sir? Exactly what do you have to go on?" asked Sammie while he stood behind the bar at its end.

"Well my good bartender, my father was a combat decorated hero from WW2."

"A noble war sir but what do, you, know of such things?" Sammie replied?

"And my uncle fought in Korea."

"An unfortunate war sir, an unfortunate war, again, what do you know of such things sir? What do you know?" Sammie's challenge's escalated.

"And my dear nephew was an officer in Viet Nam."

Malcolm turned, squinted.

"Thank him for his service, they should not be forgotten. But, again, I ask you. What do, you, know of such things?"

"What do I know?" The man angrily shot back.

"I'll tell you what I know. I pay thousands of dollars in taxes to support our countries missions—that's what I know."

"Sir, you know nothing of these matters, nothing. I think you should leave, now."

The man's face flushed, swelled as an inflated child's birthday balloon. Yellow tinted eyes, bulged. Consumed with anger, and other liquid things, his right hand slipped from its cool wet grasp of his scotch to stroke his fine wool pin striped suit jacket's left lapel. Stealthily he thought his hand slid inside over the left breast of his custom made shirt.

"That would be a mistake Sir, a big mistake. A—very—big–mistake." Sammie repeated.

This was the country. In country bars firearms were not strangers. Mr. Blowhard hadn't a chance. Twenty to thirty souls were in the bar that evening. Some regulars, the rest were weekend city visitors of different kinds, ages, types. Five locals especially looked on. Well armed, very, very, well armed.

The bobbles knowingly nodded their smug smiles to one another. Master whispered a whistle-She continued-

The man pulled an empty, trembling hand, from inside his finely tailored jacket. When he looked up he saw five single shot pistols waiting. All aimed at his mortal body. Farmer and Mr. I pointed point blank at his left and right temples. Red pointed hers at the middle of the man's forehead. Sammie's at his knee. A punitive blow if fired. Mine I placed at his heart. I'm the best marksman excluding Malcolm.

Matron smiled, blushed, continued—

Cocked pistol hammers waited instruction. Time stood still as he quaked. Both fat, over fed pudgy hands found the bars lip, yielding before he saw his maker.

"Don't shoot –please don't shoot," he stuttered a plea.

They didn't, and wouldn't. But not couldn't. Mercifully he was given time to run. Fifteen choppy steps from the doorless front door he accidently fell over someone's well placed foot. His big fat head hit the floor. Recovering to his knees he coughed. He coughed again, and spat out a gold molar. It shined in the glancing light as it lay on the floor. He scurried through the doorway, never to be seen again. The folk music continued. Malcolm loved music, mostly bluesy rock, and coffeehouse folk. The rest of the customers didn't flinch, never worried, not for a second.

Matron finished early that Sunday morning, 5:30 a.m., September 10, 2009. Cal's watch still disagreed: Tuesday 3:30 p.m., August 29, 2009. Mother frantically added. Morning light flickered. The bobbles fled in smoke. Cal went to bed sensing he was closer to going home, but trouble lay ahead.

# TWENTY-SIX

Tap Tap.... Tap, Tap, Tap.......Tap tap -tap -tap -tap –tap, Mother's telegraph tapping toe kicked up flour trapped in her stores splinting wood floor. Night rolled in, there wasn't much time left. Sweaty Cal ran in. Grabbed a stuffed roll—

"Ugh, phew, feh–" He spat it out.

"Bitter, what's this carp? I really need some NYC juice, high-test black coffee.

"Is that tuna? It tastes bad." Cal wrinkled. Mother smiled. Secrets were...secrets.

"Well, what have you learned today, Caaaaaalll?" Mother was covered in flour.

"Not sure, Mother. I know this though. If I'm not in there in a minute someone isn't going to be very happy."

"Well it's good to see you are becoming more aware of a few things anyway. Aren't you?"

"Okay, stop laughing. Yeah I suppose. Weird though. I'm remembering a lot of things I haven't thought of in a looong time, Mother."

"Good, bad?"

"Some good and, some bad but oddly some things I never paid much attention to at the time, but should have. I need to listen better."

"Yes, yes you do,"

"I'm off. I don't need another lecture."

"No, you do. Some luck also." Mother chuckled with her trademark grin and then nodded toward the door.

Cal hustled out of sight of her goodbye waving left hand fingers parted making a vee. Thumb tucked in its palm.

"Quickly, quickly, the seat, take your seat man."

"Man, hmmm?" Cal scratched his beard.

Freed his finger, and stood dressed in Master's gift, the regal hooded robe. It hung loosely on his scarecrow frame. He extended his hand with a turned up cupped palm, curled his fingers back toward him. Mary was summoned. Master's pupil, had two favorite pupils. Well worn Mary, and always testy Red. Farmer fidgeted worried he would be selected, sighed when he wasn't. Later, fragile Sammie would do more. His strained voice wore hoarse and could be used only sparingly. Reliably risky Mr. I sat in a harrumph, underutilized. Mother whistled- Matron spoke—

Muggy, late summer overcast afternoons were good times for Malcolm to prep the bar. An evening's rush was hoped for, and expected. Newbie's packed the place on the weekends. Sean would have been impressed. Original townies always salted the place.

The chosen ones proudly bobble head nodded to each other.

"Hey, where is he anyway? I, I, I think you're—-"

"—-shut up you buffooooon," Red the alto sang.

"He'll be back. He has to. Why he's the only one who knows what happened here, for real. So listen up. Maybe we can all get the he-double-ll, out of here." Sammie strained, Mother coughed-

Glasses were always properly rinsed, occasionally washed. Readied for the old times specialties of shot's, and beer's. Dusty disorganized shelves held their favorite brands of hard liquor. Some labels pointed forward, most not. Optimum expedient service was never considered but well rewarded.

The martini crowd grew. Their drink demands competed for attention, and shelf space. A particular brand of liquor counted if it were the first. The third made little difference. Malcolm or Sammie regularly mopped the bars top clean with a dirty rag. If they were to stay in business change was needed, not coinage. Needed quickly also, for this crowd of would be socialites would grow weary of bacterial or virus infections.

Six p.m. one early evening an empty bar gave Malcolm the chance to prep for the expected onslaught. His chin rested on his chest standing at the sink, rinsing glasses, lost in distant thought of distant places, of distant times. His shoes soles shuffled, and then tapped. It didn't rouse him. The dog snorting did. Malcolm lifted his head, peered over the bar. A waif of a girl by passed his early warning system.

He judged her about twenty-two. She sported a bouncing, long black pony tail. It hung on the other side of her brown eyes. Courageously she entered what was known as a mostly male establishment. Two bulldogs her bookends. A male named Ernest, and his companion the lovely Ernestine. Ernest peed on a chair. Ernestine snarled and growled at him. He sat, looked away. She knew bad manners.

~

"It wasn't really ya know, all men that is. Me, and Matron saw fit to that, and a few others."

Matron's nod's agreed with Reddy. Cal slouched playing the air guitar. Master shrugged and wagged his head. Mother giggled. Light grew brightly on the stage floor. Classical music filled the air. The Wurlitzer cruised. Mother coughed over Master's whistle. Mary went on....

~

The girl stood nervously grinning. Malcolm went about his so-so cleaning. Squinting, he cautiously stared still confused how she escaped the radar.

"What da ya want?"

She looked down, slid a foot.

"What do ya want?"

She motioned as if to sweep. Then wipe. Malcolm's forehead wrinkled. He leered.

"What, do- you- want, I said?"

Her head bowed. Then, raising a bent wrist she pointed behind her to the left front window.

"What do you want, what do you want, what do you want. I ask you, tell me now."

Malcolm's frustration rattled Destiny's walls. The girl's eyes welled. Tears fell as she gazed past the hem of her tattered brown dress, hiding her eyes, looking at her best yellow shoes. They were used when she first got them as a gift, and her only shoes.

Malcolm followed her arms direction to a red neon beer sign hanging in the window.

"Tell me what you want damn it you little bi—. Can't you speak girl? Are you a mute?"

~

"OOOOOO" seethed from the peanut gallery.

"Shut up, shut up. My goodness,"…. Master.

Mary smiled, nodded thankfully in the direction of Master then—

~

Malcolm forgot. The onslaught of new customers—weekenders mainly, put demands on his and Sammie's abilities beyond their abilities. Months after his return from California, Malcolm anemically decided to look for some part time help. One rainy day his aging bulging veined hands, with nicotine stained fingers and nails, crafted a scribbled Help Wanted sign with a nub of a pencil on frayed loose leaf paper. He posted the barely legible announcement in the left front window in front of the red neon beer sign with clear tape. One week, two weeks, and then three passed. No one applied. The tape yellowed.

Most people in those parts were fully employed, principally in farming. Newbie's, the weekenders from the city, were flush with cash. Not remembering the sign made sense as remembering for Malcolm was something he wasn't particularly good at. Forgetting, he was better. Malcolm gave up looking for help, forgot about the fading unnoticed sign, but never removed it.

~

"Funny, how we souls meet sometimes, isn't it? Yes, funny indeed. Perhaps a chance happy meeting, or an irritating encounter, both purposeful." Master rolled his left hand over and over.

"Or, maybe, just maybe it comes in a dream, day or night." Mother added, whistled.

Matron went on.

~

Slowly the girl stutter raised her head. Salty watermarks stretched from the corners of pale brown eyes, hugged her cheeks curves, and stopped at the corners of her mouth. Malcolm's eyes opened wide. The light finally went on.

She was a mute, couldn't speak if she tried. His pre-occupation with his own world prevented him from seeing hers. He was rude, not evil. He remembered the sign. Grunted a school-boy guilt ridden apology and offered her the job. Finally, he found someone foolish enough to give him the help he desperately needed. Wounded, she paused delaying an immediate acceptance. Coyly, she darted shifting eyes between red and black tiles, feigned deep thought. Malcolm fretted. Hundreds of ticks ticked. Then a nodding yes let him off the hook. Irresistibly she smiled lighting almost all four corners of the room. Malcolm's imprisoned smiled broke free.

~

"Not my corner, she could have never lit up my corner."

"Shush." Mother scolded.

"I said almost. Don't you hear well old man?" Mary lectured, Master started to cough but she went on before he could—

~

Truly, she couldn't speak but, Malcolm could never hurt her feelings. The job was to be hers at any expense, even Malcolm's. Tactics counted, and the magic of guilt. Malcolm remorsefully reached into less than clean pants. He grabbed a role of bills at the bottom of his right pocket, next to the grime. Forcibly he pressed a forgiven week's wages in her petite left hand. Compensation earned for callousness. She was not his equal, nor he, hers.

~

"Awwww" Bobbles whimpered.

Cal yawned, and then said. "I would have seen though her act in a minute. Clever waif though."

"Certainly— you would have." Master's lips squished a glass.

Mother frowned.

Cal slumped.

POP, POP- -Sail, and away, filled in blanks on the wall's neon sign. Clusters of flickering lit words, and intermingling dark blanks shaped incomplete jig-saw puzzle sentences. Cal thought more light from the dark. Mother smiled faking a whistle, Mary continued–

~

Years separated them in age, yet quickly she became very important. Two weeks evaporated from when she first arrived. Regulars debated how this angelic creature, with hips to young for her argued age, came to town? A runaway from New York City, abandoned? Some thought they saw her living in the Vaughn's woods, in a cardboard house. Soon her uncertain origin lost importance. Beer, gin, and scotch didn't. George Thorogood's song lamenting same, rocked. Within weeks, she moved to the farmhouse.

~

"UUHhhhh ooohhhhhh,"

"Stop that you idiots" Master spun.

Cal strummed his air guitar, listening, not needing notes. Master, in a mood rustled. Mother looked for a sharp object, whistled. Mary went on.....

~

Motherly Sera and Malcolm's relationship grew. Each had a bedroom.

~

"Applause," The baritone, alto and soprano, the bass slept.

"What if something did happen-so what? Jealous idiots–" Master chided.

Mary shrugged, continued, the lit floor grew brighter—

~

For no reason, other than her reason, Sera told Malcolm things from out of the blue.

"Memories, Malcolm, well they are just that and, first looks can be deceiving, beware."

Warm evening's she'd catch his eyes with reflected smiles. Her simple words calmed better than damp cool evening breeze's brushing the front porch. Sera's kitchen's calendar pages flipped. By year's end Sera was Queen of the farmhouse. She had one major discipline, Gallagher tip toed in and out.

Unusual subtle changes transpired come spring. Lush, richly colored gardens grew where Sean's drained motor oil earth forbid. Shepherds Walk borders sprouted green shoots that held plumes of vibrant yellow, red and violet flowers. They lined the pathway from the farmhouse kitchen door to the barn, as lights would a runway.

Late April, friendly four and two legged creatures visited, and stayed. Cows, sheep, pigs, dogs, cats, crows, doves, rabbits, hawks and others moved in. They loved to play, and rest in their sunny sanctuary. Afternoon sun burned the bravest. The barn's shadow offered protection to those smart enough. Gaggle's of peaceful animals, an eclectic odd lot.

Word got out through-out the county. Angelic Sera healed Shepherd's Walk. Locals nominated her mother earth. Yet, no one ever found out where she hailed from. When asked she answered with a smile. Said, here and there–the wind brought me in.

"Not a place for you." Malcolm protectively banished Sera from working at the bar. An order he demanded she respect. Her agents, Ernest and Ernestine were left there in her absence as her agents. Someone she trusted had to keep an eye on things, especially Malcolm. A good job for them, particularly Ernest, he loved night life.

The dogs slept during the daytime. A noisy affair, one snored, the other farted. An hour or so later they politely switched offenses. Each respected the other's territory, or offenses. Clumsy Ernest unique ability sensed someone not welcome in the bar, even before Malcolm. When he did, he'd clod hop to them, raised a leg and—-. Malcolm had the unwanted guest by the neck before they could retaliate. After, he patted Ernest on his slobbering head. Never a discussion, never a doubt, Ernest– was always correct and like Malcolm, Ernest always knew there was going to be a fight, ten minutes before. Ernestine had all she could handle reigning in the over-round, rough around the edges, love of her life.

Before Malcolm left the farmhouse for his night's work of pouring drinks and ending fights, he served a drink to his favorite customer first. Fine Red Zinfandel wine with shaved dark chocolate floated on top. Sera's favorite sweet, bitter sweet. Malcolm cleverly named it "The Sera."

Malcolm returned home from work, very late, one Friday night. He couldn't sleep. Lying in bed he took another drag, blew out his book propped open bedroom window with the sun warped melted glass panes. Sera wouldn't approve.

Windswept children's laughter carried from the barn, down Shepherd's Walk, and snuck inside his room. He laid his head down, listened. Thought to investigate but fell asleep. Night table draw open, pistol loaded—

~

"Blah, Blah, Blah," Master found a full case of writer's ink.

"Stop that. We want to hear." The tenor resonated.

"Well my friends. And I use that loosely. You want to hear, is it?" Master rolled his palm at them.

"Stop that this instant," Mother lunged for the bottom of his cape.

"It's not what you want– to know, that you're going to hear. Likely, it's what you need to." He twirled from her grip.

"Oooooooooooooooooo…Hey, where's all this going?"

"Not where it's going, where it's– coming from, idiots. Now, pay attention." Master nodded to Cal.

Sorcerer Cal raised his baton, pointed it at Sammie. Released Mary limped to her stool, and clung to Farmer. Sammie cavalry horse leapt over the bar, turned, Mother chuckled, and he hoarsely started—

~

Malcolm slept in most Saturdays but that morning he woke in sweat to more strange voices. They too floated on the wind from the barn, and filtered through his window. Since returning home he ventured in the barn only once to honor the Vincent's grave. Today curiosity trashed concern. On went his trousers, an unbuttoned cowboy shirt, boots. He jumped down the stairs missing many. Skidded through the kitchen, and out to Shepherds Walk. The screen door had another hole.

Malcolm picked-up the pace, closed the distance between the house and barn. The voices sharpened but still unrecognizable. He grabbed the splintering, flaky white painted creaky barn door by its rusting handle. Pulled it opened. Sera hurriedly walked out from behind it holding her left hand up in a policeman's palm signal to stop an inch from his nose. Malcolm's dusty cowboy boots heals forked the dirt. Behind her, a young teen boy about 14 wiped grease off his hands. Malcolm's eyes popped.

෴

"Oh, she's too old for him," an alto jokingly blurted.

"Shut up you idiot," Cal picked up Master's vocabulary.

He's the mechanic isn't he, Cal thought?

"Yes—Son, yes he is."

"Yes, yes." Mary confirmed. Mother coughed

Sammie went on—

෴

Sera lowered her hand. Then spoke to Malcolm in sign language she taught him. She said-

"I thought we could farm some of the acreage. I needed to repair some of the old equipment in the barn. You're not a mechanic. I heard the new owners of the Vaughn's farm had a talented son and worked inexpensively. Three days ago I walked over and struck a bargain with him and his mother."

Malcolm nodded. The boy coughed.

෴

Mother and Master looked at each other, and then nodded to Sammie.

෴

The boy extended his hand. Malcolm just stared at him holding his hands by his side. Then nodded to Sera, and walked away. Fourteen days and nights passed. Malcolm became accustomed to him. The wizard boy fixed the unfixable. But couldn't fix his relentless hacking dry cough, or why he got short winded easily. His mother called him

Red. Not for his head but his red face when frustrated. Not quite stop sign red—more muted, very noticeable.

"Why do they call you Red?" Malcolm asked.

Red didn't answer.

"Why do they call you Red?"

No answer again. His snow white face filled to a hint of cherry. His feet scuffled. Angry hands fist flexed open and closed. A strange woman charged through the farm house's screen door. Red's mother just arrived to pick him up. She and Sera were talking in sign language.

She wagged a finger screaming something not to be heard in church dressed in a yellow and blue flowered summer's dress freshly purchased from the only clothing store in town, Matrons store. The gap closed.

"He can't speak, the boy can't speak. Stand aside." She lashed.

"Born that way –born that way at birth, leave him be."

Any chance Malcolm had ridding himself of Red just vanished. He became an official member of the yard that day, he and his persistent cough.

Red worked mostly when Malcolm wasn't around. His lair, the barn Malcolm wouldn't go in. They were in there. Nighttime laughs mixing in the foggy air and serenading howling dogs.

"Great, now two mutes." Cal waved his baton with a noodle arm.

Master howled, and then groaned. Mother smiled swinging her elbow. Sammie looked, they nodded.

Red left arm in arm with his flustered mother. Malcolm stood motionless, embarrassed, and slightly ashamed. He didn't know. Should have, missed it again just like when he met Sera. He worried how, followed them leaving in their pick-up truck down the farms drive.

While tracking them he heard only what he could with no storm, thunder. The second Mother of All Battles was near."

The town clock ticked forwards to 2:45 a.m., Monday morning, September 11, 2009. Cal's watch ticked slowly backward, 3:20 p.m., Tuesday August 29, 2009.

# Twenty-Seven

His sharpened senses tasted loneliness atop Snake Hill Road, lost in the sight of an ever changing valley. Cal left the hill hungry. Mother's dubious food, suggested never dictated expert advice, waited. His questions were answered with her questions. Spoon feed her tactic, when he just didn't get it. Gently she honed with a style much different from his eminence.

"Mother— Motttheerrr," Cal's wings crisply sole razor strap slapped the floor.

"Mother, Mother," might as well been mommy.

"Yes son? Yes?" She strolled from the back.

"I ssaaaw, ugh, ugh, I saw—"Cal gagged, coughed, panted. Folded at the waist, he rasped and wheezed. His abused lungs struggled siphoning what little air they could through their clogged ductwork.

"I saw the—-"cough, blood spat to his palm in a stuttering renewed start.

"I saw the dammmest thing," finally cannoned.

Mother looked up, focused on Cal holding his right side. He struggled to stand.

"What son, what— did you see?"

"Hee–iiit—waaaaas, eeeehhee—rou—rou– rouuutine... forty-seven," he wheezed.

"Yes?"

Sixty ticks passed. Cal recovered. Caught his breath, stood, stroked his forested throat stood and—

"Mother, you know, I went up to the hill today, as usual, looked around. Always seems a little different but today—Oh- my-gosh."

"What dear, what— did you see?"

"It was all fine one minute. You know, the same and all, then-whoa. Picked my head up and nuthin was around."

"Nuthin, are you Sammie now?"

"Excuse me, nothing! Nothing was around!"

"So what, explain please."

"The tall grass, you know the stuff. Grows stupid fast overnight around here overnight."

"Yes son, I am quite aware."

"Well, as usual, it stood tall. Straight, untouched as ever. Like every day."

"Your breathing sounds better and better quit smoking. It could kill you. So you were saying?"

"It was fine one minute, as always as usual. No cows today showed up to graze. Th, Th, the, thenn it was—"

"——It was trampled when you turned your head around to look at it again. With nothing around, nothing you could see? Correct?"

Cal's eyes popped, jaw slipped, listening to Mother complete his sentence.

"I saw it on my very first trip to the hill, when I first got here. Didn't believe my eyes, thought it tiredness. I didn't want to tell to anyone. Crazy thoughts they'd think. Perhaps I am going there, crazy. But this—this I saw, clearly." Wisps of weary tears leaked from the grays. His hands gestured an apology.

"You're not crazy son. By the way, if you're not a little crazy in this world, well, you run the risk of going completely insane." she beamed

Cal pointed a wrinkled brow toward her thinking– I wonder if Master knows she's stealing his lines?

"I gave it to him."

"Ok, sure, I'm not getting involved in that, but, what happened? What didn't I see?"

"It's getting close son, very close. You'll see, soon enough. Now, what else did you see today?"

"Do I have to–say?" Cal cowered.

"No, no you don't." Mother strutted to the back wearing her patented tight lipped smile.

"Well, okay. This going to seem even crazier," Cal cracked.

"Let me be the judge of that son." She walked back to the front.

Cal sighed. His head slumped, wagged back and forth and said–

"I saw them, again. I'd seen them before."

"Who,—Who?" Mother interrogated.

"All of them, I saw the kids playing on the hill."

"Oh, My, did you really? Did they trample the grass?"

"Stop, I'm serious and nooooo- no wayyy. They were riding down the hill screaming at each other, whipping each other with willow tree branches."

"Why wouldn't you have told me that before?"

"I wawawass scared, no terrified." Cal focused on the flour dusted floor.

"I was told I would see M……."

"By whom,"

"The wind—Mother, the wind, the answers are in the wind."

"Well of course some are, silly boy. You have been listening. You are becoming— more aware then, aren't you?"

"I guess so. I hope so?"

"You've missed a lot–son, in your days."

"No, no, I've been paying attention. Really I have. I remember everything that's gone on."

"No son, not here— not over the last days. Over your life you've missed a lot, and you were told."

"Told, told to–"

"–Yes, told. You'll remember. From friends, strangers, allies, foes, someone agreeable, or irritating. Old, young, black white or yellow, maybe in daydreams. But always in your night dreams, it matters not. You'll listen now. Won't you?"

"Soooo, I'm just to listen, to anything, anybody. Agree passively, do whatever I am told. No matter from whom, or where? Is that correct?"

"Dear boy, when you ask for answers you have to think. Ask, look, listen, and think. Tune in, be aware of your surroundings, people, what you hear, what you say. Listen to your instincts. Be aware. Now go. Have a good time tonight, I may see you later."

"Good time, tonight?" Since when did we start having a good time around here he thought?

"Are we going to have a dance?"

Mother's wry tilted face raised an eye, smiled back, and stayed mum.

"Ugh," Cal walked away frustrated with the riddles. Leapt over the bakery's doorway into the day's fast fading daylight, trotted to the Bar, late.

"Come on come on hurry, hurry." Master impatiently paced. His arms flailed about, gesturing.

"Do not, dilly-dally. Times wasting, no dawdling. It's going to start without us if we're late."

"Huh?" Sweat glued Cal's shirt. Breathless, he threw himself in his electric chair. His finger plugged the first hole available. Wham.

No hard punching shock, a buzz. Master noted with a raised eyebrow. He tilted his head to the left.

"Progress–we're close Mother."

"Yes, we are, very. He'll be leaving us, soon. Time's running out. Did you hear about–?"

"—the grass bit, yes, of course." Master rolled his hand.

Mother nodded irritated with Masters bad manners. She overlooked this incident. Time was late, and running out.

Cal rapidly flipped three nickels at Master hoping to catch him off guard. Old guards, like Master are never off guard. He snagged all three, in mid-air flight. Professional, short-stop bare-backhand catches.

I know a few teams that could use him, Cal thought.

"They can't afford me. Not even the Yanks. Besides, I don't play minor leagues."

"Nooo, I meant the major leagues. The major's silly." Cal nodded confirmation.

"Soooo did I, silly boy. So did I. Your leagues aren't major leagues where I come from." Master held his hips, Santa laughed. Though he adored sarcastic wit, his comment was serious.

Mother confirmed Master's claim with her sideways pursed lips smile, and nodding head bob.

The Wurlitzer's mechanics clanked and clunked swallowing Masters first insertion. Shark hungry it needed to be well fed, especially tonight. Bobble's bobbled facing each other. Tonight they had company, more than usually. Destiny was packed. Cal stood and resumed his rightful place. Master loudly coughed.

The sixties California group Jefferson Airplanes song- Somebody to Love- rocked. It sounded so good. As if they were there, Grace Slick with short black mini skirt and all. Standing by the bar two newbie's to the scene, men, were drinking, laughing, talking.

Cal stood, walked toward them intent on a Destiny specialty, eavesdropping. Master waved his hand giving Cal permission to do as he pleased. Within ear shot he heard—.

"Ahhh, she had CBS."

"What's that my friend?"

"Cranky bitch syndrome my daddy used to say."

They smart-alecky laughed. Mary and Red glared. Mother calmly, calculatingly, stared.

Tempting fate they went on—

"She caught me buying love, so she fired me. I still have a warm spot in my heart from knowin her, and a hole in my wallet also." The shorter one ducked.

"Good." Reddy Red and Mary, soprano and alto harmonized.

The rest of the bobbles howled.

"Ahhh, damn–" Cal slipped. Thunder rumbled.

"Hey, am I in this story, or reporting it tonight? What's going on? I'm confused?"

The music screeched to record scratching halt. All turned and angrily shouted.

"Both."

Mother and Master winked at each other-"We are close."

The super trooper spot light lit all. Master sat alone on a stool. Gracefully he slid his hands up and down the neck of a 1958 Les Paul guitar looking at Hendrix's poster. Perfectly he picked the notes in sync with the music, as if he were trained by the best. Reddy Red sat next to one of the strangers. Good looking, brown curly haired, athletically built guy. A young pretty thing walked by them. Instinctively he turned his head. Red blurted–

"Hey what are you looking at? You know back in the day I was really something, myself."

"What day was that, I musta missed that one? Anonymously was screamed out."

All howled except Red. Later, Mr. I howled again. A finely sharpened pencil stuck from his leg. Strong drink fueled stronger conversations. Music punched the air. The super trooper spot light beam found him uniting him with all, except Malcolm.

"Dance Cal, Dance "Master ordered, times running out.

"Where's Malcolm? I've got to get out of here." Cal's robes hood feel off backwards.

"Heeee's around" harmonized

"Dance? OH, heck, it— is—- a—- dance."

"Yes, Cal, tis a Daaaance–" Mother shouted.

"Dance Cal Dance—Suck the marrow out of the bone of life boy-Dance." Master jumped off the stool, slide-stepped.

And with that order, Cal did. They all did, all night long. Air guitars, real guitars, drum sticks rapping the bar top. Singing alone, with someone, good, bad, didn't matter. Judgment day was coming.

"Finger wag your worries away my friend. Tonight, no issues—wave them off."

"Okay Master, well I want to, but I have baggage."

"Yes, I know boy. You all have baggage. Find someone whose baggage matches yours." Dust parachuted.

"Whaaa, why would ...." Cal dog twisted his head toward Master.

"Never mind that now. But listen, if you didn't have any baggage then you likely haven't lived now, have you?"

It was the first thing Master said that evening that made sense.

"He should know. He has enough baggage to overload a dozen caravan camels." Mother jabbed him again.

"Hey Mary M" Cal liked calling Mary the Matron that.

"What ya doing Mary M?"

"Dancin, killin time, drinkin wine, want some?"

"Better not, but thanks. Difficult enough handling these past days sober much less drunk but hey, watcha been so mad at me about?"

Matron stopped dancing in her tracks. Farmer flew, waving his arms, into the wall.

"When you're done here, soon, and you're gone, he's gonna leave. Farmers gonna leave and I'm never going to see him again."

"Whaaa...?"

"Nonsense dear," Master stepped in front of Cal. "Cal needs you, now. To clear the air, square the books, and help him get the story. You'll still be here, or there."

Mary sighed, and then chased after Farmer. Cal spoke.

~

The night went on. Music screamed through every porous thread of the old Wurlitzer's grill. Its lights blinked, flashed reds, yellows, blues, greens, and whites, all at the whim of the Wurlitzer. The colors painted the ceiling and walls, timed to the mood of the music, changed with machine gun speed. Beautiful, even the bars flies looked different in the light, alive.

Accompanying the light were flashes of conversations, especially around the pool table. That showed up exclusively for this special night with accompanying players, courtesy of Master.

Merv the curve they called him, owned a bookstore, a copy of Lady Chatterley's lover in his right back pocket of his faded blue jeans. Odd to most, Merv, a failed writer, wrote one good line once, advice from a character to another suffering a broken heart.

"Go find a spell breaker," it said. That's all. To him love was like being under a spell. The only way to break it, find someone else. Someone to, "break the spell." Best not anger him. Army taught him to be pretty good with a knife. A curved knife, cheating at the pool table was out. His shifty eyes saw all.

Gladiola Gwen stood at the far end of the green felt. Her skin, white as the petals of that plants flower. A decent pool shot but her real strength featured teasing boys. She gave them all a good look when leaning over the table to reach a difficult shot. Her top rode up, her hip hugger pants pulled down. Guys lined up to help her, from the front, behind, all genuinely offering suggestions how to make the shot thinking how they could make her. She acted unaware.

Rack them up Reggie earned his name from his many car wrecks. Not from shooting pool. A bit of a clown that routinely held up two pool balls, rolled them around in his hand and shouted– "Look at me I'm Captain Queeg." It was the only thing he learned in English class before he was thrown out of school for good. He had extra long arms, big hands and feet. Good features to help one be a natural at most things sport but now, an accomplished pool hustler. He and his friend's scammed unsuspecting marks using their unique technique that went like this–

"Although once very good, he lost his pool stroke. Doc's said his injuries would never allow him to regain those skills. We humor him. Let him play a friendly game, that's all. We can't let our friend get taken advantage of. Besides, he's always been a little off from his childhood beatings. Shame, he was very good years ago." Once his friend sold the mark, Reggie then spoke-up asking to play in a feeble way.

Friendly games, intentionally dumped, teased the mark for a money game. Miraculously Reggie magically healed during a moment of lucidity and turned into his former sharp shooting self.

"Wow, what a temporary lucky break." His friends told the ripped off mark, defending Reggie. They counted the fresh cash.

Master had access to the most unique cast of characters. Tonight he imported the best. The evening wore on. Excessive drinking combined with some friendly and not so friendly conversations.

"Menopause–? Isn't that the period of time a woman goes through before she becomes a man?" One foolish guy said to Red? Good thing the door was off or he would have been seen sticking through it. He landed in the street. Oversized pants slid ankle chaining him. His silhouette tried to pull them up as he ran.

"Come on nature, talk to me." Rack em up Reggie said taking a shot. No one but Master and Mother really knew what he meant. Reggie was an earlier pupil of Master and Mother.

An hour till dawn an older, well dressed, gentleman crossed the saddle of the doorless front door. He slapped a one-hundred dollar bill on the bar, looked intensely at Sammie.

"I need a scotch. Do you think you can make that ha—-?"

"— is that what you want?" Sammie gloated holding the man's drink.

"Thank you. Nice place, how much?" The gentleman asked.

"How much what?" Sammie wrinkled his forehead looking at Malcolm.

"How much to buy it?" The man reached in his pocket. All at the bar turned, but didn't move.

"Buy it?" Sammie wondered.

"The bar, Sir.

"Would you sell your soul?" Sammie moved closer.

"Maybe I have." He looked down. "Maybe I have." echoed.

"Well friend, the place ain't for sale. My guess though is in a few weeks—you may be back here, under different circumstances and all." Sammie looked over at Master and Mother. They both nodded back, and smiled.

"Another nickel, quickly, can't have it stop. No stopping the music." Master reached, palm out. Cal began–

"You know, I haven't heard that song in a long time. 60's I guess." The gentlemen said.

"Do you miss it?" was asked.

"What?"

"The 60's, you silly old man– do you miss it?"

"NO, but– I wouldn't have missed it."

Sammie and he doubled over laughing. Malcolm looked away trying to suppress a rising right cheek. When Malcolm tended adopted brother Sammie stood protectively close. He knew Malcolm so well he could, and often would speak for him as Malcolm wouldn't like to.

"Hey, bought a house, next town over, finally got something for my money other than a headache." The gentleman raised his voice over the ringing of the bar phone. Sammie answered.

"Is Reggie here?"

"What's left of him is."

"Well your wife is on the phone. You– were supposed to be home, an hour ago. Better get."

Reggie pecked Gwen's cheek. She swiped at him as he jogged out the door. He felt tremors of another storm brewing and raced home looking all around.

Last minutes of the party night ticked. The gentleman and Mary the M talked.

"You know, when life isn't being so desperately tragic, it can be so ridiculously funny." she said. He looked at her, she back at him.

Maybe another time, another place, maybe, he thought. He wasn't aware he'd be back. She was, and so was Farmer carefully watching.

"TIMMMMEEES UP!!" Master shouted.

"UUHooohhhhhhh," All groaned.

All house lights turned till the room was brightly lit. All, except for the Masters sliver. The Wurlitzer blared. Pulsing, flashing lights designer colored the walls. The overcharged crowd readied. The final dance, of the dance, began. Master, Mother and a grudging Malcolm hooked arms. Arms were raised, and lowered. Gwen, Mary the M, the Gentleman, Farmer Vaughn, and Reddy Red took their places on the lower spot lit floor. Mr. I pushed the chairs and tables aside. This was it.

"Time to Stroooooolll," Master showed his tonsils to all.

The nights closing dance, the stroll, was a line dance. Men stood shoulder to shoulder in a line on one side of the floor. Across from them the women did same facing their male partner. A wide passable danceable path left between them. When the music started all danced in place. Then, first couple at the head of the line left their positions, moved to one another in the space between the two lines. To the music, and the singer singing Strooooolll, they stroll danced together through the pathway, past the others, to the tail end of the lines, parted and rejoined the others. As they danced both lines moved filling the vacated spots, and then next couple in line followed the previous dancers. On it would go till the stroll ended.

A new nickel dropped–Ain't too proud to beg- played. He mouthed the words to Mother. Master loved Motown music. What a time they had. But time was up. The unexpected storms thunder rattled. Malcolm quickly walked upstairs. He needed a better view of the dance floor listening to an unfriendly noise only he could hear.

"I could hear it Master bragged" everyone looked at him with SHUUUT UUUPPP on their faces. Malcolm looked up; his nostrils flared as always when he sensed danger. His puffy bunker slit eyes squinted, waiting. A fight was coming-he knew it. Mother whistled.

Malcolm never lost a fight, with the help of the hawk, the dove, and Tien. Knowing ten minutes before one was going to happen, helped. He hurried behind the bar, grabbed his hidden pistol. Sammie panned the room nodded. Ernest growled, Ernestine next to him.

The exclusive, invite only, once in a lifetime dance ended as quickly as it started. The Wurlitzer idled, then pulsed one more time syncing with the last notes. The bar lights deeply dimmed signaling the Wurlitzer to protectively shut off. A dry storm raced raising fear in all guests. They fled. Except for Reddy, Farmer, Mary, Sammie, and a young couple who had a hard time making up their minds.

Thunder announced the riders. Malcolm hummed the tune he first unclearly mouthed after that day on the hill. He sang—

"Four horsemen came a riding, riding through the glen. Four horsemen came a riding—- to kill us— in the end!"

~

"I heard it also." Cal said then continued.

~

The riders left a trail of ricocheting thunder behind them in the wake of their motorcycles parting of the thick air. It warned the forest creatures, hell was on its way. All four pulled up in front of the bar, switched off their bikes leaving a deafening silence. Inside all eyes stared through the doorless front door, waiting for them. Anxious minutes felt like hours. Nothing happened. No noise, no visitors. More ticks ticked. Palms sweated. Then, one by one, thudding heels of black leather, silver buckled boots stomped on the doorless front doors saddle. Pixie dust parachuted.

Four sinister, smirking, riders each made their way to a different table on the first floor, one North, one South, one East, and one West. They flipped the tails of their long white dust coats to the side, sat in rapid choreographed succession. The rider of the fiery red bike went first. Coal black followed. Winter white next and then the last one, pale. All hummed the same melody as Malcolm. Long haired, steely eyed, cragged weathered faced killers robotically scanned. Malcolm kept his two eyes on all seven of theirs, and they on him.

"What are you here for?" Farmer bass bravely asked.

"We're here to see him." The pale rider nodded at Malcolm.

"You know him?" Farmer looked at Malcolm.

"Yep, guess we do!" The red rider opened the palm of his left fisted hand.

"From–" Sammie gravely interrupted.

"A very long time ago, well before you, him, her and all of the rest of you. Yes, a very, very long time ago," the white rider snapped the left arm off his chair.

"How long-" Matron's soprano voice challenged.

"We said, a very long time, are you deaf?" the black rider stroked his bearded face.

"10-15 years–?" Red's alto spoke while trying to place them.

"Not of this time, nor— of this world." Hollow eyed pale rider looked at the others sporting a snickering moustache.

Malcolm rose from a slouched perch behind the bar. "I'll kill em all when I see em, all."

Daylight broke. This was going to have to wait. The riders froze in place, alive but unable to move. Ernest walked over to the red rider and peed on his black cracked fading leather boots. All bar flies fled. Cal flew to his readied couch. Tomorrow was today. 3:50 a.m. Tuesday, September 12, 2009 told the town's clock. Cal's watch skipped a beat, backwards to 3:10 p.m., Tuesday, August 29, 2009. Mother added and subtracted the twins score. Tomorrows storm was here.................

# Twenty-Eight

Master whistled-

Dusk, Sera opened the kitchen screen door, walked onto Shepherd's walk's crust. She tilted her head skyward at the same failing daylight sky Margaret saw, the day Malcolm and Hank went to Sunbeams Hill. White puffy clouds ran away from the coming storm's blackening sky. Warrior DNA electrically filled skin tingling air. She knew. The second Mother of all battles, the one Malcolm knew would come, was here. Sera nodded to the sky thankful for the dance, and went back inside.

Only the bravest, or the most foolhardy remained in the bar that evening. The loud, over dressed, over jeweled, fled the scene. No stomach for this. No stomach for the taste of single shot 1844 A.H Waters Flat Lock smooth bore .54 caliber percussion pistols. Rules were rules and these were the only weapons allowed for this contest. The pistols slightly larger than a half inch lead ball bullet, loaded through the pistols muzzle, was prescribed to deliberately inflict as much pain to the victim, as possible. Punish warrior Malcolm. The prescribed death ballet was ordered to take time, agonizing time. The past, to be avenged as Tien was to die. Evil struggled to prevail. The snake failed. Four horsemen in California failed. Tasked again, four horsemen came a riding, told repeatedly by the wind. Only those weapons could kill a ghost, and of course, only a ghost could kill a ghost.

Malcolm, Sammie, Farmer Vaughn, Mary the Matron, Reddy Red, and the undecided couple, remained. Mr. I Imagine flew the coup the previous day after his narration. Said he had to get back to the city to take care of someone's parking space and sign. No one knew what he was talking about, figured he just wanted an excuse to leave. Six hours later, sad wind whistled news to Cal and the barflies Mr. I was killed shortly after returning home, the victim of a hold- up.

The four bikers unfroze, stood up pushing their dust coats aside. Hands hung on the grips of holstered single-shot pistols. All were right handed. The bobbles and Malcolm took cover. The man and his wife who couldn't make up their minds finally did, decided last minute to leave. They were shot in the back, in cold blood.

"The price of indecision" the pale rider said reloading.

Face down they bled, next to the lost molar. Nearby, Malcolm coolly looked at the two soon to be corpses.

"We wanted to stay, to try to help, but we had kids—we couldn't. We're sorry." The said in a unified, quiet, wheeze.

Sad, drooping eyes begged apologetically, "release us, please." They stained the floor with their life. Malcolm nodded. Their breathing labored till it could no more. Two ticks later, two hazy fogs whisked outside disappearing with the night's forgiveness.

"Funny thing about giving forgiveness," Mother said. "You never know when you're going to need it back," then whistled looking at Cal. He stood regally robed, energized. He continued knowing tonight was his last to address the class. The floor brightly lit.

No music, only sound of whirring half inch lead balls pursuing their victims. Deathly they spun and cut through the smoke filled air.

Wood paneling caught many, cracked and made some very important holes. There was nowhere to hide for the valiant who foolishly remained. What chance they against those with no souls?

Bang, bang, bang, bullets ricocheted, splintered chairs, tables and bore more holes in the walls paneling. Glass shattered. Chards flew.

Farmer's bass voice interrupted Cal. "I hid behind an upset table. It wasn't very good protection after all. A shot fired from the rider of the black bike found the middle of my head. Split it wide open. My senses deadened for all mortal time. Falling face forward, kissing the floor, instantly dead. A second later I turned to hazy smoke, like the husband and wife, but with one exception. I whistled through one of the bullet holes in the wall and have been there ever since."

A moment later, true to his description, Farmer disappeared in a smoke trail through a hole in the wall, leaving Reddy Red, Sammie, the Matron and Malcolm.

Reddy Reds alto- "I did the best I could. I knew nuthin about pistols but was there to help. A coward I ain't like some people I know." An absent perished Mr. I Imagine, the intended object for that slight. "Like I said, I had no shootin skills except the one's someone could argue that came from my mouth. I fired my gun with no success, just made a hole in the wall. So I grabbed some bottles, the cheap ones from behind the bar, and hurled them at one of the bastards, the Rider of the Red bike. I threw them the best a stocky, weeeellllI.... proportioned, buxomly woman could. Right through him, right through that sun-uf- a- bitch dey sailed. No effect on my assassin, the rider of the red bike. Dey crashed against the walls, wettin them. Left lasting memories of that day, see... over, and there...." she pointed to the stained walls. "It was like we were in an old western bar room gun fight. One difference though. These weren't ordinary gunslingers. I was desperate, needed to help, I lunged. A mistake, as the bastard showman casually slide side stepped avoiding my flight. He didn't have to, the bastard. I mid-air passed him. With a cocky grin he looked away from me, and fired. The lead ball seared into my heart. I face skid on the floor, fell silent."

She trembled for five ticks and died. Then twirled into hazy smoke, and spun home through the hole in the wall she made, right through the Mick's shirt.

"My, my, what great drama, and parlor tricks also." Jealous Master rained on Cal's parade.

"Shhhhhush you, now go on son. Go on." She muffled Master and ordered Cal.

Cal paused, looked over toward the shadow, nodded and continued.....

After those two wisped away, the Red and Black riders coldly heal stomped out. Thunder, timed perfectly, rumbled in unison with their motorcycle's engines. They fled. Mission accomplished, just another day at work.

The pale and white riders remained. Mary, Sammie and Malcolm were left. Malcolm and Mary were well experienced in pistol play. Malcolm, schooled by Uncle' Tim and Sam and Matron, Dad taught. They stood behind the Bar, ready. An always willing, but ill prepared Sammie, wisely hid behind an overturned table.

Defiant, the remaining riders stood in the open on the main lower level, hands dangling by their sides, twitching. The right side of their long white dust coats hooked over their holsters. Three against two, hardly fair odds, hardly a fair fight, for Malcolm Mary and Sammie.

Winded Cal nodded to Matron, and sat down. Matron spoke—

"Sammie broke for the door to get help, to get the cavalry like when they played. Without a scratch he made it outside. The remaining riders couldn't follow him as their principal job needed to be taken care of first, before they were free to leave.

Safety outside Sammie stopped. He just couldn't resist it. With his warriors black boot heal he kicked the pale rider's bike. It fell, toppling the white riders like dominos. A huge smile beamed from his goofy face. He always had a sense of humor. This time though it cost him, more than staying after school. Though the remaining riders couldn't leave they could get close to the doorless front door. A bullet fired from the white rider put a period in Sammie's forehead.

He turned to smoke, spun and drilled through a hole Malcolm made in the wall.

Mary Wept, Cal took over–.

The pale and white riders, unsure of their foes and the world they came from, ghostly split apart. They streaked about the room darting here and there, a defensive military hard to hit tactic. Their orders, Kill Malcolm and anyone who got in the way, they fired, struck Matron. Weak from blood loss she struggled.

Using the last of my strength I picked up my pistol. Steadied it, and pulled the trigger. The half inch, hot lead round ball flew through the pale rider, and then continued on through the Babes shirt. It was a heck of a shot.

∾

"Tsk Tsk, tsk, shame." Master twirled. Mary continued—

∾

The Pale Rider bastard just waited, watching till I dropped my too heavy to hold gun. It fell. He raised his sweeping right hand, pulled the trigger showoff style. The bullet found its mark, my chest. The assassin finished me. Groaning I fell to the floor. I laid behind the bar for twenty ticks. Enough time to look up at Malcolm. My eyes apologized.

Malcolm looked down at her with a cold nod and a grimace. Matron rightfully joined the others through a hole in the wall made by her killer's bullet. Clunking footsteps from her assassin bass drum heal thudded out the doorless front door. He cursed something in an archaic language picking up his dented bike. He sped away leaving a trail of angry thunder behind him.

Then Malcolm squinted, his killer instinct intact. He and the white rider were left. The evil power couldn't tolerate him interfering with destiny. Tien should have died. Malcolm, anointed, trained, and put in place to protect her, his raison d'être.

∾

"OOOoooooooooooooo," Harmonized from behind the wall.

Cal smirked, shook his head and continued—

Thickly calloused, nicotine stained hands set a record reloading. Malcolm used both his and the Matrons pistols. Snap turning to his right he scanned the room. A sneer cast on his etched face. Angrily he fired both pistols at a darting image. The white rider, uncertain of Malcolm's mortality, fired from behind an overturned table. A classic contest, but black and white reversed. Malcolm loaded, and reloaded. The rider responded. Single shots flew at each other one, and two at a time, over and over, back and forth. Both, well trained for this a contest, hide, seek, fire, miss, and then fire again.

Smoke hung heavily in the Destiny masking their positions. Quietly they stood waiting for the other to make a mistake. They were only fifteen feet apart when the smoke settled. They both saw and fired point blank. Ribbons of smoke plumed from the pistols barrels. Burnt gun powders sharp aroma filled the air. Each with well trained reflexes twirled out of the way avoiding the lead, but not the walls. Smoke covered, again. They battled on darting back and forth throughout the room, shielding themselves with turned over tables. It was a draw until someone made a mistake.

He looked left, dipped right. He should have went the other way. A freshly reloaded lead ball spat from the white rider's pistol. It tore Malcolm's cowboy shirt by one of the fake pearl shiny buttons lodging deep in his chest, just missing his heart. He groaned. Grabbed his chest, he hadn't felt that kind of pain since he fell in Viet Nam.

"OOoooooooooo oooooooooooooooooooooo" echoed. The walls rattled.

"Stop that, stop that." Master finger pointed.

The bobble heads sheepishly turned down their giggling heads, safe within their dimension. Mother silently coughed.

Malcolm's knees buckled. He kept balance managing a fall to one knee, paying the ordered torturous price. Moaning he thought to call for help.

Muffled sniffles were heard from behind the wall.

"AHHHHH….Siiigghhhh" Master mocked.

Mother elbowed him, he coughed. Mother nodded to Cal a go-on nod.

Malcolm dodged out of the way of another round. Tasting blood the White Rider arrogantly stood in the open now confident Malcolm was a seriously wounded mortal. Another shot hit Malcolm's arm. Then another shattered his right shin. Make him pay, the orders of the day. Uncharacteristically for his kind, the rider ad-libbed a tormenting smile.

They recorded it as Malcolm's bravest effort but the battles outcome was assured long before the first shot fired. Malcolm McKeon, a watched boy since the rain on the hill and a hunted man ever since Viet Nam. With his remaining strength he dragged himself behind the bar. Blood from his wounds streamed. The pearl button cowboy shirt soaked up his life dying it brownish red. Without immediate medical attention his fate was certain. Jesse, would have to show, and soon. Jesse was out of town.

Behind the bar he lay, legs outstretched, back propped up against the cooler, wearing an expressionless face. If Margaret saw him she would have fallen. Dazed, Malcolm hallucinated. He imagined town's people erecting a monument to him. One eventually that would be covered in pigeon shit.

"Yes my boy, pigeon shit. There's fame for you, pigeon shit. Don't let them cover you with pigeon shit boy. Be aware boy. Don't let them cover you with pigeon shit—" The man at the parks words came to him. They strengthened him, enough. Dizzy vision came and went, in and out. Guessing, he raised reloaded pistols. Waved them in the direction he expected to see his assailant show his face. A brief smile broke across his face wondering if the hawk or dove would be stopping by. They couldn't this time. He was on his own and not to be interfered with.

Malcolm's eye sight was poor, but not his hearing. Boot heals drummed across the tile floor coming toward him. It stopped. Three ticks later the cold, placid face of the white rider loomed in a leer, over the bar right, right where Malcolm expected. The hollows of the rider's sunken eyes locked Malcolm's. Purposefully the rider took slow taunting aim. He fired one shot, point blank at the center of Malcolm's forehead. Malcolm turned at the very last second. The rider's bullet striped the side of his head, split his ear. He avoided the full blow but it dazed him even more.

The confident rider sighed. Casually he reloaded without budging, unworried about Malcolm's aimed guns. He knew the balls of lead if fired would pass right through him. Malcolm fired. His bullets cut through the smoke cloud hanging over him and flew directly at the gloating, smug face of the white rider.

The white rider knew Malcolm mortal, he didn't know how strictly he was touched from another world years ago. Both shots struck the white rider. Ironically, one dotted the center of his forehead, snapped his head back. The other shot holed the middle of his chest driving him backward. He tried to stabilize, regain his balance, but fell to the ground. He lay shocked from the blows. The White Rider not moving was an error. Someone left a few details out from his orders.

The wounds would have finished any mortal. Often these warriors could self heal. Heal he could not and as a wounded animal he dragged himself down the right steps to the first level and propped up against a far wall. Panting, he hoped for help and regroup. It wouldn't come. Two strikes in this game and you're out. His back bled against the wall. Seventy ticks later he tried to stand. He stumbled, and fell again. Frightfully confused he catatonically sat, wore a quizzical bewildered look. He had no sense of this position. Cold callousness swapped places with dazed crippling pain, and powerlessness. The position reserved for his victims. Gradually his wool shirt soaked with his life turning a soft hue of blue.

For the participants the battle seemed to rage for an hour. It took an entire fifteen minutes. They sent the four very best riding day and night on thunderous horse machines, white, black, red, and one pale. From the four corners of the world, North, South, East and West, to kill him. They missed in California.

It took some doing but finally Malcolm lay bleeding with no hawk, dove or Jesse. Tributaries of blood that coursed though his body were losing. A limp left arm tingled. His fingers flinched with little tremors. Blood pooled in his palm cup. Twice he struggled and twice he failed to raise his right arm. On a third attempt he mustered all of what little strength he had and painfully held his fisted right arm up, peeled open his hand. Three fingers pointed toward heaven. Trembling tips gestured, it's done. Malcolm fell back against the cooler, his bunker slits still slightly open. He slipped into a dream waiting for Mr. Reaper. Memory's of now and then escaped his minds vault. Dillinger would have been proud.

In his delirium nameless soldier's faces, from ancient to present came to him. They spoke in tongues, laughed. The last thing he remembered before passing out were the faces of his band of brothers. The white rider, resting against the wall, groaned a haunting echo.

Cal fell over and hit his head on the floor, bled. Everyone was wounded in this battle. Mother carried him over to the couch. Master pursed his lips. "Jealous boy—oh jealous boy," Mother's eyes twinkled. Tuesday night finished at 2:45 a.m. Wednesday morning, September 13, 2009, according to the town's clock. Cal's watch, as always, begged to differ; Tuesday, 3:00 p.m. August 29, 2009. Wind chimes on the porch spoke musically. A new storm was coming and, she was not happy.

# Twenty-Nine

"Thank you. Thank you for staying with us. We hope you liked your stay. Tonight's the last night of your Vacation Package." Mother's eyes twinkled.

"Vacation Package, I'm a newspaper man, a reporter. I came here, rather was told to come here, and get a story that wasn't told fully, should have been. Man should it have been."

"Well, it's not quite finished. Are you ready to get the rest or are you going to scram? You can if you want. I think you'll find it as interesting as the rest. You do want to know about the grass don't you?"

"I know most, not all?"

"If you stay, we have something special for you, as any proper popular vacation spot would. Now, go get into Old Blue or go to the porch, your call."

Cal stared silently outside. "My call huh–Bull. See you at the porch.

"Your chair is on the porch now. Master put it close to the left side rail fencing. Go, sit and–"

"—Master lifted something? Isn't he too old, maybe hurt his back or something?"

Mother smirked, twirled an index finger.

"Oh, yeah, sorry—forgot about that. Hey— wait a sec. You mean no charge, no wall, and no juice nooooo—"

"—-no nuthin, so sit back in your chair son, close your eyes, wait." She knew like a book.

Cal punched overhead. "Yeeees, heeeeyyy wait a second, why?"

"You're flying solo tonight dear boy, you've arrived. Take it from here yourself. Our work is nearly completed. You were difficult, took longer than expected." She walked to the back of the shop out of sight. Cal heard from the back–

"Also, there won't be any customer service comment card for you answer at check out time asking, how'd we do? We think we've heard just about enough of your comments. Check-out time tomorrow is early morning. Now gooooo, night falls."

Cal skipped the wings to the bakeshop door one last time. He leapt the saddle, turned, and looked back at the floor, then ran like his life depended on it. Over the dirt front yard, up Destiny's porch steps and skidded to a ball of the foot concrete burning stop, right where his chair was waiting, just as Mother said.

"Sit down and relax, boy."

"Son, he's earned it." Mother corrected Master from next door.

"Ok, Son. Close your eyes, all of them." Master howled.

"Stretch your legs out and—"

"And—what Mother?"

"And wait, till night and day pass each other in Mother Nature's turnstile" Master jumped in

"Then?"

"Listen to the wind chimes. An angry storm is coming to take her child home." Mother finished

"How the devil am I going to write about— this?"

Cal closed his eyes, sat in his chair, tipped back rocking on two chair legs. Crossed ankles rested on the top split fence rung. Daylights last minute's sun, stroked his salt and pepper scruffy beard. Night and day do-si-doed, spun past each other. Wind turned the chimes volume up. Cal fell in a dream listening to words hung in the night's wind—-

"The bushel price of corn is—"Early morning produce quotes scratched their way through the old pickups speaker. Sera and the boy bumped along to pick up Malcolm's remains. They left the farm before the news of the battle reached the farm. The boy drove, Sera in the passenger seat. Searing morning sun painfully burnt through the windshield. They rocked and bounced, recoiling in the truck's cab.

Sera sign language ordered the boy to speed up. The ride smoothed as if the wheels didn't touch the ground. They arrived in Fate in record time and skid the truck to a dusty stop in front of Destiny. Sera jerked the doors handle, entered the bar, sounded as if swearing. The boy followed right behind her trail of anger and hate. Her presence chilled Destiny's interior. Dew hung on the walls. Sensed a strange blood smell to her left and wheeled with a crisp military head snap. There he was. The last rider, wounded, propped up against the wall, agonizing. Their eyes locked. Her stare crushed the cast aside hunter. The devils bully was no match. Panic painted his once, smug face. Wide, open-eyed, terror gripped him by his gagging throat. Useless legs slipped against the floor trying to flee but fell against the wall and started to tip, sideways, but stopped. He never took his eyes off hers. Sera had no time for him now. She sniffed, turned, faced the bar on the upper level, and sniffed again.

Six ticks later Sera peered over the countertop. Shattered Malcolm managed to properly prop himself up against the cooler. He attempted to be as presentable as possible. Heaven sent a moment of lucidity when he saw her and a wisp smile escaped turned up lips. Ones so well mated to his pale yielding face. Sera walked around the back of the bar. Malcolm rustled, tried to stand and fell backwards. Kneeling, she outstretched her left hand. He grabbed it, and rose with lent strength. The boy and she hooked Malcolm's arms around their necks, and walked him for the last time, toward the doorless front door. A snakes hissing came from the rider's direction. Sera dagger glanced. He groaned.

Sera ordered the boy to put a mattress in the bed of the truck the previous evening. Malcolm, propped against the trucks rear window, looked over the sides of the pickup as they left Fate never to return. His left hand patted his indelibly blood stained blood cowboy shirt. Peacefully he looked out at the country side recounting how he once, so mischievously, played there and masterfully ruled. Another wisp of a smile lingered.

They slowed. The truck violently bounced its final distance to the farm.

"Ahhhhhhghggh" Malcolm cried. The boy eased the truck to a stop, kicked the driver's door open, jumped out and ran to the back. After the tailgate fell he quick winked at Sera, and then black boot raced to the Barn. Sera took Malcolm's blood stained left hand, helped him slide off the mattress and out of the truck. She hooked her left arm through his right. Touching her energized him enough so they could stumble and wobble like a pair of drunks. They stopped by the kitchen door side of Shepherd's Walk.

Malcolm straightened, stood proudly in his once beautiful black and gold pearl button cowboy shirt, now bloodied and torn from the entry holes of his opponent searing lead bullets. His jeans suffered as well. Under his clothes the bullets penetrations left multicolored decorations of black, blue and red puffy donuts in his chest, shoulder, legs and back. Each tear bore honor paid to him by his assailants. Sera, stood next to him wearing a long black cape.

"I'm cold."

Sera draped a cloak around him. Fog draped his mind.

Her hand motioned toward the barn.

His bunker slits squeezed, limply locked on the barn with a lifeless expression. One well earned by a valiant time traveling warrior. Sera nodded. They began. Sera released his arm as they walked to toward the barn. Malcolm moved freely with the training wheels off, but then feebly stumbled. Shepherd Sera followed. Malcolm processed over the rich healthy earth path Margaret named Shepherd's Walk. He never knew why she called it that. Sean either, but he had a guess.

Lush Shepherd's Walk was in full bloom. Fat faced, well cushioned catcher mitt sunflowers caught all the suns fastballs it threw. In between and beneath them, pockets of kaleidoscopic multicolored blooming wild flowers. Their perfume packed the air with intoxicating scents. Stray dogs, cats, pigs, ducks and chickens came from all over. Some roamed freely, and some warmed themselves in the morning sun. Some strayed. Sera never worried about their disappearance. Usually they were unusually well trained, not always. Jealously, they fought for Sera's attention. Today's orders, be on your best behavior.

Mistakes would not be tolerated. They had this well practiced, Sera saw to it that they were ready for a day they knew would come.

Malcolm approached. They fell in line, the smallest to the largest. Along both sides of Shepherd's walks path as school children on a class trip. Warrior royalty, barely clinging to life, graced its hallowed ground. Sera followed a few paces behind and to the left.

As he neared each successively knelt in a curtsey or bow as best they could. On one leg, or two paws, claws or hooves dug in the earth. Chins or beaks tucked and turned avoiding eye contact finishing the royal genuflect.

Malcolm stopped, stood and watched each twist to a spin. Around and around, each turn spun faster than the previous till only diffused smoky whirlwinds danced on the dirt. Once completely translucent, the spinning mini-twisters slowed, stopped and reversed. Hazy forms gradually thickened to shape, ghostly human shapes.

Poised Malcolm watched the transformations without shock or surprise. Eyes of a few of the transformed locked to his. Mother Margaret's secret was finally exposed. Shepherds of the Walk, materialized. People he hadn't seen in some time-some. Many passed years ago. Aunt Jean, mom's sister who died of breast cancer, Uncle Vic, the World War Two Veteran, a hero, who died later in life in a car wreck. Mrs. Winston, Cecil Rhodes, who drowned as an eight year old in the quarry one awful summer's day, Sally Crenshaw as a young child– long before she died of a heroin overdose in the early 70's. She clung to the back of her deceased mother's leg. Famed rock stars immortalized in posters in his bar; Lennon, Hendrix, Joplin, Morrison, Brian Jones, Croce, and Harrison and of course, his friend-the third Mothers son, Johnny Shake, properly reassembled. Malcolm caught his eye, nodded a big grin. Many were there, but no sign of Mom or Dad.

Malcolm and Sera continued. Flowers petals fell. The wind snatched them before they hit the ground, dried them to a crackle, and swept them into the late morning sky filling it with their bright colors. The ghosts spun dissolving into black miniature twisters. They sped off as dark bolts of light against the sky's colorful background.

A few yards away from the forbidding barn door Malcolm stopped. The scar on his face pulsed, throbbed, and began to fade.

Sera clutched his cold palm, led him past the barns threshold. They stopped in front of Winters Eve's tomb. The old lock that sealed it lay on the floors straw. Sera nodded. Malcolm pulled the stall door. Its old wood creaked. Malcolm wavered, poked his head inside but his eyes refused to look ahead and fell to the ground as memories rekindled.

Tobacco smoke filled his nostrils. The scent stood the hair up on his neck. He snapped his head, glanced at Sera. She motioned for him to move. Malcolm didn't fear much but this he did and slowly raised his head as if in church. Puffed squinting eyes confronted his past.

"Come in Malcolm, come in. She's all ready for you." The boy sat on the Vincent, big smile and all, smoking, occasionally with that oh too familiar cough.

The Vincent proudly gleamed, back to its original condition. No mention of damage anywhere.

"Farm equipment mechanic my eye." Malcolm choked.

The spotless black beast's front wheel, and gleaming headlight, faced forward pointing toward the stall door.

"Just right, if you need to make a fast get away that is." The boy laughed.

"She's all ready." he coughed, took another drag sliding off the seat.

"All ready," his hand patted the seat.

"Git on er, go ahead, and git on er."

What a mechanic. How in the wor–? Confused Malcolm stutter thought. The boy winked at Sera.

"Come on lad," Come on. She's ready. So are you, ready to ride— to ride my, your—- Winters Eve."

Malcolm stopped, right in his tracks, stone still. A broad smile looked back. Malcolm's right eye leaked. Malcolm grabbed Sera's hand, released it and climbed on the Vincent using borrowed strength. She was all set up. All Malcolm had to do was kick start her over. All riders had to start the Vincent— themselves. He stood on the foot-pegs, hooked his boot heel on the kick-start lever, jumped and pressed his tortured leg down depressing the kick start. No luck.

"Help," grimacing lifeless Malcolm uttered.

Sera sternly nodded, try again. Malcolm thought, remembered tickle the carbs a little. Pump fuel in the engine. Not too much or she would flood from the magneto's weak spark. He stood, pressed, kicked. Thump, thump, thump. Bloody, his right hand twisted the throttle and then allowed it to roll back. Again and again, each time a little further feathering it till it warmed and ran smoothly. When it was it drummed the most beautiful, resonant, rhythmic sound. Sera climbed on behind Malcolm.

"Come, Malcolm. Take me for a ride." She playfully asked. Mute no more.

Malcolm looked at the boy with wonder in his eyes. The boy looked back again, with the broadest of proud smiles, nodded approval. Malcolm's foot pressed the bike into gear. The three sped off out the barn. After the dirt farm road kicking up dirt and stones they turned left onto the country road heading to Snake Hill Road, on their way to Spirit Trail Road.

The Vincent hummed beautiful notes. Effortlessly its power carried its package through the cool shaded areas of the forest. Ahead, wisps of smoky ghostly images lined both sides of the road, waiting. As the bikers closed the gauzy images morphed into human figures and honored the passerby's with a bow or courtesy. Malcolm slowed Winters Eve trying to catch a familiar face wondering who they were. "Overactive imagination," he remembered his elementary teacher brand.

Wait, I know him—I knew her—that's Mister—- and his wife Misses—. Oh, there—Misses-, my English teacher, and math and history teacher. They all came back, to him, for him. He knew them all. The way it was back then in a small town— smaller school. You knew everyone, and everyone, knew you.

He cracked the throttle, threaded through the cool shadows of the tree lined road. Then saw something. He wasn't sure at first but then he was. The boy mechanic, he turned to fog, and then back. Dad, Sean?

Was it—himself, as he was sometimes called? Malcolm blinked, and then again. It looked like him. He was with someone and the sight of them together made Malcolm think the loss of blood surely caused him to hallucinate. Then again he saw. It was Dad, ghostly him. He was holding something out. What? Oh my god Malcolm thought—a neck, he's got someone by the neck. Sean's anvil mitts were around a neck of Cromwell. Damn, Dad hated him so. He finally got his chance but dad grinned. Cromwell looked bored. Yet another, of Dads jokes.

Malcolm's throttle hand twisted. The large shiny speedometer jumped, 80, 90 mph, fast, very fast. How? He worried no one could, roads to twisty, to narrow, to bumpy but yet he did. The Vincent roared toward Malcolm's destiny, its riders pinned majestically aboard. Behind them bright daylight faded.

The sun fought for its place but lost ground as the ticks ticked. Replacing it, a sculpted plum colored sky. It looked as if an old theaters velvet curtain. Fine threads of brilliant reds, blues and yellows and complementing muted earth tones spun from the flowers of Shepherds Walk wove throughout. Daylight was nearly finished, replaced with that of fine fabric suitable for a nineteenth century elegant mother's evening gown, perfect as a backdrop for the coming, promised, huge thunderhead.

The rich graying to black cloud was edged with crimson. It tracked Malcolm and Sera as the tasked Vincent rolled in a warning stalk that a violent event is coming. It snuffed out the little lingering trickle of the afternoon sun. The riders, sealed as one, rode the road holding on for their remaining dear lives.

The Vincent's back tire sawed a groove in the road, threw gouged dirt and gravel against the inside of the rear fender and wheels spokes. A musical tingling sound changed to rhythmic drum rapping beats, like a drummer boy drumming signaling a battle charge. Malcolm's ears perked.

An aged suspension shook yet maintained traction hitting rut after rut, and every crevice of the parched grooved dirt road. Eve would wobble, but never slip for real, teasing it's riders as if children on their first amusement park ride. Threatened disaster, wrapped in fun.

Ominously the cloud streaked closer. Brother thunder heralded the traveler's arrival. Sister Lightening flashed pencil thin spiderweb flashes of light. Shadow from the swelling black cloud raked the ground. Winters Eve raced away thunderously vibrating, shaking and twisting the sparse woods as they hurtled past. Wind filtering through the teeth of the treed area escaped the forests grasp with harmonic eerie notes of whining music. Greater winds above howled. The trio left the forested area to watch a wave sweep through the pasture, bending its high grass.

Malcolm glanced. More clouds showed hauntingly similar to those responsible that frightful day. They hovered. The terrorizing agents hung above all Mother Nature placed below. Sera watched, they floated lower as if to land and whispered–

"Ride Malcolm ride. Stephanie is waiting. The ball field is waiting."

Malcolm twisted the throttle, the Vincent rear suspension squatted, and then the three shot like one of sister's bolts to the top of Snake Hill.

∾

One road in, two roads out— Cal ran away for 3 ticks.

"Shhhhhhhhhhhhh, get back to it. We're so close." hushed from behind the walls.

Okay, he answered in a fog

∾

The two sat on the third and climbed to the top of Snake Hill Road. Malcolm depressed the clutch, footed the rear brake. Resting, he listened to the Vincent's bup- bup- bup music. Memories of his last time on the Vincent repeated over and over.

"Go ahead." Sera tugged his shirt.

Malcolm remained motionless lost in memory of his lost band of brothers and the great downhill races. His courage never weakened. With remaining borrowed strength he boot toe pushed the Vincent. Winters Eve spoke as a full horse whinny when he twisted the throttle. Left, right, the stallion followed the roads notorious snaking curves. The wheels hopped and recoiled deep inside the fenders over a terrible rutted road, worse than ever. Go they must, and go they did. All was under control, for a moment.

Fifty yards ahead it lay across the middle of the road as a log. Slipped from the roads hollow shoulders where it cowardly hid. Thick, black, long, a snake thought merely folk lore with beady eyes watching for prey hissed with fangs exposed. The snake sought its redemption. Malcolm stopped. His eye slits widened.

"It's alright, ride on, ride—" Sera two arm squeezed his wet waist.

The Vincent rolled. The wheels hopped as they built momentum through the remaining twisting lefts and rights. Malcolm had an eye on the road and one on the snake. It morphed, looked as a fire truck hose. As Winters Eve closed the snake turned its head, fangs dripping, hissing, ready to duel. The buffer of fifteen yards shrank. Determination clamped Malcolm's jaw he would not run.

Ten feet left and Malcolm gripped the handlebars in preparation for impact, but the Vincent struck something else, first.

"Noooonoooo, not another crash, I can't, we can't."

Sera smiled, hugged his waste tightly.

"Hang on Malcolm, hang on." She laid her head on his back.

The Vincent left the ground with the assistance of an elf head no one saw. The engine screamed a frightening sound of a wounded animal. Vincent struck the ground with a jarring landing when its short, airborne heavenly flight ended. Its rear wheel guillotined the back of the black snakes head. The wounded satanic, panic stricken helix slipped away. Coiled hiding in the drainage ditch it must have thought this explanation was going to be tougher than the last. Much time would pass before it tried that parlor trick again.

~

Shame, Cal mentally smart mouthed.

"Shut up, shut up. You're ruining allll the good parts damn it." Thunder rolled. "Oops, my apologies," Master answered back.

POP, POP, POP, four more dark words neon lit up on the sign inside, "winds in your" and "bowlines." Master mentally whistled.

~

Sera tugged, they stopped, looked back, beamed at each other and sped off. The pond wrapped with willows lay ahead. Spirit Trail Road, next.

At the bottom of Snake hill Malcolm stopped, dismounted, looked around remembering good times, and others.

"What a waste Mom, I did nothing-nothing at all." He looked at the sky.

"Climb aboard, get back on Winters Eve, Malcolm. I'll tell you about a young girl, Tien, and life saving research she's doing that likely will save even those who would have killed her." Sera kissed his ear.

The three curved around the pot belly turn and cranked it up on Spirit Trail Road. Malcolm grabbed a last look at the Vaughn's grazing fields where they all played the battle of the cows, and—- where he liked to day dream as a kid on warm summer's afternoons lying in the hill. Lips once turned down, pursed, smiled.

"I used to see faces, and things in the clouds." Malcolm confided to his mother Margaret when he came home.

"Of course Malcolm," she would answer looking out the kitchen window. She knew.

Malcolm caught a piece of the hill where the rainstorm pelted him and Hank, and then looked above at today's tracking black cloud.

It caught them, hovered over their heads. Without as much of the slightest of breeze the cloud split apart into multiple shapes. The diffusing shapes gently reached for and grabbed earth. Then, as if a spirited magician waved a wand the diffusing cloud offered what only those prepared to see could.

The procession began with waves of cold, pale-faced, drummer boys and girls leading the honoring parade. Standing in place, their legs kneed the air. Each row stretched the width of the flat field. On a thunder claps cue they began marching. Precise phalanxes marched. They were dressed in once fancy bright uniforms but now time suffered to dull tatters and held closed by reflecting brass buttons. Snare drums rapped–buda bup…buda bup—rap rap, buda bup...buda bup...rap… rap, left hand, right hand. Up, down. Arms and elbows flew in alternating rhythm as if climbing a rope. Show-off's twirled their sticks, lofted them, and gracefully caught them without missing a note. They were the lead of the honoring ceremony that led the rest toward Heavens Hill. They trampled the ground and disappeared.

Another scattered piece of a cloud fell carrying with it sounds of racing horses. Malcolm looked. When the cloud cleared legions of ancient Egyptian, Greek and Roman warriors rolled over the grazing grass of the wide open fields. They parade rode chariots, large steeds, or marched in orderly, as if in a great pageant. Steadfastly they kept pace with Malcolm, and Eve. The chariots steeds, harnessed with gold and silver reins, jammed pounding large claw hoofs to the ground. Chariot drivers wore plumed, red feathered golden strapped helmets. They whipped their horses till the animals twisted their heads back in protest, wishing to taste their master's flesh. With open, frightened eyes, they strained against their bits. Nostril's desperately flared trying to siphon much needed air. They broke pace, charged a warriors charge in honor of the returning warrior. Outstretched arms gloved swords high in a superior salute. This majestic welcoming committee too, stamped and trampled the fresh new grass of the night shaking the earth with quake vibrations. All mortals, hid. The tall grazing grass lay trampled.

"OOoooooooo" echoed from behind the walls.

Three of the parading chariots parted from the rest, rode close to the fence, and looked at Malcolm. They mouthed something he couldn't hear over the hooves. Smiling bearded faces laughed tauntingly as if a prank played. They fell back into line, and disappeared as the drummers had.

New clouds reshaped, fell. New greeters appeared. The first sat atop his Arabian, the great Moslem warrior, Saladin.

"Sali always loved riding Arabian's." Sera whispered. Malcolm agreed, shaking his head.

At chill from his right grabbed his attention. A splintered cloud twisted, hazed into Stephanie's smiling tomboy figure. Sera smiled back. Soon, their jobs would be over. Stephanie nodded to Sali. They both morphed, he to a hazy smoke and she—-to a white dove. They flew off.

On the far side of the field a faint outline of a tank came charging. Its metal tracks nosily but barely touched the ground as if floating on air. General Georgie commanded, hanging on for dear life on the back, a waving smiling Sammie. He looked so very happy reunited with the band. The two spun away.

The next clusters touched earth. An English King in shiny dress battle armor rode a charge to the fence. Henry the Fifth flipped his helmets face shield up while following the fence line, keeping pace with the slow cruising Winters Eve, then rode ahead. Malcolm approached and was greeted with the broadest of familiar smiles. The knight unsheathed his sword and charged forward, pointing, saying—

"Charge, Charge Malcolm, the final Great Downhill soon, will be over."

A two tick smile hung on the king's face. He winked. Flipped his face shield down, kicked his horse and joined the others who all came back flooding the field.

Magnificently dressed legions of soldiers, ancient and modern, friends and foes, all charged across the field toward Heavens Hill in his rightful honoring. All came to take him home in a glorious sight. Then all as moist tissues dissolved to nothing.

"Sniffle, sniffle," Master was overcome.

"OOooooooooo," the Bobbles spoke numbly.

Astonished, in a trance, Cal's nub of a note taking pencil fell out of his hand.

A new, weighty rich black cloud hovered slightly above Mother Earth. It fell. Malcolm gasped looking at its exposed belly of bursting brilliant explosive reds, blues, greens and ambers, a universe's fiery colored womb.

~

"Can we move this along please Hey that's my fishing spot" Master pointed.

"Owwww" Mother momentarily fixed the interruption.

POP, POP, POP–That you didn't, lit up from the dark and posted on the neon sign.

~

Sera's arms wrapped tightly. The side of her face flattened on the back of Malcolm's shoulder. Reaching, her right arm slid over his, gripped his, and tugged.

"Faster Malkie, twist the throttle. Go faster. Ride Malkie ride, ride like the wind you were born on—RIIIDDEEE…"

~

"Ohhhh" hummed from behind the wall.

"Malcolm, not Malkie!" squawked an anonymous critic.

No, it's ok. It's ok. Think, think, Cal dream fired back.

"Oooooooo" sniffled, then silence.

~

Malcolm listened, snapped the throttle open trying to make a run for it. The Vincent responded like a switched race horse. Its heart, the engine, pounded. Eve surged. Cracks in Malcolm's face faded. Original passion of his reckless youth reinvaded. A gleam returned to old tired eyes. A last ride—a last chance.

"Ride Malkie ride."

Over and over her words rang out. Each time she with greater strength. Strength only a mother could give. The Vincent hustled. Sean improved its capabilities, but the boy, took it to a different level attaching a unique part under the engines primary case. At speed it spun, around and around with the engines revolutions sending silent vibrations of harmonic notes only few morals could hear. It sang out, cried out, and called out to all. Time has come. Old reported top speed capabilities crumbled. 120,130 140-150 mph, they were gone–

However fast they couldn't outrun the ominous cloud. It stretched the length of ten football fields, hunted and caught them. After it fell to earth it shrank around them, swallowing them in its mist.

Cocooned inside, Malcolm rode with strained leaking eyes. Salty water spread across his face washing away craggily lines. Puffed eyes firmed, gave way to smooth supple taut skin. Crevices etched into his pale cheeks, flattened. Rich color of Heaven's Ocean refilled pale pupils, his hair thickened and returned to straw. Finally, the great metamorphous attacked his great scar. The roadway indelibly gouged so deeply into his face from eye to lip softened, faded, and vanished. It left a child's mischievous innocent gleam used so well for getting out of trouble.

Still captured within the clouds foggy womb an eerie chill shivered Malcolm's failing body. He stopped, put his feet to the ground, and twisted. A portal in the cloud opened. He looked through it and over the hazy fields all the way back to the top of Snake Hill Road. There, silhouettes of a man and a woman stood motionless, and then waved. They raised their arms and hands over their heads. The man, dressed in a cape, the woman with pixie powder on her chest, danced. Their hands and arms taunted the sky then waved them as conductors and stirred the darkened sky. It grew black coffee dark, and then swirled as if cream were poured in. The sky rhythmically pulsed, sending surging waves over the field. This storm was well brewed.

Nudged Malcolm turned and faced forward. Sera clung. They rode off down the last distance of Spirit Trail Road. Late visitors came to wish them well along the final leg of the procession. Warriors, alive or souls, all proudly stuffed in their tight uniforms. Some Viet Nam Vets wore sleeveless motorcycle jean vests with sewn MIA and POW badges on then. Many sported gray ponytails, some—- an occasional earring.

The Vincent's BSA siblings were there, the 441 Victor and the Gold Star. When the Vincent rocketed by them they whimpered. Deceased legends of rock and roll showed, late as usual and had to leave as fast as they got there, a gig to do for someone more important.

Howard Raymond Davies showed, the British flying officer who founded the motorcycle company which eventually built the Vincent, by building the HRD in the early 1900's. Phillip Vincent, the man who took Davies Company and made the HRD Vincent also stopped to pay his respects.

The shepherding cloud tightened. Malcolm and Sera on, the Vincent sped forward recording speeds un-recordable—and not of this world.

"Booom, boom—" Thunder spoke. First as a whisper, and then as if Zeus himself was there.

Warm cousin rain fell, soaked them. Time neared. Blood stains from Malcolm's clothes washed away. Sister Lightening, high above Heavens Hill, showed with a mammoth jagged bolt. It lit the entire county's sky.

"Bang, Bang." minor claps of brother thunder helped the announcement.

Malcolm's famous rich blue eyes focused on the road underneath. The Vincent's tires barely touched. Reddish sandy blonde straw hair kite tailed behind him, occasionally whipping and lashing bare eyes. Taut skin, without scar, returned as the canvas of his Jack-o-Lantern grin. It hung from ear to ear.

"Race with the devil, ride with the wind Malkie, Ride your Eve," Sera ordered "Ride Malkie, ride."

Tuned notes of the Vincent's tailpipes changed. Thunderous guttural exhaust tones mixed with echo's of haunting notes. Gradually they mixed producing deep resonate organ tones. An ordinarily dim headlamp projected a laser beam of bright light clearing a tunnel to follow through the web of the dark shrouding cloud's belly.

Sera released her clasp, flung her arms outward. Lightly she pressed her toes on the Vincent's rear passenger foot pegs, and stood. Sturdily, she leaned headlong into the pressure of rushing wind. Rushing air caught her black cape and streamed it as a kite's tail in the trailing wind. Her human arms morphed to brown feather hawk wings, and then to white angel's wings. She reached and folded them over Malcolm' shoulders.

Blindly they sped forward on the final leg of Spirit Trail Road. Malcolm banked his EVE in a soft right turn that bent around Heavens Hill and disappeared from sight. They reached their end.

"Boooom," Brother offered homage. The massive vibration rang the town bell. A new name etched on the memorial plaque in town. Sisterly lightning struck. She again brilliantly lit the sky for as far as the eye could see and so Malcolm could see one last time where he spent so much time in his life. Then darkness reclaimed its dominance.

"Booom, boom, boooom," spoke again. Against the dark backdrop of the black sky a bright silver flash bolted from the ground to eternity from behind Heavens Hill. A long trail of red, gold and orange streaked behind. The dove to its right, the riders were gone.

Back at Destiny the wounded white ghost rider continued his stopped slide. His blood stained shirt windshield washer swept the wall coloring the wood paneling with a curving blue brush stroke. He struck the floor with a deadening thud. Lay on his side, oozing blood that pooled free form on the wood splintering floor. The defacement annoyed the Wurlitzer. An angry bolt of non-sisterly lightning ignited his bike into flames. Its black ash blew away with the remaining wind of the fleeting storm. The white riders pale stunned face compressed on the floor pushing his lower jutting jaw to the right. His eyes froze fright wide open, mouth hung open as if asking, how. He was dead. A moment later his lifeless body suffered the same fate, in Fate, as his bike. He should have realized, only a ghost——can kill a ghost.

Cal woke to Fate's new noisy farm town day, Thursday, 9:00 a.m. September 14, 2009.

Cal's watch slowly crept counterclockwise. Tuesday, 2:45 p.m. August 29, 2009. The sand in his hour glass was nearly empty.

# Thirty

Cal screamed. He grabbed his furry cheeks, and lost his arms to his chairs side.

"Jeasus H Christ, Jeasus H. Christ." Knee stiff locked legs crossed tightly at the ankles frozen in a tense Crucifix sprawl. The wings tips pointed toe up.

"AGAGAHHAGAH—" He squashed his tongue between smoke stained teeth, in a raspberry ballooning clench.

Cal listened all night to the last part of the story as it was promised, in the wind. If he didn't see it, hear it, smell it, or be touched by it, he never would have believed it. No one would have.

"Carp, I think, I hope at least I can—I can remember enough to write this. I've got to, Big Pete will kill me. Double Carp, he may kill me once he reads it?" Old Cal thawed inhaling and exhaling questions, spoken out loud and answered back, out loud. Hope they like it, he wondered?

"Who is gonna read this? Who is gonna believe it. I freakin wouldn't, sounds like carp."

"Eh hem, we'll see son. We will see." Master's shadow cast on Cal. His index and middle finger of his right hand bent slightly at the tips, pressing under his chin, supporting his wrinkled pondering face.

"Would I have enough time to get home and——?"

"My son, go put it down on paper."

Huh?

"Son, yes—," Master warmly confirmed.

"Damn," Cal forgot the mind reading parlor trick and the game over so no thunder, or points.

"What's the matter son?"

"I'll never have time to write it. Big Pete will blow it off when he hears what it's about. You know he's really tough, and a bit of a jerk. I'm gonna be fired for sure."

"He is a jerk, yes and———"Master's silhouette turned a smirking face away with a beckoning finger.

"If not fired, then locked up insane, or maybe I'll have enough time to write it but nowhere to publish it, or—-" Cal leapt over the door saddle following instructions.

Master looked over at his lady. On her arm hung a woven basket covered by a white cloth, on her face hung another smirking smile. Cal didn't get, didn't get the inside joke.

"Hey, this is serious, very serious." Their misplaced parental attitudes ticked him off.

"Hey, you get to stay up here in Alice in Freakin Wonderland. I have to go back to all that crap again. Err, carp, carp."

"Would you like to stay?" Master spun an open palm around Destiny's interior.

"Well, err, ah, hmmm, yeah. Yeah, I would in fact."

"Well, you can't. You've moved on. We need the room" Master closed his palm to a tight balled fist.

"Children must leave the nest you know?" Mother took the basket from her arm, handed it to Cal. He looked at the floor.

"But we have a bit of news for you that may make things a little better. Now, take Mother's basket. She baked specially for you, for your ride, back."

Cal grabbed the wicker basket by its large arched fibrous handle, turned, nodded thanks with a child's grin.

"Ok, soooooo—- what's the news? What in the woooorld could possibly top alllll this?" Cal poked his finger under the towel covering the baskets contents.

"We don't think your boss will be bothering you about this, or anything else for that matter."

"No, as Mother said, we don't think so at all. In fact he won't be there when you get back. Heard they're looking for a new editor and your name is high on the list. If we could bet –we can't, they're rules everywhere in this universe, well, we would bet on you. Call it inside information." Master twirled his left index finger, chuckling.

"How do you kn—" Cal's eyes caught them staring at him, with a come on are you kidding look on their faces.

"What happened to him?"

"Well, you remember when Master went on that fishing trip?"

"Of course I do, of course."

"Master was a little lonely. Soooo— he took someone with him."

"Yeah aaaand—ooohhhhhh heeeeyyy, you didn't do that just for me? I mean, I would feel terrible if–"

Mother and Master held up their left hands, fingers making a vee, thumb tucked in, in a stop gesture.

"No son, not just for you. He has some work to do as well. Not here, there." The magical garage door roof flopped open.

"Boy I wish I could do that."

"Someday, you will son, someday."

"Damn, hey, no thunder? Hmmmm, I'll never get used to that." Cal ducked.

"NOW...!" Mother.

"GO!" Master.

"LEAVE!" Mother.

"SHOO!" Master.

The wind picked up as it did last time the roof opened.

"Creates a terrific draft in here don't you think? Hahahahahaha," Master grabbed Mother's arms loudly laughed, Mother softly.

"I don't know why you're not, but all you humans, should be astronomers. Look up darn you.

People, look —up." Master looked out the roofs opening.

POP, POP, POP, POP, the rest of the words of the neon sign on the far wall blinked to life in perfect multicolored neon filling in the rest of the missing words. Cal shook his still somewhat foggy waking head, and read aloud.

"Twenty years from now you will be more disappointed by the things you didn't do, than by the ones you did. So throw off the bowlines. Sail away from the safe harbor. Catch the trade winds in your sails. Explore, Dream, Discover."

"I know that saying from many years ago at school. Mark Twain wrote it."

"He means Samuel Mother, doesn't he?"

"Yes, Samuel Clemens, his birth name?"

"You know him?"

"He's becoming more aware isn't he?" Rhetorically she asked Master.

"Yessssss, of course we know him. For many years in fact, Mothers pet." Master pouted.

"He's a real treat to be around. Came in on Haley's Comet one day we figured. We may see him later. He's so funny we just don't know where he gets it from?" Mother turned facing Master. Each other smiled and shook their heads back and forth no.

"He's a handful. You may see him som—-"

"—-but you have something to do, correct Master?"

"Will I see you again?"

"Not likely." Master grinned "But, if you need us? Go outside, no matter what the weather, sunny days are appreciated. Lay on your back, on ground of your choosing son."

"Grass would be a good idea." Mother mothered "Perhaps on a sunny hill, or under a shade tree. However, be certain to have a great view of the sky's ocean."

"You mean out there, look up out there?" Cal pointed.

"Yes, out there, and there and here, for here is there, and there is here. Yes, well then, Mother we must go."

"And look up of course—look up –way up. Out, deeply into the great universe of which you have been a resident of for so very long. Close your eyes and let your mind race, race like the wind in day-dream. Ask your questions, await your answers, they'll come some-way, somehow—from somewhere, on the wings of the wind most likely." Mother strolled toward Master.

"You just may hear from us. Not directly necessarily, but you just may. Be aware. Aware I tell you. You mortals spend so much time looking straight ahead, or down. You never look up. Be aware of where you are. This, is—- a very big place boy." Master open palm pointed through the roofs opening.

"Son," Mother corrected "He's earned it and yes, very big indeed, and beautiful. Now, go finish writing your story, son, before the angels dance the dance of the sweet surrender, and call for the fog to take your mortal soul."

"Gooooooooo–" They harmonized.

"Oh, by the way, last thing." Mother said looking up.

"Ahhh, what is it this time? Cal.

"Be sure to leave the nickels on the bar. They all stay here. All twenty, count them—they're all there, in your pocket. I promise." Master flipped his hair.

A mini tornado topped through the doorless front door. It split in two. One part engulfed Mother, the other Master. After twisting them tightly in cocoons they shot like comets through the bars garage door open roof. Mother first, Master followed. They were gone. Cal would never, ever, see them again, in this lifetime.

Clutching the basket by its long handle he walked to the bar. Hand plunged deep into his pocket, scooped out all the nickels. Turning his hand sideways, uncurled his fist. One by one each passed through the opening by the fat of his hand. He relaxed his grip. More quickly fell each striking the bar top, each making its own unique musical note. They were all there somehow. Mother was right, wasn't she always.

"Just one, they won't miss it-a memento." He stopped at nineteen. A petty theft, no punishment if found out, it was only a —-nickel.

"Heck, thunder and lightning lost their scoring power. No one was here to know anyway." Cal spoke directly at a tired looking Jimmy Hendrix.

Shiftily eyed he looked around double checking.

"Good, no one here, it's mine." He palmed the nickel, stuffed it back in his pocket, a latent teenage heist success.

He turned his attention to the bar another time before he left. He started at the neon sign and spun surveying the empty shot up bar that had been his home, stopping looking forward through the doorless front door. A soft shake of his head confirmed his disbelief.

Double checking, his mind raced backwards in a video rewind of all the past day's events. Then fast forwarded rerunning and remembering the time he spent here.

As slowly, and carefully, as the first day he first he slipped into Destiny, Cal walked away. A few quick light footed steps took him down the left side short stairs to the first level. The wings briskly pressed on shuffling past the broken tables, chairs, side stepping the tooth. He spun, looked back at the bars interior. Sighed, spun and stood facing outside looking through the doorless front door thinking about last night.

Outside summer's morning sunlight warmed the earth, toasted his face, and woke sleeping smells of the farm country teasing his nose. He stood motionless at the doorless front doors saddles edge reluctant to leave, as he was to first go in.

"I feel like I'm leaving home not going home."

"Ooooouuuttttt," Boomed from space, rattled the rafters and pushed his back.

Cal wobbled, struggled to maintain his balance not wishing to fall on the saddle. His toes an inch shy of the doorless front doors saddle. Stabilized, he frowned and then looked over his shoulder inside.

"Ouuuttt," pushed again. Cal turned around, faced inside, and carefully stepped backwards over the saddle, onto the concrete porch floor. Immediately a red hot searing burn torched his leg.

"Aghaghaghagh," Cal grabbed his leg, bit his tongue.

"We said—— all stay."Mother and Master chorused with spectacular clarity. Reprimanded, Cal leapt back over the doors saddle and came to a shoe skidding halt inside. At bar's counter top he straightened from being doubled over, panting. Lingering pain lingered, but lessened, after he returned the stolen goods.

"YOU HAD BETTER REMEMBER HOW TO LISTEN." Master was not pleased.

Cal nodded acknowledging the value of sage advice. Smartly he leapt back over the doors saddle and ran to the hopefully well rested, and up to the long ride to come, Comet.

Comet's door creaked.

"Damn, hmmm, thought that was fixed? No matter, I'm outa here. Somehow I have to get this down on paper before I forget. Hey, wow, no thunder and now no answer? They must be gone for real."

"Yoouuu won't forget boy." The building violently shook, cedar shakes flew.

"SON," Mother corrected.

Cal's face hit the passenger seat fearing Destiny toppling. The place he feared that first day peacefully stabilized. He looked through the Comets windshield, fought a wet eye. A small salty river managed to escape from the corner of his left one. It flowed curving over his cheek and stopped at the corner of his mouth as if a scar cut by a knife. He fired up Old Blue and listened to its rumble. It didn't sound as calm as before, but wasn't as bad as when he left the city. With a sighing chest Cal backed up, started out of town on the other road out.

"Not that way you idiot."Master scolded.

Cal slammed his foot on the brake. "Hey, wadda mean, one road in- two roads out, right? Aren't I to go home this way? The map said….."

"—Looook again son, look again." Mother's distant voice faded.

"OH, maybe we should have kept him another few days, damn, oops, soooorrryyyy…."Master groaned.

Distant thunder warned. Cal scrambled for the map through his mess on the seat.

"Somewhere, it's freakin here somewhere." He pushed the papers, used paper coffee cups, tissues and all, till some disqualified themselves from the Easter egg hunt fleeing to the floor.

"Ah, I've got it," there it was. He grabbed it, it shook.

"Where is it, I know what I said. It was on here, I know?" Cal focused on the smudged note he confidently concluded said "One Road In and Two Roads Out." And there it was. Completely legible and filled in, "One rode in, two rode out."

Cal blinked, and blinked, and blinked again, again, again, and again, with what he was sure were lying eyes. After four more hard pressed blinks it read the same.

"One rode in, two rode out? What? What the heck?"

Mixed among rattle of the coming summer's storm Cal heard.....

"One rode in–son, and yes, two rode out." Master and Mother harmonized hyena laughs, accompanied with a flash of Sister's heat lightening, and Brother Thunder's bellow.

"What the h– does that mean? That's not fair you tricked me."

"Did we? Or did you, yourself? Be aware boy, things aren't always what they seem."

Confused exasperated Cal shook. He looked in the rear view mirror. Backing up, thought, time for me to get home and write this damn–he ducked but no thunder—story. What in the world is Big Pete gonna think? Far out, he's not there. Far out, I haven't said that in years.

Cal drove through Fate, and headed home to face his new boss that Thursday morning. He passed by the town clock, 10:30 a.m. September 14, 2009. He looked at his watch which slowed to a backwards sludgy crawl. 2:40 p.m. Tuesday, August 29, 2009.

"If I make time, and the Comet doesn't break down, I'll have a few hours."

# Thirty-One

Cal headed up the hill, and out of Fate on the road he came in on. The one he thought," the one road in."

Who's the new boss? How am I going to explain this? Big Pete is—well, history. Who is gonna back me up, Cal worried?

"If I keep chewing my cheeks my face won't that be attractive. How the heck am I gonna write this, sell it? It sounds like complete carp, err, crap. I'm good but this ...well it's just too much, they'll think I made it all up."

How am I gonna be able to remember?

Cal bounced between self talk and self thought. He had his story and it, him. More than his pencil had lead, his note pad had lines, his head could hold.

"They'll never believe it, never. I am so screwwwwwed."

Old Blue creaked and squeaked complaining, about Cal. The two rusty relic adventurers stole out of town on the road they came in on. The trip shook Cal to a stir but Blue seemed— quite pleased.

Cal's cracked lips gingerly wrapped around one of Mothers freshly baked, crispy, flaky rolls.

"Owwww" He looked down at the trail of crumbs clinging to his overripe shirt, leading to his very loose pants. Thought how much easier it was to follow that, than the past day's events.

"CARP, oh heck-crap. I wish I had one of those nickels. Good evidence."

Big Fat head, hmmm—well maybe? Full, anyway.

The smell of a cup of NYC coffee obsessed. Mother knew best, sent him off with her special brew of tea. At least that's what she called it.

"Maybe this is tea, but not from here."

The cup sat on the Comets healed dash. It never tipped.

Old Blue built to speed. Cal snapped from his work worry. A half a mile out of town a big bright beam of super trooper burning white light raced head-on.

"Hmmm, Blue. What do you make of that? A big sassy single motorcycle headlight no doubt?"

They rolled toward the luring light, and it, them. The gap quickly closed.

"Looks like two riders." He yielded the center, moved to roads right. Playfully the riders wiggly and wobbled their machine, swaying back and forth, but staying on their side of the road. Cal slowed to a crawl in the shade of the wet thick forest. Perfectly balanced, the biker ballet dancers teased some more, slowed, came dangerously closer to Blues drivers door. The driver had their hands wrapped around the handlebar grips. The passengers, around the driver, fingers tucked through the belt loops. They over- slowed, nearly stalled, the motorcycle almost slid into the Comet.

The driver recovered with an experienced maneuver, twisting the throttle but not too much, or quickly. They stabilized, peered inside the Comet as they safely passed. Cal's salt and pepper bearded face hauntingly stared back, then flashed to the bikes black fuel tank. "VINCENT," below that, white windswept lettering. The bike passed before the grays could make out what it said. Hyena laughter screamed from within the black helmets so powerfully it echoed through the heavy suffocating air left from a powerful fleeting storm.

His shoulders stuffed in his neck, Cal watched them speed away in the driver's door mirror. The reflected blurry figures waved hello, or good-bye, with their left hands. Then the driver of the black bike switched the black beast with a full throttle twist. Its back wheel spun, they jolted forward and roared away through the cool glen toward town.

They left, "Hi Cal," lingering in the heavy wet air.

Wait a New York City minute. Where are they coming, going, damn this isn't over just yet?

Cal thought hard and swallowed hard. Thunder rumbled. Cal ducked smiling he was not forgotten. Curiosity won. Blues brakes were put to the test. Muddy tires twisted to a creaking three point turn. The tea cup tipped, but spilled coffee. He raced back to town with some questions. Surely they would be there.

Cal and Blue sloppily rolled down the last tier of the road through the glen and slid into the town they left only minutes ago. He crawled to where Destiny once stood. Much to the dismay of the Comet he jammed the gear shift in park before they came to a full stop. There they sat, in the middle of Fate's dusty town road, in a cloud. The glens air hadn't reached, yet. No bike anywhere. No town either.

Comets creaky door opened. Cal lit his first cigarette in days briskly walking to where he was standing a short time ago. Only charred remnants of a burned out, field stone foundation, building remained. Destiny's sign lay shattered on the dirt lawn.

"God damn, Carp. What the he–" Then his left ear clipped something coming, from the left.

"A bike, please. But doesn't sound like a bike? I know that sound. Rumbling farm equipment maybe?"

Well spent time trained his ears to the sounds, and smells of country life. In a few ticks Cal would be certain of what he would know anywhere. Sure enough, there it came, charging full speed. An elderly, long white haired man sat on top of a big blue tractor, raising the dust. The ticks ticked off, the driver wrestled the blue tractors steering. He headed to carve a path between where dumbfounded Cal stood, and the remains of Destiny. Last minute, as he passed in-between, the rider pressed two fingers of his right hand together and raised them in a salute. Cal waved a relaxed low hand wave back, assuming the man would stop. He didn't.

"Stop, stop. Please stop, you there—stop." Cal stopped running, placed his hands on his knees sucking in dusty air, out of breath.

Ten yards away the tractor hopped to a halt. Billowed dustcoated the driver. He casually looked straight ahead, twisted back, then forward again. Matched to his blue bib overalls he wore a straw hat curled to in front to a loose point. Cal straightened up. Ran to and stood in front of the rumbling blue beast, facing the driver.

"Can I help you there stranger? What's got you to these parts pray tell. You look like a city boy?"

"Where is it? UUhhhh, where's the bar, Sir. Where's the bake shop– –nothings here? It was just here—just minutes ago. I left, came back a few minutes later looking for this—" Cal's dry mouthed stopped. He worried if he tried to explain anymore Jesse would show.

"Easy there my friend, no worries boy, go on."

Cal grabbed his chest. His heart beat as a gong, then as a fast drum beat from the adrenaline surge.

"What's that you say boy?"

Ahhh, what the hell Cal thought?

The farmer shook his head in a–that's a mistake son.

"Uh, it was here, a little while ago. This nice—err—ah, old gentleman explained what happened here—over there—there—inside that –that that—bar? It was right there." Cal dropped his head as he spoke.

The Farmer continued his stare. Then a gleam came to his eye.

"Son, that bar–hasn't been there for nearly thirty years, yep, about forty I reckon. Terrible fire one night, hit by lightning we all thought. No matter, the owner hadn't been there ever anyway. Moved away, thought kilt in Nam—yep."

"No it was just there I swear, and a motorcycle just passed me as I was leaving. They were coming to town. I turned around to see if it was him." Cal panted a worried explanation

The farmer looked down.

"What've you been smoking, anyway, boy? No motorcycle tracks here friend. Look around. And who's him?" The old man teased a smile.

"Malcolm," Cal barked, looking at the ground for motorcycle tracks

"No need to shout boy. Malcolm huh, well boy, ain't no buildin been there for nearly thirty I reckon, or more, as I said. Now, I dunno what you been drinkin, or smoking, but you better stop, because you're seeing things. Or maybe you need to start if you don't. Either way—ain't been there for nearly thirty. Well, got to be gettin back. Waitin for me, yep –waitin. Over there on the farm—Shepherd's Walk—they're waitin for me. See ya son. Take my advice, leaaaveee—- nowwww."

Cal's hands limply fell. Index fingers on each of his peck typing hands twitched, simultaneously. Only those two, no others. The farmer looked up at the sky. Spat out a big HOOT of a laugh.

"Look boy, it's been a privilege knowing ya. Now once you can say that about yourself, well, your life will change for all eternity. Now, I gotta be gettin off now. Shepherd's walk, it'll be waitin."

A big wind whipped out of the calm, hot morning air. It spun, twirled, and whirled the roads dust into mini twisters. They danced like small tops. The unexpected wind lifted the right pant leg of the farmer's well wore faded overalls for three ticks. Cal got a glimpse, just for a three ticks, long enough for him to see the farmer's leg as if it was meant to be. Blue, it was blue, space blue. Boy's pajama's with the stars, moons and rocket ships. The pant leg fell. The driver screamed a deafening, echoing, howling, ricocheting laugh that carried throughout the valley. It kicked up a dust storm. He flipped his silver locks. Cal jumped out of the way when the man jammed the tractors shifter in its difficult gear box. After grinding it he drove through a dust curtain into a wind spun tunnel. It closed behind him. The dust settled as quickly as it kicked up. Not a tire track of evidence remained.

Cal's sand caked face looked as if a white tank commander in Africa. He back-hand wiped the grays, pointed the Comet home, out the—one road in.

"Time to head home Old Blue, time to head home, and face the music. Let's see what's on?"

Sly and the Family Stone–I wanna take you higher. Cal sang along in much improved voice.

He looked at a big bright blue sky. Searched for the town clock, it too was gone. Cal heard in a daze, a woman's voice.

"Doc Jack, are you telling what I think——"

A radio announcer interrupted- "Its Tuesday 2:30 p.m., August, 29, 2009."

The Comet's clock read 2:30 p.m.

Cal's watch back ticked one last time, froze at Tuesday 2:30 p.m., August 29, 2009.

# THIRTY-TWO

"Rachel, he'll be coming around. Please make some of your special tea."

"Cal—Malcolm. Cal Malcolm McKeon on the count of three, I will snap my fingers. You will wake, refreshed" Doc Jack Master whispered in Cal's ear.

He nodded to Rachel, his brown eyed motherly buxom assistant. She gathered her notes from the session, and left the room stepping over the saddle of the offices missing door, into an outer office.

"ONE, TWO," Cal, the electrified voyager, sniffed. Doc Masters pipe smoke, and coconut incense, twitched his nose, opened his eyes.

"I SAID ON THREE, THREE, AND THREE! DAMN IT CAL. Don't you ever—listen?" He threw his snapping fingers at him. It sounded like two drum sticks rapping against each other.

"Anyway—— weeeellcome back, boy. How do you feel?" Doc finger combed his flowing, neck length wavy, silver hair.

The volume dialed up on the office Wurlitzer. "I Wanna Take You Higher" punched out through the chrome speaker cover. A poster of Sly Stone dancing on stage hung on a blue wall. It fluttered from the fan's waves. Rachel returned with cups of some sort of brew and powdered donuts, some of which covered her dress. Cal munched and sipped. Rachel asked—

"So Doc, what's the answer?"

"What's the question?"

"To the last question you asked. You asked if you love someone, and they you, do you think it wrong if each is married to another?"

"No, I didn't."

"Yes you did. I remember."

"No I didn't. I said, do you think it wrong if you loved someone and they you, but both are married to another?"

"Yes, Doc, now I remember. I was quick to think it wrong but now—-"

"—now you re-asked the question. Things aren't what they always seem, are they?"

"No, they're not. You may have known the other before," she said.

"Yes, maybe, and maybe will again. We stay in touch, don't we? But maybe you didn't understand the question completely."

"Think about it-we'll talk."

Doc nodded asking her to excuse herself. This time she purposefully thudded her heavy shoe on the doors saddle. Cal trembled lounging on the crushed red velvet dirty couch. He jack-knifed, spun his wings to the black and red tiled floor. Tuesday 2:31 p.m. August 29, 2009 blinked from the therapist's desk clock.

"How long was I under for?"

"There and back; a fortnight and four"

Cal blankly stared at Doc whose expression suggested he try to remember.

"Let's see, we started at 2:00 p.m., seconds to put you under then—oh would you excuse me. I have to stop the tick tock metronome."

"Thank you, yes where was I? Oh, yes, and then add eighteen odd nights- jammed into thirty minutes approximately. It seemed like thirty days to me, so real."

"Wasn't it, Cal?" Doc nodded, and then switched off the fan.

"What happened? What did I say?"

"Quite a lot, boy—and, quite a bit," Doc's disbelieving, gaunt face, looked at his desk where his motherly assistant returned her notes. With a boney left hand he clutched them by their left edge.

"Yes, quite a lot, and quite a bit. By the way, how are the twins?"

Cal looked at him.

"Yes, I know about them. They always need management. Always at it, aren't they Cal?"

"Who won?"

"Rachel says the game is still being played. I think it a copout but—mothers and children you know. By the way, Malcolm, does your family still have its summer place upstate New York?"

"No."

"What happened to it?"

"Burned down,"

"So, what do you remember?" Doc stared at Cal, then at the pile of pencil written notes.

"Oh, um, oh, oooohh— boy, you see, this farm town, Fate, and this old bar named Destiny. This guy, Master, and his wife, Mother, and these kids an——" Cal stopped, thought he'll commit me for sure, maybe all a dream?

"Was it? Doc answered.

"HOLY CARP, Did you just read my mind?"

Doc Jack Master parted his clown mouth. Cal struggled like a drunk to get to a wobbly stance.

"Cal, what would you have changed?"

"Dunno, regarding what?"

"Why are we here Malcolm? Would you have thrown yourself on the land mine, if you could have to save Johnny?"

"Oh, forgot. Yes, in a tick, yes of course."

"Never mind that for now. We have a lot to work to do. Stumbled on some things, just scratched the surface. Peeled back a few layers, now, moving forward Cal, I received back the results from your ancestral DNA test."

"Cool, and?"

"Well it seems you're made up of some pretty old DNA." Doc laughed

"How old..?"

"Says here your Y chromosome results identify you as Hapolgroup R1b, M343 (Subclade R1b1b2, M269). Your first common mutation (marker they like to say) is M168. It reaches back roughly SIXTY THOUSAND YEARS. It's the first common marker of all non-African men. Your lineage tells us your people left Africa, hit what we know as the Middle East, headed to the Far East a bit, then a little into Asia then turned left and wound up in Europe. M343 is your last marker. So Cal, who are you?"

"Who are any of us, Doc?"

"Good answer. Well, we've just scratched the surface as I've said, and a lot of work to go."

Doc Master stood to shake hands goodbye. Static electricity pinned one of his pant legs high up on his calf exposing his leg for a second, then it fell. Cal's eyes caught a glimpse of it.

BLUE, you too, Cal thought. Doc peered over nose held tortoise shell glasses, paused for two ticks, smiled and nodded toward the door.

"OUT, oooouuuttttt you go"

The wings soles slowly shuffled toward the doorway. Above it hung a sign. It read–ONE RODE IN-TWO RODE OUT. Cal looked at it, twisted looking over his left shoulder. "It's not all random is it?"

"NO—-no it isn't. Now I ask you friend, where are you going?" Doc spun his left hands index finger, smirking.

Cal looked forward through open doorway. "To a high school reunion but I have a stop first. Have to cover an economic summit."

"The one upstate, it's a secret. No one knows where it is being held?"

"There are no secrets in my land. I'll find it. I'm taking three finger Ned with me."

"Malcolm, don't do it. You're a writer. Your pen is mighty than the sword you carry in the trunk of your car with the sight. You're not evil."

"Ha, you know of that then do you. Well, we're all a little evil. I have to have a conversation with some people. Then I'll decide."

Cal inched to the edge of the saddle, twisted around and waved goodbye holding up his left hand. Index and middle finger pinched together, fourth and pinky also. The two pair split apart making a vee, thumb tucked into his palm. Doc did the same.

As he lowered his hand he lifted his left wing, pushed it over the doors saddle planting it safely on the other side. The right followed. He disappeared.

Doc Master stood with folded arms waiting. Twenty ticks passed. Cal backed up into the room stepping over the saddle. Then started to leave again but this time he forcefully stomped the sole of his right wing on the saddle, cringed and waited.

"BOOOM," Doc Master joked while flipping his hair. "Malcolm Cal McKeon, the tyranny of the innocent, weak, fragile and vulnerable can have no place in his world friend. However there is no greater injustice, no greater tyranny that can be imposed upon someone than that which one imposes upon them self. That is the tyranny of undeserved guilt. You're free, son. The TYRANNY OF YOUR GUILT is gone. The burden of Johnny's death is gone and the chains of your guilt, with it. You perfectionists are all the same. Now go spend, not live, what's left of the time you have left. It grows short."

Doc masterfully flipped his hair pointing for Cal to leave and said, "You didn't have to go."

"Yeah I did Doc, we all agreed...they were my brothers...and I forgot about Johnny."

"Did you, you certain?"

"People don't forget things, do they Doc?"

"No, we misplace them. Anyway, Mr. Lucky, you came back and did what you said you were going to do."

"Yeah, guess I did." Cal unraveled from his cringing curl and offered Doc a thankful smile with soft eyes. The door snapped closed behind him.

"That's a dandy finger." Doc twirled his left index finger.

On his way out of the office building Cal looked down at his shirt.

"Heeeeyyy, where did these crumbs come from?"

He skipped toward Old Blue looking into a bright blue sky and heard—

"Be mindful, Cal. Be mindful of what's you within you, what's hid in your Id, what you carry in mankind's black box. Live it better this time or—-. Now go, get going before your Winters Eve comes and fetches you." Mother.

"And look up BOOOY. OWWWW" Mother found his rib.

Cal ducked his crew cut salt and pepper head into the Comet, and drove it to its new home. A newly painted parking spot courtesy of

Mr. I. Seems he didn't die after all. The sign on the concrete wall in front of the blue floor parking space read:

Reserved for MALCOLM (CAL) MCKEON

And of course for OLD BLUE, complete with a dog eared copy of Catcher in the Rye, resting on the passenger seat.

"Doc Jack?"

"Yes Rachel."

"I know it's only a theory but, you never said why you think we come back?"

"Doc Jack?

"Doctor Jack!"

# ALBERT ZAYAT

Albert Zayat was born in Brooklyn, New York in 1950. Shortly thereafter his family moved to Northern New Jersey. His father, Arthur, was a beer salesman/manager for Ballantine Beer and thus Al was born a New York Yankee fan as Ballantine Beer was a major sponsor of the Yanks, "back in the day." His mother, an editor and author, always insisted on literacy for her children. The Webster's dictionary, and mom, made certain misused, and or mispronounced words were immediately corrected.

Al spent most of his time in New Jersey until he left for a New England prep school in 1966. After returning home he moved to Manhattan's rocking lower East side (the East Village) in the late sixties. Always a worker, he had different jobs. Two of the more notable, an usher at the famed rock venue- the " Fillmore East," and then as a production assistant on the film "Woodstock."

As such, Al had many various film company duties. He was one of the projectionists and other important responsibilities included picking up the late night crew's dinner, often Chinese. After Al's film career ended he headed back to New Jersey and the pursuit of real life in business. Along the way he had a run in with Alopecia which cost him his hair, for good. For nearly the last 30 years Al has been a professional in the investment community. He is an avid fan of cars, motorcycles, various genres of music, baseball, stout, good Scotch or Irish whiskey, and of course–his two kids.

"One Rode In" started with the development of one character, on a lonely divorcee's snowy evening. One shoot of very green strongly-rooted grass grew, and grew. Thanks Mom, thanks Webster, thanks Alopecia, thanks life, says Albert Zayat!

CPSIA information can be obtained at www.ICGtesting.com
Printed in the USA
BVOW021756050712

294468BV00001B/22/P

9 780983 687320